Dear Reader:

So, you think you'd like to pursue an exciting career in para-archaeology? Explore the eerie ruins of the Dead City of Old Cadence? Maybe indulge in a discreet affair with one of those sexy ghost-hunters hired to protect you while you work?

Think again.

Sure, it sounds exciting, but let me tell you, it isn't easy dodging energy ghosts down there in the glowing green passageways of an alien world. This is a high-stress job. And, okay, so it's true what they say about those hunters—they are pretty amazing in bed and they certainly are handy to have around when things turn dicey underground. But let's face it, there are some very compelling reasons why nice girls shouldn't get involved with guys who zap energy ghosts for a living. For one thing, these professional bodyguards can be a lot more difficult to handle and every bit as dangerous as the ghosts.

But, hey, a lady has to make a living, and at least this job is never dull.

If, like me, you sometimes relish your romantic suspense with a paranormal twist, welcome to Harmony. The rules are a little different here. . . .

Yours very truly,

Jayne Ann Krentz
writing as Jayne Castle

. . . and Jayne Ann Krentz

"GOOD FUN."   *—Cosmopolitan*

"A delight."   *—Publishers Weekly*

"ENTERTAINING."   *—People*

"Lively . . . filled with strong protagonists and witty dialogue."
—Library Journal

"FAST-PACED . . . interesting characters . . . a good time is had by
the reader."   *—Chicago Tribune*

"Along with Nora Roberts, Krentz is one of the most reliably satisfying romance writers publishing."   *—Sunday (CA) Times*

"AN ABSOLUTELY, POSITIVELY FUN READ . . . Krentz's characters are always people you'd like to meet for yourself and know
more about."   *—The Southern Pines (NC) Pilot*

Harmony

Jayne Ann Krentz
writing as
Jayne Castle

BERKLEY BOOKS, NEW YORK

A Berkley Book
Published by The Berkley Publishing Group
A division of Penguin Putnam Inc.
375 Hudson Street
New York, New York 10014

PRINTING HISTORY
Berkley trade paperback edition / July 2002

Visit our website at
www.penguinputnam.com

Library of Congress Cataloging-in-Publication Data

Castle, Jayne.
    Harmony / Jayne Ann Krentz writing as Jayne Castle.—Berkley trade pbk. ed.
    p. cm.
  "Includes the New York times bestseller After dark and her beloved novella Bridal jitters"—
Cover.
    ISBN 0-425-18477-3
    1. Love stories, American. I. Castle, Jayne. After dark. II. Castle, Jayne. Bridal jitters. III.
Title.
  PS3561.R44 H37 2002
  813'.54—dc21

                                                        2002024501

PRINTED IN THE UNITED STATES OF AMERICA

10   9

CONTENTS

After Dark

CHAPTER 1

IF IT HAD NOT BEEN HORRIBLY OBVIOUS THAT CHESTER
Brady was already dead, Lydia Smith might have strangled him herself.

Her first assumption when she rounded the corner into the shadowy Dead City Tomb wing of Shrimpton's House of Ancient Horrors
was that Chester was pulling another scam. It had to be some bizarre
con tactic designed to steal her new client prospect right out from
under her nose before she could get his name on a contract.

It was so typical of the little sneak. And after all she'd done for
him.

She came to a halt and stared at the leg and arm hanging limply
over the side of the ancient sarcophagus. Maybe it was just a weird
gag this time. After all, Chester's sense of humor did lean toward
childish pranks.

But there was something a little too realistic about the way he was slumped in the not-quite-human-shaped coffin.

"Maybe he just fainted or something," she said, without much hope.

"Don't think so." Emmett London glided around her and walked forward to gaze down into the green quartz burial box. "He's very dead. You'd better call the authorities."

She took another cautious step forward and saw the blood. It had drained from Chester's throat into the bottom of the coffin.

The reality of what she was staring at hit her with a numbing jolt. She could not believe it. *Not Chester.* He was a thief and a con artist, the kind of shady character who gave a bad name to all legitimate antiquities dealers and respectable para-archaeologists, but he was a friend too. Sort of.

She swallowed heavily. "An ambulance?"

Emmett looked at her. Something about his gaze made her uncomfortable. Maybe it was the eerie gold-green hue. It was a little too close to the color of her pet dust-bunny's second pair of eyes, the ones it used for hunting.

"There's no rush on the ambulance," Emmett said. "I'd start with the police if I were you."

Easy for him to say, Lydia thought. The problem was that the first person the cops would want to talk to would probably be her. Everyone on Ruin Row knew that she'd had a furious argument with Chester last month because the little creep had snaffled off her first potential client.

Oh, God, Chester was dead—genuinely *dead.* It was difficult to grasp the concept. This wasn't another one of his convenient disappearing acts designed to keep him one step ahead of an enraged client. This time his death was for real.

She suddenly felt light-headed. This could not be happening.

Deep breaths, she thought. Take some deep breaths. She would not fall apart. She would not lose it. She was not going to crack under stress the way everyone expected her to do.

With an effort she pulled herself together.

She glanced up from Chester's body and found Emmett London watching her. His expression was oddly thoughtful, even mildly curious in a detached sort of way. It was as if he was waiting to see how she would react, as if her response to the sight of a dead body in a sarcophagus was merely an interesting academic puzzle.

Unconsciously, her gaze went to his wrist. She had caught a glimpse of his watch a few minutes ago. The dial was set in an amber face. No big deal, she thought. Amber accessories were fashionable. A lot of people wore amber simply because it was stylish. But some people wore it because amber was the medium that powerful para-resonators used to focus their psychic talents.

Another shiver went through her.

"Yes, of course, the police," she whispered. "There's a phone in my office. If you'll excuse me, Mr. London, I'll go call them."

"I'll wait here," Emmett said.

So calm and unruffled, she thought. Maybe stumbling across dead bodies was routine for him.

"I'm really very sorry about this." She didn't know what else to say.

Emmett regarded her with that unwavering expression of polite interest. "Did you kill him?"

The shock of the question left her momentarily speechless.

"*No,*" she finally gasped. "No, I most certainly did not kill Chester."

"Then it's not your fault, is it? There's no need to apologize."

She got the distinct impression that he would not have been especially troubled if she *had* admitted to murdering poor Chester. She wondered uneasily what that said about him.

She turned away to walk back along the gloom-filled display gallery to her office. Her glance fell on Chester's foot propped on the edge of the green sarcophagus. The foot was encased in a boot made of some sort of cheap imitation lizard skin.

Chester had always been a flashy dresser, Lydia reflected. To her surprise, she felt a pang of wholly unexpected sadness. True, he had been a sleazy, opportunistic hustler. But he was only one of many who eked out a living on the fringes of the booming antiquities trade here in Cadence. The eerie green quartz ruins of the long-vanished alien civilization that had once flourished here on Harmony provided a variety of profit niches for industrious entrepreneurs. Chester had not been the worst of the lot who worked in the shadow of the Dead City wall.

He had been a nuisance, but he had been colorful. She was going to miss him.

AT FIVE O'CLOCK THAT AFTERNOON, MELANIE TOFT stood in the doorway of Lydia's tiny office, her dark eyes alight with curiosity. "What did they say? Are you in the clear?"

"Not entirely." Exhausted by the hours of police questioning, Lydia sagged back into the depths of her chair. "Detective Martinez said they think Chester was murdered sometime between midnight and three A.M. I was home in bed at the time."

Melanie made a tut-tutting sound. "Alone, I suppose?"

Melanie was never loath to bring up the subject of sex. Six months ago she had terminated her third, or maybe it was her fourth, Marriage of Convenience. She made no secret about the fact that she was open to the notion of a fifth.

On the basis of her considerable experience, Melanie had appointed herself Lydia's personal sex advisor. Not that she had any great need of the expertise, Lydia thought. Her sex life, never what anyone would term lively, had become downright moribund in the past year.

Lydia absently fingered the amber stones in her bracelet. "How does a person verify that she was innocently asleep in her own bed when someone got murdered?"

Melanie folded her arms and leaned against the door frame. "It would certainly be a whole lot easier to prove if you had not been alone in said bed. I've been warning you for months about the dangers of not having a more active social life. Now you see the risks of being celibate for extended periods of time."

"Right. A person never knows when she's going to need a good alibi for murder."

Concern replaced some of the fascinated interest on Melanie's face. "Lydia, are you—you know—okay?"

It was starting already, Lydia thought. "Don't worry, you don't have to call the folks in the white coats yet. I'm not going to have a nervous breakdown in front of you. Thought I'd save it until I get home tonight."

"Sorry. It's just that you told me that the para-rez shrinks had advised you to avoid stressful situations."

"What makes you think I've had a stressful day? All I've done so far is find a dead body in the Tomb Gallery, spend a few hours being grilled by the cops, and probably lose my shot at signing up a private client who could have single-handedly elevated my financial status into the next tax bracket."

"I see your point. Nothing stressful about a day like that. Not in the least." Melanie straightened away from the door frame and moved into the office. She sat down in one of the two chairs in front of the desk. "Just a walk in the park."

A new worry descended on Lydia. She could not afford to lose this job. "I wonder what Shrimpton will say when he gets back from vacation tomorrow and finds out what happened."

"Are you kidding? Shrimp will probably give you a raise." Melanie chuckled. "What better publicity for Shrimpton's House of Ancient Horrors than the discovery of a murder victim in one of the exhibits?"

Lydia groaned. "That's the sad part, isn't it? If this makes the evening papers, there will probably be a line of people around the block tomorrow morning."

"Uh-huh." Melanie's expression turned serious again. "I thought the police questioning was strictly routine. Are you really a suspect?"

"Beats me. I'm still sitting here behind my desk, which means no one's arrested me so far. I take that as a positive sign." Lydia drummed her fingers on the arm of her chair. "But the cops knew about my flaming row with Chester in the Surreal Lounge last month."

Melanie frowned. "Not good."

"No. Fortunately, Detective Martinez also seems to be aware of the fact that Chester had a lot of disgruntled clients and more than a few enemies on Ruin Row. It'll take her a while to sort out all the possible suspects. It's going to be a long list."

Melanie shrugged. "I doubt the police will spend too much time on the case. Chester Brady wasn't exactly a high-profile victim or an upstanding member of the community. He had several brushes with the law, and his name was compost with the Society of Para-archaeologists."

"True. I imagine the only people at his funeral will be the folks he ripped off. They'll attend just to make sure he's actually dead."

"Probably hold a celebration at the nearest bar afterward."

"Probably." Lydia sighed. "I don't think there will be any family at the graveside, either. Chester once told me that he had no close relatives. He was always saying that was one of the things he and I had in common."

Melanie snorted softly. "You and Chester Brady had nothing at all in common. He was a classic loser, always looking for the big score and always screwing it up whenever he came close to getting it."

"I know." Not so very different from her at all, Lydia thought glumly. But she refrained from saying that aloud. "It's weird, but I think I'm going to miss him."

Melanie rolled her eyes. "I don't see how you can summon up any sympathy for the little jerk after the way he stole your first client away from you last month."

"He just looked so pathetic lying there in that sarcophagus, Mel. The blood and everything." Lydia shuddered.

"It was awful. You know, Chester was pond scum, but I'm surprised that he actually made someone mad enough to murder him."

"Among his other glowing qualities, Brady was a thief. That tends to irritate folks."

"There is that," Lydia conceded. "And as a parting gift to me, on his way to the afterlife he managed to sabotage the sweet deal I had going this morning."

"Think you've lost the client who came to interview you today?"

"For sure. The poor guy had to spend an hour with the cops because of what happened. He was polite about it, but I got the impression that Mr. London is not accustomed to tolerating that kind of inconvenience. He's a rich, successful businessman from Resonance City. When he phoned earlier he made it clear he prefers to keep a very low profile. He wanted all sorts of assurances about discretion and confidentiality. Thanks to me, he'll probably wind up in the evening papers."

"Not real discreet or confidential," Melanie agreed.

"Considering the circumstances, he was amazingly civil about the whole thing." Lydia propped her chin on her hands. "He didn't say anything rude, but I know I'll never see him again."

"Hmm."

Lydia cocked a brow. "What's that supposed to mean?"

"Nothing, really. It just occurred to me to wonder why a rich, successful businessman who likes to keep a low profile would contact a para-archaeologist who worked in a place like Shrimpton's House of Ancient Horrors."

"When he could have had his pick of university consultants from the Society of Para-Archaeologists?" Lydia asked grimly. "Okay, I'll admit I sort of wondered about that, too. But I didn't want to push my good luck, so I refrained from posing such delicate questions."

Melanie leaned across the desk to pat her arm. "Hang in there, pal. There will be other clients."

"Not like this one. This one had money, and I had plans." Lydia held up her thumb and forefinger spaced an inch apart. "I was this close to giving my landlord notice that I would not be renewing my lease on that large closet he calls an apartment."

"Bummer."

"Yeah. But maybe it's all for the best."

"What makes you say that?" Melanie asked.

Lydia thought about the too casual way London had asked her if she had murdered Chester. "Something makes me think that working for Emmett London might have been almost as stressful as finding dead bodies in the Tomb Gallery."

CHAPTER 2

AN HOUR LATER LYDIA EMERGED FROM THE STAIRWELL on the fifth floor of the Dead City View Apartments.

She was gaining stamina, she thought as she walked down the dark hall to her front door. She wasn't panting nearly as much after the five flights of stairs now as she had in the first week after the elevator had stopped functioning. Better than a gym workout, and much cheaper.

It was important to stay positive.

She slid the amber key into the lock, gave it a small pulse of psychic energy, and opened the front door.

Her pet dust-bunny, Fuzz, drifted toward her across the floor. If she had not been anticipating his greeting, she would not have seen him until he appeared at her feet. None of his six paws made any sound on the tile floor of the postage-stamp-size foyer.

Fuzz's daylight eyes were open, glowing a brilliant, innocent blue against his dull, nondescript fur. He was fully fluffed, making it impossible to see his ears or his paws. He looked like something that had just rolled out from under the bed.

"Hey, Fuzz, you are not gonna believe the day I had." Lydia scooped him up and plopped him on her shoulder. "Oomph! Been into the pretzels again?"

The sturdy weight of the little beast always surprised her. One tended to forget that the scruffy, unprepossessing exterior of a dust-bunny concealed the sleek muscles and sinews of a small but serious predator.

"Chester Brady got himself murdered in my new sarcophagus. The one I told you I got for Shrimp's museum super cheap from the University Museum because they had two hundred extra ones in the basement. Plus they owed me, on account of I found a couple of dozen of their best examples in the first place."

Fuzz rumbled cheerfully and settled into a more comfortable position on her shoulder.

"I know, I know, you never did like Chester, did you? You were in good company. Still, it's strange to think that he's gone."

Several months ago she had stopped worrying about whether or not her one-sided conversations with Fuzz were an indication of deteriorating mental and psychic health. She'd had more pressing matters to occupy her attention. Chief among them had been finding a job and stabilizing her personal finances after the disaster.

Besides, as far as everyone else was concerned, she had cracked up big time after her Lost Weekend. Given the diagnosis she had gotten from the shrinks following the incident, talking out loud to a pet seemed pretty close to normal.

The disaster in the Dead City six months ago had not only destroyed her career at the university and wreaked havoc on her personal finances, it had also left phrases like "psychic dissonance" and "para-trauma" sprinkled liberally about in her medical records.

The doctors had recommended that she avoid excessive stress. Unfortunately, that was easier said than done when one was trying to forge a new career on the ruins of one that had crashed and burned.

For all their pompous-sounding pronouncements, Lydia knew that the rez-shrinks didn't have a clue about the true state of her mental and psychic health. Neither did she, for that matter. She remembered almost nothing about the forty-eight hours that had passed after she fell into the illusion trap.

The doctors said she had repressed the memories. They claimed that, given her high-rez psychic profile, it was probably better that way.

The paranormal ability to resonate with amber and use it to focus psychic energy had begun to appear in the human population shortly after the colonists came through the Curtain to settle the planet of Harmony. At first the talent was little more than a curiosity. It was only gradually that the true potential of the phenomenon became apparent.

Today, almost two hundred years after the discovery of Harmonic amber, it was routinely used for everything from switching on car engines to running dishwashers. Any child over the age of four could generate enough psychic energy to "rez" untuned amber. Few people, however, could summon enough psi power to do more than use it to drive cars or operate a computer. But there were exceptions.

In some people the ability to para-resonate took odd, extremely powerful twists. Lydia was one of those people. In technical terms, she was an ephemeral-energy para-resonator. The common term was "trap tangler." For some unknown reason she could use tuned amber to resonate with the dangerous psychic illusion traps that had been left behind by the long-vanished Harmonics. Being able to de-rez the nightmarish snares practically guaranteed that a person would end up in the field of para-archaeology. The alternative career path was dealing stolen antiquities.

Until six months ago, she had been advancing quickly through the hierarchy of the academic world. It had been only a matter of time before she made full professor in the Department of Para-Archaeology.

And then came the disaster.

Her only clear recollection of what she privately called her Lost Weekend was that of coming to in a Dead City catacomb and discovering that not only was she alone but she had somehow lost her amber. Without it she faced the nearly impossible task of finding her way to one of the exits.

But Fuzz found her. She had never figured out how he got out of the apartment, let alone prowled the Dead City until he discovered her. But he had. He had saved her life.

She was not the first strong para-archaeologist to lose control and be overwhelmed by the alien nightmares enmeshed in the traps, but she was one of the few who had not wound up in an institution after the ordeal.

Lydia removed Fuzz from her shoulder and dumped him on the bed while she changed clothes. If it weren't for his bright blue eyes he could have been mistaken for a large ball of lint sitting on the quilt.

"Bad news on the client front today, Fuzz. Looks like we won't be moving into that spiffy new apartment at the end of the month after all. And I may have to cut back your pretzel ration."

Fuzz rumbled again. He watched without much interest as she kicked off her low-heeled shoes and climbed out of her business suit.

She pulled on a pair of well-worn jeans and an over-sized white shirt, then resettled Fuzz on her shoulder.

Barefoot, she padded into her pint-size kitchen, poured herself a glass of wine from the twist-cap jug she kept in the refrigerator, and fixed a plate with a couple of crackers and some cheese. She removed the lid from the pretzel jar and grabbed a handful of munchies for Fuzz.

When that was done, she carried the makeshift hors d'oeuvres and the wine out onto the minuscule deck. Sinking into one of the loungers, she fed a pretzel to Fuzz, propped her feet on the railing, and settled back to watch the sun go down behind the great green quartz wall that surrounded the Dead City.

Her small apartment was overpriced, considering its size, the outdated kitchen, and the bad section of town in which it was located, but it had two important features. The first was that it was within walking distance of Shrimpton's House of Ancient Horrors, which meant she did not have to buy a car. The second, and in some ways more important, feature was that it was located in the Old Quarter, near the western wall of the Dead City. From her balcony she had a tiny sliver of a view of the ruins of the Dead City of Old Cadence.

It seemed to her that the ancient, mysterious metropolis was at its most hauntingly magnificent when it was silhouetted against the light of the dying sun. She contemplated the narrow wedge of the wall that she could see from the balcony and watched the last of the daylight illuminate the emerald glow of the stone. The nearly indestructible green quartz had been the Harmonics' favorite building material. The four dead cities that had been discovered thus far—

Old Frequency, Old Resonance, Old Crystal, and Old Cadence—had all been constructed of the stuff.

Aboveground the architecture of the various alien buildings assumed a dazzling variety of fanciful shapes and sizes. No one knew how the Harmonics had actually used any of the structures that were being painstakingly uncovered by the archaeological teams contracted to the university.

The only thing para-archaeologists could be sure of was that whatever had gone on aboveground in the eerie ruins, it was nothing compared to what had gone on underground. By several estimates, less than twenty percent of the catacombs had been explored. Illusion traps and energy ghosts made the work slow and fraught with danger.

She had told the doctors that she had no memories at all of what had happened during the forty-eight hours she had spent in the glowing green catacombs, but that was not entirely true. Sometimes, when she sat on her deck like this and watched night descend on the Dead City, fleeting images came to hover at the farthest corners of her mind. The wraiths always stayed just out of sight, disappearing whenever she tried to draw them into the light of day.

A part of her was more than content, even eager, to leave them in the shadows. But her intuition warned her that if she did not eventually find a way to expose them, the phantoms would haunt her until the end of her days.

She sipped her wine, gazed at the green wall, and felt the familiar little shivers go down her spine.

The knock on her door startled her so profoundly that wine sloshed over the edge of her glass.

Fuzz rumbled in annoyance.

"Could be Driffield." Lydia sucked the drops off her fingers as she got to her feet. "Maybe he got my last letter threatening to call a lawyer and decided he'd better do something about the elevator. Naw, I can't see him climbing five flights of steps to tell me he's going to get it fixed."

With Fuzz on her shoulder, she went back into the apartment and crossed the miniature living room. When she reached the door she stood on tiptoe to peer through the peephole.

Emmett London stood in the hall. He did not appear to be breathing hard after the five-story climb.

For a few seconds she just stared, unable to believe her eyes. Emmett gazed calmly back. He was not exactly smiling, but there was a trace of amusement in his expression. He was obviously aware that he was being observed.

She noticed that he had picked up the evening edition of the *Cadence Star*, which had been left on her doorstep, and held it absently in one hand. She could read the headline of the lead story: MUSEUM ASSISTANT QUESTIONED IN MURDER.

She wondered if London had stopped by to tell her just how much he disliked being connected to a murder investigation.

Taking a deep dreath, she summoned up enough bravado to open the door.

"Mr. London." She gave him her best professional smile. "What a surprise. I wasn't expecting you."

"I was in the neighborhood," he said dryly.

Not bloody likely, she thought. Hers was not the sort of neighborhood that attracted upscale businessmen who were inclined to worry about getting mugged.

On the other hand, something told her that Emmett didn't fret too much about street crime. He looked quite capable of taking care of himself.

Fuzz rumbled. It wasn't a warning. The dust-bunny sounded inquisitive.

"I see." Lydia looked at the newspaper in Emmett's hand. "It really wasn't necessary to go out of your way to tell me that you've changed your mind about hiring me as a consultant. I already assumed I wouldn't get the job."

"Did you?"

"You, uh, indicated that you were real big on discretion. I sort of figured that what with the dead body and the cops and the evening headlines, you might conclude that discretion wasn't my strong point."

"Apparently not." He glanced back along the shabby hallway and then looked at her. "I would prefer not to continue this conversation out here in the hall. May I come in?"

"Huh?" At first she thought she had misunderstood. "You want to come inside?"

"If you don't mind."

She flushed and hurriedly stepped back. "Oh, sure, sure. Please, come on in."

"Thank you."

When he moved into the foyer, he made no more noise than Fuzz did. That was where the resemblance ended, Lydia decided. Emmett London did not in the least resemble a dust-bunny blowing across the floor. There was nothing haphazard, fluffy, or scruffy about him.

He looked like someone who made his own rules. The expression in his uncompromising eyes and the severe lines of his face told her that he also lived by those rules. An ominous sign, she thought. In her experience, people who adhered to a rigid code were not particularly flexible.

Emmett studied Fuzz with a thoughtful expression as Lydia closed the door. "I assume he bites?"

"Don't be ridiculous. Fuzz is perfectly harmless."

"Is he?"

"As long as all you can see are his daylight eyes, there's nothing to be concerned about. The only time you have to worry about a dust-bunny is when he stops looking like a wad of dryer lint."

Emmett raised his brows. "They say that by the time you see the teeth it's too late."

"Yes, well—as I said, there's no need to be alarmed. Fuzz won't bite."

"I'll take your word for it."

The conversation was deteriorating, Lydia thought. She needed a distraction. "I just poured myself some wine. Will you join me?"

"Yes, thank you."

She relaxed slightly. Maybe he wasn't here to tell her that he was annoyed with her for getting him involved with the cops. Surely he wouldn't accept an offer of hospitality and then inform her that he was going to sue her and Shrimpton's House of Ancient Horrors.

Then again, maybe he would do exactly that.

"When I heard your knock, I thought you were my landlord." She went into the kitchen, yanked open the refrigerator, and removed the jug of wine. "I've been after him to get the elevator fixed. It isn't working—but I expect you noticed."

Emmett came to stand in the doorway. "I noticed."

"Driffield is a lousy landlord." She poured the wine into a glass. "I'm trying to get enough cash together to move soon. In the mean-time, he and I are locked in an ongoing war. So far he's winning. I've given him so much trouble lately that I have a hunch he's looking for an excuse to evict me."

"I understand."

Oh, sure. She seriously doubted that anyone had ever tried to evict Emmett London, but she decided it would probably not be politic to say so.

"Enough about me," she said smoothly. "It's a dull subject. Let's go out onto the balcony. I've got a view of the ruins."

He followed her outside and carefully lowered himself into the other lounger.

It was amazing how much smaller her treasured balcony seemed with him occupying such a large portion of the limited space. It wasn't that he was an especially big man, she thought. He probably qualified as medium on most counts. Medium height, medium build. It was just that what there was of him was awfully concentrated.

She had a feeling that with Emmett, like Fuzz, by the time you saw the teeth it was too late.

In spite of having spent nearly half an hour with him this morning, she knew little more about him than she had when he'd called her office and made the appointment. He had told her only that he was a business consultant from Resonance City who collected antiquities.

"We didn't have a chance to finish our conversation this morning," Emmett said.

Lydia thought about Chester's body in the sarcophagus and sighed. "No."

"I'll come straight to the point. I need a good P-A and I think you'll do."

She stared at him. Apparently he wasn't going to sue her, after all. "You still want to hire me? In spite of the fact that I got you into the evening papers?"

"I'm not in the papers." He sampled the wine. "Detective Martinez very kindly refrained from giving my name to the press."

She whistled softly. "Lucky you."

"Luck had nothing to do with it."

She relaxed slightly. "Well, if it makes you feel any better, I'm really very good at what I do."

"I'm glad to hear that." His smile lacked all trace of true humor. "It's not like I've got a lot of choice."

That gave her pause. She recalled Melanie's question that afternoon. Why hadn't he gone to the Society or to a classy museum to find a para-archaeologist?

She cleared her throat. "I don't want to talk myself out of a job, Mr. London, but you do seem to be, for want of a better phrase, financially comfortable."

He shrugged. "I'm rich, if that's what you mean."

"Yeah, that's what I mean. Let's be honest here. With your money you could go to the Society of Para-Archaeologists and pick a private consultant who has established a reputation with big-time collectors."

"I know," he said simply. "But I need one who isn't too particular."

She chilled. "Too particular about what?"

"About getting involved in the illegal side of the antiquities trade."

Lydia went very still. "Oh, damn. I knew you were too good to be true."

CHAPTER 3

HE HAD NOT HANDLED THAT WELL. EMMETT REALIZED his mistake immediately. Lydia looked as if she had been flash-frozen in her chair. She did not move so much as a single muscle.

The dust-bunny on her shoulder stirred, but since it didn't open its second pair of eyes Emmett figured he was safe for the moment.

Lydia's lagoon-blue eyes gleamed with anger, however. It was probably just his imagination or maybe a trick of the evening light, but he could have sworn that her red-gold hair had turned an even more fiery shade. Unlike the dust-bunny, she did look dangerous.

"Perhaps I should explain," he said gently.

"Don't bother. I get the picture." She narrowed her eyes. "You're under the impression that I'm a thief? That I deal in illicit antiquities?"

Obviously a bit of diplomacy was required at this juncture, Emmett decided.

"I think you have connections in the underground market here in Cadence," he said deliberately. "I need those contacts, and I'm willing to pay well for them."

She slammed down her wineglass. "I am not a ruin rat. I'm a respectable member of the Society of Para-Archaeologists. Okay, so I haven't worked on any licensed excavation teams lately, but I am in good standing with the Society. I've got enough academic credentials to paper a wall, and I've worked with some of the most noted experts in Cadence. How dare you imply—"

"My mistake." He held up one hand to silence her. "I apologize."

She was clearly not mollified. "If you want to hire a thief, Mr. London, I suggest you go elsewhere."

"I don't want to hire a thief, Miss Smith. I want to find one. Preferably with as little publicity as possible. To do that, I figured I'd need someone who knew the underground side of the antiquities business."

"I see." Her voice was as brittle as glass. "What made you think that I could help you?"

"I did a little research."

"You mean you went looking for a P-A who was not employed by a legitimate excavation team?"

He shrugged and took a sip of the truly awful wine. He congratulated himself on not wincing.

Lydia's smile was getting colder by the second. "Did you work on the assumption that any P-A who could not get respectable employment on a team or in a museum must be involved in the illegal trade?"

"It seemed like a reasonable theory. I regret any misunderstandings."

"Misunderstandings?" She leaned forward slightly. "Calling me a thief comes under the heading of *insults*, not misunderstandings."

"If it makes any difference, I'm not especially concerned with your professional ethics."

"It makes a difference, all right," she said ominously. "A big difference."

"Be fair, Miss Smith. No one expects to find a legitimate para-archaeologist working at a place like Shrimpton's House of Ancient Horrors." He paused. "And then there was that business with the body in the sarcophagus this morning."

"I knew you were going to hold that against me." She flung out a hand in disgust. "One lousy body and you leap to the conclusion that I'm up to my ears in the illegal trade."

"It wasn't finding the body that made me think you might have some contacts in the business, it was the fact that you seemed well acquainted with the victim. I'm told that, among other things, Chester Brady was a ruin rat."

Her mouth opened, closed, and then opened again. "Oh." After a moment she settled wearily back into her chair. "I suppose that could lead a person to some inaccurate conclusions."

"I appreciate your cutting me some slack on that point." He took another cautious swallow of wine and pondered the razor-thin view of the Old Wall. "So how did you come to know Brady?"

Lydia slanted him a meditative glance. Out of the corner of his eye he studied her expressive, intelligent face. He got the feeling that she was debating just how much to tell him. He would no doubt get the highly edited version of the story, he thought. She had no reason to confide in him.

Not that he didn't already know a good deal about her. In the past twenty-four hours he had made it a point to learn a lot. He was

24

aware of the two days she'd spent trapped underground in the Dead City six months ago. His people in Resonance had briefed him on her medical reports—reports that were supposed to be private and confidential but that were extraordinarily easy to come by if you had money and connections. He had plenty of both.

This morning when he'd walked into her office and seen the gutsy determination in her eyes, he'd immediately dismissed the opinions of the para-rez psychiatrists. Whatever else she was, Lydia was not weak or delicate. He knew another fighter when he saw one.

The little rush of pure sexual awareness that went through him in that first moment was a warning. He had chosen to ignore it. That, he reflected, might not have been one of his smarter decisions. But he knew himself well enough to realize that he was not going to change his mind.

"I met Chester a few years ago," Lydia said after a while. "He was a strong ephemeral-energy para-resonator."

"A tangler?"

"Yes. But he came from nothing. No family, no proper schooling. He never went to the university. Never studied archaeology the way most good tanglers do. He was never allowed into the Society."

"That's not exactly a mark against him. Everyone knows the Society of Para-Archaeologists is as arrogant and elitist as they come."

She glowered. "I agree that the Society is inclined to be a bit stiff-necked, academically speaking. But it's because of their high standards and strict admission requirements that tanglers haven't got the same disreputable public image as those ghost-hunters in the Guilds."

"The Guilds have standards," he made himself say in a neutral tone.

"Hah. What the Guilds have are bosses who run things the way gangster bosses run their gangs, and everyone knows it. In this town, the Guild boss is Mercer Wyatt, and I can assure you that whatever standards he imposes have nothing to do with academic qualifications or credentials."

Emmett contemplated the bright flash of anger that lit her eyes. "It's no secret that there's a lot of professional rivalry between hunters and tanglers, but you seem to have taken it to an extreme."

"Whatever else you can say about the members of the Society, we're respected professionals, not members of an organization that is only one step above an underworld mob."

"I believe that we were discussing Chester Brady."

Lydia blinked a few times, scowled, and then subsided back into her chair. "Yeah, Poor Chester."

"You said he never gained admission to the Society?"

"He preferred to work the, uh, fringes of the antiquities trade."

"Meaning he was a thief?"

"Well, yes. But I sort of liked him anyway. At least, when I wasn't mad as hell at him. He really was an incredible tangler, you know. Very few could resonate with the ephemeral energy in the illusion traps the way he could. I once saw him de-rez a whole series of vicious little traps in one of the catacombs." She broke off abruptly and dabbed surreptitiously at the corner of her eye with the sleeve of her shirt.

"How did you become friends?"

"He runs—ran—a little shop in the Old Quarter near the east wall. Sort of a combination pawnshop and antiquities gallery. Small-time stuff. Anyhow, a couple of years ago he ripped off a little tomb vase from the lab where I was working. I traced it to his shop. Confronted him. We got to talking, and one thing led to another."

"You bonded with a small-time thief? Just like that?" Emmett said in surprise.

Her jaw tightened. "I got my tomb vase back first. As a gesture of thanks for not handing him over to the authorities, Chester did a small favor for me. As time went on, he did other favors."

"What kind of favors?"

She turned her glass between her fingers. "He knew everyone involved in Dead City work, legal and illegal. He knew who could be trusted and who would rip you off without a second thought. He also knew who was hiding a major find and who'd just secured funding from questionable sources. There's a lot of competition among the excavation teams, you see. Inside information is useful."

"There's always a lot of competition when there's a lot of money at stake."

"It's not only the money. Careers are made and broken out there on the sites."

"So good old Chester clued you in on the players in the business?"

"Something like that."

Emmett looked at her. "What did you do for him in return?"

"I . . . talked to him. And once I listed him as a consulting source in a paper I published in the *Journal of Para-Archaeology*." She smiled sadly. "Chester really got a kick out of that."

"You said you talked to him." Emmett paused. "What did you talk about?"

"Lots of things. Chester spent years underground. Illegally, of course, but he sure knew a lot of stuff. Sometimes we talked about how it felt to go into para-resonate mode with the really old illusion traps. The kind that can suck you into a nightmare before you know what hit you."

"I see."

"Chester was a loner, but even loners get lonely occasionally. And tanglers need to talk to other tanglers sometimes. The Society provides more than just decent career opportunities for ephemeral-energy para-resonators. It functions as a club. A place where you can meet and talk to other people, share experiences."

"But Brady wasn't a member of the club."

She shook her head. "No. So he talked to me instead."

"In other words, Brady was an outcast tangler who sometimes pined for company, and you provided it?"

"That about sums it up."

"Any idea who might have wanted to kill him?"

"No. But there was always someone around who was unhappy with Chester." She made a face. "Including me. I've been struggling to get a private consulting business up and running. Last month he lured away my first important client. I was furious with him for a while. But it was hard to stay mad at him."

"I see."

Lydia straightened in her seat. "I think it's time you told me exactly why you wanted to hire me, Mr. London."

He leaned back in his chair and propped his feet up on the railing. "Recently a family heirloom was taken from my private collection. I have reason to believe that the thief brought it here to Cadence and sold it on the underground market. I want it back."

"You want me to help you trace it?"

"Yes."

"It's a Harmonic artifact, I assume?"

"No. As a matter of fact, it's not an antiquity from the ruins. This particular artifact came through the Curtain with my ancestors."

Her eyes widened. "You're looking for something pre-colonial? An object from Earth?"

"Yes." The barely suppressed excitement in her voice amused him. "It's not nearly as old as anything from the Dead Cities here on Harmony, of course. But it is, obviously, extremely valuable."

"Naturally." Enthusiasm lit her face. "Anything from the Old World is worth a fortune to collectors. So little remains."

"Yes."

Everyone knew that after the mysterious gate between worlds known as the curtain closed forever, the settlers on Harmony had found themselves stranded. Lacking replacement parts, the equipment the colonists had brought with them had ultimately failed. Everything that could be used had been stripped. Many valuable artifacts had been lost during the violent, tumultuous period known as the Era of Discord. Most of the rest had been discarded, lost, or destroyed in the two hundred years that had passed since colonization.

"What was it?" Lydia demanded eagerly. "One of the computers? An agricultural tool of some kind?"

"It's a box," Emmett said.

Her face fell. "A box?"

"A very special box. Hand-carved from some sort of golden-brown wood and trimmed with gold and silver metals. It's called a cabinet of curiosities. It contains dozens and dozens of small secret drawers. My great grandmother claimed that no one in the family had ever found and unlocked all of them."

Lydia frowned. "I don't understand. It sounds like a work of art, not a piece of Old Earth equipment or a mechanical device."

"It is a work of art. Handmade by an Old World craftsman some four hundred years before the Curtain opened. One of my Earth-side ancestors had the wood especially treated to preserve it indefinitely."

"But that's not possible." Lydia's voice gentled, although she did not trouble to hide the disappointment in her eyes. "You know as well as I do that the settlers brought no art with them. Space on the transports was too limited. And the Curtain closed before trade between the two worlds could be established. Perhaps it's something one of your ancestors made after arriving here on Harmony."

"No," Emmett said. "The cabinet of curiosities is from Old Earth."

"But how did your ancestors get it here?"

Emmett glanced at her. "I'm told that my several-times-great-grandfather had no choice. He married just before he came through the Curtain, and his new wife insisted on bringing the cabinet with her. Apparently she was a strong-willed woman. Somehow, she convinced my ancestor to smuggle it on board the transport."

Lydia looked politely doubtful. "I see."

"You don't believe me?" he asked skeptically.

"Every family has a few quaint legends concerning its Old World history."

"You think I'm looking for a colonial-era box that one of my forebears crafted right here on Harmony, don't you?"

She gave him a breezy, reassuring smile. "Don't worry. It really doesn't matter what I think about the provenance of your missing artifact. I don't have to believe that it came through the Curtain in order to find it for you."

"True, but there's a small problem with that approach."

"What problem?"

"If you really think that I'm semidelusional or just overly sentimental about an old family antique, you probably won't be sufficiently careful."

"Why do I need to be careful?"

"Because there are collectors who do believe that the box dates from pre-Curtain Earth. Some of them would no doubt kill to get their hands on it."

CHAPTER 4

"A SMALL CHEST, YOU SAY." BARTHOLOMEW GREELEY folded his hands on top of the locked glass case. His broad, ruddy features assumed a meditative expression. "Made of a yellowish wood. With a number of tiny hidden drawers."

"That's how my client described it." Lydia glanced at her watch. She had only twenty minutes left on her lunch hour. "Apparently it's been in his family for several generations. Between you and me, he's convinced it's an Old World antique."

Greeley looked pained. "Highly unlikely."

"Yeah, I know. Probably a nice heirloom-quality piece made right here on Harmony less than a hundred years ago but with a history that has been, shall we say, embellished by a long series of grandfathers and grandmothers." Lydia nodded. "You know how families are when it comes to that kind of thing."

"Indeed." Bartholomew's eyes gleamed. "But if the particular family in question actually believes the item is of Old World manufacture—" He let the sentence trail off suggestively.

Lydia got the point. "Rest assured, my client is convinced that the cabinet came from Earth, and he is prepared to pay well to get it back."

"How well?" Bartholomew asked bluntly.

"He has instructed me to put out the word that he will top any offer from a private collector."

"What about an offer from a museum?"

"My client says he can prove ownership of the cabinet and will go to court to get it back if necessary. No curator will touch it if he or she thinks the museum will lose it in a legal battle. What with the initial expense plus legal costs, it wouldn't be worth the price."

"True. Not unless the artifact in question actually is a work of art from the home world."

"As you said, highly unlikely. The thing to keep in mind is that my client *believes* it's from Earth. That means there will probably be some other collectors who can be persuaded to believe it too."

"Hmm." Bartholomew pursed his lips. "So you need concern yourself only with the private market."

"Not just the private collector market, Bart." Lydia gave him a meaningful look. "A very special segment of that market."

He did not pretend to misunderstand. "The segment that does not ask too many questions."

"Right. We both know that you would never get involved in questionable transactions, of course."

"Absolutely not. I have my reputation to consider."

"Naturally." Lydia was proud of the fact that she did not even blink at that statement. "But a dealer in your position sometimes hears things. I just want you to know that my client is prepared to compensate you for any information that leads to the recovery of his antique box."

"Indeed." Bartholomew glanced around the cluttered interior of Greeley's Antiques with an air of satisfaction. "You're quite right, of course. A dealer in my position occasionally picks up rumors."

Lydia followed his gaze. The display cabinets were crammed with odd bits and pieces of rusty metal and warped, faded plastic. She recognized some of the items in the cases, including what looked like the remains of an Old World weather forecasting instrument and the hilt of a knife. They were typical of the kind of basic tools the settlers had brought through the Curtain or crafted shortly after their arrival on Harmony.

A torn, badly stained shirt with a round colonial-style collar was displayed in one of the glass-topped counters. Next to it was a pair of boots that looked as old as the shirt. Neither the shirt nor the boots bore any traces of artistic adornment. The colonists had tended to be an austere lot. They'd become even more focused on the basics of survival after the Curtain had closed.

She took a step closer to the case that held the shirt and boots, widening her eyes at the neatly penned description and price.

"You're selling these as genuine first-generation apparel?" she asked politely.

"Both the shirt and the boots have been authenticated," Bartholomew said smoothly. "Excellent examples of early colonial-era work. There is every reason to believe that they were crafted within the first decade after the closing of the Curtain."

"I'd say it's a lot more likely that they were made last year by a forger who didn't do enough research."

Bartholomew scowled. "No offense, Lydia, but you're an expert in Harmonic antiquities, not colonial antiques."

"Give me some credit, Bart." Lydia eyed him. "Just because I specialize in ruin work doesn't mean I don't know a fake human antique when I see one. I was trained to recognize all kinds of frauds."

Bartholomew's wide face reddened in outrage. "What makes you think that shirt is not first generation?"

"The color. That particular shade of green wasn't used in the early colonial era. It appeared about forty years after the Curtain closed."

Bartholomew sighed. "Thank you for your opinion."

Lydia chuckled. "Hey, don't go changing the price on my account. Like you said, I'm no colonial-antiques expert."

"Quite true," Bartholomew said a little too readily. "And I won't be changing the price."

She took another look at her watch. Fifteen minutes left until she had to be back at Shrimpton's House of Ancient Horrors. There had been time for visits to only two antique galleries on her lunch hour today. She had deliberately chosen to start with Greeley's Antiques and Hickman's Colonial Artifacts because both proprietors dealt in Old Earth and first-generation artifacts and because neither gallery owner was overburdened with scruples.

"I've got to get back to the office," Lydia said. "We've been swamped at Shrimpton's today. You will let me know right away if you hear anything, won't you?"

"You have my word on it, my dear." Bartholomew looked at her. "Speaking of your job at Shrimpton's little museum, mind if I ask a question?"

"I didn't murder poor Chester."

Bartholomew gave her a limpid glance. "Good heavens, Lydia, I wasn't about to suggest that you did."

"Why not? Everyone else has felt free to suggest exactly that."

Bartholomew leaned forward and rested his elbows on the counter.

"The thing is, why was he found in that tacky little establishment where you work?"

"Haven't got a clue." Lydia turned to walk toward the front door. "But I'll tell you one thing. If I had killed Chester, I wouldn't have left his body just down the hall from my own office. A little too obvious."

Bartholomew looked thoughtful. "I suppose that's true. But it does raise another interesting question."

"I know." Lydia opened the door. "What was Chester doing in Shrimpton's in the first place?"

"What do the cops think?"

"They think he went there to steal something. Granted, we're not a front-rank museum, but we do have some interesting items in the collection, especially in the Tomb Gallery. I wouldn't put it past Chester to lift a couple of vases or some tomb mirrors."

"I wouldn't put anything past Chester. But why was he murdered, do you think?"

Lydia shook her head. "Who knows? Detective Martinez believes that one of his truly annoyed clients followed him and killed him in the museum."

"Poor Chester. He never got that big break he was always looking for, did he?"

"No," Lydia said quietly, "he didn't."

She stepped out onto the sidewalk and closed the door behind herself. She was satisfied with what she had accomplished. Both Greeley and Hickman operated in the gray area between the world of respectable galleries and the illegal underground of the antiques business. By tonight, the news that she was looking for the cabinet of curiosities would have reached every dealer in Cadence.

She shot another glance at her watch and smiled to herself. So what if she was a suspect in a murder investigation? Things were looking up. Counting travel time to and from Ruin Row, she was about to post her first billable hour to Emmett London's account.

Her first job as a private consultant was off to a nice start. She could only hope that she wasn't successful too soon. The less time it took to track down the London family heirloom, the less she could charge Emmett for her services. She pursed her lips. Maybe she should have done a fixed-price contract.

EMMETT EMERGED FROM THE CROWDED BAR AND walked down the cracked sidewalk. The weak streetlamps in this section of the Old Quarter made only small inroads in the dark valleys of the night, and the light fog didn't help. It created impenetrable pockets of shadow in the unlit doorways of the looming buildings. It was a little like moving through a Dead City catacomb, Emmett thought, but without the green glow and the eerie, alien quality.

He crossed the silent street, automatically adjusting his balance so that his boot heels did not echo on the pavement.

He walked deliberately back to where he had parked the Slider, but he did not hurry. He was in no great rush to return to his hotel. He needed to think, and it was easier to do that out here in the shadows.

Things were becoming complicated, he reflected. Hiring Lydia Smith had not been part of the original plan. But with Brady dead, the only thing he could do was improvise.

The prickle of awareness at the top of his spine interrupted his thoughts. It got his immediate and complete attention.

The telltale whiff of synch-smoke told him that the watcher was somewhere in the shadows to his left. He continued along the sidewalk without pause, but he took his hands out of his pockets.

A figure stirred in an unlit doorway.

"Mr. Emmett London?"

Well, that was a first, Emmett thought. Small-time thugs who preyed on late-night bar crawlers rarely addressed their intended victims by name, let alone in a polite, damn near deferential tone.

Which meant that the young man in the shadows of the doorway was probably not a garden-variety street thief.

Emmett came to a halt and waited.

The man stepped out of the shadows into the pale glow of the streetlamp. He was thin and lanky, and he had the trademark ghost-hunter slouch down cold. He also had the wardrobe. He was dressed in khakis, boots, and a supple black leather jacket with the collar pulled up around his ears in a rakish manner. His long hair was tied back at his nape with a black leather thong. He wore his amber in a belt buckle the size of a car.

The size of one's amber wasn't important. It took only a small chunk of the stuff to focus psi power and convert it into a usable energy field. But try telling that to the flashy dressers.

"Didn't mean to alarm you, sir. My name is Renny. I'm just the messenger."

"That can be a high-risk profession."

"That sounds like something the boss would say," Renny replied.

"Who's your boss?"

Renny scowled. "I'm a guildman. My boss is Mercer Wyatt."

"Really?" Emmett smiled slightly. "You take orders from Wyatt?"

Renny flushed. "Well, not directly, of course. Not yet, at any rate.

But I'm movin' up fast in the Guild. One of these days I'm gonna take orders from the big man himself. Meanwhile, I get 'em through Bonner."

"And what exactly did Bonner tell you to tell me?"

Renny drew himself up as if preparing to recite from memory. "Mr. Wyatt requests your presence at dinner. His place."

"Let me be sure I've got this straight. This is an invitation."

"Yeah, right."

"So why didn't Wyatt just pick up the phone and call me at my hotel?"

Renny looked slightly taken aback by that suggestion. "With all due respect, sir, Mr. Wyatt is real big on tradition, y'know? He likes to do things in the old ways."

"You mean he likes to run things the way they were run in the days following the Era of Discord. Somebody ought to tell him that times have changed."

Renny's brow furrowed deeply. "Just because the Resonance City Guild decided to turn itself into some kinda wimpy business corporation doesn't mean the other Guilds got to do things that way. Here in Cadence, we're into tradition."

"Well, Benny—"

"Renny."

"Excuse me. Renny. Tell you what. Go ahead and honor your traditions. In the meantime, not only is the Resonance Guild making money hand over fist, but one of the vice presidents is getting ready to run for a seat on the Federation Council."

Renny's mouth dropped open. "The Council? Are you serious? A guildman is running for public office?"

"He's mounting a campaign, and the latest polls show he's probably going to get elected. You know why? The voters think he's had a lot of good, solid business experience because of his executive position in the Guild."

"Well, shit." Renny shook his head. "If that don't beat all. How the hell did they do it?"

Emmett shrugged. "Let's just say that the last boss of the Resonance Guild decided he didn't like being regarded as the CEO of a racketeering mob. He decided to upgrade the Guild image. You know, mainstream the organization."

Renny's face scrunched up into a puzzled frown. "Mainstream?"

"Never mind. Look, it's getting late. You've delivered your message, so why don't we just say good night?"

"Wait—you haven't accepted Mr. Wyatt's invitation."

"I'll go back to my hotel and think about it. If I decide I can fit it into my busy social schedule, I'll give him a call." Emmett started to move on. "You know, on the phone?"

Renny looked alarmed. "Mr. Wyatt will be real disappointed if you don't have dinner with him, sir."

"Good old Mercer. He always was the sentimental type."

Renny cleared his throat. "One more thing. I'm supposed to tell you that if you accept Mr. Wyatt's invitation, he might be able to help you out with your business here in Cadence."

Emmett stopped and looked back over his shoulder. "Is that a fact?"

"Yes, sir."

Emmett considered that for a moment while Renny twitched uneasily. Striking a bargain with Mercer Wyatt definitely came under the heading of risky business. But if he got some assistance from the Guild out of the deal, it just might be worth it.

"Tell Wyatt I'll call him in the morning," Emmett said.

Renny blinked a couple of times. "You mean you ain't gonna accept right now?"

"No. I want to think about this for a while." Emmett turned away again.

"Mr. Wyatt's not gonna like being told he's gotta wait," Renny called out behind him.

"I warned you that being a messenger was a high-risk job," Emmett said. He walked off into the fog.

CHAPTER 5

LYDIA WAS NOT SURE WHAT IT WAS THAT AWAKENED her. It could have been Fuzz shifting his weight at the foot of the bed. She lay unmoving and opened all of her senses.

The unmistakable aura of psi energy vibrated in the air around her.

"Damn."

She knew this prickling sensation all too well.

"Fuzz. Don't move."

The dust-bunny made a low rumbling sound, not a purr but a hissing growl. Lydia sat up cautiously, searching the shadows swiftly for what she knew had to be there.

The bedroom was not very dark. After the Lost Weekend incident, she had altered more than one routine. These days she left the light on in the adjoining bathroom all night long. In addition, she slept with the curtains open to allow the reflected glow of the street-lamps and some moonlight into the bedroom. There had been other changes, too. She wore one of her personalized amber bracelets to bed and kept half a dozen others scattered around the apartment.

Forty-eight hours in the catacombs had left their mark.

She saw Fuzz's eyes first—his second pair, the ones he used for hunting. They glowed a fiery gold in the dimly lit room. Fuzz was seriously concerned. That meant that she was not overreacting.

She swept the rest of the bedroom, seeking the telltale glow. Nothing.

The whisper of energy shimmered again in the air. Lydia concentrated. No doubt about it, a ghost had invaded her bedroom. But it had not yet materialized.

"Just a tingle. A small one, Fuzz."

Of course it was a small ghost, she thought, desperately trying to reassure herself and the dust-bunny at the same time. Here in the Old Quarter, psi energy leaked freely out of unseen cracks in the Dead City. Nevertheless, even a strong ghost-hunter could summon only a small manifestation of dissonance energy outside the catacombs.

But the conclusion was obvious. If there was a ghost in the vicinity, there was a ghost-hunter somewhere nearby. Unstable Dissonance Energy Manifestations did not appear on their own outside the catacombs. And the only folks who could manipulate energy ghosts were ghost-hunters.

A shadow moved on the balcony outside her window. Lydia turned her head quickly, but she caught only a fleeting glimpse of a figure.

"*Pervert!*" she shouted.

The shadow disappeared from sight.

She longed to give chase, but she had to deal with the ghost first. Even small UDEMs could do a considerable amount of damage.

She eased aside the bedclothes, got to her feet, and scooped Fuzz off the quilt. The dust-bunny did not relax in her arms. His hunting eyes were twin flames in the shadows. His small body trembled. Lydia caught a glimpse of fang. He was staring at the space above her pillow.

The ghost began to materialize. Acid-green energy pulsed erratically. Lydia edged back toward the door. Fuzz hissed.

"Take it easy. There's nothing either of us can do except stay out of its way until it vaporizes. It really is pretty small. I doubt it will last more than a few minutes."

She did not turn her back on the ghost as she retreated into the hall. The green glow of the coalescing form grew steadily more intense.

"That bastard out on my balcony probably thinks this is very funny. If I find out who it is, I'm going to turn him in to the cops. Summoning ghosts outside the Dead City is illegal, and everyone knows it."

But the vow was a waste of breath. Even if she managed to discover which of the neighborhood toughs had pulled this vicious trick on her tonight, the police were unlikely to get involved. At most, someone would contact the Guild authorities and report the incident. The Guild might or might not take action.

Fuzz growled again. His hunting eyes gleamed more fiercely.

In the air above her bed, the green ball of energy started to move. There was an audible crackle as it floated closer to the wall. Lydia grew more uneasy. There was no sign that the ghost was weakening. More disturbing was the fact that it did not seem to be moving randomly now.

Fuzz stared, unblinking, at the pulsating energy ball over the bed. Lydia knew that there was nothing either of them could do about the ghost except stay out of its way and hope that it did no serious damage. Only a dissonance-energy para-resonator—a ghost-hunter—could summon one; only a hunter could de-rez it.

The small, pulsing green specter was almost touching the wall over the bed now. Lydia watched in frustration.

Then she smelled scorched paint.

"My wall!" Lydia whirled and ran down the hall, barely avoiding a collision with the small end table she had put there because there was no other space for it.

She dashed into the kitchen, tossed Fuzz onto the counter, flung open the door under the sink, and grabbed the household fire extinguisher, then raced back toward her bedroom.

Fuzz gamely tumbled down from the counter and scampered after her.

"It can't last much longer," she told him. "It just *can't*. Not here, outside the wall."

The smell of burning paint reached her before she got back to the bedroom doorway. She rounded the corner just in time to see the eerie green glow wink out of existence.

"It's gone." She breathed a sigh of relief. "Told you it couldn't last, Fuzz."

The odor of charred paint was unpleasantly strong. Lydia groped for the light switch, flipped it. And then groaned when she saw the scorch marks the ghost had left on the formerly pristine white surface of the wall.

With the immediate danger past, she whirled and went to the window. She was just in time to see a figure garbed in dark clothing vanish up a rope ladder that dangled from the roof. As she watched, outraged, the ladder was pulled up and out of sight. She yanked open the window and leaned out.

"Little punk! If I ever get my hands on you—"

But the jerk was gone, and she knew the odds of learning his identity were virtually zip.

That was when the full implications of the situation hit her. She had given her landlord so much trouble lately that he would probably seize upon any excuse to terminate her lease. Fire and smoke damage no doubt came under the heading of "willful destruction of property by tenant" or some other vague clause in the contract.

"If Driffield finds out about this, we're fried, Fuzz."

EMMETT GLANCED AT THE AMBER FACE OF HIS WATCH AS he got out of the Slider. It was barely seven o'clock. The morning sun had not yet penetrated the blanket of fog that had crawled in from the river late last night.

He walked across the small, cramped parking lot of the Dead City View Apartments, let himself in through the broken security gate, and started up the stairwell.

He had called twice before leaving the hotel, but Lydia had not answered her phone. Probably in the shower, he thought. He had considered waiting until she got to work before he talked to her, but in the end he'd decided it would be better if he spoke to her outside Shrimpton's museum.

He was halfway down the dingy corridor to her door before the obvious explanation for Lydia's failure to answer her phone this morning occurred to him. Maybe she had spent the night somewhere other than her own apartment.

For some obscure reason, that possibility irritated him. She was *his* consultant. He had first claim on the hours that she did not spend at Shrimpton's House of Ancient Horrors.

He started to lean on the doorbell, recalled that it did not function, and knocked instead. The door opened with unexpected speed. He caught a whiff of fresh paint.

"Stop by to see the damage you caused, you little thug?" Lydia jerked the door wide. "If you think I won't go to the cops just because you're a kid, you—" She broke off, her eyes widening in shock. "Mr. London."

He studied her with deep interest. Clearly, she had not yet dressed for her job at Shrimpton's. She wore an old denim shirt and a pair of well-worn, faded jeans. Her fiery hair was held back off her face with a wide blue band. The style underscored the intriguing angles of her face. There was a paintbrush in her left hand.

The dust-bunny was perched on her shoulder, looking like a dirty cotton ball. Blue eyes blinked innocently at him.

"Little thug?" Emmett repeated politely.

A deep red blush crept up Lydia's throat into her cheeks. "Sorry about the greeting," she said gruffly. "I, uh, was expecting someone else."

He glanced at the paintbrush. "Does this mean you won't be going to your office at the museum today?"

"I wish." She wrinkled her nose. "Unfortunately, I've got less than two hours to finish repainting my bedroom wall, get changed, and get to work. Look, I know you're here because you want an update on how my search for your heirloom is going, but I really don't have time to talk right now."

"I can see that. Mind if I ask why you didn't wait until the weekend to undertake a major household-remodeling project?"

"I don't have much choice. One of the neighborhood ghost-hunter wanna-bes paid me a visit last night. Pulled a particularly nasty prank."

Emmett moved into the small foyer without waiting for an invitation. "What kind of prank?"

"He managed to summon a small ghost. It materialized in my bedroom. I don't know if he meant to do damage or if the UDEM just got away from him. Whatever, my wall looks like someone tried to use it for a barbecue grill. If my landlord finds out about the damage, he'll probably try to use it as an excuse to cancel my lease."

"I'll give you a hand," Emmett said.

"I beg your pardon?"

Her astonishment amused him for some reason. "I can paint a wall."

"Oh." She glanced uncertainly down the hall. "It's very nice of you to offer to help, but—"

He removed the brush from her hand. "Let me have that." He started down the hall.

"Wait." She hurried after him. "You'll ruin that spiffy jacket. It looks like it cost a fortune. I can't afford to replace it for you."

"Don't worry about the jacket." He came to a halt in the bedroom doorway and studied the scene.

He had invited himself inside because he needed to see the evidence of ghost damage. Neighborhood punk or not, the fact that his new consultant had received a "visitation" within twenty-four hours of going to work for him set off several alarm bells.

Even though he was here to examine the wall, the first thing he noticed was the unmade bed. There was something very intimate about the sight of the tangled white sheets and rumpled quilt. Lydia had slept here last night. Alone, from all indications. He felt the same whisper of sexual awareness that he had experienced the other morning at Shrimpton's when he had interviewed her. The sensation was stronger this time. He wondered how much of a complication it would prove to be.

Lydia came up behind him in the doorway. He forced his attention back to the matter at hand.

The bed had been pushed away from the wall. A sheet spread out on the floor served as a makeshift tarp. A bucket of white paint sat on the sheet. Rags were piled in a heap.

Emmett looked at the smoky traces on the wall. Three wavy lines. A chill settled in his gut.

"We've got a problem," he said.

"I know I've got a problem. His name is Driffield. But as you can see, I'm almost half finished with that wall. If you'll just get out of my way—"

Emmett shook his head a single time, his gaze still on the marks that had been burned into the paint. "Your landlord is not your biggest issue right now."

"What are you talking about?"

He did not answer right away. Hell, maybe he was wrong, he thought. Maybe he was letting his imagination run riot. It was just barely possible the marks were merely random.

He walked slowly into the room, examining the singed paint. The more closely he looked, the more he knew that his first reaction had been the right one. The marks were not the haphazard scorching of a small out-of-control ghost. Admittedly it was sloppy work, but he could make out the design. The three wavy lines were unmistakable.

"Your neighborhood punk didn't do this," Emmett said.

"Don't bet on it. We've got some strong young budding ghost-hunters around here. Future hoodlums, all of 'em. And all itching to join the Guild."

"I don't care how strong they are. Those burn marks are deliberate. They aren't random scorches. Whoever summoned the ghost had it under full control. No untrained dissonance-energy para-rez could have managed that degree of accuracy with a wild ghost."

She eyed him uneasily. "Do you really think so?"

"Yeah," Emmett said very quietly. "I really think so. We need to talk."

She studied him for a long moment. "You think this has something to do with your missing cabinet, don't you?"

"Yes."

She hesitated. "Okay, we'll talk. But the conversation will have to take place some other time. Right now I've got to get this wall painted, and then I have to get to work."

She snatched the paintbrush back out of his hand, stepped around him, and started toward the wall.

His first impulse was to grab the brush again, but he resisted the temptation. Maybe he'd been wrong about her relationship with Chester Brady. Maybe he'd been wrong about some other things as well. He was still winging it, he reminded himself. Still playing it by ear. So much depended on hitting the right notes.

"I'll take you to dinner tonight," he said. "We'll talk then."

She frowned. "What is this? Has something changed since yester-day?"

He glanced at the design that had been etched into her wall. "Maybe. Maybe not."

She gave him a steely look. "I'd better remind you that we have a contract, Mr. London."

"I'm aware of that, Miss Smith. Like I said, I'll fill you in this evening. In the meantime, don't make any further inquiries concern-ing my cabinet."

Alarm flashed in her eyes. "Why not?"

"There isn't time to go into it now."

"Wait just one damn minute here." Her voice heated swiftly. "I've got plans to talk to three more antique shop owners today."

"Forget them."

"But—"

He turned to face her. "That is a direct order, Miss Smith. I don't want you making any more inquiries on my behalf concerning the cabinet until we've discussed the matter tonight. Is that understood?"

Most people backed down when he used that tone. Lydia's jaw tightened, but she did not give so much as an inch.

"No," she said, "it is not understood."

"Let's get something clear here. I'm the client. I'm telling you that I will not pay you another cent if you continue talking to dealers about the cabinet."

"But we have a contract," she protested.

"Paint your wall, Miss Smith. I'll pick you up tonight at seven."

CHAPTER 6

"SO WHO'S THIS GUY YOU'RE GOING OUT WITH TO-
night?" Zane Hoyt helped himself to a can of Curtain Cola from
Lydia's small refrigerator. "Someone you met at the museum?"

"Sort of. He's a new client." Lydia peered into the hall mirror and
adjusted the gold hoop in her ear. "It's a business meeting, not a
date."

"Sounds boring."

Whatever else Emmett London was, Lydia thought, he was definitely not boring. She met Zane's gaze in the mirror and smiled.

Zane had just turned thirteen. Dark-haired and dark-eyed, he was
slim, energetic, and hitting the awkward stage when he badly needed
a man's firm hand on his shoulder. Unfortunately, there was no adult
male in the picture. His father, a ghost-hunter, had been killed years
ago in the catacombs. His mother had died in a drunk-driving acci-

dent shortly thereafter. Zane was being raised by his aunt, Olinda Hoyt. They lived downstairs on the third floor.

The majority of Lydia's so-called friends and colleagues at the University had disappeared after the Lost Weekend incident. Zane and Olinda had befriended Lydia at a time when she had found herself badly in need of friends. She was deeply grateful.

"The important thing is that Mr. London is going to pay me big bucks to help him find a lost family heirloom," Lydia said.

"Huh. Still sounds boring." Zane paused hopefully. "Unless we're talking about something from the catacombs?"

"Nope. It's an Old Earth antique."

"Why do you want to mess around with Old Earth stuff? I thought you wanted to get back underground."

"I do. But before I can attract that kind of business, I need to establish my reputation as a private consultant. That means I'll take any business I can get."

"I guess." Zane took a swallow of cola and wrinkled his nose. "So is it okay for me to study here tonight with Fuzz while you're out?"

"Sure." Anything to encourage his educational efforts, Lydia thought. "Fuzz enjoys the company."

Zane was a budding dissonance-energy para-rez. Unless he was forcibly prodded into a different path, his career prospects were all too obvious. It was almost a given that he would join the Guild when he turned eighteen and become a ghost-hunter. To make matters worse, he was thrilled with the image of himself in leather and khaki.

Lydia was doing her utmost to discourage him. At best, ghost-hunters were little more than high-priced bodyguards, in her opinion. Bodyguards, furthermore, who could not be depended upon in a crunch, as she had discovered at her own expense six months ago. At worst, they were gangsters.

Zane was too bright to waste his life in a dead-end muscle job. She might not be able to keep him from doing some ghost-hunting on the side, but she was determined that he get a college degree and study a respectable profession.

She sat down in the chair across from him. "Zane, before Mr. London gets here, I want to ask you a question. This is real serious, okay? So please don't tease me."

He gave her a quizzical look. "Something wrong?"

"Maybe. Last night someone summoned a ghost and sent it into my bedroom to frighten me. Today, at work, I got a weird phone call about it. I think it must have been someone from the neighborhood. Any idea who it was?"

Zane sputtered on a mouthful of cola. "Are you kidding? None of the guys I hang with are strong enough yet to actually summon a ghost."

"How about one of the older boys? Derrick or Rich?"

Zane took another swig of his soda while he pondered that. "Jeez, I dunno, Lyd. I don't think so. Maybe it's someone new in the area."

"I was afraid you'd say that," Lydia muttered.

"A lot of the guys would probably *tell* you they could do it, but don't believe 'em. They like to flash a lot of amber around, but I've never actually seen any of 'em do much except maybe get a couple of flickers going." Zane eyed her closely. "You sure that wasn't what you saw? Some flickers?"

"Positive." Lydia knew that Zane and his buddies used the word "flickers" to describe the tiny, harmless scraps of energy that were too small to be classified as real ghosts. They lasted, on average, for only a few seconds before winking out of existence. They were too little and too weak to be manipulated. Even the youngest and weakest hunters could summon flickers by the time they reached puberty.

"You're sure it was a real ghost?" Zane looked doubtful.

"Trust me on this, Zane. If there's one thing I can recognize on sight, it's a real ghost."

"Yeah, sure," he said much too quickly. "I believe you, Lyd."

But she caught the flash of concern in his gaze and knew what he was thinking. Zane was her friend and loyal defender, but deep down he, too, was worried that she had been badly damaged by whatever she had experienced during her Lost Weekend in the catacombs.

Until she got back underground and faced a few traps, she could not prove to herself or anyone else that she wasn't going to crack under pressure.

The knock on the front door interrupted her before she could grill Zane further.

"That will be my hot date." She started to get to her feet.

But Zane leaped off the sofa and charged toward the door. "I'll get it."

He opened the door with a flourish. There was a moment of acute silence while man and boy regarded each other.

"Hello," Emmett said. "I'm here to pick up Lydia."

Zane grinned. "Hi. I'm a friend of Lydia's. Zane. Zane Hoyt."

"Nice to meet you, Zane. I'm Emmett London." Emmett glanced at the large chunk of amber that hung around Zane's neck. "Nice necklace."

"Thanks. I'm a dissonance-energy para-rez. Gonna join the Guild and become a ghost-hunter when I turn eighteen."

"That right?" Emmett asked politely.

Lydia frowned. "You're only thirteen, Zane. You'll probably change your mind about what you want to do a thousand times before you turn eighteen."

"No way," Zane said with absolute conviction. He grimaced at

Emmett. "Lydia's not real keen on ghost-hunting. She had a bad experience a few months ago, you see, and she blames—"

"That's enough, Zane," Lydia cut in swiftly. "I'm sure Mr. London has dinner reservations. We'd better be on our way."

"Yeah, sure," Zane said. He looked at Emmett with a proprietary gleam in his eyes. "Lyd's ready to go, Mr. London. She looks real nice, doesn't she?"

Emmett swept Lydia with a considering expression. His eyes gleamed, too. Lydia was pretty sure she saw amusement in that amber-colored gaze, but she thought she also saw something else, something that might have been masculine appreciation. She grew unaccountably warm.

She wasn't blushing. She could not possibly be blushing. This was business, after all.

Maybe she should have worn a business suit instead of the little aqua dinner dress. She had bought it just before the disaster in the catacombs, right after she and Ryan Kelso had started dating. But Ryan had eased himself out of her life in the weeks following her Lost Weekend, and she'd never had an opportunity to wear the dress.

When she had taken the frock out of the back of the closet where it had been hanging unworn for more than six months, it had seemed discreet enough for a business dinner. The long sleeves and the high neckline gave the garment an almost prim look. At least, that's what she had told herself. Suddenly she was not so sure.

"Yes," Emmett said, "she looks very nice."

Nice? What did "nice" mean? She wondered. She eyed his slouchy, unconstructed black linen jacket, black T-shirt, and black trousers. Definitely not nice, she decided. Dangerous, sexy, intriguing, but not nice.

She cleared her throat. "We'd better be on our way. Zane, you can do your homework here and keep Fuzz company until it's time for you to go back to your place. But no watching the rez-screen. Understood?"

Zane made a face. "Jeez, Lyd, I don't have enough homework to fill up the whole evening."

"If, by some bizarre chance, you happen to finish your schoolwork early, you can read a book until it's time to go home," she said heartlessly.

Zane groaned. "Okay, okay. No rez-screen." He paused speculatively. "How about ice cream?"

Lydia grinned. "Sure. As long as you leave some for me."

"No problem." Zane waved her through the door with a gallant motion of his hand. "Have a good time."

Lydia grasped the strap of her purse tightly and moved out into the hall. When Zane closed the door very loudly behind her, she was suddenly conscious of being alone with Emmett. Without a word, she walked beside him to the stairwell.

"Known Zane long?" Emmett asked as they started down to the fourth floor.

"I met him and his aunt right after I moved into this apartment complex. He and Olinda were very kind to me at a time when I, well, when I needed friends."

"Olinda is the aunt?"

"Yes." Lydia stepped into the elevator. "She's okay. A good-hearted soul. Runs the Quartz Café down the street. But I'm afraid she's got plans for Zane, and they don't include a college education."

"What kind of plans?"

"Olinda makes no secret of the fact that she can't wait until Zane is old enough to join the Guild and train as a ghost-hunter. A good one can make excellent money, you know."

"So I'm told."

Lydia grimaced. "Unfortunately, Zane shows every sign of becoming a very powerful dissonance-energy para-rez."

"In other words, good old Aunt Olinda thinks Zane's going to become an asset to the family's cash flow as soon as she gets him into the Guild."

"Exactly." Lydia glanced at him. "Don't get me wrong. I'm very fond of Olinda, but she and I are engaged in an undeclared war. I'm fighting to make sure Zane goes to college before he even thinks about becoming a ghost-hunter. Olinda wants him to join the Guild the day he turns eighteen."

"I get the picture."

"I'm doing my best to discourage his fantasies about ghost-hunting, but I'm not making much headway. Young boys are so impressionable. All that macho hunter stuff really appeals to them, especially at Zane's age."

Emmett slanted her an enigmatic look as they exited the stairwell and walked out into the parking lot.

"Being a dissonance-energy para-rez isn't something you can ignore. Sooner or later Zane will have to come to terms with that side of his nature. He won't be able to pretend his talent doesn't exist, no matter how much he tries."

His calm logic irritated her. "Zane's a bright kid. He could be a doctor or a professor or an artist. I'm not saying he can't exercise his talents on the side. But I don't want him to become just another high-priced, overrated bodyguard."

"I realize the profession doesn't rank very high with you, but bodyguards occasionally have their uses."

"Huh. That's a matter of opinion."

He stopped beside a dark gray Slider and reached out to open the passenger door for her. "If you were going to continue as my consultant, you might need one."

She paused, one high-heel-shod foot inside the car. "What are you talking about?"

"I'm afraid I'm going to have to fire you."

Outrage and disbelief swept through her. "You're taking me out to dinner to tell me that you want out of our contract?"

"That pretty much sums it up. Those burn marks on your wall have changed everything, Lydia. There's some stuff I haven't told you about this job."

CHAPTER 7

HE'D CHOSEN THE RESTAURANT WITH THE HELP OF THE concierge at his hotel.

"The kind of place where the university crowd hangs out; you know, the professors, not the students."

"Don't worry, I know the perfect restaurant, sir. A charming little bistro. It's called Counterpoint. Specializes in New Wave cuisine. Excellent wine list. Very popular with the university crowd."

Lydia said nothing as she followed the maitre d' to a table near the window. Emmett knew that she was fuming. But beneath the simmering anger, he caught the glint of recognition in her expression. He made a mental note to tip the concierge. The guy had nailed it with the restaurant.

Emmett's gaze swept the room, assessing the polished wooden floors, the intimately lit tables, and the waiters dressed in black and white. In recent years he had finally grasped the concept of casual chic. He knew it when he saw it—and Counterpoint was definitely it. The sort of place that served a lot of pasta and did terribly clever, artistic things with miniature vegetables.

Lydia managed to contain herself until after the waiter had taken the order. Then she folded her arms on the table and narrowed her eyes at him over the candle flame.

"Okay, talk," she said. "What's all this about firing me?"

He had given a lot of thought to the problem of how much to tell her. In the end he had decided it would be best to go with at least a measure of the truth. He couldn't think of any other way to convince her that she did not want the job.

"I told you that I came to Cadence to search for a family heirloom that had been stolen from my collection," he said.

Her fingertips did a quick staccato on the table. "Are you going to tell me that your story about the missing cabinet of curiosities wasn't for real?"

"It's for real, all right. What I didn't get around to mentioning was that the person who took it was my nephew, Quinn."

That information made her blink a couple of times. "Your nephew?"

"My sister's kid. He's . . ." Emmett paused, thinking. "Eighteen as of last month."

"I don't understand. He stole a family heirloom?"

"I doubt if he looks at it quite that way."

"What other way is there to look at it?"

"Technically, what he actually did was pawn it. He dropped a copy of the receipt into the mail to me. Just in case, he said."

"Just in case of what?"

"I'd better start at the beginning. A few months ago Quinn took up with a new friend, a young lady named Sylvia. My sister and her husband did not approve. The long and short of it is that Sylvia came here to Cadence, apparently looking for work. Quinn followed."

Lydia frowned. "What kind of work?"

"Don't know. Quinn told me that she's a fairly strong ephemeral-energy para-rez and she dreams of working in the field of para-archaeology. But she's untrained and uncertified. Unfortunately, her resources are quite limited. No family to speak of. When Quinn met her, she was barely keeping herself off the streets by working as a waitress."

"Okay, so she came here to Cadence, and Quinn followed. With your cabinet."

"Right. And now he's disappeared. No one's heard from him for nearly two weeks. My sister is getting frantic. Her husband is concerned."

Lydia studied him. "So you agreed to come look for him?"

"Yes. As near as I can tell, he sold the cabinet to a dealer in the Old Quarter and used the money to get a hotel room. But he only spent two nights at the hotel, and then he just vanished."

Lydia looked thoughtful. "What about the dealer who bought the cabinet? Have you talked to him?"

"I went to his shop, but he wasn't there. Neither was the cabinet."

She stared at him, understanding dawning in her eyes.

"Are you talking about Chester? Was he the dealer who bought the cabinet from Quinn?"

"Yes." He watched her face. "His shop was closed when I arrived. I went in anyway, to have a look around."

"You broke into his shop?"

"I didn't want to waste any time."

"Good grief!"

He reached into the inside pocket of his jacket. "I didn't find the cabinet or any clue to who might have bought it off Brady, but I did find this."

He removed the photo he had found on the wall behind Brady's shop counter and placed it on the table in front of Lydia.

The picture showed a woman with brilliant red hair seated in a booth in what looked like a seedy nightclub. She was smiling ruefully into the camera. Next to her sat an oily little man with slicked-back hair and a cheap, flashy sport coat. The man was grinning from ear to ear.

Lydia glanced down at the photo and then looked up swiftly, her eyes darkening. "That's a picture of Chester and me at the Surreal Lounge. We were celebrating my last birthday. He was always asking someone to take pictures of the two of us together there. It was his home away from home."

"When I couldn't locate Brady, I decided to look for you instead." Emmett picked up the picture and tucked it back into his jacket. "You weren't hard to find. But right after I located you, Brady turned up dead in that sarcophagus."

Anger flushed her cheeks. "My God, it was all a sham, right from the start, wasn't it? You came looking for me because you thought I was involved with Chester. You pretended to be a genuine client, but all along you thought I could give you a lead on your missing cabinet and your missing nephew."

"I didn't have much else to go on," he said quietly.

"I knew it."

"Knew what?"

Her hand tightened into a small fist on the white tablecloth. "You really were too good to be true."

He shrugged and said nothing.

"What made you decide to end the charade tonight?" she demanded fiercely.

"The scorch marks that ghost burned into your bedroom wall."

Confusion defused some of her outrage. "What in the world does that have to do—"

She broke off as the waiter returned to the table with the appetizers. Emmett looked at the dish that was set in front of him. The menu had listed it as Prawns in Three-Part Harmony.

None of the three perfectly cooked prawns sitting atop the bed of thin-sliced radishes appeared to be singing, in three-part harmony or otherwise, but he decided not to make an issue of it. New Wave cuisine was a state of mind, he reminded himself.

Lydia leaned forward impatiently as soon as the waiter had vanished. "All right, explain yourself, London. What did you mean about my scorched wall changing things?"

"The mark that ghost left on your wall was not a random design, Lydia. If you looked at it closely, you could make out three wavy lines. It was a sloppy job. The hunter obviously didn't have complete control of the ghost, but I'm sure about the lines."

"So?"

"I think someone may have tried to leave you a message."

She looked wary now. "You're saying that you recognized these three wavy lines?"

"Yeah." He took a bite of one of the prawns. "I've seen them before."

"Where?" Her voice was very tight.

He put down his fork, opened his jacket, and removed the scrap of notepaper he had found on Quinn's desk. Without a word he handed it to Lydia.

She snapped it out of his fingers and glanced at the three wavy lines. She raised her eyes. "I don't get it."

"I found that mark on a pad of paper next to the phone in Quinn's room. I think he made the notation after taking a phone call from Sylvia. He disappeared a few hours after he got that call."

"Do you know what the lines signify?"

"No. I'm looking into it. But the fact that someone used a ghost to burn them into your wall tells me they're probably important. And possibly dangerous."

Absently she tapped the piece of paper on the tablecloth. "It also tells you that I probably don't know what happened to your cabinet or to Quinn after all, right?"

He shrugged. "It did strike me that if someone had risked warning you off with an illegal manifestation, you might be in danger because you'd started asking questions. And if you had to ask questions, you probably don't know where my cabinet or my nephew is."

"Guess that explains the phone call I got at work this morning," she said reluctantly.

"What call?"

"I thought it was a crank call." She moved one hand in a dismissive gesture. "It was a man's voice. A young man, I think. I didn't recognize it. All he said was, 'No more questions.' Then he hung up."

"Damn it, why the hell didn't you tell me?"

She glared at him. "I just finished explaining that I thought it was a crank call. It didn't make any sense. I didn't connect it to my inquiries about your missing cabinet."

"The hell you didn't. You're too smart not to have figured out the connection."

Annoyance strained her voice. "Okay, okay, I admit the possibility crossed my mind. But I was afraid that if you thought I might be in danger, you'd fire me."

"That's exactly what I'm going to do. It's pretty clear now that I miscalculated. You weren't involved in this until I involved you."

"You think you can un-involve me be reneging on our contract? Is that it?"

"I want you out of this, Lydia."

He was prepared for the stubborn anger that blazed in her face. What surprised him was the flash of something else. Desperation?

"Even if you're right, it's too late," she said quickly. I've talked to some dealers. The word is out that I'm looking for the cabinet."

"Tomorrow morning you can put the word out that your new client fired you and you are no longer looking for his heirloom."

"What makes you think that will work? The word is already out in the antiquities community. I can't cancel it just like that. If someone knows anything about the cabinet, I'll be contacted, whether or not you fire me."

"Tell your contacts to get in touch with me."

"The ones who are most likely to know anything useful won't want to talk directly to you." She leaned forward, determination vibrating around her in an almost palpable energy field. "I know this crowd. They trust me, but they don't trust outsiders. You need me, London."

"Not badly enough to put you at risk."

"You didn't mind putting me at risk when you thought I might be in cahoots with Chester."

"That was different," he muttered.

"It was a very small ghost."

"Even the weak ones can cause a very unpleasant reaction. They can freeze you, knock you unconscious for as long as fifteen or twenty minutes."

"Fainting or temporary paralysis are common, transient side effects of direct contact with a weak UDEM," she said primly. "Permanent damage is rare."

"You sound like you're quoting from a textbook or an emergency room pamphlet. Do you know what it really *feels* like?"

"Yes." Her eyes were cool. "I know what it really feels like. It feels like all of your psychic senses have been rezzed to the breaking point. Everything is too bright, too hot, too cold, too dark, too loud. Sensation overwhelms you and you pass out. Unless, of course, you're a very strong ghost-hunter, in which case I understand you have some limited immunity."

He drew a deep breath. "Okay, so you do know what it feels like."

"Let's get something straight here. I spent most of the past four years of my working life in the Dead City. No para-archaeologist, regardless of how effective the team's hunters are, can spend that much time in the field without brushing up against a few small ghosts."

He was not going to get far with logic and reason, he realized. Might as well cut to the chase. "You don't seem to get the picture here, Miss Smith. I'm firing you."

"You're the one who doesn't get it, Mr. London. You can't fire me. We've got a contract."

"Don't worry. I'll compensate you for your time."

"There's more than money involved now. If what you say is true, it's possible that poor Chester was killed because of your cabinet—" She broke off abruptly.

He realized she was looking at someone who was approaching the table.

"Hope I'm not interrupting anything, Lydia. Saw you from across the room and had to say hello."

The voice was easy, refined, masculine. The kind of voice that projected well, Emmett thought. The voice of a man accustomed to the lecture hall. An educated voice.

"Hello, Ryan." Lydia forced a chilly smile. "It's been a while, hasn't it? This is Emmett London. Emmett, this is Professor Ryan Kelso. He's head of the Department of Para-Archaeology at the university." She paused delicately. "A former colleague."

And formerly something more than a colleague, Emmett thought. He didn't consider himself the intuitive type, but even he couldn't miss the undercurrents swirling around the small table. A disturbing tendril of possessiveness uncoiled deep inside him. Probably not a good thing. He could have done without the added complications.

He took his time getting to his feet, absorbing the salient points of Ryan Kelso in a single glance. Tall, athletically fit, dark hair, gray eyes. Chiseled features.

Ryan looked every inch the fashionable academic in a brown turtleneck, a tweed jacket, and a pair of trousers that rode low on his hips. He wore amber in a chunky wristband on his left arm.

Emmett shook hands briefly. "Kelso."

"A pleasure, London."

Ryan gave Emmett a quick, assessing survey and then switched his attention back to Lydia. "What's this about finding a murder victim in that peculiar little place where you work? Saw something about it in the papers."

"His name was Chester Brady," Lydia said stiffly. "I doubt if you knew him."

"Can't say that I did." Ryan's mouth curved with amused disdain. "The papers implied that he was a ruin rat who had probably been killed by one of his criminal associates. What was he doing at Shrimpton's? Trying to steal one of your acquisitions?"

"Chester was a friend of mine. A very strong trap tangler," Lydia said in a steely voice. "One of the most powerful I've ever met. Who knows? If he'd had access to a decent education, he would have been a first-rate para-archaeologist. Probably could have been chairman of the department at the university by now."

Ryan dismissed that with a chuckle. Then his eyes softened with concern. "It must have been very traumatic for you, finding the body and all. I mean, the shock of that coming on top of what happened six months ago—"

"Not everyone thinks I'm fragile," Lydia said with conviction. "Believe it or not, the detective in charge of the case put me on her list of suspects. Apparently she believes I'm fully capable of handling the stress of murdering an old pal and stuffing his body into a sarcophagus."

"Uh—" Ryan floundered briefly, clearly unable to figure out where to go with that.

"I have to tell you, it was almost flattering in a way," Lydia continued.

She was on a roll. Emmett was amused. Nevertheless, it was time to intervene.

"Cops always question the people who find the victim," London said easily. "Naturally they talked to Lydia. They also talked to me. I was with her when she discovered the body. But the detective in charge made it clear that she's not seriously interested in either of us. We both have alibis."

"Some of us have better alibis than others," Lydia murmured.

Emmett ignored that. He kept his attention on Ryan. "Apparently Brady had a lot of disgruntled friends, clients, and associates. The police think one of them did him in."

"Makes sense." Ryan seized the opportunity to change the subject. "Anyway, it's great to see you looking so well, Lydia."

"Amazing, isn't it? I managed not to go stark-staring bonkers after all. At least, not yet. But never fear, there's always hope. I might still go over the edge one of these days."

Ryan had the grace to turn red. "You can't blame your friends for worrying about you."

"If my so-called *friends* had been genuinely worried about me, they would have seen to it that I got my old job back after the doctors turned me loose," she said much too sweetly.

She was not going to let up, Emmett realized. He wondered how Ryan had ever come to the conclusion that she was too delicate to continue in her archaeological work.

Kelso managed an expression of polite confusion. "I'm not sure what you're implying, Lydia. The decision to, uh, release you from your university contract—"

"You mean fire me."

"The decision was made by the administration," Ryan said quickly. "You know that. It wasn't a departmental decision."

"Give me a break." She made a small but unmistakably disgusted sound. "We both know the administration takes the recommendation of the department heads. Why don't you just be honest about the whole thing? You figured I was a candidate for the funny farm, and that's what you told the academic council."

"Lydia, we were all devastated by what happened to you."

"But not devastated enough to let me come back to the department."

"As chairman of the department, I have a grave responsibility. I couldn't take the risk of sending you out with the team after what happened. I had to keep your best interests in mind."

"If you were really that nervous about my para-psych profile, you wouldn't have had to send me back out into the Dead City right away. You could have let me work in the labs for a while until everyone was convinced that I wasn't going to freak under stress."

Ryan's frown of earnest concern darkened into annoyance. He glanced hastily around the restaurant, clearly uncomfortable, searching for an excuse to get himself out of what had become an awkward situation.

"Policy is policy," he said stiffly. "What you've got to remember, Lydia, is that your para-psychological health is the most important element in the equation. You went through a brutal experience. Got to allow yourself plenty of time to recover."

"I'm fully recovered, Ryan."

"Tell you what," he said a little too heartily. "Give yourself another six months and then reapply to the department. I'll make sure your application gets special consideration."

"Gee, thanks, Ryan. But six months from now I won't need my old job. I expect to have my own full-time consulting business up and running."

He looked slightly disconcerted. "You're going private?"

"That's right. I'm already working at it part-time."

"I hadn't realized—"

"Two months ago I registered as a private consultant in para-archaeology with the Society." Her eyes gleamed. "Mr. London here is my first client. Isn't that right, Emmett?"

He had to hand it to her, Emmett thought. She had backed him rather neatly into this corner.

"Lydia and I signed a contract two days ago," he said.

"I see." Ryan frowned at Emmett and then looked at Lydia. "What about your job at Shrimpton's?"

"As soon as I build my private business into a full-time enterprise, I will, of course, resign my position at Shrimpton's. In the meantime, I need the money. I was pretty well wiped out financially after losing my job at the university, you know."

"I see," Ryan started edging back. "Well, that's great. Just great. Say, the department occasionally uses private consultants and outside experts. Maybe we'll have occasion to call on you one of these days."

"I will, of course, be happy to consider contracts with the university," she said with grand aplomb, "but bear in mind that the private sector commands very high fees. Just ask Emmett."

Emmett managed not to choke on the swallow of wine he had just taken. He shot her a warning look across the top of the candles. *Don't push your luck, lady.*

"Worth every penny," he said aloud, with what he thought was commendable gallantry under the circumstances.

Lydia rewarded him with a triumphant smile that outshone the candles.

Ryan studied him with wary curiosity. "What do you collect, Mr. London?"

Emmett saw Lydia's mouth open. But he'd had enough of her reckless conversation. Beneath the table, he brought his shoe down on the toe of one of her sexy little black evening sandals with enough force to get her attention. Her eyes widened, but she closed her mouth.

Emmett looked at Ryan. "I'm into tomb mirrors."

"Tomb mirrors." If the amused condescension in Ryan's voice had been any thicker, it would have dripped onto the table. "Well, that's very interesting."

"Got a room full of 'em at home in Resonance City," Emmett

continued expansively. "Had the walls lined with real mirrors, put the tomb mirrors on little stands in front and then lit the whole gallery with green lights. Really impresses guests."

Across the table, Emmett caught Lydia's attention and knew that she was torn between irritation and laughter. She knew even better than he did that tomb mirrors were among the most common and least valuable Harmonic artifacts. They were also among the most commonly faked. Reproductions and frauds abounded in the shops near the Dead Cities. Only novices and the most unsophisticated private collectors bothered to acquire them.

"Green lights?" Ryan looked pained. "How original."

"Cost a bundle, but I'm pleased with the effect," Emmett said. "The lights and the wall mirrors give the gallery a real weird feel, know what I mean?"

"I can imagine," Ryan murmured dryly.

Lydia smiled blandly. "Sounds like you've achieved exactly the sort of creepy effect that we strive for at Shrimpton's, Emmett."

" 'Creepy'—that's the word." Emmett looked at Ryan. "I need a few more pieces to fill out the collection, though. That's why I'm here in Cadence. Lydia thinks she can turn up some choice mirrors for me."

"I'm sure she will." Ryan glanced over his shoulder. "If you'll excuse me, I'd better get back to my companion. Nice to meet you, London."

"Sure," Emmett said.

Ryan turned to Lydia. "It's great to see you getting out again, Lydia."

He leaned down with the obvious intention of giving her the sort of casual peck on the cheek that constituted a friendly farewell between old friends, but he missed his target. At the last possible instant, Lydia, acting as though she was entirely unaware of his intent, reached out to pick up her fork, and her elbow somehow connected with his groin.

"Umph." Ryan took a hasty step back, started to put a hand gingerly on his crotch, then apparently thought better of it and took some shallow breaths instead.

"Oh, sorry." Lydia paused with the fork in midair. "Didn't realize you were standing quite so close. It was terrific seeing you again too, Ryan. Give my regards to everyone at the lab."

"Right." He backed away from the table. "Catch you later, Lydia. Good luck with the consulting work."

Turning on his heel, he moved quickly off through the maze of small tables. Emmett watched him go and decided that Ryan had the air of a man making a strategic retreat. Or maybe it was more of a desperate flight to safety.

CHAPTER 8

SILENCE DESCENDED ON THEM. EMMETT LOOKED AT Lydia. She met his eyes. A moment of perfect comprehension, he thought.

The waiter returned with the entrees. When he was gone, Lydia refocused her attention on her food.

"He thinks I lost my para-rez pitch because of something that happened to me six months ago," she said after a while.

"I got that impression."

"I had a bad experience in the Dead City."

"I know," Emmett said quietly.

"You do?" She looked up quickly, frowning. "I hadn't realized—" Then she grimaced. "Yes, I suppose you would know."

"I called one of my people back in Resonance City. Had him take a quick look into your background."

"I see."

"The report said you were surprised by an illusion trap. It overwhelmed you, and you disappeared into the catacombs before anyone else on the team realized what had happened. There was a search, but you had vanished. Two days later you walked out on your own."

She shrugged. "So they say. To be honest, I can't remember anything about the forty-eight hours I spent underground. The para-rez shrinks said it's probably better that way."

"What do you think happened?"

She hesitated. "I may have gotten caught in a trap. I'm good, but no tangler is perfect. But there's another possibility."

"What's that?"

"I could have gotten badly fried by a really powerful ghost. That would also account for two full days of amnesia."

He frowned. "Couldn't have been a ghost. You were with a university excavation team. The report said you had two fully qualified ghost-hunters."

She cocked a brow. "You read the official report of the inquiry council, didn't you?"

"Yes."

"It's supposed to be confidential, you know."

"I know."

She let that go. "You're right. There were two hunters with us. They claim they accompanied me to the entrance to the tomb chamber. They told the committee that while they were dealing with a couple of small ghosts at the entrance, I disappeared into one of the antechambers. That was the last they saw of me."

Emmett waited.

"They said I didn't follow standard safety procedures." Her mouth tightened. "They implied I behaved recklessly."

Emmett nodded. The two hunters swore that, in her eagerness to explore the newly discovered antechamber, Lydia had gone ahead without waiting for them or any of the other members of the team. The conclusion of the report had been blunt: she had gotten herself into trouble.

He watched her twirl pasta around the tines of her fork. "Must have been an illusion trap. If it had been a real monster ghost the two hunters would have detected traces of energy in the vicinity."

"So they say." She ate some pasta.

"Are you telling me that you don't believe the hunters' version of events?" Emmett asked very neutrally.

She put down her fork. "I'm saying I don't know what happened. I've got no clear memories of what occurred in that antechamber. I've been forced to take the word of the others who were on the team that day."

"No *clear* memories?" Emmett watched her closely. "A moment ago you said that you couldn't remember *anything* about the forty-eight hours you spent in the catacombs."

She said nothing for a time, just looked at him. In the light of the candle her face was shrouded in mystery. He thought about what it must have been like to lose forty-eight hours out of your life and then wake up in the endless green night of an alien catacomb without amber. A lot of people who got lost underground never returned. Those who did find their way out were usually so psychically traumatized that they wound up in para-rez wards for a long time.

For a few seconds he thought Lydia was not going to respond to his question. Then she appeared to come to some inner decision.

"I've never told anyone else, but lately I think I've been getting little bits of memory." She gazed into the heart of the candle flame.

"The only problem is, I can't make them out. It's like catching a glimpse of a ghost, the old-fashioned, horror-story kind—a shade or a phantom, not a UDEM."

"Have you gone back to the doctors?"

Her mouth twisted. "The last thing I need is another note in my para-psych file telling the world that I'm showing increasing signs of post-para-traumatic stress. I've already lost one good job because of the shrinks' report."

"And because the chairman of your former department was not willing to give you a chance to prove the doctors were wrong," Emmett reminded her.

"Ryan and I used to be colleagues. He got promoted to chair of the department one month after my Lost Weekend. That's when he apparently decided that I'm too fragile to do my job."

"I see."

"I can't really blame him. Everyone in the department is convinced that no tangler can go through what I did and come out of it with all para-faculties intact. No one wants to work on a team with someone who's—" She broke off to twirl her fingers in a circle. "You know, unreliable. A team member who loses her nerve or her edge in the Dead City puts everyone else in danger."

Emmett thought about how he had found her repainting her bedroom wall that morning to remove scorch marks left by a ghost. Whoever had summoned the UDEM must have known about her terrifying experience six months ago, he reflected. Most people could be expected to panic at the sight of a wild ghost, no matter how small, in their own homes. Anyone who had spent forty-eight hours alone in the catacombs would be especially vulnerable to that kind of small-scale terror.

Before this was over, he thought, he would very much like to get his hands on the hunter who had cold-bloodedly attempted to frighten her.

"If it makes any difference," he said, "I don't think you're delicate or fragile or inclined to fracture under stress. In my opinion, you are one very gutsy lady."

"Hey, that's great." She smiled with iron-willed intent. "I'm so glad you think I can do my job. Because we've got a contract and I'm not going to let you fire me."

He groaned. "So we're back to that, are we?"

"Sorry." She took another bite of pasta. "But it is the subject that is uppermost in my mind tonight."

"Lydia, you're missing the point here. I'm the reason someone sent that ghost to your bedroom last night. Don't you get it? If you continue to work with me, there may be other incidents. Someone is trying to make it plain that he or she doesn't want you to help me search for the cabinet."

"True. I wonder why not?"

He shrugged. "It's obvious. Whoever is behind this is afraid that the cabinet will lead me to Quinn. From now on, I have to go on the assumption that someone doesn't want me to find him."

She tapped one glossy green-and-gold-tinted nail against her plate. "If there is someone out there who feels that strongly about it, your nephew may be in serious danger."

"Yes. Until now, I've assumed he was just a lovestruck kid with rampaging hormones chasing after a girlfriend. But after what happened in your bedroom last night—"

"You need me, Emmett." She aimed the fork at him. "Admit it. You need all the help you can get."

"Maybe. But I don't want to be responsible for putting you in danger."

"That didn't worry you when you believed that I was working with Chester."

"That's different."

"No, it's not. Nothing has changed except that you no longer think I know the whereabouts of your cabinet. Look, I'm an adult and I'm a professional. I can make my own decisions."

"Lydia—"

"I won't let you push me out of this, Emmett. I need this job and you need me. I'm going to continue looking for your cabinet, regardless of what you choose to do."

"There's a word for that kind of threat."

"Yeah. Blackmail. You can't stop me. If there is any real danger involved, it will be safer for both of us if we work together. We should share information."

He studied her for a long moment. He knew beyond a shadow of a doubt that she meant every word. She would continue to search for the cabinet, with or without his permission. He should have known that it was not going to be easy to fire her.

"All right," he said after a while. "Okay. You win."

She felt triumphant.

"But as you said," he continued evenly. "it will be safer if we work together."

"Right. No problem. I'll keep you informed—"

"You should be reasonably safe during the days while you're at the museum," he said, talking straight over the top of her eager promise. "There's obviously a renegade ghost-hunter involved in this somewhere, but he isn't likely to try to terrorize you when there are witnesses around."

She quirked a brow. "No?"

"I doubt it. Too much chance of getting caught. Hunters have to work at close range, you know that. Even a strong, well-trained, very experienced one can't summon a ghost and manipulate it from more than half a city block away, even when he's working near the Old Wall. And I don't think we're dealing with a well-trained one here."

"You sound like an authority on the subject," she said coolly.

"Use your head. You know as well as I do that it's illegal to summon ghosts outside the Dead City. Any renegade hunter doing so risks drawing the attention of the Guild authorities. They tend to frown on that kind of thing."

"Especially if there's no profit in it for the Guild," Lydia shot back. "But what if he's not a renegade? What if he's working for the Guild?"

"You really don't hold ghost-hunters in high esteem, do you?"

"Let's just say that I don't think the Guild is above allowing its members to get involved in a few personal financial adventures on the side, provided, of course, that they cut the Guild in for a percentage."

"Are all para-archaeologists here in Cadence that cynical about the Guild?"

"No." She dunked a chunk of bread into the olive oil. "A few of my former colleagues think hunters are sort of sexy, believe it or not. They've actually had affairs with some of them. My friend Melanie Toft at Shrimpton's told me that she once dated a hunter for several weeks."

For a few seconds he thought she must be teasing him. Then he realized she was serious. "I take it the idea of having an affair with a hunter doesn't appeal to you?"

She blew that off with a wave of her hand and bit down on the bread. "Forget my personal opinions on the subject. We've got more important things to worry about."

"All right. As I said, I'm not too concerned about the days, provided you're willing to follow some reasonable precautions. It's the nights that are a problem."

"So?"

"So," he said deliberately, "if you insist on carrying out the terms of our contract, as of tonight you've got a roommate."

She gaped at him in stunned silence. Maybe it hadn't occurred to her that he could play tough too, he thought. Damned if he would let her blackmail him without paying a price.

Not a very big price, of course. Her dumbfounded expression was no doubt as much satisfaction as he would get.

CHAPTER 9

"Don't you think you're overreacting here, London?"

"No." Emmett reached into the backseat of the Slider to retrieve his small duffel bag.

On the way back to Lydia's apartment, he had stopped off at his hotel long enough to collect the things he figured he would need tonight. A razor, a change of clothes, and the other small paraphernalia a man required for an overnight stay in a lady's home.

He would pick up the rest of his stuff in the morning when he checked out of the hotel. Assuming he did check out. There was, he assured himself, always the possibility that Lydia would lose her enthusiasm for this consulting job after she discovered what it was really like to give up her sofa and share her bathroom. Her apartment, after all, was very small.

"Well, if you're going to be stubborn about it—"

"I am," he assured her. "Stubbornness is one of my most distinctive personality traits."

"I believe it." She threw him a pointed look and jerked the door handle.

He popped open his own door and got out of the car. Automatically, he examined the small, ill-lit parking lot. It was crowded tonight. Tenants' vehicles, the majority displaying worn paint and battered fenders, loomed in the shadows. A large refuse container occupied one of the spaces near the side wall. It was filled to overflowing. Empty cardboard boxes that had apparently not fit into the bin were stacked beside it.

There was an air of resignation about the Dead City View Apartments. It was as if everyone inside had abandoned all hope of upward mobility.

Everyone except Lydia. It didn't take much to figure out why she was reluctant to let go of him as a client. It wasn't just the money. He'd offered to buy his way out of the contract. He was certain that she had her own agenda, no doubt aimed at getting herself back underground and working in the catacombs. He was her ticket out of Shrimpton's House of Ancient Horrors.

He walked beside her to the door with the broken security lock. "I assume you've mentioned this to your landlord?"

"In the same letter in which I mentioned the broken elevator and several other problems," she assured him.

They started up the first flight of stairs.

"I'll get the lock repaired first thing tomorrow," he said.

She glanced at him in surprise as they turned up the second flight. "It's not your problem."

"It is now. You could say I've got a vested interest in security in this building."

She looked as if she wanted to object, but in the end she did not comment. Probably wanted to save her breath for the long climb to the fifth floor, he thought.

He didn't blame her. On the third landing he glanced at her. "How long has the elevator been out?"

"Couple of months. It was never what you'd call reliable, even before that."

"No wonder you're in such good shape."

"Thanks. I guess." She gave him a strange look. "Staying with me means you're going to have to climb these stairs on a regular basis. I wouldn't count on Driffield getting the elevator fixed anytime soon."

"You're not going to scare me off that easily," he replied.

She groaned. "I was afraid of that."

They made it to the fifth floor side by side, then headed down the dark corridor.

"Maybe I'll see about getting some new bulbs for the overhead lights in this hall too," Emmett said.

"What are you, Mr. Fixit?"

"I've always sort of enjoyed fixing things—" Emmett broke off as he caught the telltale trace of ghost energy.

"Ah, shit." He dropped the duffel. "Give me your key."

"What?" She had her apartment key out, but she made no move to hand it over. "What's wrong?"

"Give it to me." He snapped the key out of her hand and started forward. "Stay here."

He did not wait to see if she would obey orders. It was probably a fifty-fifty proposition at best. He got the feeling she did not take direction well.

But there was no time to enforce the directive. Unstable dissonance energy shimmered in the vicinity. The odds that it was seeping out of Lydia's apartment were much too good.

He made the door, shoved the key into the lock, rezzed it with a small pulse of psi power, and twisted the knob.

A poisonous green glow spilled through the opening.

He slammed the door wide and saw the ghost.

The garbage-lid-size ball of green throbbed in the corner. In the eerie glare Emmett could see the two figures against the wall. Zane was curled into a hard, tight ball. Fuzz's hunting eyes gleamed from the shelter of his arm. Small white fangs glistened. Neither could move. The leading edge of the ghost's energy spasms was only inches from Zane's arm as he struggled to protect Fuzz.

Emmett concentrated briefly. Sought and found the violent energy pattern of the UDEM. It was uncomplicated and weak. The work of an untrained, inexperienced amateur. That did not mean it could not do some unpleasant damage if it touched Zane or Fuzz.

He resonated for a few seconds with the wildfire energy that was the essence of a ghost. When he was fully turned to it, he sent out the dissonant psychic waves that would disrupt and destroy the harmonic resonance pattern. The amber in his watch warmed slightly.

The ghost flared, winked out, and disappeared as though it had never existed.

In the sudden darkness Zane and Fuzz were no more than shadows in the corner.

"Zane?"

"He's in the bedroom," Zane whispered, his voice strained and hoarse. He lurched to his feet. "He's got a knife, Mr. London. He said he'd gut Fuzz if I even—"

"Get out of here. Take Fuzz. Go."

Zane did not argue. Clutching the dust-bunny, he ran toward the open door. Fuzz's amber hunting eyes blazed in the darkness.

"Zane," Lydia shouted from the doorway, "what happened? Are you all right?"

"Sure, Lyd."

Metal scraped. The sound emanated from the bedroom, echoing loudly in the dark hall. Emmett remembered the window. It was five stories above the ground, but only a short distance from the roof.

It was a risk, but if the intruder was sufficiently agile and sufficiently bold, he might figure that he could wriggle out the window and scramble up to the roof.

The front door was the only other way out of the apartment.

Emmett went down the hall, listening carefully.

Another scrape, followed by a dull thud. The intruder had gotten the window open.

Emmett flattened his body against the wall beside the doorway and gathered himself to go in low and fast.

"Emmett." Lydia's slender figure materialized at the other end of the hall, blocking some of the light. "What do you think you're doing? For God's sake, get out of there. Zane says he's got a knife."

Without warning fresh ghost energy sizzled in the hallway, inches away from Emmett. A poisonous green glow announced the new UDEM. Smaller this time, Emmett noted. The intruder was weakening. Or maybe he was distracted with the task of trying to escape.

"Look out," Lydia shouted.

Zane bounced up and down behind her. "Holy shit, another ghost! Watch this, Lydia."

Emmett concentrated briefly and then swatted the new ghost with a pulse of psi energy.

"Man, that is so dissonant," Zane crowed. The fear that had underscored his words a moment earlier had been replaced with excitement. "Did you see what Mr. London did?"

Emmett did not hang around to catch Lydia's response. This far from the ruins, it was harder to conjure a ghost than it was to banish one. The use of so much psychic energy drained the body's resources quickly.

The intruder had wasted a lot of his strength on the task of summoning the second UDEM, strength that he should have saved for crawling through the window. There would never be a better opportunity to take him.

Emmett shot through the doorway into the bedroom.

The ghost-hunter had one leg through the open window. The dark outline of his body was clearly visible against the night sky. He scrabbled wildly, trying to find leverage.

Emmett seized one booted foot and yanked hard. The hunter tumbled back into the room and landed on the carpet with a heavy thump.

The man stared up at him through the eyeholes in his stocking mask. Moonlight gleamed on the knife in his hand. Emmett circled warily, watching for an opening. The hunter rolled once and surged to his feet.

He made no move to close with Emmett.

"Stay back, you sonofabitch," he warned. He shifted toward the door of the bedroom. "Just stay outta my way and nobody will get hurt."

He was tightly wound, Emmett thought. Not in full control. Maybe having two of his ghosts neutralized in quick succession had made him nervous.

"What are you doing here?" Emmett moved toward him, staying just out of range of the knife. "What the hell is this all about?"

"None of your business." The hunter made a short, brutal, slashing motion with the knife. "Get back, damn it."

"Talk to me," Emmett said quietly. "Or you'll end up talking to the cops and to the Guild."

The hunter laughed, a harsh bark of sound. "The cops can't hurt me, and the Guild can't touch me."

He was at the doorway now. He eased through it, into the hall, never taking his eyes off Emmett.

"You were the one who summoned the ghost here last night weren't you?" Emmett kept his voice casual, almost conversational. "Why the warning to Lydia?"

"Shut *up*. I'm not answering any of your stupid questions." He risked a hasty glance over his shoulder, apparently checking to see that the path was clear.

When he turned back, Emmett had a ghost waiting for him. A big one.

Green energy pulsed in front of the intruder, filling the room with the strange light that was the hallmark of a dangerously intricate ghost.

"Oh, *shit*! No one said anything about this." The hunter whirled and fled down the short hallway.

He collided with the small table there, staggered, righted himself, and dashed into the foyer. He was clearly in the grip of panic. He did not even bother trying to neutralize Emmett's ghost.

The problem with ghosts was that although they could be maneuvered, it was impossible to make them move quickly. The hunter could easily outrun the UDEM Emmett had summoned.

In the meantime, it was blocking Emmett's path. He zapped the energy pattern. The ghost winked out, enabling him to plunge through the doorway and out into the hall.

Ahead of him the intruder pounded toward the stairwell. Emmett gave chase.

"Let him go, Emmett," Lydia called. "I saw the knife in his hand."

It was not the knife that worried him, Emmett thought. It was the fact that the intruder was already at the stairwell, about to disappear down it.

A robust middle-aged woman built like a monument to the colonial settlers hauled herself out of the stairwell just as the hunter reached it. A T-shirt emblazoned with the message DISSONANCE HAPPENS in sequined letters heralded her ample bosom. In the weak light of the dimly lit hallway, Emmett saw the other man's start of panicky surprise. And then the unmistakable hesitation.

It hadn't taken the hunter long to realize that he had just been handed a potential hostage, Emmett thought.

"Get down," Emmett shouted to the woman. "Hit the deck. Now!"

To his great relief, the newcomer assessed the situation with commendable speed and came to the correct conclusion. There was an audible thud as she dropped to the floor like a block of marble.

The ghost-hunter started to reach down for a fistful of the woman's jacket, belatedly realized he could not possibly haul her to her feet, and abandoned the hostage idea.

He whirled and leaped into the stairwell. The echo of his boots rang loudly as he plummeted downward.

Emmett had to vault the prone woman to reach the opening.

"What the hell's going on here?" She sat up warily. "Who are you?"

"Later." Emmett gripped the railing to control his swift descent.

The sound of the hunter's footfalls was already receding into the distance. He would never catch him now, and he dared not risk another ghost. There was no telling who else might enter the stairwell from one of the other floors. A brush with a UDEM would not endear him to the neighbors. And then there were the awkward legalities to be considered.

He was on the second landing when he heard his quarry slam through the broken security door.

I'm going to lose him, Emmett thought.

The intruder was fast. He moved with the speed and agility of a young, athletic male. But he had not yet learned to marshal and control his psychic energies. He had freaked at the sight of the large ghost that Emmett had conjured. He obviously lacked the kind of practical experience that came only with extensive work in the field. Which put him in his late teens.

About the same age as Quinn.

Emmett glanced over the railing in time to see the masked figure dash out into the parking lot. When he reached the ground floor he heard the whine of a highly revved mag-rez engine and knew that he had lost whatever small chance he'd had. A long, six-inch-wide band of bright light appeared suddenly in the darkness, the distinctive glowing tube that marked the front grill of a Coaster.

The vehicle's passenger door slammed shut. The Coaster glided forward between the rows of parked cars, heading straight for Emmett.

He threw himself into the dark space between an ancient Lyre and a small Float. The Coaster howled as it went past, a hungry beast that had been denied its intended prey.

It did not turn back. Emmett stood between the Lyre and the Float and watched the car roar out of the small lot and into the street. A few seconds later it disappeared around the corner.

He was still standing there, thinking, when Lydia, followed by Zane, dashed out of the stairwell to join him.

"My God!" Lydia stared at the empty street. Then she swung around to face him. "Are you all right?"

"Yeah." Emmett drew a deep breath, exhaled slowly. "Yeah, I'm okay."

It was not as though he could have kept it a secret for much longer, anyway, he thought. Lydia was smart. Sooner or later she would have figured out that he was a ghost-hunter.

CHAPTER 10

"NO NEED TO LET IT GET YOU DOWN." OLINDA HOYT clapped Emmett on the shoulder. "Hell, even if you'd caught him, he'd have been out on bail by morning."

Emmett managed, barely, not to stagger beneath the blow. Olinda was no dainty pigeon. Years of wielding commercial-weight pots and pans and waiting on customers in her café had endowed her with a respectable layer of muscle.

The sequined DISSONANCE HAPPENS T-shirt Emmett had glimpsed earlier when she had emerged from the stairwell glowed even more brightly in the lights of the living room. Tight jeans cinched with a glittering rhinestone-studded belt sheathed her full-figured thighs. She wore a pair of running shoes decorated with neon-pink shoelaces. Her long gray hair was tied back in a ponytail.

Definitely not a woman who would go unnoticed in a crowd, Emmett thought.

He nodded absently in response to her observation. "Yeah, probably."

"Man, that was one amazing ghost you threw at him, Mr. London," Zane observed for what must have been the hundredth time. "You shoulda seen it, Aunt Olinda. It was huge. It filled the whole doorway—and we're not even inside the Dead City."

"Sorry I missed it." Olinda winked broadly. "But don't worry, Zane, my boy, one of these days you'll be summoning ghosts that size yerself."

"Made the other guy's ghost look like nothing," Zane crowed.

Emmett saw Lydia's jaw tighten as she set a cup of tea down in front of Zane, but she made no comment on the battle of the ghosts.

"You're sure you're all right?" she asked Zane again. "That man didn't hurt you?"

"Heck, no. I'm fine." Zane ignored the tea. He could not seem to take his eyes off Emmett.

Emmett stifled a groan at the unabashed hero worship in Zane's gaze. Lydia was not going to like this turn of events.

"Let's go through this from the beginning," he said quietly. "Tell me exactly what happened, Zane."

"Sure. Like I said, I'd finished my homework and was just getting ready to go downstairs. I opened the door and there was this guy in the hall. All I could see was his eyes, on accounta the mask. Fuzz didn't like him one bit. He started growling right off."

Emmett crouched down in front of him. "What did he say? Did he ask for Lydia by name? Do you think he knew who lived here or was he just looking for an empty apartment to burglarize?"

"I dunno. At first he seemed as surprised to see me as I was to see him. Guess he'd figured there was no one home. But before I

could ask him what he wanted, he summoned the ghost. I tried—"
Zane stopped suddenly. "But I couldn't do anything, y'know?"

"It's okay, Zane." Emmett put his hand on the thin shoulder. "A
man's got to work with what he's got. You don't have the strength or
training yet to neutralize a ghost. So you did something more important. You kept your head. You didn't panic. And you probably saved
Fuzz's life."

Zane looked up quickly. "Fuzz wanted to attack him, but I knew
that if I let him go, the guy would fry him with that ghost. And I
was pretty sure a UDEM that big would kill something as small as
Fuzz."

"Emmett's right." Lydia stroked Fuzz's ratty gray fur. "You saved
Fuzz. If you hadn't been here, I'm sure he would have gone for the
burglar, and that would have been the end of him."

Zane looked at the dust-bunny perched on Lydia's knee. "The
sucker used the ghost to pin me and Fuzz in the corner. Then he
started tearing the place apart. I figured he was looking for stuff he
could sell, y'know? But he didn't pay any attention to your rez-
screen."

"Not surprising," Lydia remarked. "It's at least eight years old. I
got it at a rummage sale a few months ago. I can see why a burglar
would pass it up."

Olinda snorted. "I told you I could get you a deal on a nice new
model not more than a few months old at most."

"And I told you I'll pass," Lydia said. "I prefer to purchase appli-
ances that did not fall off the back of a truck. That way I've got a
shot at the warranty."

"Yeah, sure. Whatever. I just don't see why you gotta deprive yerself of some of life's little pleasures just because you don't like the
notion of not knowing exactly where they came from, is all."

Emmett silenced them both with a look and turned back to Zane. "You don't have any idea what the burglar might have been looking for? He didn't say anything at all while he was tossing the place?"

"Not really." Zane bit his lip, thinking hard. "He swore a lot. He was kinda nervous, y'know? I guess that guy in the Coaster was waiting for him to hurry up and finish."

"I think you're right." Emmett glanced at Olinda. "You didn't see anything?"

"No." She shook her head. "First I knew somethin' was wrong was when I closed up the café and hiked up those damned stairs to see why Zane here hadn't come back down. Thought maybe he'd gone to sleep in front of the rez-screen. At the top of the stairs I saw the guy with the knife and heard you yell to get down. That's all I know about the situation."

"All right." Emmett got to his feet. "There's no point going over this again tonight. We all need some sleep."

"You gonna call the cops?" Olinda asked in a very neutral tone of voice.

Emmett turned toward Lydia. "We can call them, but I doubt that it will do any good. No one was hurt and nothing was stolen. They probably won't even bother to send out an officer to take a report."

"Huh. Not to this neighborhood, that's for sure," Olinda muttered. "Now, if this apartment complex was up on Ruin View Hill, they'd have someone out quicker 'n a man can say he's gotta take a leak."

"Thank you for that insightful observation," Lydia said. "Let's not forget that we do have a clue or two. He used a ghost in the course of an attempted burglary. We know he was a hunter."

"And a young one," Emmett added absently. "With a very limited amount of training."

"You're certain?"

"Reasonably certain." Emmett went to stand at the sliding window that opened onto the balcony. "But those two facts leave us with a very large group of suspects. The cops will be too busy to bother with this, but we've got another option."

There was a short, stark silence behind him.

"Are you suggesting that we take this to the Guild?" Lydia asked eventually.

"It's local Guild business when a hunter uses his talents to commit crimes," Emmett reminded her.

"What makes you think we'll get the time of day from those thugs?" she demanded. "No offense, Emmett, but for all we know, the Guild itself is involved in this."

"No way, Lydia." Zane's voice was hot with feeling. "The Guild polices its own. Everyone knows that. Ever since the Era of Discord, the hunters have taken care of any member who went renegade."

"Yes, of course," Lydia said dryly. "How could I forget my history so easily? We all know the Guild deals with its own internal problems. I can't imagine what got into me to even suggest that it wouldn't fall all over itself to help outsiders prove one of its members was a knife-wielding burglar who likes to terrorize people with ghosts."

Emmett ignored the sarcasm in her voice. "I'll talk to the head of the Cadence Guild tomorrow."

"Mercer Wyatt?" She stared at him in disbelief. "You think you can just walk up to his front door and ask to speak to him? You're crazy. And you're also from out of town. That means that even though you're a hunter, you're not a member of the local Guild. What makes you think Wyatt will see you?"

"Professional courtesy."

She blinked. "I beg your pardon?"

He shrugged. "You can come with me if you like."

She looked slightly stunned. But she recovered swiftly. "Sorry. I've got a funeral to attend."

Olinda looked blank. "Anyone I know?"

"Chester Brady."

"Oh, yeah, right. Chester." Olinda shook her head. "Reckon you were the closest thing he had to a friend. Not that that's saying much about Chester's circle of acquaintances."

"I'll go with you," Emmett said. "My meeting with Wyatt isn't until seven o'clock in the evening."

Lydia frowned. "You've already got an appointment with him? At night?"

"I've been invited to dinner," Emmett said.

They all stared at him this time. The only one whose eyes were not opened unnaturally wide was Fuzz.

"Holy shit!" Zane mouthed in awe. "You've been invited to dinner with Mercer Wyatt?"

"I'll be damned," Olinda breathed.

"Exactly," Lydia said. "Better take a very long spoon."

She was in the tomb chamber again. Ancient though it was, it glowed faintly with the mysterious ambient green light emitted by the quartz walls. She knew the eerie luminescence was dangerous because it masked the energy of the illusion traps and the ghosts the Old Ones had set to guard their underground maze.

She could see the dark opening to the antechamber. She went toward it, just as she always did in this dream; and then she sensed the presence behind her, just as she always did. She started to turn, glimpsed the shifting of shadows, felt the cold chill . . .

She woke with a start, shivering. For a moment she could not think where she was. The disorientation was stronger this time. The chilly sensation was new, though.

Another cold draft swept across the bed. Then came the muted sound of the sliding glass door closing out in the living room. Belatedly she recalled that she and Fuzz were not alone in the apartment tonight. The knowledge that Emmett was here was as disconcerting as the dream. Maybe more so. She sat up slowly, aware that the whisper of cold night air and the sound of the door indicated that Emmett had gone out onto the balcony.

She glanced at the clock. Three A.M. They had gone to bed at one. She had been adamant about restoring order to her apartment before retiring. No one had argued. No one had suggested that the task could wait until morning. Instead, they had all pitched in to help her clean up the mess the intruder had left in his wake. It was as if everyone understood that it would have been impossible for her to sleep in the midst of the chaos. It had taken nearly two hours to get things back into their proper drawers and cupboards.

Three o'clock in the morning was a weird time to go outside for a breath of fresh air. She wondered if her new roommate had any other odd habits.

"Fuzz?"

At the foot of the bed Fuzz yawned and opened his daylight eyes. They gleamed colorlessly in the moonlight.

"Okay, okay, go back to sleep. Sorry I woke you."

She pushed aside the covers and got out of bed. She started toward the door without thinking and then paused to grab her robe. Sharing the small living space with Emmett required a few modifications in her own habits, she thought. She could only hope he didn't get in the way too much.

She slid her feet into a pair of slippers, belted the robe, and padded out into the front room. The curtains were open. Moonlight spilled across the sofa, revealing that the makeshift bed was empty.

She looked out at the balcony and saw Emmett. He had pulled on his jeans, but that was all. He leaned negligently against the railing, gazing out at her sliver-size view of the green Wall. In the light of the moon his shoulders looked very broad.

She hesitated, struggling briefly against the impulse to take a closer look at his back. What the heck? she thought. This was her apartment, her balcony. If he was going to wander around half naked, he had to expect that she would notice.

She hadn't been getting out a lot lately, after all.

She walked closer to the glass door and peered through the window at sleek lines of moon-sculpted masculine muscle. A man's back, at least this particular man's back, said a lot about him, she decided. There was power, both psychic and physical, in him. And a riveting sensuality.

There was also grace. An easy, unconscious grace, the kind that came from full control, the internal kind. Something about the way he held himself—even now, when he was simply lounging against a rail—spoke volumes about that inner control. She searched her brain for the right description.

"Centered." That was as good a word as any. This was a man who knew his own resources, made his own decisions, his own judgments of others. He had not accepted the experts' verdict on her parapsychological health, as Ryan and her other former colleagues had done. He had not bought the usual assumptions about people who had survived forty-eight hours alone in the catacombs. He didn't think she was too delicate to do her job.

Okay, so Emmett was a ghost-hunter, and a strong one at that. No one was perfect.

She opened the sliding glass door and stepped out onto the balcony.

He did not turn around. "Everything okay?"

She had the uneasy feeling that he had known she was there, watching him through the window, all along.

"Not quite." She joined him at the rail. "I don't think I ever got around to thanking you for what you did for Zane and Fuzz this evening."

"If it makes you feel any better, I doubt that the intruder intended to hurt either of them. He just wanted them out of the way while he went through your place."

"Maybe. But I don't think he would have hesitated to singe them if they had gotten in his path."

Emmett did not deny that. He lifted one shoulder, the movement of muscle and bone fluid in the moonlight.

Take deep breaths, she instructed herself. Lots of deep breaths.

Silence fell. Lydia focused on the dark silhouettes of the nearby buildings. She wondered why Emmett did not seem to feel the chill in the night air.

"You want to know why I didn't tell you, don't you?" he asked eventually.

She knew what he meant. "Why you didn't tell me that you're a dissonance-energy para-rez? I know why. I made my opinions about ghost-hunters fairly obvious right from the start. I don't blame you for keeping quiet about your talent. It was a perfectly reasonable decision for you to make under the circumstances."

"I thought so."

She fiddled with the belt of her robe. "The rest of it, the part about being a businessman from Resonance City. That's all true, isn't it?"

"Yes."

She relaxed. "Mind if I ask why you don't make your living as a ghost-hunter?"

"I did for a while."

"What happened?"

"I quit."

She looked up at the stars. "Okay, I know a dead-end conversational wall when I see one."

There was a short silence.

"You think that those two ghost-hunters who were on your team six months ago are responsible for what happened to you in those catacombs, don't you?" Emmett said.

She gripped the railing. "I told you, I don't know what happened to me six months ago. I can't remember."

"But you blame the hunters."

"They blamed my recklessness. We all agreed to disagree."

He nodded. "I'm not the only one with dead-end conversational walls."

"No, you're not." She turned sideways and studied his unforgiving profile. "So let's change the subject again. You think there's a connection between what happened here tonight and the ghost who appeared in my bedroom last night."

"Sort of obvious, don't you think?"

She tightened her fingers around the rail again. "I've tried to talk myself into believing that the two incidents could be unrelated. But I've got to admit I haven't been able to convince myself."

"The ghost last night was intended as a warning." Emmett gazed out into the night. "Presumably meant to stop you from looking for the cabinet. But why did someone search your apartment tonight? What was he looking for?"

"I haven't got a clue." She contemplated the night for a time. "Maybe we should take this to the police, Emmett."

"The cops can't handle it. Hell, they can't even find the guy who killed your pal Brady. This involves hunters. And hunters stick together. We need the Guild's cooperation. Here in Cadence, that means we need Mercer Wyatt's help."

"But maybe the police could talk to him."

"No," he said. "No cops. Wyatt would view it as an infringement of his own authority. Besides, we don't have much to give the police. The ghost last night and the break-in tonight won't amount to much in their eyes."

"What about the fact that your nephew is missing?"

"There's no evidence of foul play. Quinn is eighteen years old, not a little kid. The cops don't have any reason to look for him. They'd say it's a family matter. And they'd be right. Finding Quinn is my problem, not theirs."

"What about the cabinet of curiosities?"

"Same thing. A family problem. It wasn't exactly stolen, after all. It was pawned. I've got a copy of the receipt. No, we can't go to the cops. At least not until I figure out what the hell we're up against."

Some of her gratitude gave way to irritation in the face of his hardheaded attitude. "What harm can it do to at least talk to them?"

"For starters, it might get my nephew killed."

She stilled. "What do you mean?"

"Bringing the cops into it now will drive everyone involved further underground. Whoever's behind this might decide that the easiest way to deal with the problem is to get rid of whatever it is that's drawing the attention of the authorities."

She sighed. "In other words, your missing nephew."

"Yeah."

"All right. Oddly enough, I can see your point of view. No cops. Not yet."

He turned partway around to face her. "Thanks. I appreciate your cooperation."

"Hey, I'm your high-priced private consultant, remember? A satisfied client is my only goal."

He ignored that. "I wish like hell that I could get you out of this."

"I told you, you can't fire me."

He watched her with somber intensity. "Even if I could, it's too late."

"What's that supposed to mean?"

"After what happened here tonight, we have to assume that for some reason you're in this up to your neck."

Another chill went through her. This one had nothing to do with the temperature. "I sort of came to that very same conclusion myself this evening. It's not always real obvious, but I'm actually pretty smart, you know."

"I know. Looks like we're going to be sharing a bathroom for a while."

She had a sudden thought and found herself grinning.

"What?" he asked.

"Just make sure you stay out of sight if my landlord comes to the door. I'm not supposed to have long-term houseguests. Driffield says it's a violation of the lease to have anyone living in the apartment who's not named in the lease."

"I'll hide under the bed if he shows up."

"You won't fit. Relax. Odds are, he won't make it up all five flights of stairs." She turned away, intending to go back through the door. Then she paused. "I almost forgot. In addition to saving Zane and Fuzz, I wanted to thank you for something else."

"And that is?"

"For not labeling me delicate." She smiled tremulously. "That counts for a lot in my book."

"Even if the compliment comes from a hunter?"

"I thought you said you were a businessman."

He smiled slowly. "That's right."

She took hold of the handle, started to open the door.

"One more thing," Emmett said softly.

She glanced back inquiringly and discovered that he had moved away from the rail. He was standing very close to her now. Almost touching her. Totally blocking the night view. If she moved, she would brush up against his bare chest.

Deep breaths, she reminded herself. More deep breaths.

"What?" she asked. Damn. So much for deep breaths. She was suddenly breathless.

"Given that you're not the delicate type, and all," he began deliberately.

She searched his face. "Yes?"

"Do you think that you're likely to faint if I make a pass?"

She was no longer just breathless, she discovered. She was out of oxygen altogether. "Is this a hypothetical question?"

"No."

His hands closed around her shoulders. A sizzling charge, more shocking in its own way than a jolt of UDEM energy, shot through her. Every nerve resonated in response. She wondered if her hair was standing on end.

Like brushing up against a ghost but without the pain. No pain at all. Just an exquisite sense of excitement. Very high-rez stuff, she concluded. Very high-rez indeed.

He bent his head slightly. His mouth closed over hers in a kiss that held the concentrated essence of everything she had deduced from her intensive study of his back. Control, power, sensuality.

To hell with deep breaths. It had been a long, long time since she'd been involved in anything that could even remotely be described as an intimate relationship. And this was *her* balcony, after all.

She flattened her palms on his chest. The heat of his skin burned nicely. She let her mouth soften beneath his.

He groaned. It was the unmistakable sound of hunger stirring in the depths. It should have made her cautious, but instead it only heightened the thrill. Experimentally, she flexed her fingers, savoring the feel of muscle beneath skin.

He tightened his hold on her immediately, wrapping her in his heat and strength. One of his hands slid down her spine, glided over her buttocks, cupping them.

Her lower body was suddenly tight against his. Even through the layers of his jeans and her bathrobe, she was intensely aware of his erection.

And just as intensely aware of the sudden dampness gathering between her legs.

He took one hand off of her long enough to grasp the door handle. "Inside," he muttered against her mouth. "No room out here."

She did not argue. It *was* a very small balcony.

He got the door open, got her into the living room. She was conscious of movement. Her feet left the floor. And then she felt the tumbled bedding and the cushions of the sofa beneath her. She turned her head into the pillow and caught his scent—heady, utterly male, unique. As exhilarating as the tangled energy in an illusion trap. And no doubt just as dangerous.

His hands left her. She was once again conscious of the coolness of the room.

She opened her eyes and looked up. Emmett loomed over her. His fingers were busy at the fastening of his jeans.

The unmistakable frisson of psi energy sparked invisibly in the vicinity. She glimpsed tiny flickers in the air just behind Emmett. He was causing them, she realized. *Probably wasn't even aware of it.*

The little flashes of green light brought her back to reality with a jolt. From out of nowhere came a sharp memory of Melanie's description of a sexual encounter with a hunter who had recently summoned a ghost. *Using their talent gives them a hard-on like you wouldn't believe. Makes 'em sexy as hell. Something to do with the aftereffects of exercising dissonance energy. The experts think it's linked to their hormones or something.*

Lydia froze. She could not abide the thought that Emmett's eagerness to go to bed with her was just a by-product of his earlier use of his paranormal talents. It was too depressing to think that *any* woman might do for him right now.

"Time out." She sat up quickly and shoved her fingers through her hair to get it out of her eyes. *Deep breaths.* "This is not smart. This is definitely not smart. Everyone knows that this sort of thing plays havoc with a business relationship."

His hands stopped moving at the waistband of his jeans. For a long moment he said nothing. Behind him, the little green sparklers winked out.

"You're right," he said eventually. "Everyone knows that."

He didn't have to agree with her so readily, she thought, irritated.

It wasn't as if there weren't several good counterarguments he could have made.

With an effort of will she summoned what she prayed was a nonchalant nod and managed to struggle up off the sofa. "I realize that this was a unique situation. It's not your fault. I completely understand."

"Good to know," he replied as she gathered her robe more snugly around her and edged toward the hall. "Nothing like an understanding woman, I always say."

"My friend Melanie explained everything to me."

"Terrific. Mind if I ask exactly what she explained?"

"You know, all that stuff about how using your particular type of psi energy affects your, uh, libido."

"Lydia—"

"It's okay. Really." She flapped her hands at him as she backed away. "Every type of psi talent produces certain eccentricities."

"Eccentricities," he repeated in that oddly neutral tone.

"Don't worry. I'm sure you'll be back to normal in the morning."

"You really think so?"

"Melanie said the effects are transitory." She paused to give him a chance to respond, and when he didn't she whirled and fled back to the safety of her own bed. She forgot about the little table until her knee glanced painfully off the corner. She knew she would have a bruise in the morning. More than one kind, she thought, thinking of how close she had come to letting Emmett seduce her.

She could only hope that none of the bruises showed.

CHAPTER 11

PERPETUAL RESONANCE CEMETERY HAD HISTORICAL SIG-
nificance because it dated from Settlement days, but it was no longer
the most fashionable final address in town. The oldest headstones,
the ones that marked the graves of several pioneers, were chipped,
scarred, and weather-worn. Graffiti had been liberally spray-painted
on some of the markers. Weeds grew with carefree abandon on most
of the plots.

The day had dawned sunny and bright, but clouds were moving
in from the west. There would be rain by nightfall. A bitter breeze
was already rustling the leaves of the trees.

The only fresh flowers in sight were the ones Lydia had picked up
on the way to the funeral. Tears burned in her eyes, surprising her,
when she bent down to place the bouquet on Chester's grave.

She straightened and fumbled for a hankie. Belatedly she realized
she hadn't thought to put one in her shoulder bag before leaving the

apartment. But, then, she hadn't planned to cry. Not at Chester's funeral. Chester had been a thief, a liar, and a bloody nuisance.

Oh, God. Bloody. A vision of Chester's body in the sarcophagus appeared in her mind. The tears burned hotter in her eyes and spilled down her cheeks. Whatever else you could say about Chester, he had never killed anyone. No one had had any right to kill him.

Emmett put a large square of white cloth in her hand.

"Thanks." She hurriedly blotted her eyes. "He wasn't a very nice person, you know."

"I know."

"When you don't have any family of your own, you sometimes hook up with odd people." She blew her nose, realized what she had done, and hastily stuffed the hankie into her bag. "I'll wash it and return it."

"No rush."

She looked around, eager to change the subject. Things had been somewhat strained since they had bumped into each other coming and going from the bathroom that morning.

After she had gone to bed for the second time last night, she thought long and hard about how to handle the situation between them. She concluded that by morning Emmett would have recovered from the aftereffects of using his para-rez talent and would no doubt be embarrassed by his psi-driven pass last night.

Aware that he would probably regret everything, she had determined to pretend that nothing had happened. Unfortunately, as far as she could tell, her strict avoidance of any reference to the steamy kiss had done nothing to improve his mood. He had been grim and taciturn all morning.

"Olinda was right about one thing," she said as they turned to walk back to the car. "We were the only ones who came to the funeral."

"Not quite," Emmett said, looking past her toward the parking lot.

Startled, she followed his gaze to where the familiar figure of Detective Alice Martinez lounged against the fender of a nondescript blue Harp.

"Great," Lydia muttered. "Just what I needed to brighten my day. I wonder what she's doing here. She didn't even know Chester when he was alive."

"Might as well say hello, since we all seem to be in the same neighborhood."

Emmett took Lydia's arm and steered her toward the Harp. Martinez watched their approach through a pair of wraparound dark glasses that concealed her expression.

"Good morning, Detective." Lydia refused to be intimidated by the shades. "Nice of the department to send a representative to the funeral. I didn't know the police had a budget that allowed them to provide professional mourners."

"Take it easy, Lydia," Emmett said. "I'm sure Detective Martinez is here in an official capacity. Isn't that right, Detective?"

"Hello, Miss Smith." Alice nodded at Emmett. "Mr. London. As a matter of fact, I'm here on my own time today."

"Working on the old theory that murderers often show up at their victims' funerals?" Emmett asked casually.

"You never know," Alice said.

"Emmett and I were the only ones who showed up today."

"Couldn't help but notice that," Alice said.

"I assume this means that you're no further along in solving this case than you were on the day of the murder. You're still looking at the same two suspects. Emmett and me."

"Not exactly," Alice said. "Mr. London is not on my list. He never was. His alibi checked out. Yours, of course, is a little harder to verify.

Something about being home in bed, wasn't it? Alone. That kind of story is always hard to substantiate."

"Hard to disprove, too," Lydia shot back.

Emmett interrupted. "Taunting the investigating officer is not generally considered to be a sign of good citizenship and willingness to cooperate with the investigation, Lydia."

Lydia felt herself turn red. "I happen to think Detective Martinez is wasting her time here. What kind of murderer would be dumb enough to show up at the funeral?"

Alice straightened away from the fender and opened the door of the Harp. "You'd be surprised how often the old theories prove to be true. Worth a shot, at any rate."

"Have you turned up any clues at all?" Lydia demanded.

"Nothing you'd call real useful," Alice said. "There was one small item of minor interest, however."

"What was that?"

"We went to Brady's apartment and his shop to take a look around," Alice said. "But someone else had been there first, looking for something, I think. The place was a shambles."

Lydia felt Emmett go very still beside her. She stared at Alice. "Why would anyone have searched Chester's place?"

"No idea," Alice said. "Don't suppose you could shed any light on the subject?"

"Chester didn't hang out with a lot of sterling citizens," Lydia said.

"Present company excepted, of course," Emmett inserted softly.

Lydia glanced at him quickly, realized he meant her. She noticed that Alice was watching the byplay very closely.

"Chester was a ruin rat," Lydia said. "Once in a while he came across some moderately valuable artifacts. Whoever went through his things was probably someone who had heard about his death and decided to see what he could find before the cops got there."

"Or it could have been the killer." Alice got behind the wheel. "Making certain there was no evidence to point back to him." She started to close the door.

"Wait a second." Lydia stepped closer to the Harp. "What did you mean about being here on your own time?"

Alice turned her head to look out over the forlorn cemetery. Sunlight glanced off her shades. For a moment Lydia thought she would not answer.

"My boss tells me I've got to learn to prioritize," Alice said.

"And Chester Brady's death doesn't rank very high on your boss's list of high-profile investigations, does it?" Lydia said acidly.

"No. In fact as of Monday, the Brady murder officially goes on the back burner. The department doesn't have the time or the manpower to spend on it. Too many other cases need attention. But I had the morning off, so I figured it wouldn't hurt to attend the funeral. Like I said, you never know."

It occurred to Lydia that maybe she could learn to like this woman after all. "Speaking as a concerned citizen, thanks."

Alice nodded once and rezzed the Harp's ignition.

Lydia watched the car move off down the narrow road that led away from the cemetery. Then she turned to Emmett.

"Whew, that was close," she said.

"What do you mean?"

Lydia frowned. "You heard Martinez. They know someone searched Chester's shop and apartment. You told me you went through his things looking for a lead on your cabinet, remember? That's how you found that photo that led you to me."

"Someone else must have gone in after me." Emmett looked thoughtful. "I left everything exactly the way I found it, except for the photo."

"Are you sure?"

"Of course I'm sure."

Lydia nibbled on her lower lip. "That means that someone else—"

"Uh-huh. Maybe the same someone else who tore your place apart last night."

Lydia shivered and looked out at the deserted cemetery. "Too bad the old cop theory about the killer attending the funeral didn't work this time."

Emmett removed his sunglasses from the pocket of his jacket and put them on. He took Lydia's arm again and walked toward the Slider.

"I'm not so sure the theory failed," he said quietly.

"What do you mean?"

"If you look up at that stand of trees on the hillside above the cemetery, you can see sunlight reflecting off something. Metal, maybe. Or glass."

"Are you serious?" Squinting against the glare, she studied the trees for a few seconds. "I don't see anything." She started to turn back. Light winked at the edge of her vision. "There. Yes. I caught it. Could be anything."

"Anything including the lenses of a pair of field glasses."

"A bird-watcher? Kids playing in the woods?"

Emmett said nothing. He opened the door of the Slider.

"Okay, okay." Lydia got into the car. "It could have been someone watching the funeral with a pair of field glasses. But why?"

"Maybe because he knew Martinez was here and didn't want to

take the risk of being seen. Or—" Emmett closed the door and walked around the front of the Slider.

"Or what?" Lydia prompted the instant he got behind the wheel.

"Or maybe he was there for the same reason Martinez was."

"He wanted to see who showed up at the funeral?"

"Yeah."

"Kind of gives you the creeps, doesn't it?"

Emmett did not reply. He rezzed the ignition. Flash-rock melted. The big engine whined hungrily.

He swung the Slider out of the small dirt lot and drove toward the narrow road. Lydia sank back into her seat and took one last look at the sad little cemetery.

She thought about the very abbreviated graveside service the funeral home had arranged. The check she had written to cover the cost of Chester's funeral had taken her account dangerously low. She hoped she wouldn't have to cut back Fuzz's pretzel ration.

Then she thought about how she was the only one who had attended the funeral for personal reasons. Emmett and Alice didn't count. They both had other agendas.

She shouldn't have been surprised by how pathetically lonely the short service had seemed. It was only to be expected. That was the way it was when you didn't have any close family or friends.

Memories of something Chester had once said to her over a couple of glasses of cheap wine at the Surreal Lounge returned. *You and me, Lydia, we got something in common. We're both alone in the world. Got to stick together.*

She wondered how many people would have turned up today if it had been her funeral. Mentally she started to tick off potential mourners. Olinda and Zane would probably have attended. Ryan?

No, he wouldn't have bothered to come. A couple of others from the para-archaeology department might have shown up, though. Melanie Toft? Maybe. They had worked together for several months now.

Emmett glanced down at her hand on the seat. "What are you doing?"

"What?" Briefly distracted from her reverie, she looked at him. "I was just thinking about something."

"You were counting."

"Counting?"

"On your fingers," he said.

She looked down at her left hand where it rested on the seat beside her thigh and was embarrassed to see that she had extended her first three fingers.

"Math was never my strong suit," she said. Very deliberately she splayed all five fingers on the car seat.

Emmett, thank heaven, did not push it. She did not want to have to tell him that she had been trying to figure out how many people might show up at her funeral. The last thing she wanted to do was give the client any reason to believe the rumors that she was not mentally stable.

Nevertheless, for the first time in several months she thought she detected a hint of the dull gray mist that had obscured her world for a while after her Lost Weekend. She knew from experience that it was better not to examine the fog too closely. Better to focus on something else.

"I think Detective Martinez may actually be sincere about wanting to find Chester's killer," she said. "But it doesn't sound like she's going to get much support from her superiors."

"Priorities," Emmett said. "Everyone has them, including cops."

"Yeah, right. Priorities. You know, Emmett, I don't think Detective Martinez is going to find Chester's killer."

Emmett said nothing.

Surreptitiously she fished his limp handkerchief out of her pocket and mopped up a few more ridiculous, totally unwarranted tears.

CHAPTER 12

SHORTLY AFTER FIVE THAT AFTERNOON, EMMETT EASED the Slider into a loading zone on the street a short distance from the entrance to Shrimpton's House of Ancient Horrors. He got out, leaned against the fender, and folded his arms. Waiting for Lydia.

After the small funeral that morning he had dropped her off at Shrimpton's and told her that he would pick her up after work. He had spent the rest of the day plotting a new strategy for finding Quinn. At least that's what he had told himself he was doing.

He had been reasonably successful in focusing his attention on the mess he had come to Cadence to resolve. The problem was that Lydia was part of that mess, and every time he thought about her things got a lot messier.

Her words from last night reverberated dissonantly in his brain, disrupting the rest of his orderly thoughts. *Every type of psi talent produces certain eccentricities. . . . Don't worry. I'm sure you'll be back to normal in the morning.*

Damn. Did she really think the passion that had resonated between them was the result of a peculiar para-rez eccentricity that affected only ghost-hunters?

He forced his mind away from that line of thought and studied the outrageous, over-the-top imitation Dead City facade of the structure that housed Shrimpton's. In his opinion, the building itself, with its garish domes, phony spires, and fake arches, qualified as a horror, architecturally speaking. It was supposed to be a replica of a ruin, but the only thing vaguely authentic about it was the green paint on the walls. It lacked the characteristic grace and Harmonic proportions of the aboveground Dead City structures.

As he watched, Lydia walked out through the front gate, spotted the Slider, and hurried toward him.

How the hell had she ended up working in a place like this? he wondered. Then he reflected on what he knew of her personal history. He thought about how and why she had formed a bond with a character like Chester Brady and knew he had already answered his own question. She was alone in the world. When disaster had struck six months ago, she'd had no family and very few resources to cushion the fall.

Ryan Kelso had certainly not rushed to her aid. Emmett found that interesting. He knew from the hastily assembled background report his people had prepared that Lydia and Kelso had worked on the same team together for nearly a year. They had coauthored several papers on Harmonic excavations. Apparently after the Lost Weekend, Kelso had concluded that she would be of no further professional use to him. What was it Martinez had said? *Priorities.*

Sonofabitch.

"Something wrong, Emmett?" Lydia came to a halt in front of him, frowning in concern. "Did you get a ticket for parking in a loading zone?"

"No." He shook off the ambient hostility that he felt toward Kelso, straightened, and opened the door for her. "My record as an upstanding pillar of the community is still clean."

He closed the door behind her and went around to the other side of the Slider. She looked better than she had that morning, he decided. The worrisome shadows had retreated from her eyes. He had the feeling that they were still there, somewhere, but the familiar look of determination had returned. Definitely a fighter.

"How did things go at work?" he asked as he pulled away from the curb.

"Quiet." She made a face. "Shrimp is whining because the little flurry of business we had following Chester's murder has faded. I almost slugged him. Probably would have if Melanie hadn't stopped me."

"Good way to lose a job."

"I know." She fell silent for a while. "I've been thinking about Chester all day."

"What about him?"

"I want his killer found, Emmett."

"Martinez is doing her best."

"Martinez as much as admitted that she's got nothing. I've been thinking about hiring a private detective. How much do you think it would cost?"

"A lot more than you can afford," he said gently. "We've got other problems at the moment, Lydia. Stay focused."

"Yeah. Focused. Maybe it's all connected, Emmett. Maybe when we find your nephew and your cabinet we'll find Chester's killer."

"Maybe," he said cautiously.

"I'd like that." She flexed her hand. "I'd really like that."

He did not want her to start obsessing on that aspect of the case, he thought. According to the reports he had read, she was inclined to take risks in pursuit of a goal.

"With luck I'll get some information out of Wyatt tonight that may give us a lead," he said.

Her head came around very quickly. "Are you nervous about the dinner with Mercer Wyatt?"

"No. But I'm not exactly looking forward to it."

"I don't blame you. I can think of a thousand other things I'd rather do, including go to the dentist."

"What makes you say that?"

"Mercer Wyatt is very powerful in this town. That means he's dangerous."

"All of the heads of the Guilds wield a lot of economic and political influence in their cities."

"Wyatt runs the Cadence Guild as if it were a private fiefdom. Everyone knows it. He's grown enormously wealthy off Guild income. Politicians jump through hoops when he suggests that they do so."

"So he's a man with a lot of clout. Every community has its movers and shakers." He was in no mood for this. "No offense, Lydia, but your anti-hunter paranoia is showing."

Her mouth tightened in an annoyed line. For a couple of seconds he thought she was going to tell him that he was free to fire her after all.

Instead, she said, "I've changed my mind. I'm going with you."

He was so surprised that he nearly missed the turn into the Dead City View Apartments parking lot.

"Not necessary," he said brusquely.

"No, it's okay. You're my client, after all. And this is a sort of business dinner, isn't it?"

He thought about just how complicated this dinner was going to be. "Sort of."

He slid his vehicle into a slot beside an aging Float, de-rezzed the engine and opened the door. Lydia got out on her side. Together they walked toward the security door.

Lydia stopped and stared in astonishment. "It's fixed."

"Zane and I took care of it today while you were at work," Emmett explained. "Unfortunately, I don't know much about elevator repair." He de-rezzed the lock.

"Hey, Lydia. Mr. London." Zane waved to them from the third-floor landing.

"Hi, Zane. Nice job on the security gate."

"Mr. London helped," Zane said proudly. "Guess what?"

"What?" she asked.

"A letter came for you. A guy from Resonance Relay Messenger Service brought it. He wanted someone to sign for it, so I did."

"Wow." She gave him a wry grin. "Probably my invitation to the Restoration Ball. I've been wondering what happened to it. Dang, I just hope it isn't too late for me to get a decent ball gown. The good ones are probably all gone by now."

Zane guffawed. "No, no, this is for real. I'll get it." He whirled and ran off down the hall.

Emmett looked at Lydia as they started up the stairwell. "Restoration Ball?"

She wrinkled her nose. "Big society shindig at the end of the year.

Seventy-five years ago it started out as part of the annual festivities staged to celebrate the end of the Era of Discord, but somewhere along the way it became *the* social event here in Cadence. Everyone who matters in local politics and business will be there."

He nodded. "Got it. Do you usually attend?"

She gave him an amused look. "Don't be ridiculous. I was just joking. Of course I don't go to the Restoration Ball. What do I look like? Ameberella? Fairy godmothers don't hang out in this neighborhood after dark."

Zane popped into the stairwell waving a brown envelope, saving Emmett from having to respond to what he was pretty sure was one of those awkward rhetorical questions.

"Who's it from?" Lydia asked.

"Don't know." Zane handed it to her. "The return address is one of those box numbers they use at those private mail service operations."

Lydia eyed him as she took the envelope. "Already checked, did you?"

"Sure. We don't get a lot of deliveries from outfits like Resonance Relay. I think the guy was a little nervous about being in this neighborhood. That's why he made me sign for it. He didn't want to have to make a return trip."

"Wimp." Lydia tore open the envelope. A key fell out. It clattered on the step.

"I'll get it." Emmett scooped up the amber-and-steel key.

"Thanks." She opened the single-page letter that she had withdrawn from the envelope. The amusement evaporated from her eyes. "My God, it's from Chester."

"Brady?" Emmett closed his fingers around the key. "When was it written?"

She scanned the note. "His writing is terrible. I don't see a date. Oh, yes, here it is. Last Monday."

Emmett calculated quickly. "The day before he was killed. Wonder why you didn't get it until today?"

Lydia scanned the note quickly. "He says he left instructions for it to be delivered after his funeral."

Emmett propped one shoulder against the stairwell wall. "Let's hear what he has to say."

Lydia took a breath and started to read the note aloud.

Dear Lydia:

If you're reading this letter, it means I've gone back through the Curtain the hard way. You can consider this my last Will and Testament. I know we've had a few run-ins, but that was just business.

I never told you this, but sometimes when we talked about stuff over drinks at the Surreal, I used to pretend that we were out on a real date together. Sometimes I went back to my place and thought about how things could have been if you weren't so nice and I wasn't so screwed up.

I always told you that you're too good for your own good. I still say being honest and loyal and hardworking and all that shit won't get you far. But, I got to admit that it was kind of nice to know that there actually are people like you out there in the world— and I'm not saying that just because I made a lot of easy money off folks like you.

Anyhow, what all this is leading up to is that if anything happens to me I want you to have the assets in my retirement plan.

After Dark

It's at the Bank of Rose. Use the key to get into it.
Good-bye, Lydia. And thanks for everything.

Love,
Chester

P.S. I still say you're better off without that son of a bitch Kelso
hanging around. You'll see. He's a user, Lydia. I know his kind.
Maybe it's because I'm one of them.

Lydia stopped reading suddenly. There was a short pause during
which Emmett watched her dig out the handkerchief he had given
her at the funeral. Zane looked alarmed when she brushed away the
fresh tears. He opened his mouth to say something but subsided
when Emmett caught his attention and shook his head.

After a while Lydia stuffed the handkerchief back into her purse
and took the key from Emmett.

"Well," she said, "this should be interesting. I wonder what kind
of assets Chester would keep in a retirement plan?"

He glanced at his watch. "Too late to find out tonight. The banks
are closed."

"Not the Bank of Rose," she assured him. "It never closes."

CHAPTER 13

THE SURREAL LOUNGE WAS EVERYTHING ONE WOULD have expected in a place that had served as Chester Brady's home away from home, Emmett decided an hour and a half later. The atmosphere reeked of second-rate liquor, synch-smoke, and rancid cooking grease. The place was drenched in the perpetual gloom that was the quintessential hallmark of cheap nightclubs.

It was nearly seven o'clock. The regulars had already begun to settle in for the evening. The shabby booths were populated with men whose hair gleamed from too much pomade and women whose dresses fit too snugly. There was a small stage. A sign announced that a musical group calling itself the Earth Tones was scheduled to play at nine. In the meantime, some surprisingly good rez-jazz emanated from a pair of speakers.

Emmett thought about the photo of Lydia sharing a drink with Chester Brady in one of the red vinyl booths.

"Come here a lot?" he asked dryly.

"Couple of times a month for the past two years," she said quite seriously. "The music's good."

"Two years?"

"I told you, that was how long I knew Chester."

"Ah."

He adroitly eased both of them out of the path of a waitress. The woman carried a tray laden with bottles of White Noise beer and a bowl filled with bite-size chunks of something that had been deep-fried beyond recognition.

"Which one is Rose?" Emmett asked Lydia.

"Behind the bar." She led the way through the crowded room with the ease of someone who knew her way around.

Emmett watched her as she moved ahead of him. She made an incongruous picture here in this sordid setting. Her red hair glowed like a cheerful bonfire in the sickly yellow gleam of the table lamps. She had dressed for the dinner with Mercer Wyatt as though she were going to meet with her lawyer or banker. All business in her trim, dark-brown business suit and demure pumps, she looked wildly out of place. But the waitress gave her a friendly nod. Lydia returned the gesture.

"Hi, Becky."

She came to a halt at the far end of the bar. Emmett stopped beside her.

"That's Rose," she said, indicating the huge man with the shaved head pouring whiskey at the other end.

Emmett contemplated the thick neck, mountainous shoulders, and tattoos on biceps that bulged beneath the sleeves of a lime-green T-shirt.

"By any other name," he muttered.

"Rose is really very sweet," Lydia confided.

"I'll bet."

"He's a musical-harmonic para-rez," she said. "Trained as a classical musician. But he prefers rez-jazz."

That explained the excellent sound track playing in the background, Emmett thought. Rose knew music.

"Hey, there, Lydia." The big man's face lit up when he spotted her at the end of the bar. "Glad you could drop by. Thought maybe we wouldn't see much of you what with Chester gone and all."

Emmett watched Rose glide toward them. The bartender moved in a soft, easy, coordinated way that belied his size.

"Hi, Rose." Lydia stood on tiptoe and leaned across the bar to brush her lips lightly against Rose's cheek. "Hard to believe Chester's gone, isn't it?"

"To tell you the truth, I'm surprised he lived as long as he did." Rose folded his big arms on the bar. "In the course of his long and varied career, Brady managed to piss off just about everyone who knew him." Rose looked at Emmett. "Who's your friend?"

Emmett put out his hand. "Emmett London. I'm a client of Lydia's."

"Client, huh?"

Rose shook hands firmly but politely, making no attempt to demonstrate his strength with a crushing grip. Emmett concluded that Rose was a man who was comfortable with himself and his size. He thought he understood why Lydia liked him.

"We're on our way to a business dinner," Lydia said.

"No kidding." Rose surveyed her from head to toe. "No offense, Lyd, but brown is not your color."

"I'll remember that next time I go shopping. Rose, we don't have a lot of time. I've got the key to Chester's locker. Mind if I pick up his things?"

"Nope. He once told me you'd be by for them if anything ever happened to him." Rose glanced at the waitress. "Keep an eye on things, Becky. I'll be right back."

Becky raised a hand to indicate she'd heard him.

"This way to the Bank of Rose," Rose said to Lydia.

He unlocked a door behind the bar and led the way into a dark hall. Lydia followed. Emmett trailed after her.

The door was surprisingly heavy. It closed behind the trio with a solid thud. Mag-steel, Emmett thought. It would take a blowtorch or a small bomb to get through it. The walls of the hallway were lined with the same material.

Rose rezzed a switch. The cold light of a fluo-rez tube in the ceiling illuminated the hallway, revealing two rows of mag-steel lockers. All of them were secured with heavy mag-rez locks.

"Looks like a bank vault," Emmett said.

"With twenty-four-hour security." The fluo-rez light gleamed on Rose's bald head as he walked down the aisle between the lockers. "To get in here, you got to get past me or my partner. The Surreal Lounge is open day and night, so there's never a time when there's no one behind the bar. Proud to say the Bank of Rose has never been robbed."

"Or audited or insured or taxed or licensed, either, I'll bet," Emmett concluded.

Rose came to a halt in front of a locker. "Nope. We here at the Bank of Rose don't have much to do with the various regulatory authorities."

"Rose caters to a rather select clientele," Lydia murmured as she reached into her shoulder bag.

"We rent out lockers to folks who prefer not to patronize what you'd call a more traditional bank," Rose explained.

"Probably because most of 'em would get arrested on sight if they went through the front door of a real bank." Lydia held out the key that had come in the brown envelope. "Any idea what Chester kept here?"

"No." Rose took the key from her. "Bank of Rose policy is not to ask any awkward or embarrassing questions. So long as you pay your rent on time, you're a valued customer."

The lock clicked as the key briefly disrupted the pattern of its internal resonance. Rose opened the door. Lydia stepped forward to peer into the small locker.

"Looks like an old duffel bag," she said. She started to reach for it.

"I'll get it," Emmett said.

She got out of his way so that he could haul the small, battered canvas bag out of the locker. It was not very heavy.

Lydia looked at the old bag. "I wonder why he wanted me to get this."

"Not like he had anyone else to leave his stuff to." Rose closed the locker door. "You were the closest thing to a friend that old Chester had. He always told me that the two of you had a lot in common."

LYDIA SET THE DUFFEL BAG IN FRONT OF HER ON THE floor of the Slider. She unzipped it while Emmett got in behind the wheel and rezzed the engine. In the reflected glow of the dashboard she could see a bulging envelope and a small paper sack.

"Maybe you're about to become the lucky owner of a winning lottery ticket," Emmett said.

"I won't hold my breath." Lydia removed the envelope. "Chester was not what anyone would call lucky."

She broke the seal on the envelope and took out the handful of yellowed papers inside. She glanced at the first one. The tide of gloom that had ebbed and flowed around her all day rose once more, swamped her again for a moment.

"What are they?" Emmett asked.

"Chester's applications for membership in the Society of Para-Archaeologists. And the rejections the Society sent back to him." She shook her head, amazed. "He always talked about how much he disdained the Society. But according to these, he applied for membership every year for twenty years."

"And got rejected every year?"

"Uh-huh. Poor Chester. Deep down, he must have desperately wanted to become legitimate."

"I doubt if those papers constitute his retirement plan."

"Probably not."

She put the papers back into the envelope and reached into the duffel for the paper sack. She froze the instant she touched it. A thrill of awareness sang through her nerves. Psi energy.

"Oh, my," she whispered.

Emmett glanced at her sharply. "What is it?"

"Something old." Very gently she put the paper sack on her lap. "Something very, very old."

"Harmonic artifact?"

"Yes." There was no mistaking the resonance. She was a para-archaeologist, after all. One of the best. "But there's something different. I could swear I'm picking up a trace of trap energy. But that's impossible. No traps have ever been found outside the Dead Cities. No way to anchor them."

"Never say never when it comes to the ancient Harmonics. There's still one hell of a lot that we don't know about them. Be careful, Lydia."

"Hey, I'm the expert here, remember?"

"I remember," he said. "Be careful anyway."

"I'll bet you were a real pain to work with when you ghost-hunted professionally."

"It was mentioned from time to time," he agreed. "On the plus side, I never lost a single para-archaeologist."

She ignored him, turning the paper sack cautiously in her hands. Then she opened it very carefully and looked inside. In the dim light she could just barely make out a dark, rounded object about the size of her two hands clasped together.

"There's something strange about the resonance," she said. "It's definitely genuine. Very, very old. But the vibrations are different from anything else I've ever sensed from artifacts this old."

"Still catching traces of trap energy?"

"I'm not sure. There's too much else going on here. It feels almost like—" She broke off abruptly. It was never good policy to make a fool of oneself in front of the client.

"Like what?"

"You wouldn't believe me if I told you." Lydia held the paper sack cradled in both hands and tried to get a grip on her runaway imagination. Impossible, she thought. It couldn't be.

But what if?

Her euphoria evaporated as another *what if* occurred to her. What if she really had lost her para-rez pitch, just as Ryan and the others assumed? What if the disaster six months ago was only now produc-ing a delayed reaction? What if she was wrong?

"Lydia? You okay?"

"Yes."

"What's inside the sack?"

Emmett's calm voice brought her out of the downward spiral. She stared through the window of the Slider and saw that they had left the busy city streets behind. They were climbing one of the hills above town, a neighborhood of exclusive estates. Massive gates guarded the long drives that led to the mansions.

"Lydia? Are you going to tell me what's inside the sack?"

"Yes." There was only one way to find out if she held something truly incredible in her hands or if she should check into a nice, quiet para-psych ward first thing tomorrow morning.

Deep breaths.

She took one, steeled herself, and reached into the sack. Another, much stronger shock of tingling excitement went through her when she actually touched the warm, smooth surface.

"It feels like a bottle," she whispered.

Emmett did not take his eyes off the winding road. "What about the trap energy you said you felt?"

"Stop worrying. I know what I'm doing."

He said nothing, but he pulled the Slider over to the side of the road and de-rezzed the engine. He turned in the seat to watch in-tently as she slowly removed the artifact from the paper sack.

She saw at once that she had been right about the bottle shape.

"What the hell is it?" Emmett asked softly.

"An unguent jar, I think." She studied it more closely, trying to focus on the shimmering surface. "But not like any that I've ever seen."

She stared at the thing she held. In the dim backwash of illumination provided by the dashboard the sealed jar seemed to glow with an inner light of its own. Colors shifted, stirred, and swirled on the surface. She saw shades of reds and golds that had no name. They flowed into strange greens and blues before she could describe them.

She swallowed hard. "Emmett? Please tell me I'm not seeing things. I really don't want to have to go back into therapy."

He gazed fixedly at the jar. "Hell, that's not—It can't be. We need better light."

He reached into the console between the seats and removed a small flashlight. He rezzed it and aimed the beam at the ancient jar.

For a long moment they both just sat and stared at the artifact. In the bright light of the flash, the colors on the surface of the bottle leaped into full, pulsing life. A restless sea of light and darkness surged around the widest portion of the elegantly shaped jar. Each hue seemed to be animated by its own inner energy source. Vast depths of dazzling light and color appeared and disappeared.

"Dreamstone," Emmett said in a voice that held no inflection at all.

"Impossible," Lydia said again.

"You know as well as I do that there's nothing else it could be." He took the jar from her and turned it slightly so that the flashlight beam played across its surface. "Pure worked dreamstone. Damn. Talk about a retirement plan."

Lydia shook her head slowly, unable to believe her eyes or her para-rez senses.

Dreamstone was well named. Small deposits of it were occasionally found, usually embedded in clear quartz in the vicinity of dead volcanoes. Not only was it extremely rare but it had thus far defied any attempt to extract it from the protective quartz. It shattered at the slightest touch, simultaneously appearing to melt and fracture into microscopic shards.

No technology yet devised by the human population on Harmony had been able to handle it without destroying it. For prospectors and mining companies, it was indeed the stuff of dreams. Beautiful to look at when it was found, it evaporated the instant you reached out to touch it.

But the unguent jar in Emmett's hand was firm and solid proof that the ancient Harmonics had discovered how to work dreamstone.

Lydia felt the hair stir on the nape of her neck. "Maybe this is what got Chester killed."

"I'd say that is an excellent possibility." Emmett gave the jar a quarter turn. "Incredible."

"Do you realize what this means?"

"It means that if Chester had lived long enough to sell this to a museum or a private collector, he would have been set for life."

Lydia waved that aside. "The monetary value is beside the point. You can't put a price on it, since nothing else like it has ever been found."

"Trust me, Lydia, you can put a price on anything."

"But the significance of worked dreamstone is absolutely extraordinary. Don't you see? This jar means that it can be done. There must be a way to psychically tune dreamstone so that it can be manipulated like other raw materials. Who knows what properties it has in this form?"

"Good question." He did not look up from his examination of the jar.

"Somewhere in their past, the Harmonics found a way to actually mine the stuff."

"Yes."

She frowned. He did not seem to be as impressed by the full implications of this staggering discovery as she was. Then again, he was a businessman, not an archaeologist. Make that *ghost-hunter-businessman*, she amended silently. Probably took a lot to impress him.

Emmett gave the jar another turn. "I wonder where Brady found it?"

"Who knows? Chester was a ruin rat. He was always exploring illegally on his own. He must have stumbled across this jar on one of his forays into the catacombs."

She watched as Emmett gave the jar another quarter turn, bringing another section into the beam of the flashlight. When she saw the figure of a bird in flight imprisoned forever within the shifting rivers of color, she nearly stopped breathing altogether.

"Emmett."

"I see it," he said.

Now he did sound impressed. As well he should be, she thought. In all the years in which humans had been excavating the ruins of the Harmonics, no one had ever come across any indication that the ancient people had indulged in representational art.

The long-vanished inhabitants of the Dead Cities had left no pictures or drawings of animals, plants, or themselves. There were no seascapes or landscapes, no scenes of what the world had looked like to them or images of how they had seen themselves in their environment—at least none that humans could interpret.

Until now.

Now there was a small bird flying in the depths of a sea of colors flowing across the surface of a little jar that should not exist.

Emmett straightened slowly and clicked off the flashlight. "Looks like your pal Brady made the most significant discovery since Caldwell Frost blundered into the ruins of Old Frequency and decided that someone had made him a god."

"I'm stunned," Lydia whispered. "This is so amazing."

"Anything else in the duffel bag?"

"What? Oh, right, the bag." Lydia peered into the unzipped canvas carryall again and rummaged around. Her hand brushed against another envelope. "There's something."

She withdrew the envelope and opened it. A photo fell out. She held it to the light and saw another picture of herself and Chester in a booth at the Surreal Lounge. There was a familiar volume of the *Journal of Para-Archaeology* propped in front of Chester, who was beaming proudly.

"He did like photos of the two of you together, didn't he?" Emmett said.

"Yes." She got teary again as she examined the photo.

"He had several pictures taken of us."

"Must have fed his fantasy that the two of you were a couple."

"Probably." She blinked rapidly to clear her eyes. "This was a special one, though. I had just published a paper in the journal. Coauthored with Ryan, naturally. I had to fight tooth and nail, but I made sure that Chester got credit as a consultant on the project."

"Probably his only brush with legitimacy."

"I hadn't realized until now how important it must have been to him," she whispered.

"You'd better put the jar in your purse until we get home." Emmett handed it to her. "And whatever you do, don't say anything about it in front of Mercer Wyatt and his wife."

"What do you think I am?" she asked as she rewrapped the jar and stashed it inside her purse. "Crazy?"

Emmett's mouth curved slightly as he rezzed the engine and pulled back onto the road. "No, I don't think you're crazy."

Lydia settled into her seat, clutching her purse very tightly. Excitement snapped and sizzled through her again. Euphoria followed in its wake. Worked dreamstone. And a picture of a bird.

"Thanks," she said, feeling very smug. "I appreciate that."

CHAPTER 14

MIDWAY THROUGH THE PAINFULLY FORMAL DINNER, Lydia reached a major conclusion about her hostess. She did not like Tamara Wyatt. More precisely, she did not like the way Tamara looked at Emmett when she thought no one was watching.

The speculative gleam in Tamara's gaze reminded Lydia of the way Fuzz looked when he peered at the pretzel jar. As if he was willing to devote a lot of thought and energy to a consideration of ways and means of removing the lid.

Tamara was sleek and polished, with an indefinable edge of glamour that would set her apart in any room. Her dark hair was bound up in an elegant chignon that accented her aristocratic cheekbones and fine jawline. A fortune in gemstones sparkled at her throat. She wore amber set in gold in her ears. The deep décolletage of her gown stopped just short of being indiscreet.

Lydia had realized when they had arrived an hour and a half earlier that Emmett had met both the Wyatts previously. Mercer and Emmett had greeted each other with polite civility. But something else had been going on between Tamara and Emmett just beneath the surface.

It had taken her a little longer than it should have to recognize the resonance patterns between these two, Lydia thought. She excused herself for the delay. After all, she had been seriously distracted this evening. Approximately one-third of her attention was focused on the bizarre experience of being entertained by the head of the Cadence Guild. The remainder was consumed with speculation about the extraordinary little jar Chester had bequeathed to her. It was all she could do not to excuse herself every five minutes to run down the hall to check the elegant armoire where the butler had placed her purse.

Calm down, she told herself as a white-gloved waiter removed the plate in front of her. If the jar wasn't safe here in Mercer Wyatt's mansion, it wasn't safe anywhere. The only other place she'd seen with so much security was the University of Cadence Museum.

"So, Lydia, you're in the private consulting business?" Mercer asked with seemingly polite interest.

Tamara smiled. "Rather young to have left university work, aren't you? Most consultants tend to be older. More experienced."

Lydia pulled herself away from concerns about her purse. She ignored Tamara and studied Mercer instead.

Mercer Wyatt had to be at least forty years older than his wife. Silver-haired, with hawklike features, he was a man who was clearly accustomed to the accoutrements of money and power. He wore his amber on his hands in the form of large, heavy rings. As head of the Guild, he would necessarily have to be a very powerful dissonance-energy para-rez, she thought.

"It's not routine for a para-archaeologist my age to go into the private sector," Lydia said, "but it's not unheard of."

Conversation to this point had consisted of the sort of superficial patter she had learned to tolerate at faculty teas. Lydia had a feeling that the real talking would be done after dinner.

"Some people don't fit into the academic bureaucracy very well," Emmett said casually. "Just as some can't tolerate the corporate environment. Lydia has what you'd call an entrepreneurial spirit."

Tamara gave Lydia a polished smile. "How did Emmett find you?"

"I'm listed with the Society of Para-archaeologists as a consultant, and I advertise in the *Journal of Para-Archaeology*," Lydia said smoothly.

"That's hardly a guarantee of honesty and integrity, is it?" Tamara said. "There are so many frauds and scam artists in the antiquities trade."

"Very true," Lydia murmured. "But on the whole, I'd have to say that one's odds of getting a dishonest P-A from the Society's lists are considerably lower than the odds of getting a dishonest hunter from the Guild hall."

Tamara's eyes darkened with anger. "The Guild maintains the strictest standards."

"Uh-huh." Lydia spooned up a bite of the fruit ice that had been served for dessert. "Is that why I've had at least two break-ins recently by ghost-hunters?"

Mercer pinned Emmett with a cold glare. "What the devil is she talking about?"

Emmett shrugged. "You heard her. She's had some unfortunate experiences with hunters recently. Kind of soured her view of the profession, I'm afraid."

Mercer turned back to Lydia. "Kindly explain yourself."

Lydia put down her spoon. "As the head of the Guild here in Cadence, you must be aware that there are some ghost-hunters running around the city committing illegal acts. What's more, they are summoning ghosts to aid in the commission of those crimes. My apartment has been vandalized twice."

Mercer's jaw clenched. He flicked a quick look at Emmett and then went back to Lydia. "Are you absolutely certain ghost-hunters were involved?"

"I saw the ghosts they summoned," she said very steadily. "Ask Emmett. He chased off one of the hunters. Would have caught him if the little sneak hadn't had an accomplice waiting for him in the parking lot."

Mercer's piercing gaze swung back to Emmett. "Is this true?"

"All true," Emmett said easily. "I assume you can assure us that the intruders were not working for the Guild?"

"Of course they weren't working for the Guild." Mercer flung down his napkin and stood abruptly. "I assure you, I will have my people look into the matter. The Guild polices its own."

"How convenient," Lydia said politely.

Mercer glowered at her.

Lydia turned toward Tamara. "So, what's it like being the wife of the head of the Cadence Guild? What do you do besides go to the Restoration Ball every year?"

"I manage to keep busy," Tamara said coolly.

Mercer studied her with obvious pride. "Tamara is an executive in her own right. Thanks to her, the Guild has established a very active foundation that funds several Cadence charities. She oversees the administration of the Foundation."

Tamara's expression warmed noticeably under the praise. "I don't do it all alone, of course. I am extremely fortunate to have Denver

Galbraith-Thorndyke as my chief administrator. I'm sure you're aware of the Galbraith-Thorndyke family's long history here in Cadence?"

"As in the Galbraith-Thorndykes who pretty much dominate the social scene?" Lydia was impressed in spite of herself. "Give tons of money to charity? Patrons of the University Museum, sit on all the important boards, et cetera, et cetera? Of course I've heard of them. I didn't know they were connected to the Guild."

Mercer chuckled. "They weren't—until Tamara approached them and asked young Denver to take over the job of administering the Guild Foundation."

"Nice move, Tamara," Emmett congratulated her.

"Thank you," Tamara murmured. "I see it as a major first step toward elevating the image of the Guild in the community."

"Indeed," Mercer said briskly. "A brilliant first step, if I do say so myself. Young Denver is a lawyer. He has connections with all of the movers and shakers in town."

"So how come he went to work for the Guild?" Lydia asked bluntly.

Tamara looked annoyed, but Mercer merely chuckled.

"Usual story," he said easily. "Young scion of a rich and socially prominent family longs to prove himself to his father. Denver did not want to join the family law firm. Didn't want to go to work for good old Dad, I suppose. He wanted to stand on his own two feet. Tamara offered him the Foundation job and he grabbed it."

"He's very committed," Tamara said.

Mercer turned to Emmett. "You and I need to talk privately. Tamara, please take Lydia into the salon for tea. We will join you later."

"Of course, my dear." Tamara rose gracefully from her chair and began to usher Lydia out of the room.

Lydia glanced at Emmett. He inclined his head a bare half inch. She had no problem at all reading his message. She hesitated and then decided that he was right. They might learn more separately than they could together. Without a word she followed Tamara out of the dining room.

They walked down a hall paneled in a dark, richly grained wood that had been polished until it glowed. Tamara led the way through double doors set with squares of beveled glass into a room done in yellow and maroon.

A frisson of awareness sparkled across Lydia's nerves. She turned and saw the cabinet filled with ancient Harmonic artifacts. So many of them grouped in close proximity produced more than enough resonance energy to reach her here on the other side of the salon. Automatically she went toward the cabinet and came to a halt in front of it.

"A magnificent collection," she murmured.

"My husband started it years ago, long before we were married." Tamara picked up the pot that had been placed on a small round table. "Tea?"

"Thank you, yes." Lydia studied an oddly shaped green quartz panel that had probably formed a portion of a tomb chamber door. "You and your husband were married a year ago, weren't you? I seem to recall seeing something about it in the papers. You're not from Cadence, are you?"

"No. I was living in Resonance City when I met Mercer." Tamara walked forward, a cup and saucer in one hand. "He attended a meeting of the Guild Council there. We were introduced at a reception."

"I see."

"The reception was held to announce the engagement of the head of the Resonance Guild," Tamara clarified softly.

An icy sensation swept through Lydia. She watched her fingers to make certain that they did not tremble when she took the cup and saucer from Tamara. It wouldn't do to spill rez-tea on what was no doubt a fabulously expensive carpet. The Guild would probably send her a bill that she would not be able to pay.

"No kidding." Lydia sipped tea. It was, as everything else had been at dinner, excellent. "Whom did the Resonance Guild boss marry?"

Tamara looked amused. "He was engaged to marry me. But things did not work out. We ended the engagement soon after the reception. I moved here to Cadence a short time later."

"I see." Stop right now, Lydia told herself. Just because you see an accident waiting to happen doesn't mean you have to help it along.

But she couldn't stop. She had to know for certain.

"So, who was this Guild boss you were going to marry back in Resonance?"

"Emmett, of course," Tamara said sweetly. "He was the head of the Resonance Guild for six years until he resigned ten months ago."

MERCER LOWERED HIMSELF INTO THE PLUM-COLORED leather of the massive reading chair. He raised his brandy glass to his mouth and studied Emmett above the rim. "I will get right to the point. I had two reasons for asking you to come here tonight. One of those reasons is that I wish to offer you a bargain, son."

"I'm not your son." Emmett rested an arm along the top of the mantel. "And I sure as hell won't agree to any deal until I know all of the terms."

Mercer exhaled deeply. "I'll level with you, Emmett. I need your help. And I think I can help you in return."

"Why do you need me? You've got a Guild full of people you can call on for help."

Mercer shook his head. "Not for this. Let me explain. I haven't yet made any official public announcement, but I intend to step down sometime during the coming year. Only the members of my personal staff are aware of my decision. They have all been sworn to secrecy."

This was the last thing he had expected to hear tonight, Emmett thought. Mercer Wyatt had held the Cadence Guild in an iron grip for more than three decades. It was widely assumed that he would die at the helm.

"You're going to retire?" Emmett said warily.

"I've been running this show for a long time. Until recently the Guild was always the most important thing in my life. My first wife was a wonderful woman, but I never took the time to know her. After her death I was left with two children. I let someone else raise them. They're both grown now, and I've got three grandkids, but I hardly know any of them."

"Let me guess. You've finally decided to stop and smell the roses, is that it?"

"You find that amusing?"

"Let's just say it's unanticipated. What the hell brought on the sudden change? Get a health scare from your doctor?"

"Nothing like that. I got a new wife."

"Oh, yeah, right. Must have slipped my mind."

"I am in love for the first time in my life, Emmett," Mercer said very seriously. "My marriage to Tamara is a Marriage of Convenience at the moment, as you know, but we plan to convert it into a Covenant Marriage."

Emmett stared at him. "You want more children?"

"There are other reasons for entering a Covenant Marriage besides the desire to have children," Mercer reminded him.

Emmett grunted. "True love? Give me a break. Aren't you a little old for that kind of romantic nonsense, Mercer?"

"You are not a romantic man, Emmett."

"Neither were you, last time I checked. Terminating a Covenant Marriage is a legal and financial nightmare." He did not add what they both knew, which was that adultery was one of the very few legally accepted reasons for dissolving a Covenant Marriage. "What's the point of getting into one if you don't want kids?"

Mercer stretched out his legs and gazed into the fire. "Obviously you do not understand, so we'll drop the subject. The bottom line here is my intention to step down."

"No offense, Mercer, but I find it a little tough to grasp the concept."

"Why? I'm forty years older than Tamara. I don't know how long I'll have with her. I intend to enjoy every minute of whatever time I have left, however. I've got money, I've got my health, and I've got a beautiful woman at my side. I'd be a fool to continue to devote myself to the Guild."

Emmett contemplated him for a while. "Does Tamara know of your decision?"

"She knows."

"Huh." He shrugged. "So what does this have to do with me?"

"I want your help. And I'm willing to bargain for it. I know why you are here in Cadence. My people told me about your missing nephew. I may be able to assist you."

Tonight was turning out to be one big surprise after another, Emmett thought. There was nothing he could do but go with the flow. "Before we talk about doing any kind of deal, you'd better tell me what you want from me."

Mercer nodded slowly and sipped his brandy. After a moment he set the glass aside. He propped his elbows on the arms of the heavy chair and steepled his fingers.

"As I said, I am preparing to step down. But I intend to do so in an orderly manner, one that will leave the Guild on the right course for the future."

"In other words," Emmett said, "you want to handpick your successor."

"Precisely. I have worked for years to create a strong organization that can take care of its own. To a large extent, I have achieved my goals. All members in good standing can be assured of an excellent pay scale and a safety net of benefits for themselves and their families."

"So long as they follow orders, don't ask any questions, and don't cross you," Emmett said.

"I have always rewarded loyalty well."

"And crushed anyone who stood up to you or questioned your decisions. You're a real old-fashioned kind of guy, Mercer."

"I will admit that in the past you and I have differed on the subject of how an organization such as the Guild should be run."

"You could say that. Your approach is about seventy years out of date."

"It is true that I have honored tradition during my tenure as chief of the Cadence Guild."

Emmett grunted again. Hard to argue that one.

"It may interest you to know, however," Mercer continued, "that I have concluded it is time for the Cadence Guild to change."

"I'll believe that when I see it."

"I intend for Cadence to follow the lead of the Resonance Guild,"

Mercer said steadily. "I want to see it restructured and modernized along the same lines."

Emmett searched his face. "You're serious, aren't you?"

"Entirely serious. But sudden shifts cannot be effected overnight. Furthermore, they must be accompanied by strong leadership. I shall begin the process of change this year, with Tamara's help."

"You mean her Guild Foundation work?"

"It's a start, and she is very committed to her charities. Her Foundation will go far toward helping to change the image of the Guild here in Cadence. But the task of restructuring the organization itself cannot be completed in the few months during which I will remain as head of it. Therefore, I must make arrangements to, as you say, handpick my successor."

A sudden dark suspicion sparked. Emmett folded his arms across his chest and leaned one shoulder against the mantel. "Got someone in mind for the job?"

"Yes, of course." Mercer smiled humorlessly. "You."

Emmett exhaled slowly. "I hate to have to be the one to tell you this, Mercer, but I think you may have accidentally gotten fried the last time you summoned a ghost."

"I realize my proposal is coming as something of a shock. But surely you can see why I want you to consider it. That's all I'm asking at the moment. There's no rush. We've got a year to make plans. Plenty of time to work out the details."

"There's nothing to work out. I'm giving you my answer right now. I don't want the job. I've gone into the private sector, Mercer. I'm just a businessman these days."

Mercer unlocked his hands and leaned forward. His fierce eyes glowed with energy and determination. "Listen to me, son—"

"I am not your son," Emmett repeated through his teeth.

"Sorry. Slip of the tongue."

The hell it was, Emmett thought. They were both aware of the gossip and rumors that had circulated for years. He had no intention of going down that road tonight. Not with Mercer Wyatt.

"As I was saying," Mercer continued, "I want to leave the Guild in good hands. Hands that can steer it on a new, modern course. You are the best possible person to do that."

"No."

"You're the one who single-handedly restructured the Resonance Guild when you took charge. You're the one who established the new ways, turned it into a business, made it respectable. I want you to do the same for the Cadence Guild."

"In case you haven't heard, I'm out of Guild politics. I'm a business consultant now."

"That is precisely what I want," Mercer said seriously. "A business consultant who is uniquely qualified to help transform the Cadence Guild into a respected business enterprise."

"Forget it, Mercer. I don't want any part of your plan. I wish you luck with it, but I don't want to be involved."

"I see." Mercer sat back in his chair. He did not look defeated; he looked more like a man who was content to bide his time. "We'll leave that for the moment, then. Let's move on to other matters."

Emmett came away from the mantel. He walked to the window and looked out over the lights of the city below. "Do you really know something about my nephew, Mercer? Or was that just a lure to get me here tonight so that you could try to talk me into taking over the Guild?"

"I'll be honest with you. I have no direct knowledge of young

Quinn's whereabouts. But my sources tell me that he followed a young woman here to Cadence. True?"

"Yes."

"The young lady apparently disappeared, and your nephew, who, I understand, is a dissonance-energy para-rez, vanished shortly thereafter, according to my information."

Emmett looked out at the brooding, moonlit ruins of the Dead City. "Your information is good."

"There are some advantages to having been in my position as head of the Cadence Guild for so long," Mercer said dryly. "I've had plenty of time to set up reliable information networks both inside and outside the organization."

Emmett turned slowly to face him. "What do you know?"

"I know that Quinn's lady friend is not the first young person to disappear here in Cadence in recent weeks," Mercer went on. "No one has taken much notice of the fact because none of the missing persons was underage and none appears to have had much in the way of concerned family."

"Until now."

"Until now," Mercer agreed. "In addition, there has been no indication of foul play."

"How many have turned up missing?"

"I can't be certain. You'd be amazed at how many young people disappear every year. Had no idea myself until I started looking into it. Most of them wind up on the streets or in Curtain cults. Some go to another city. No one seems to notice."

"Why did you suddenly decide to take notice?"

"Because when I heard that you were in town looking for your nephew, I made a few inquiries. I learned that some of the young people who have disappeared in recent weeks have been dissonance-energy para-rezes. Untrained ghost-hunters who were in the process of applying to the Guild. They never appeared for basic training and indoctrination. My first assumption was that someone had enticed them into a gang or cult or an unlicensed excavation team. The Guild takes a dim view of outsiders using ghost-hunters for illegal purposes."

"Bad for the public image," Emmett said dryly.

"Yes. This sort of thing has occurred occasionally in the past. It's been relatively easy to put a stop to it. But this time there are complications."

"Tried going to the police?" Emmett suggested mildly.

Mercer gave him a disgusted look. "Of course not. If I did that, the media would get wind of it in no time. I won't have the papers running headlines declaring that the Guild can no longer police itself. Not on my watch, by God."

"Right." Mainstreaming the Cadence Guild was not going to be easy, Emmett thought. Not with attitudes like this at the top.

"As I was saying," Mercer continued, "I have concluded that you and I might be able to work together."

"You mean you're willing to give me access to the resources of the Guild to help me look for Quinn?"

Mercer closed his eyes briefly. When he opened them there was a bleak rage in his gaze. "I only wish it were that simple. I am sorry to tell you that the resources of the Guild cannot be relied upon at the moment."

Emmett watched him for a long time as the full implications of that statement sank in. "Maybe you'd better explain."

"I have reason to believe that there is a traitor in my organization," Mercer said wearily. "Someone close to me."

Emmett said nothing. He knew what it must have cost Mercer to acknowledge such a thing.

"I had to go outside my own Guild just to discover what little information I managed to learn about the situation involving your nephew," Mercer said. "Someone I trust is plotting against me, Emmett."

"Every Guild chief has enemies. Fact of life."

"Of course. And I have dealt with many in the past. But this is different. More insidious. I have been unable to isolate the traitor. It could be anyone on my administrative staff. *Anyone.*"

"Someone who knows about your plans for the future of the Cadence Guild and doesn't like them?"

"I believe so. But it may be more than that. It may be personal. I simply don't know at this point. I only know I can no longer trust my staff."

"What does that have to do with luring young, untrained hunters off the street?"

"It has occurred to me that this traitor, whoever he is, may be trying to create his own private army of hunters who will take orders directly from him and who will be loyal only to him."

"Set up a rival organization? Hell, Mercer, that's a little over the top, isn't it?"

"Think about it," Mercer insisted. "If this bastard wishes to go against me, he will need a power base. That means he will need his own trained ghost-hunters. What better way to do that than to grab young ones who have not yet been indoctrinated into the Guild?"

Emmett whistled soundlessly. "Are you sure you're not sliding into paranoia here, Mercer?"

"I'm being careful. There's a difference."

There was a difference, Emmett reflected, but it was not always easy to see it when you were a Guild boss.

Mercer Wyatt was not a stupid man, he reminded himself, even if he was seriously lovestruck at the moment. Wyatt was smart, powerful, and, above all, he was a survivor. If his instincts told him he had a traitor on his staff, chances were good that he was right.

Emmett studied the pattern of the carpet beneath his feet for a while. Then he looked up. "What all this boils down to is you want me to get rid of your so-called traitor for you."

"I won't deny that I need your assistance in this unpleasant affair, since I can no longer trust my personal staff. The way I see it, our interests are aligned, son. You want to find your nephew. I want the person who may have caused him to disappear."

Emmett ignored the *son* reference this time. He had other priorities now. He contemplated the city lights for several long seconds while he weighed the pros and cons of getting more closely involved with Mercer Wyatt.

The truth was, he had very little choice. Quinn's safety came first.

"What information can you give me?" he said at last.

"Not much, I admit. As I said, I had to go outside the Guild to get even that. On your own, you will no doubt stumble onto the few facts I've got. But at least I can save you some time. And time may be of the essence here."

Emmett looked at him over his shoulder. "I'm listening."

Mercer leaned forward in his chair, his expression intense. "The day your nephew disappeared, he paid a visit to a youth shelter in the Old Quarter near the east wall."

"What's the name of the place?" Emmett asked swiftly.

"It's called the Transverse Wave. It was founded years ago by the

Anderson Ames Trust. It's a place to start looking, Emmett, but I want your word that you will be discreet."

"Why the hell do you care if I'm discreet?"

Mercer sighed. "Two years ago Anderson Ames died. When the lawyers finally unraveled the trust, which took several months, it was discovered to be nearly bankrupt. The Transverse Wave Youth Shelter was in danger of closing last year, but at the last minute new funding was found for it. Just in time to enable it to remain open."

"Oh, shit." He had the whole picture now, Emmett realized. "You're going to tell me that the Guild Foundation stepped in and is now supporting the Transverse Wave, aren't you? The reason you want me to be discreet is because the shelter is one of Tamara's new pet charity projects."

Mercer narrowed his eyes. He suddenly looked like the ruthless specter-cat that he was. "Tamara knows nothing of my suspicions. I want this mess cleaned up without any publicity that might embarrass her or the Guild Foundation. Is that understood?"

CHAPTER 15

LYDIA CLUTCHED HER PURSE VERY TIGHTLY ON HER KNEES and smiled blandly through the window at the guard as Emmett drove out through the front gates of the Wyatt mansion.

Silence welled up inside the car. It thickened rapidly.

"If I had to rate the evening on a scale of faculty social events at the university, I would have to say it scored a two," she said finally.

"That high?" Emmett asked.

"Somewhat less tolerable than the monthly sherry hour but not quite as bad as the weekly coffee hour in the Department of Para-archaeology."

"Personally, I'm giving it a one," Emmett said.

She glanced at him. "You mean it was worse than your engagement party where your fiancée decided she was in love with Mercer Wyatt instead of you?"

"So you heard about that, huh?" Emmett downshifted for a curve. "Sounds like you and Tamara got friendly in the salon."

"Actually, the subject of your engagement came up right at the beginning, and conversation sort of fizzled after that. I spent a lot of time admiring the Wyatt collection of Harmonic antiquities. Fortunately, I can talk about relics for hours on end. By the time you came out of the library with Mercer, Tamara was half asleep from boredom."

"Tamara has a short attention span if the subject is not one of great personal interest to her. Take our engagement, for example."

"Something tells me she can be very focused if the subject *is* one of great personal interest to her." Lydia paused. "She wears amber. Is it for real or just for looks?"

"It's for real. She's a strong dissonance-energy para-rez."

"I see." It figured, Lydia thought. Statistically speaking, most ghost-hunters were male, but she had worked with more than one female hunter in the catacombs. "Well, if she was engaged to you, I'd say she must have been extremely interested. Probably liked the thought of becoming the wife of the Resonance Guild boss."

A cold smile came and went at the corners of Emmett's mouth. "You did pick up a lot of trivia over tea."

She whipped around in the seat, anger sweeping away her control. *"Why didn't you tell me?"*

"Couple of reasons." He sounded far too casual. "First, given your general opinion of ghost-hunters, I didn't see any reason to bring up Guild politics. Second, I didn't think it had any direct bearing on the situation."

She stared at him. "I don't believe this. You're an ex-Guild boss and you don't think it has any *bearing* on our business arrangements?"

"Does whatever happened to you during those forty-eight hours you spent underground six months ago have any bearing on them?"

"That's entirely different."

"Each of us has a past. Neither of us can change it. But we've both moved on. I'm no longer in the Guild."

"The heck you aren't. Once a guildman, always a guildman."

"Some people say that once a tangler's been badly fried in a trap, she's never the same again."

"Stop trying to pretend there's a parallel here," she shot back.

"What do you want to do, Lydia? Do you want out of the contract?"

"No, damn it, you're not going to get rid of me that easily."

"Then we have to find a way to work together."

"How can we do that when you keep springing these surprises on me?" she demanded furiously.

"Just because we have a contract doesn't mean we have to tell each other every damn personal thing that ever happened to us, does it?"

"The fact that you're a Guild boss is not exactly a private, personal matter."

"I'm an ex-Guild boss."

"How come I never heard of you?"

"Can you name the heads of the Frequency or Crystal City Guilds?"

"Well . . . no." She frowned. "I admit, I've never paid much attention to Guild politics outside of Cadence. I had heard something to the effect that the Resonance Guild had instituted some changes, but—"

"But you were skeptical, so you didn't take any notice. Is that it?"

"It wasn't that so much as that I didn't think those changes would have any influence on the Cadence Guild. At least not while Mercer Wyatt is in charge."

"If it makes you feel any better, you probably wouldn't have remembered my name, even if you had followed the news." Emmett guided the Slider through an intersection. "I kept a low profile while I held the position."

"I see."

There was another brittle silence. Lydia fumed.

She had a contract with a Guild boss.

Make that *ex*-Guild boss.

A freelance consultant had to be flexible, she thought. She was no longer safely ensconced in academia, with its rigid hierarchy and social rules, both written and unwritten. If she was going to establish herself as a private consultant, she would have to take a few risks.

"Why did you decide to step down?" she asked gruffly.

"I ran the Resonance Guild for six years. It took me that long to get it restructured organizationally. When I was finished, I wanted out of the job. So I turned down the board's offer to renew my contract, and I made sure they appointed Daniel instead."

"Who's Daniel?"

"My younger brother."

"So you handpicked your successor?"

"Daniel and I think alike when it comes to Guild politics. He'll keep the organization moving forward in the new direction. In a few more years no one will even remember the old days. The Resonance Guild will be just one more major corporation in the city."

Lydia hesitated, but morbid curiosity got the better of her. "When did you tell Tamara that you were planning to step down?"

"A few days before our engagement party. Since she did not immediately give me back my ring, I assumed she understood and supported my decision."

"Probably thought she could talk you into changing your mind."

"We had a few conversations on the subject," Emmett admitted. "I didn't change my mind."

He eased the Slider into the parking lot of Lydia's apartment complex. "In the six years I spent reorganizing the Resonance Guild, Tamara was my one major miscalculation."

"No kidding."

He brought the car to a halt and shut off the engine. For a moment he just sat there behind the wheel, saying nothing. Lydia got the feeling that he was thinking. Hard.

"You figure I should have known right from the start that it was the idea of being married to the head of the Guild, not me personally, that she loved?" he asked neutrally.

"Hey, don't feel bad." Lydia gripped the handle and opened the door. "I wasn't any smarter about Ryan. He was only interested in me as long as I was moving up in the para-archaeology department and could write papers that got our names in print."

"You wrote the papers?" Emmett inquired.

"Ryan's a good P-A, but he's not as good as I am," she said evenly. "After my Lost Weekend, it was obvious that I was not going to be real useful to him as a coauthor, at least not for a long time. But it all worked out very nicely. He got promoted, based on our last paper together. Now, as head of the department, he gets his name on every paper that is published by the people under him. They do all the research, he gets the credit. Pretty neat, huh?"

She got out of the car, keeping her arms wrapped tightly around her purse. Emmett climbed out from the driver's seat, closed and locked the door, and came around the vehicle to join her. Together they walked toward the stairwell.

"I could have clued you in on Ryan Kelso if I'd been around when you were dating him," Emmett offered.

"I could have told you that Tamara is a shrewd, ambitious woman who won't let anyone or anything get in her way. She's into power. It attracts her."

Emmett de-rezzed the security door. "You can tell that after spending one evening in her company?"

She cleared her throat and strove for an academic tone. "In parapsychological terms, she no doubt connects sex with power and vice versa."

"In other words, when I resigned as head of the Guild, I no longer looked quite as sexy. Is that it?"

Lydia hugged her purse as they started up the stairwell. "Power is always interesting, but it comes in two different forms, the personal, internal kind and the kind that depends on the trappings."

"The trappings?"

"You know—office, position, social standing. That sort of thing. Some people are only attracted to that type of power. I'd say Tamara is in that crowd."

"You may be right." Emmett climbed the stairs beside her. "I know she sure as hell lost interest in me after she found out that I intended to become a business consultant."

"Live and learn," Lydia said.

"So do we still have a contract?"

"Yes," Lydia said, "we still have a contract."

They reached the fifth floor together in silence and turned to walk along the corridor to her front door.

Lydia looked down at the purse she had clutched to her bosom. "I've got to find a safe place for this until I decide what to do with it."

"Why don't you put it in a real bank safe-deposit vault tomorrow morning?"

"Good idea. But I can't leave it there indefinitely. This is an incredible find, Emmett. It needs to be properly studied."

He gave her a wicked, knowing grin. "Hey, I've got an idea. You can turn that dreamstone jar over to the university and let Ryan Kelso and his staff write it up for the *Journal of Para-Archaeology.*"

"Over my dead body," she muttered. Then she thought about Chester and winced. "Guess that wasn't really a good metaphor under the circumstances."

His grin vanished. "Guess not."

"I can't think clearly about the problem of what to do with the jar tonight. I do believe I've had a little too much high-rez input this evening. My nerves aren't accustomed to so much excitement."

"Excitement?"

"Yeah, you know, excitement. This artifact, dinner with the head of the Cadence Guild, the discovery that my first consulting client is the ex-CEO of the Resonance Guild. It takes its toll, you know."

"I see," he said. "Excitement."

"I live a quiet life, for the most part, these days. Oh, now and again I come across dead bodies. And there are the occasional moments of hilarity when I get the odd ghost burning holes in my bedroom wall. But that's about it."

"Sounds quiet, all right." He inserted the key into the lock.

She gave him a sharp glance. "By the way, I almost forgot to ask—did you learn anything useful about your nephew from Wyatt?"

"Maybe."

"That's all you can say? Maybe?"

"He gave me a possible lead," Emmett said casually as he opened the door. "I'll check it out tomorrow."

Lydia stepped into the foyer. "And just what did Boss Wyatt want in exchange for this so-called lead?"

"Has anyone ever told you that you have an extremely cynical streak in your nature?"

"What I've got is a good working understanding of how Guild politics work."

He looked at her, saying nothing.

"At least I know how they work here in Cadence," she amended. "Mercer Wyatt doesn't do anything for anyone out of the goodness of his heart."

Emmett shrugged. He reached down to pick up Fuzz, who was drifting around at his feet. "We made a deal."

Lydia froze. "What kind of deal?"

"It doesn't concern you," he said quietly. "It's Guild business."

"Damn it, don't you dare pull that 'Guild business' routine with me. I'm your consultant in this thing, remember? I have a right to know what's going on."

"My arrangement with Wyatt falls outside the terms of our contract."

"I'm not buying that. Not for one minute."

"That's your problem." He went into the kitchen and took the lid off the pretzel jar. "Because that's all I'm selling."

She opened her mouth to continue the argument, but the blinking light on the telephone answering machine caught her attention.

She crossed the room and pushed the button.

"This is Bartholomew Greeley of Greeley's Antiques calling about the item we discussed when you visited my shop. I have received word re-

garding its present whereabouts. I am told that the collector who bought it will be willing to sell for the right price. I will be happy to act as a go-between and to accept the finder's fee you mentioned. Please meet me at my shop tomorrow morning. I will open early to conduct the negotiations. Shall we say ten-ish?"

Triumph flashed through Lydia. "Sounds like I've found your cabinet for you, Emmett."

Emmett glanced at the answering machine. Then he gave her a level look. "If that's true, then your job is done, isn't it? That will simplify things. Tomorrow we'll collect the cabinet and I'll give you your check. Our contract will be legally terminated and you'll be out of this."

Her triumph evaporated in a heartbeat. He was right. Once the cabinet of curiosities was back in his hands, their contract would be fulfilled. There was nothing she could do about it.

Why the hell did she want to do anything about it, anyway? He was an ex-Guild boss, for crying out loud. He did social dinners with Mercer Wyatt. Worse yet, he did deals with Mercer Wyatt. His ex-fiancée was married to the boss of the Cadence Guild. Things couldn't get much messier.

Yes, sir, she wanted this contract to end just as quickly as possible. With the fees Emmett would pay her she could move into a new apartment. With his name on her list of satisfied clients, she would be off to a stunning start in her new career as a consultant. Life was looking up.

So why wasn't she thrilled?

She flashed him a brilliant smile. "Looks like I'll be getting my sofa back tomorrow night."

CHAPTER 16

THE SOUND OF THE BEDROOM DOOR BEING STEALTHILY opened brought him out of his brooding thoughts. His first reaction was a small rush of relief. He had been sinking deeper and deeper into the morass of possibilities, angles, problems, and risks since he had stretched out on the sofa and turned off the light.

His contemplation of how to juggle the search for Quinn with his bargain with Wyatt had been continually interrupted by the memory of Lydia's flashing smile when she agreed that their contract would be terminated tomorrow. *Looks like I'll be getting my sofa back . . .*

She didn't have to be quite so thrilled at the prospect of getting him off her sofa. Hell, she was welcome to it. The damn thing sagged in all the wrong places. It was lumpy and it was too short.

He caught the faint thump of a bare toe striking a wooden table leg in the hall. The small sound was followed by a stifled groan and a muffled curse. He moved one arm from behind his head and glanced at the fluorez-lit face of his watch. Two in the morning. Apparently Lydia had not had any more luck getting to sleep than he had.

All the plans and contingency schemes he had been crafting receded in the face of the more immediate question that had just arisen. Why was Lydia coming down the hall?

He was keenly aware that the question was not the only thing that had arisen. The knowledge that she was up and moving toward him had been enough to give him an erection.

He wondered if she was still angry. Then he wondered if it had occurred to her, as it had to him, that they had no logical reason to see each other again after they retrieved the cabinet tomorrow. Did she even give a damn? She had looked extremely pleased by Bartholomew Greeley's call. Just delighted at the news that their contract was about to end.

He lay unmoving, conscious that his blood was heating up with what had to be really stupid anticipation. What the hell did he think was going to happen now? Was he really dumb enough to believe that she might be coming out here to join him on the sofa?

More likely she was headed for the kitchen. Only logical destination under the circumstances. She couldn't sleep, so she was going to get herself a nice glass of warm milk. Or something.

He saw the pale outline of her white robe as she tiptoed around the corner, the shadowy blob that was Fuzz perched on her shoulder.

He held his breath and willed Lydia to come toward the sofa.

She headed for the kitchen.

He exhaled deeply and watched her disappear through the doorway. A few seconds later he heard the refrigerator door open. Light glowed briefly from the opening to the kitchen and then disappeared again. There was a soft clink. Lydia had removed a glass from the cupboard. Then he heard the lid of the pretzel jar.

Well, hell. Did she really expect him to sleep through all that racket?

He eased the covers aside and got to his feet. Halfway to the kitchen he remembered that he was wearing only his briefs. He glanced down and noticed that they did not provide much in the way of camouflage for his aroused body. Suppressing a groan, he reached into his open carryall and snagged his jeans. He yanked them on quickly.

"Didn't mean to wake you," Lydia said from the kitchen doorway.

He kept his back to her as he struggled carefully with the zipper. "I wasn't asleep."

At last he managed to get the pants fastened and turned to face her. She looked so good that it was all he could do not to take a bite.

She had a glass in one hand, a couple of pretzels in the other. She fed one of the pretzels to Fuzz.

"Mind if I have one?" Emmett asked, disgusted by his inability to come up with a more stimulating conversational gambit.

"Help yourself."

His arm brushed against the sleeve of her robe as he went into the kitchen. It was as though he'd touched a live wire and sent a jolt of raw energy straight to his already over-rezzed body.

He yanked the lid off the pretzel jar and started to reach inside.

"I don't think you want one of those," Lydia said. "Fuzz has probably drooled on them. Get one out of the bag in the oven. That's where I keep mine. Fuzz isn't strong enough to open the door."

Emmett replaced the lid and jerked the oven open. He gazed at the bag of pretzels inside. "Ever accidentally turn this thing on while the bag was in here?"

"Once," she admitted. "I keep a fire extinguisher under the sink now."

He helped himself to a handful and closed the oven door.

He could tell that she was still pissed. All because he hadn't told her the details of his deal with Mercer Wyatt.

What did he have to lose? he wondered. She probably couldn't get much more ticked off. It was Guild business, but maybe she had a right to know some of it.

"Okay, I'll tell you about my deal with Wyatt," he said around a mouthful of pretzel.

She lifted her chin. "Don't bother. You made it perfectly clear that you don't consider it any of my affair."

"It isn't. But the cold-shoulder treatment is working."

"I'm amazed. A Guild boss who's susceptible to the cold shoulder?"

"Ex-Guild boss." He crunched another pretzel. "In a nutshell, Mercer found out that Quinn disappeared shortly after visiting a youth shelter in the Old Quarter. A place called the Transverse Wave."

She looked thoughtful. "I know it. It's been around for several years. They offer social services to street kids."

"Wyatt thinks there's some connection. A couple of other young, untrained dissonance-energy para-rezes have disappeared too. They'd also had some contact with the shelter. He wants me to find out what's going on. But he wants it done discreetly."

She tipped her head to one side. "Why discreetly?"

"Because, as of a few months ago, the Cadence Guild Foundation began funding the shelter."

"Ah."

"Right. Ah." He shoved another pretzel into his mouth.

"Could be real embarrassing for the Guild if it turns out something illegal is going on at the shelter."

"In particular, it could be very awkward for Tamara." Emmett hesitated. "Mercer's in love with her. He wants to protect her."

"Hard to picture Mercer Wyatt in love with anyone except the power he exercises as a Guild boss."

"People change."

"Some do. Some don't."

"Little cynic. There's more. Wyatt thinks he's got a traitor on his administrative staff. He believes that person is responsible for whatever is going on at the shelter."

"Uh-oh. I think I know where this is going."

"In exchange for the lead on Quinn, I agreed to try to uncover the traitor on Wyatt's staff."

She blew out a deep breath. "I see. So now you're a spy for the Cadence Guild boss."

He said nothing, just munched.

"Okay, okay, I don't blame you," Lydia said.

That surprised him. "You don't?"

"No. In your shoes, I'd have made the same bargain. After all, your primary responsibility is to find your nephew. And it does sound as though Wyatt may have given you a solid lead. No one gets anything for nothing in this life. And that goes double where the Guild is concerned."

"That's kind of how I viewed it." He swallowed the last of his pretzel. "Sorry I got edgy earlier."

"You're probably not accustomed to having to explain yourself."

He looked at her. "It wasn't that. I didn't want to go into the details because I know how you feel about Wyatt and the local Guild."

"I admit I wouldn't trust Mercer Wyatt any farther than I could throw him. But—"

"But what?"

She smiled wryly. "But you're not Mercer Wyatt."

Something eased deep inside him. "Does that mean you do trust me?"

She lifted one shoulder in a small shrug. "A lot further than I would Wyatt."

Okay, so she wasn't declaring her undying faith in him. At least he wasn't in the same category as Wyatt.

"Tomorrow, after we pick up the cabinet, I'll check out the youth center," he said.

"Sounds like a plan. I wish you luck, Emmett. I hope your nephew is okay."

He waited a beat or two. "Something I think you should know before we terminate our contract."

"What's that?"

"I want to correct a slight misconception you have about ghost-hunters."

She watched him from the shadows. "If this is another lecture on Guild politics—"

"It's got nothing to do with politics."

"No?"

He leaned back against the refrigerator and folded his arms. "It's about that little eccentricity problem you mentioned last night. I don't know where you got your information, but you've been misinformed."

"Melanie." She cleared her throat. "Melanie Toft mentioned the eccentricity thing. She seemed very sure of her facts."

"Summoning a ghost or neutralizing one does generate a buzz," he said very deliberately. "But the point I want to make here is that the effect is short-lived."

"How short?"

"Half hour, max."

She considered that. "Come to think of it, I don't believe Melanie mentioned the time factor."

"Yeah, well, I just wanted to make it clear that the effect wouldn't last anywhere near long enough to account for what happened between us last night."

"I see," she whispered.

He unfolded his arms and took one step toward her. Given the small confines of the kitchen, that was enough to put him directly in front of her. The warm scent of her sent a thrill of hunger through him. He knew she sensed it, but she made no move to dodge him. Fuzz eyed Emmett for a few seconds and then tumbled off Lydia's shoulder and disappeared in the direction of the pretzel jar.

"And it sure as hell wouldn't account for this." Emmett pulled her into his arms and covered her mouth with his own.

For a couple of what he decided were some of the worst seconds of his life he thought she was going to push him away.

Then he felt her soften against him, and suddenly everything was all right. Better than all right. Very, very good.

Her arms went around his neck, her fingers slid into his hair. Her lips parted. He could taste her now. Need roared through him. A euphoric excitement followed. He was pretty sure that he could summon a dozen, hell, a *hundred* ghosts right now—but he was otherwise occupied.

Long periods of abstinence were probably not good for a man his age, he thought. A man his age was not supposed to be engaging in occasional flings. A man his age was supposed to be married. A man his age was supposed to have a wife in his bed. He was supposed to be getting sex so regularly that it became routine, maybe even a little dull, like eating breakfast.

Breakfast had never tasted so good.

Lydia was warm and she smelled of night things, female things. Things that were unique and astonishing and mysterious, things that he had never inhaled before in his entire life and that he was pretty sure he would never forget.

He moved his hand down over the full curve of her hip and closed his fingers around her thigh. She stirred against him. Her toe touched his foot. He eased her back against the counter, kissed her throat.

He reached between their bodies, found the sash of her robe, and untied it. She cupped his face in her hands.

"No, Emmett."

He stilled. Then he raised his head to look down at her. "No?"

She smiled wistfully. "I really don't think this is a good idea. Technically speaking, we're still involved in a business contract."

"That ends tomorrow morning."

"I know. But until then we're business associates."

Anger and frustration uncoiled deep within him. "What the hell is this? You want me. I want you. Where's the problem?"

"The problem," she said steadily, "is that we don't know each other very well. The problem is that you're a client. The problem is that I don't want a one-night stand."

"Why don't you be honest about it? The real problem is that I'm ex-Guild, isn't it?"

"No."

"The hell it isn't." He released her abruptly, pushed himself away from the counter. "You're so damned biased against anyone connected to the Guild that you can't even let yourself have a normal physical relationship with a hunter."

"Don't you dare blame this on me." She retied the sash of her robe with short, violent motions. "Just because I'm not into flings with men I hardly know doesn't mean I'm not normal, damn it."

"Shit." He shoved his fingers through his hair. "I didn't mean to imply you weren't normal."

"Yes, you did. That is exactly what you said. Bad enough that my former colleagues think I've lost my para-harmonic pitch. I don't need to be told that I'm not *normal* in other ways as well. If you'll excuse me, I've had enough. I'm going back to bed."

He watched helplessly as she whirled and stomped out of the kitchen. Then he looked down at Fuzz, who was gazing at him from the countertop.

"Ever had the feeling that you just screwed up bigtime?" Emmett asked.

CHAPTER 17

LYDIA AWOKE TO THE RINGING OF THE BEDSIDE PHONE. Her hand smacked the table, groped briefly, found the instrument.

She managed to get the receiver to her ear in time to hear Emmett answer on the living room extension.

"London," he growled.

Horrified, Lydia sat straight up in bed. "Hello? Hello?"

"Excuse me," Ryan Kelso said brusquely. "I believe I have the wrong number."

"Ryan?" Lydia said quickly. "Wait."

"Is that you, Lydia?" He sounded confused now.

"It's me. Emmett, I've got it. You can hang up now."

"Sorry," Emmett said easily. "I'll get breakfast started while you two talk. Take your time. I haven't even had my shower yet."

There was a click as he hung up the phone. A short, stark silence ensued during which Lydia knew that Ryan was absorbing the implications of Emmett's having answered the phone in her apartment at this hour of the morning. With a supreme effort of will she resisted the urge to storm into the other room and scream at Emmett.

She composed herself and swiftly considered the possibilities. Maybe Ryan was calling to tell her that the department had decided to give her back her job. Maybe he was calling with the offer of a private consulting contract with the university. Maybe her new career was finally about to take off.

"Sorry," she said crisply. "Someone else picked up the phone by mistake."

"The man who answered, he was the one who was with you the other night at the Counterpoint, wasn't he?"

There was a note of disapproval in Ryan's voice now. It irritated Lydia. As if he had a right to comment on the situation.

"Mr. London is my guest."

A shadow loomed. She looked across the room and saw Mr. London filling her doorway. He was wearing only the jeans he'd had on last night. She waved him off. He did not budge.

"What was it you wanted, Ryan?" she asked.

He cleared his throat. When he spoke this time, his tone was a bit too affable. "As a matter of fact, I was calling to suggest that we get together for lunch."

"Lunch?"

"Seeing you the other night made me realize how long it's been since we had a chance to sit down and talk," he said quickly. "Got a lot of news to catch up on."

"I see." She couldn't decide if he was hinting at a business discussion or just being friendly. "When did you want to do this lunch?"

"How about today?" Ryan said.

Lydia thought about the dreamstone jar that she had to get safely stored in a bank vault this morning and the cabinet of curiosities that she and Emmett were going to retrieve from Bartholomew Greeley. And then there was her job at the museum. She would be going in late today. She probably ought to work through lunch.

"I'm pretty tightly scheduled today, Ryan. How about tomorrow?"

"Damn it, Lydia, I've got to talk to you." He sounded both annoyed and urgent. "Today. As soon as possible. I could come to your apartment."

Ryan was definitely anxious about something. She tried to ignore Emmett, who had propped one shoulder against the doorjamb and was watching her with deep interest.

"What's this all about, Ryan?" she asked.

"It involves a professional matter," he said stiffly.

She tried to conceal her eagerness. "Are you saying you want me to consult for the department?"

There was a slight but meaningful pause. "Not exactly."

Her enthusiasm waned abruptly. "Ryan, I've got a busy day ahead. I don't have time for games."

"Wait, don't hang up, Lydia. This is important. Maybe the most important thing that's ever come along. I don't want to discuss it on the phone. But trust me, we're talking about a major Harmonic find."

Lydia tightened her grip on the phone. "What kind of find?"

"We can't talk about it now. I've got to see you." Ryan hesitated. "There's a rumor. I can't say any more about it, but I can tell you this much. If it's for real, it could remake your career for you."

Lydia felt her confidence return in a rush. Ryan needed her. That meant she was in control here. She had to play her cards carefully.

"Tell you what, Ryan, I'll give you a call later in the day when I've got my schedule nailed down for the week."

"Lydia, wait, don't hang up. Damn it, *don't hang up*. Both of our futures are riding on this."

"I'll call you later, Ryan." Very gently she replaced the phone. She looked at Emmett.

"What?" he said.

"I have a nasty feeling that Ryan may have heard some rumors about my bequest from Chester."

"You think he knows you've got the jar?"

"No, but I got the impression that he thinks I may know something about it."

"That's bad enough." He came away from the door, walked to the bed, and tossed her robe to her. "Rise and shine, my little sex goddess. We're going to be standing at the door of the bank when it opens. I want that jar in a safe-deposit box before we do anything else."

Lydia clutched the robe and met his gaze. " 'Sex goddess'?"

"You prefer the term 'sex kitten'?"

"No, that's okay. 'Sex goddess' will do."

THE CADENCE CITY BANK OPENED PROMPTLY AT NINE. By nine-twenty Lydia had filled out all the paperwork required for a safe-deposit box. The clerk showed her and Emmett into the hushed solitude of the vault room and left them alone.

Lydia removed the dreamstone jar from the paper sack for one last look before she sealed it safely away in the safe-deposit box.

"I still can't quite believe this is real." She studied the small streams of ever-changing colors that encircled the jar like tiny alien seas. "Solid as a rock and yet it's pure dreamstone. How is it possible?

By rights it should have melted and splintered into a gazillion different molecules."

"I don't know if it's all that unexpected," Emmett said.

"Unexpected? The ability to work dreamstone is unheard of."

"Think about it." Emmett studied the jar in her hands. "We humans have only been here a couple of hundred years, but we've already developed ways of resonating psychically with rez-amber. We use the stuff every day to do everything from turning on the rez-screen to cooking dinner and hunting ghosts. The Harmonics probably evolved on this planet."

"We don't know that for certain," Lydia said quickly. "They may have come through the Curtain thousands of years ago, the same way we did two centuries ago. The experts say there's no telling how many times the Curtain has opened and closed in the past or which planets it linked when it was open."

Emmett shrugged. "Whatever. Any way you look at it, the Harmonics could have been here for thousands of years, right?"

"Right."

"Plenty of time to get psychically tuned to the basic harmonic frequencies of the planet. Who knows what they could do with rez-amber? Hell, we still can't even figure out how they created ghosts or the illusion traps. Some of us can manipulate them, but no one has come up with a way to create a ghost or a trap from scratch."

"True."

Lydia looked at the jar she held. She could feel the weight of the centuries and the echoes of a creativity that was not quite human but that nevertheless resonated on a very human frequency. "Maybe they discovered or invented something even better than rez-amber to help them focus their psi talents."

"Wouldn't be surprised. Given a couple of thousand more years

here, we'll probably come up with something more efficient, too."
Emmett glanced at his watch. "It's almost nine-thirty. Greeley will
be waiting for us."

"Yes." She could come back here later to look at her fabulous jar,
Lydia reminded herself. She started to rewrap it in the paper sack.
Midway through the process she paused.

"What's wrong?" Emmett asked.

"I'm not sure." She removed the jar from the sack again and hefted
it in her bare hands. She sent out a gentle psychic probe. Her amber
bracelet grew warm against her skin. Cautiously, she felt for the
harmonic pulse of the energy that emanated from the jar.

The amber grew warmer. A small chill went through her. "Oh,
jeez."

Emmett moved closer, intent on her face. "What are you picking
up? The age of the thing?"

"No. Something else. Remember, last night I told you it felt
strange? Almost like a bit of illusion trap energy. I thought it was
just something unique to dreamstone. But now I'm not so sure."

He glanced at the jar, and then his eyes lifted swiftly to meet hers.
She saw that he understood the implications of what she had just
said.

"Not ghost energy," he said with absolute certainty. "I'd sense it
more clearly than you would."

"No," she whispered. "Illusion energy."

"Illusion traps are very rare outside the catacombs."

She nodded mutely. He was right. Even so, she could not help
looking around the vault room. She studied every corner intently,
amplifying and focusing her para-resonating senses through the amber bracelet. She saw no pools of darkness in the corners. There
were no inexplicable shadows under the table or near the ceiling.

Of course there weren't any illusion snares in here, she thought. They were standing in the middle of the Cadence City Bank, for crying out loud.

But the amber in her bracelet was very warm against her skin. Traces of energy shimmered in the room.

She looked down at the jar. Then she looked at Emmett.

"Something to do with worked dreamstone, maybe?" Emmett asked. "Some property that we don't know about because no human has been able to manipulate the stuff?"

She held the artifact up to the light. "There's a lid, I think. It really should be removed in a lab. I don't want to risk damaging the jar."

"It's lasted this long," Emmett reminded her. "It can't be too fragile."

"I'll give it a try."

She set the jar on the table and very gingerly pried at the tightly closed lid. To her surprise it came off easily. She found herself looking down into the dark—very dark—interior of the little artifact.

"Hmm."

She picked up the jar and angled it so that light from the overhead fixture shafted into the interior. It could not penetrate the darkness. There was no gleam or sparkle from the dreamstone inside the jar. Just thick, impenetrable, black mist.

There were two possibilities, she thought. She was either losing it, para-rez-wise, just as Ryan and the others suspected, or she was holding a jar filled with an illusion trap.

"Uh-oh," she said.

"The real thing?" Emmett asked quietly.

"Yeah. Not much of it. Just enough to fit inside this jar."

He hadn't questioned her judgment, she thought. He'd accepted her verdict even though he had every right to doubt it.

He watched as she very carefully set the jar back down on the table. "What do you think?"

"I don't know. Like everyone else, I've never seen much of this stuff outside the Dead City. The very fact that it exists inside this jar may mean that this trap is different from the others I've worked with. It must be anchored somehow to the dreamstone. Only one way to find out."

He looked at her over the top of the jar. "Go for it."

"Might be better if you stepped into the other room. Just in case."

"Not a chance. I'm staying right here."

"Suit yourself."

She took another breath and concentrated on sending psi energy through the amber on her wrist. The stones warmed quickly again. The unmistakable pulse of resonating energy vibrated through her. Weak, but steady and clear.

"It's such a small trap," she whispered. "It's only giving off a trickle of energy."

"Even a trickle can cause some very unpleasant effects," Emmett warned.

She said nothing. They had both worked in the catacombs. They knew what the ancient Harmonic snares could do. Alien dreams. Alien nightmares.

She channeled psi energy steadily through the amber while she gazed down into the palpable night inside the jar. After a few seconds she saw something stir in the depths. The dark itself appeared to be condensing and coalescing. It was reacting to the pulses of energy she was forcing through it. If she screwed up at this stage, she could all too easily spring the trap.

If she triggered the illusion trap, she would have only about one second to realize she was in trouble. There would be no time to do anything about it. The darkness would snap back along the psi-frequencies that she herself had provided it. The stuff would swamp her mind before she could react.

If it was sufficiently powerful, the snare would not only plunge her into a disorienting illusion that her human mind could not accept for long but it would use her own psi energy to trap anyone else who had the misfortune to be standing nearby. Emmett, for example.

How long the nightmare would last or what form it would take was anyone's guess. Given the size of the trap, one could only hope that the dream it produced would be correspondingly limited and short-lived.

But she knew that even if it lasted for only a few minutes, it would take days to recover.

Using her para-rez senses, she edged deeper into the little patch of darkness. She sifted through the cloaking ephemeral energy until she caught the telltale echo of resonance. She fine-tuned her probe, found the hidden design inside the masking pattern, and fed energy into it, dampening the wave motion.

Slowly, carefully, she began to adjust the resonance frequency of the trap. It grew weaker, flattened.

The darkness inside the jar winked out abruptly.

Lydia released the breath she had not realized she was holding. She looked up and saw Emmett grinning at her.

"Nice work," he said.

It was then that the elation ripped through her. This was the first time she'd had a chance to work illusion trap energy since the Lost Weekend. The first time she'd been able to prove to herself that she still had her harmonic pitch. She hadn't lost her edge.

She tried to stay cool, tried not to let her bubbling excitement show. "It's been a while," she said offhandedly. "I was afraid I might be a little rusty."

"Rusty, hell. Screw the whole damn University of Cadence Department of Para-archaeology and the ghost they rode in on. You haven't lost your touch."

She gave up trying to squelch the delight and relief that were surging within her. With a small shriek, she flung herself into Emmett's arms. They closed swiftly around her.

"I'm okay," she whispered into the fabric of his jacket. "I really am okay. I can still handle the stuff." She was laughing now.

He hoisted her off her feet and laughed with her. "You can say that again." He slid her back down the length of his body and kissed her hard.

For a moment she clung to him, savoring the triumphant, congratulatory embrace. She knew then that there was no one, no one else at all, with whom she would rather have celebrated that moment.

When the initial blast of euphoria finally began to subside, she became conscious of the fact that she was kissing Emmett in the middle of a bank vault. Reality returned with a jolt. Slowly, reluctantly, she stepped back, flushed and breathless. She was supposed to be a professional, she thought. Professionals didn't behave this way.

Emmett seemed unaware of her chagrin. He glanced at the jar on the table. "Anything else inside besides the de-rezzed trap?"

Lydia hurried back to the table. She picked up the jar and angled it once more toward the light. "I don't see anything. No, wait—there is something. It looks like a piece of paper."

"Paper?"

"Yes." She lowered the jar and tipped it upside down.

They both stared at the slip of paper that fell into her palm. It was ordinary, everyday paper. It certainly was not thousand-year-old paper. No one had ever found anything that resembled paper in the ruins.

"Chester," Lydia whispered. "He could have de-rezzed the trap, stuck the paper inside the jar, and then reset the snare."

She put down the jar and carefully unfolded the paper. A familiar scrawl sloped across the page. There were three lines of jumbled letters and numbers. They were followed by a short message:

Dear Lydia:

Hell of a retirement plan, isn't it? Just wish I was there with you to enjoy it. I promised you that one day I'd surprise all those bastards up at the university. The really big news is that I think there's more where this came from. The bad news is that some other ruin rats are already excavating the site illegally. But it's going to take them weeks, if not months, to get all the dreamstone out. From what I could tell, every damn corridor in that catacomb branch is crawling with illusion traps and ghosts. I've never seen anything in the underground city that was this well guarded. Whatever you do, don't go in alone. You'll need a ghost-hunter to help you, and even then it will be dangerous. Whoever you choose, make sure you can trust him or her with your life. There's enough dreamstone involved to make your best friend contemplate murder.

The coordinates above are in code. Sorry. Had to do it this way. I can't be sure that someone else besides you won't find this jar first or that whoever it is won't get past the little trap inside. Nasty little bugger, wasn't it? It's anchored to the dreamstone. Amazing.

You'll need a key to the code. I didn't want to leave it in here

with the coordinates for obvious reasons. But don't worry, I'll make
sure you get it.

Be careful when you go after the rest of the dreamstone. The
other ruin rats at the site are real SOBs. I don't think they'd hes-
itate to cut your throat if they caught you.

Love,
Chester

"My God!" Lydia whispered. "There's a whole site full of this stuff."

Emmett studied the three lines of letters and numbers Chester
had written. "He says he'll make sure you get the key to those coordinates."

Lydia's jaw dropped for a few seconds as lightning struck. "Emmett, maybe that's what Chester was doing in the museum the night
he was killed. Maybe he came there to leave the key in my office.
The killer must have followed him, murdered him, and taken the
key."

"Okay, I'll buy that. But getting the key didn't do the bastard any
good, because the coordinates were hidden inside the jar." Emmett
glanced at his watch. "Let's go. We've got an appointment with Greeley."

CHAPTER 18

THE MORNING FOG OFF THE RIVER HAD THICKENED SINCE she and Emmett set out for the bank an hour ago. It was so dense now that Lydia could not see to the end of the block. The shops along Ruin Row were still dark. By mutual agreement and long-standing tradition, they did not open until eleven. Behind the low buildings the massive green walls of the Dead City loomed in the mist.

She rubbed her arms briskly against the chill as she got out of the Slider. She noticed that Emmett had put on his black leather jacket. She reached back into the vehicle for her coat before she joined him on the sidewalk. Together they walked toward the front door of Greeley's Antiques.

Emmett glanced at the amber face of his watch. "Not quite ten."

"Ruin Row doesn't really get humming until noon. But I'm sure Greeley will be in his shop."

They walked to the front door. The shop was unlit inside. Lydia tried the door. It was locked.

"I was certain he'd be here early." She cupped her hands on the glass and peered into the dingy interior. "I'll bet he's in his back room. Try knocking."

Emmett made an easy fist and rapped loudly. Lydia watched closely, but no one emerged from the gloom behind the front counter. She stepped back from the window.

"He's getting a little hard of hearing," she said. "Let's try the rear door."

She led the way to the corner and turned down the narrow service alley that ran behind the shops. Here the fog seemed even heavier, and the close confines heightened the gloom. The fleeting traces of stray energy leaking from the Old Wall made her feel edgy. Emmett followed close behind.

A frisson of awareness wafted through her. Para-rez energy. Her own amber was still at skin temperature.

"Emmett? Is that you?"

"Sorry," he said absently. "Just checking."

She glared at him over her shoulder. "Checking for what?"

"Dissonance energy. Thought I caught a trace."

"Hold it right there." She stopped, spun around, and shoved her hands into the pockets of her jacket. "Are you telling me that there's a ghost-hunter working somewhere near here?"

"Not at the moment. If there was one here, he's either gone or he's stopped working."

She contemplated the fog-filled alley uneasily. "A lot of kids hang out in this part of town. They like to play with the energy that leaks through the Dead City walls. Young dissonance para-rezes like Zane come here to practice summoning flickers."

Emmett nodded. "It's the same way near the walls of Old Resonance. Maybe I picked up the traces of some would-be junior hunter."

He did not sound convinced, Lydia thought. But who was she to argue?

She turned around, pulled up the collar of her coat, and started walking again. When she reached the rear entrance of Greeley's Antiques, she came to a halt and knocked forcefully on the door.

No answer.

"Damn," she said. "He said he'd be here around ten. Looks like we'll have to wait in the car. I don't think he'll be very late. Greeley's got a short list of priorities. Money is right at the top."

Emmett studied the closed door for a few seconds, saying nothing. Then he pulled a pair of gloves out of the pockets of his jacket.

Lydia suddenly felt very cold. She cleared her throat. "Speaking as your consultant, I really can't recommend breaking into Greeley's Antiques. No point in it. Bartholomew wouldn't have left anything as valuable as your cabinet in his back room overnight. Trust me on this, Emmett."

"I believe you." He reached for the doorknob with his gloved hand. "About the cabinet. But I'm still getting traces of rez energy. Don't you feel it?"

She frowned. "No. I felt your energy when you used it a minute ago, but I'm not picking up anything now."

"Probably because you're a tangler. These are hunter vibes."

She hunched deeper into her coat. Most people could pick up faint traces of psi energy when someone in the vicinity was actively working with amber. But the average individual was far more sensitive to others who had similar paranormal talents. Ghost-hunters could more easily detect the energy trail left by another hunter.

Ephemeral-energy para-rezes such as herself were more likely to be aware of another tangler working nearby.

But even the most powerful para-energy trace dissipated quickly after the user had stopped resonating through amber. If Emmett was picking up a hint of dissonance energy, it meant that the hunter had worked somewhere close by and sometime in the past few minutes.

Lydia watched Emmett twist the doorknob. It turned easily in his fingers. Too easily.

"I don't think the fact that the back door is unlocked is a good sign, Emmett."

"Funny you should say that. I was coming to the same conclusion." He pushed the door open wide and gazed into the back room of Greeley's Antiques.

Lydia stood on tiptoe so that she could see over his shoulder. At first she could make out nothing except the shadowy shapes of cartons and some green quartz vases.

Then she saw the body sprawled on the floor.

"Oh, my God, Emmett!"

Bartholomew Greeley lay facedown in a pool of rapidly drying blood. His throat had been slit.

"Oh, God!" Lydia exclaimed again. It was hard to catch her breath. Her fingers shook so hard she had to cram them back into her pockets. "Just like Chester."

"There is a pattern here, isn't there?" Emmett contemplated the scene. His intent, focused awareness was clear.

"What is it?" Lydia demanded. "What are you picking up?"

"A hunter worked amber in this room. Not long ago. Probably summoned a ghost to stun Greeley before he cut his throat. Whoever he was, he must have been in a hurry."

"Why do you say that?"

"He singed something. Can't you smell it?"

Lydia inhaled cautiously, caught a whiff of charred packing-crate filler. "Yes."

Emmett glanced at her. "You okay?"

"Yes." That was a flat-out lie, she thought. Her stomach was roiling. The sheer cold-blooded brutality of the scene was making her nauseous.

"Don't get sick here," Emmett warned.

"I'm not going to throw up."

He gave her a doubtful look. Then he stepped into the death room, blocking her view.

"Wait! What are you doing?" She glanced urgently back down the alley. "This is a crime scene."

"I know. I just want to take a quick look around before we leave."

An ominous feeling settled on her. "Leave?"

"Yeah." He edged cautiously through the gloom, avoiding the blood.

"What about the police? You're the one who insisted we call them when we found Chester, remember?"

"There wasn't any choice then. This time around, though, we've got an option. We'll call from a pay phone after we're out of the area."

She realized where he was going with this. The unpleasant sensation in her stomach worsened.

"Anonymously, I take it?" she said dryly.

Emmett leaned down to examine the floor near the body. She thought she saw him pick something up, but she could not see what it was.

"Under the circumstances," he said, getting to his feet. "I think anonymity is our best bet. Detective Martinez hasn't had any breaks in the Brady case. I got the feeling that she's hungry for one. If she finds out that you've turned up yet again as the first person on the scene of a second murder—" He let the sentence trail off meaningfully.

"She's going to move me up into first place on her list of suspects, isn't she?"

"Probably."

Lydia thought about that. "I'm not the only person who's turned up twice at a recent murder scene."

"You don't need to remind me." He straightened and moved toward a desk littered with papers. "I skated the first time, but something tells me Martinez won't let me off the hook so easily again."

"Especially since you've been keeping company with me," Lydia said glumly.

"Uh-huh." He riffled through the papers gingerly with his gloved fingers.

"There's no hard evidence to tie either of us to the murders. Surely Martinez will acknowledge that. She's got nothing solid to use against either of us."

Emmett left the desk and walked to the door. Without a word he opened his hand as he came back through the opening.

Lydia stared at the rez-amber bracelet in his palm. Six good-quality stones, each with her initials inscribed on it, set in inexpensive imitation gold. Another wave of sick dread rose up inside her.

"That's one of my bracelets," she whispered.

"I was afraid of that." He dropped the amber into her hand and then took her arm, leading her quickly away from Greeley's back door. "What do you want to bet the ghost-hunter who tossed your apartment took it?"

"And planted it at the scene of this murder?"

"I doubt if it was the same guy. He was just a kid."

"Kids can kill."

"But usually not as efficiently as that." Emmett glanced back over his shoulder. "The kid in your apartment was probably working for someone else."

"Someone tried to tie me to Greeley's murder." She was shivering so hard now that she almost dropped the bracelet. "I can't believe it. Why would anyone do that?"

"Probably to make sure you'd be very busy for the next few days. Too busy to pay attention to little things like a priceless dreamstone jar or my cabinet of curiosities."

She tried to think logically. It wasn't easy. "There's another reason why he might have left my bracelet near Greeley's body. If Martinez gets called in on this murder, she's going to find that charred paper on the desk. She'll suspect a ghost-hunter was involved."

"Yes."

"And she knows that you and I have been working together lately."

"Yes."

She glanced at him. "Tying me to the murder scene is a good way of implicating you too."

"The thought did cross my mind."

"Oh, damn."

"My sentiments exactly," Emmett said.

TEN MINUTES LATER LYDIA SAT TENSELY IN THE PASSENger seat of the Slider and watched Emmett hang up the pay phone. He left the booth and walked back to the car, his face hard.

He glanced at her as he got in behind the wheel and rezzed the ignition. "You sure you're not going to throw up?"

"Pretty sure. What did you tell the cops?"

"I reported an unlocked back door at Greeley's Antiques. Anonymously." He eased the Slider away from the curb. "Suggested it looked like a burglary-in-progress. They'll send a car to take a look."

She forced herself to think. "Maybe that's what it was, Emmett. Maybe Greeley surprised the killer when he opened early to get ready for us. If I hadn't agreed to meet with him this morning—"

"Stop right here. You had nothing to do with this. It was Greeley's idea to do the deal for the cabinet before he opened the shop, remember?"

"Well, yes, but—"

"But nothing. He set up the schedule." Emmett slowed for a corner. "And he may have invited the killer inside."

"What are you talking about?" she said in disbelief.

"Let's go someplace where we can get coffee. I need to think."

CHAPTER 19

THE AMBER SKY CAFÉ WAS ONE OF THOSE COMFORTABLE places where you could sit in a booth and huddle over a cup of rez-tea and a jelly doughnut for at least an hour before the waitress started to glare. Emmett did a quick survey and spotted a quiet booth at the back.

He studied Lydia's face as she ordered tea. She seemed to be holding up well, but he was worried about her. The strain showed on her face. She was amazingly resilient, but the shocks were coming fast and hard. A lot of people he knew would be in screaming hysterics by now. He wondered how much she could take. Everyone had a breaking point, even intrepid para-archaeologists who could de-rez Harmonic illusion traps while standing in the middle of a downtown bank.

To make matters worse, he didn't think she trusted him completely. She probably couldn't bring herself to trust anyone with Guild connections.

They sat in silence until their refreshments arrived. Lydia picked up the steaming cup of tea. She ignored the doughnuts.

"Tell me why you think Greeley may have known the killer," she said steadily.

He thought back to the grisly scene at Greeley's Antiques.

"It looked like the killer went through Greeley's desk in a hurry," he said. "The papers were scattered and mixed up on top. Two of the drawers were half open."

"What do you think he was looking for?"

"No way to be certain, but several sheets had been torn from the desk calendar. Yesterday's and today's pages were missing. So were two or three on either side."

"You think the killer was concerned that whatever was written on one of the pages had left an imprint on the next one?"

"It's a possibility." Emmett paused. "I wonder if Greeley tried to set up an auction in order to drive up the price of my cabinet?"

"Wouldn't put it past him." She drummed her fingers on the table. "If he did, it's entirely possible that he made a note about the auction on his desk calendar. He was very methodical. He could have written the killer's name and phone number on today's date."

"As well as our names and your phone number."

She shuddered visibly. "Whoever killed him knew that we were due to arrive at ten. He must have contacted Greeley yesterday. Arranged the whole thing. Oh, God, Emmett, that means—"

"It was a setup."

Lydia pondered for a while. "I can see someone murdering poor Chester for the key to the dreamstone coordinates. I can even envision someone killing Greeley for the cabinet. It's not exactly price-less, but it is extremely valuable. But what's the link between the two?"

"You," Emmett said. "And me. And the dreamstone."

"And a supposed traitor inside the Cadence Guild," she added.

"What do you mean, 'supposed'?" he asked.

"It's possible we've been suckered into some illegal antiquities op-eration run by Mercer Wyatt," she said coolly.

Emmett felt his jaw tighten. Her dislike and distrust of all things related to the Guild was not news. He would not let himself get drawn into an argument on the subject of hunter ethics.

"If the Guild was involved in this," he said in his most reasonable tone, "Mercer Wyatt would not have invited me to dinner. He would not have told me that Quinn had been seen at the Transverse Wave. He would not have made a deal with me."

"You can't be sure of that. Who knows what Wyatt's real agenda is? He told you he wanted you to help him squash some rival who's supposedly training young ghost-hunters without Guild approval. But what if he lied to you? What if he's trying to set you up for murder?"

"Believe me, the last thing Wyatt wants to do is get me arrested for murder. He needs me. And not just to help him get rid of a renegade ghost-hunter."

She sat back against the plastic seat. Her gaze turned very cool. "You didn't tell me everything about your bargain with Wyatt, did you?"

Anger roared through him. He leaned across the table, pinning her without touching her. "I told you the truth about the arrangement I made with Mercer Wyatt."

"What didn't you tell me?"

"Damn it, the rest of it has nothing to do with this."

"Tell me."

He sat back slowly. With an effort of will he brought himself under control. "Wyatt told me that he's planning to retire in a year."

She made a soft, disgusted sound. "That's good news, I suppose. I, for one, won't miss him. But what has that got to do with you?"

"He claims he has some big plan to restructure the Cadence Guild along the same lines as the Resonance Guild before he steps down."

"Really . . . He wants you to do a little business consulting for him, is that it? Help him modernize things?"

Emmett hesitated. "He wants a little more than just some consulting."

"Damn. He wants to handpick his own successor, doesn't he? And he wants you for the job."

Her stunned outrage aroused the anger he thought he had suppressed a moment ago. He tossed a meaningful glance to the side to remind her that they were not alone in the restaurant.

"You might want to keep your voice down. We've got enough problems on our hands without starting wild rumors about internal Guild politics. Mercer Wyatt wouldn't like it."

"I don't care what Mercer Wyatt likes or doesn't like."

"More to the point," he said softly, "I wouldn't like it."

"Are you, by any chance, trying to intimidate me?"

"Yes."

She gave him a ferocious glare. But when she spoke, her voice was barely above a whisper. "What did you tell Wyatt when he informed you he wanted you to take over the Guild?"

Emmett picked up his tea. "I told him I didn't want the job."

"You think that's going to stop him from trying to make you take it?"

"I can handle Mercer Wyatt." He set his cup down a little harder than necessary. "Look, the future of the Cadence Guild is not the main issue here. In case you've forgotten, we're trying to keep ourselves from getting arrested for murder."

"Must have slipped my mind," she said into her tea mug.

"I have a hunch that Detective Martinez is one of those real dogged types. If she gets wind of Greeley's murder and makes a connection to the Brady case, you can bet she'll come around asking questions. We need to get our stories straight."

Lydia sighed. "What kind of stories are we going to tell her?"

"The truth, insofar as we can."

"Sounds tricky."

"It's always safer to stick as close to the truth as possible. Less chance to screw up that way."

"You've had a lot of experience in this kind of thing?"

He said nothing, just looked at her.

She flushed. "Sorry. I'm a little tense today."

"I'm not exactly at my best, either." He rested his elbows on the table. "Here's how it goes: We were together all last night and this morning. First at your place, then at the bank. We had tea here, and I dropped you off at Shrimpton's. We simply don't mention the few minutes we spent at Greeley's Antiques. We should be covered. Plenty of witnesses. Kelso's call earlier, and the people at the bank will back us up. I'll leave a good tip here so the waitress will remember us. The missing time in between we'll attribute to traffic congestion."

"What if someone on Ruin Row saw us?"

"I doubt if anyone noticed us in the fog. None of the other shops were open. We should be in the clear."

"You think so?" Lydia looked worried. "Your story is going to raise some questions in other people's minds."

"Such as?"

"Such as, why were you at my apartment last night and why were you still there this morning? Why are we sitting here in a café together when I should be at work? You know—questions like those."

"Fortunately, those questions have a real easy and obvious answer."

"They certainly do. For crying out loud, Emmett, everyone will think we're having an affair."

"Better they think you're sleeping with me than have them conclude that you're murdering your associates in the antiquities field."

She paled. "Point taken."

"You and I are each other's alibis."

"Great. My alibi is that I'm sleeping with my first major client. Heck of a way to launch my new career as a private consultant. Can't wait to see what type of high-class clientele I attract after this gets out."

THE MESSAGE SLIPS ON HER PHONE WERE AN OMINOUS sign. Lydia sat down very gingerly at her desk and reached for the sticky little papers. She flipped through them quickly. Two calls from Ryan and a message from a woman who wanted to schedule a tour of Shrimpton's for her seven-year-old son's birthday party. The good news was that there were no messages from Detective Alice Martinez.

Lydia allowed herself to relax ever so slightly.

Her life had certainly undergone some major alterations lately. Who would have thought that there would come a day when she would be hanging out with a past and possibly future Guild boss and ducking phone calls from the cops?

She stared at the bookcase on the other side of the office and thought about the blood on the floor of Greeley's back room.

Melanie opened the office door and put her head around the edge. "Well, well, well. I see you finally decided to come to work."

Lydia started. "I had a breakfast meeting with my client. The time got away from me."

Melanie glanced over her shoulder, apparently checking the hallway, and then bustled into the small room. "Thought I saw you get out of London's car a few minutes ago. Breakfast meeting, huh?"

"Yes." Lydia got up and went over to the hot plate that sat on top of the bookcase. She didn't really want any more tea, but she needed to do something, anything, while she endured the inevitable inquisition.

"So, how is the consulting project going?" Melanie asked a little too brightly.

"We're making progress." Lydia spooned tea leaves into a pot.

"I just wondered," Melanie said.

"What did you wonder, Melanie?"

"Why Mr. London gave you a lift to work. Usually you walk."

If she couldn't handle Melanie, Lydia thought, she wouldn't have a snowball's chance in a very warm place of handling Detective Alice Martinez. *Think of this conversation as a good chance to practice your story.*

She put down the pot, turned around, and leaned back against the bookcase. She braced her hands on the wooden shelving behind her and smiled at Melanie.

"Mr. London very kindly offered to drop me off here after our breakfast meeting."

"That was nice of him."

"Yes, it was."

"Don't imagine too many high-end clients could be bothered to chauffeur their consultants around. Just think of all the trouble he went to. He had to get up early, leave his hotel, drive to the Old Quarter to pick you up, drive you to the café, drop you off here—"

Lydia took the plunge. "Mr. London is staying with me while we work on his project."

Melanie's face lit up with horrified fascination. "Omigod, you're sleeping with him, aren't you? You're having an affair with your new client. I knew it. I knew it the minute I saw you get out of that Slider this morning."

Lydia was saved from having to respond by the sight of the six-and-a-half-foot-tall skeletal shadow that darkened the glass panel of the office door. A bony hand lifted to knock.

"Come in, Mr. Shrimpton," Lydia called. The more, the merrier. Martinez would probably show up any minute now.

The door opened. Winchell Shrimpton looked at her with his undertaker's gaze. "You're here."

"Sorry I was a little late getting in to work this morning. I had some personal business. Don't worry, I'm going to make up for it by working through lunch."

Shrimpton inclined his skull-head in a glum gesture. "Don't suppose it makes much difference. As you may have noticed, business has fallen off again. Customers are not exactly thronging the galleries anymore."

Shrimpton's chronic pessimism was more irritating than usual this morning. The last thing she wanted to do was listen to her boss whine about the fall-off of business. It wasn't as if she didn't have her own problems, Lydia thought. It was all she could do not to yell at him. *You want something to whine about? Try walking into a murder scene first thing in the morning. Try finding out that the killer left one of your personalized amber bracelets next to the body. Try worrying about whether you're going to be arrested at any moment. Try wondering if the man who is sleeping on your sofa and using your shower is scheduled to become the next boss of the Cadence Guild.*

Lydia pulled herself up short and gave herself a mental shake. It was not Shrimpton's fault that he not only looked as if he had just walked out of a crypt but had a personality to go with his looks. The man had given her a job when she desperately needed one. That counted for a lot in her book. Besides, as a boss, he literally and figuratively towered over a lot of the egotistical academics she'd worked with at the university.

"Don't worry, Mr. Shrimpton," she said, struggling for a note of professional good cheer. "The spring holidays are coming. Things always pick up during school vacations. Kids love this place."

Shrimpton did not brighten noticeably, but his cadaverous features realigned themselves into a thoughtful expression.

"It was the body in the sarcophagus in the Tomb Gallery that caused business to pick up for a day or two," he said. "I wonder if there's any way we could arrange for another little *incident*."

Lydia felt her jaw unhinge.

Melanie bounced with excitement. "What a great idea, boss! You know, if a second body turned up here at the museum, we could probably get a good legend started."

Shrimpton looked at her hopefully. "What sort of legend?"

"Something along the lines of an ancient Harmonic curse would probably work best." Melanie tapped her finger against her cheek. "People love that sort of thing, you know. Maybe we could mount an ad campaign based on the Curse of the Harmonic Sarcophagus."

Shrimpton nodded. "I like it. It has possibilities."

Lydia dropped her head into her hands.

CHAPTER 20

THE DAMP FOG HAD DRIVEN OFF THE USUAL DENIZENS OF the tiny park, but Emmett and Zane had to weave a path through a maze of discarded bottles of Night Vibe wine and Acid-Aura beer.

"The Transverse Wave?" Zane looked away from Fuzz, who was investigating the grass around a tree. "Yeah, sure, I know it. A lot of street kids hang there. They've got free food and video games and a neat gym. I used to go there sometimes after school until Lydia found out."

Emmett shoved his hands into the pockets of his leather jacket. "Lydia doesn't approve of the place?"

"Nah." Zane rolled his eyes. "She convinced Aunt Olinda it wasn't a good *environment* for me."

"Ah."

"She said it was a place for kids who didn't have a home. She said I've got one."

"Guess there is some logic to that."

"Maybe. Aunt Olinda bought it, at any rate."

Emmett watched Fuzz tumble toward them across the scraggly lawn. "Is it open twenty-four hours a day?"

"Used to be. But a few months ago they started closing it at midnight. Someone said the lady who runs the place claimed there were new legal problems and restrictions on all-night shelters."

"Think you could describe the interior of the place to me?"

"Sure." Zane squinted up at him. "How come you want to know about the Wave?"

"I'm thinking of dropping in to take a look around."

"Lydia probably won't like that."

"Probably not."

They headed back to the Slider, leaned against the fender, and watched Fuzz bob happily around the empty bottles.

"Lydia thinks I should go to college," Zane said after a while.

Emmett nodded. "Doesn't surprise me."

"I don't want to go to college. I want to join the Guild."

"No reason you can't do both."

Zane snorted. "College is a waste of time for a ghost-hunter."

"Lot of hunters lose interest in full-time ghost-hunting after they've done it for a while. Or they get fried one too many times and decide to call it quits. If they haven't trained for anything else, they have a tough time finding another job."

"I can't imagine ever getting tired of hunting."

"It's okay once in a while. But it's not exactly the most intellectually challenging occupation in the world."

Zane gave another snort. "Who cares about intellectual stuff?"

"Being good at ghost-hunting is sort of like being good at crossing a busy street in the middle of the block. If you're fast you don't get clipped too often. Sure, it's kind of exciting for a while, but do you really want to spend your whole life doing it?"

Zane glowered. "It's not like that at all."

"It's no different from being able to de-rez illusion traps the way Lydia does. She's good at it and she could probably make a living doing nothing but springing traps, but she'd get bored if that was all she did."

"I won't get bored ghost-hunting," Zane vowed.

Emmett shrugged. "Maybe not."

"Did you go to college?"

"Yeah. I zapped ghosts in the Resonance catacombs on the side. Did it full-time for a while after I graduated. But I got tired of seeing the para-archaeologists get all the credit for the discoveries."

Zane scowled. "What do you mean?"

"No one gives the hunters any credit when a new catacomb is excavated. We're just hired muscle as far as most people are concerned. It's the P-As who get their pictures in the papers and write the articles in the journals."

"That's not fair."

"I know," Emmett said. "But that's how it works."

"PLEASE COME IN, MR. LONDON." DENVER GALBRAITH–Thorndyke rose from behind the broad desk. He pushed his glasses up higher on his nose and motioned Emmett to a chair. "I got a call from Mr. Wyatt telling me to expect you."

"I won't take too much of your time." Emmett surveyed the plush offices of the Guild Foundation. Tamara had certainly pulled out all the stops in her goal to start reshaping the Guild's image. The rich paneling, expensive carpets, and deeply polished wood furnishings had obviously been chosen by a designer who had been instructed to project Expensive Good Taste.

Denver Galbraith-Thorndyke fit in naturally with his surroundings. The years of private schooling and social connections were evident. But there was an earnest, determined quality about him also. Mercer had gauged him correctly, Emmett thought. This was a young man out to prove himself. He wanted to make it on his own. Tamara had offered him the means of doing just that.

"I understand that you're interested in the details of our contributions to the Transverse Wave Youth Shelter." Denver adjusted his gold-rimmed glasses again and opened a thick file. "I don't know exactly what it is you want, but I've got a full financial summary here, if that will help."

"I'd like to see it." Emmett reached across the desk to take the report. He glanced through it quickly. "I assume any prospective charity is well researched before you authorize funding?"

"Of course. I verify all of the relevant facts personally. Background checks on the individuals associated with the organization are always performed, as are financial checks. The objective is to assure ourselves that the institution is legitimate. There are a lot of scam artists out there, you know."

"I know." Emmett scanned the financial data in front of him. "I see that the Transverse Wave was in financial trouble when the Foundation began funding it."

"Yes." Denver leaned back in his chair. "When the founder died, the finances were in chaos. We almost didn't go through with the project because of that. But historically the shelter has had a good reputation for getting kids off the street, and Mrs. Wyatt was determined to fund a project that was oriented toward street youth. We decided we could work with Miss Vickers to get the Wave back on its feet. We've been quite successful."

Emmett looked up. "Miss Vickers?"

"She's the person responsible for the day-to-day operation of the shelter. She went to work for it shortly before Ames died. A very dedicated woman."

LYDIA GAZED DOWN INTO THE SARCOPHAGUS WHERE Chester's body had been found. The janitorial staff had done an excellent job. The bloodstains were gone. But, after all, the translucent green quartz the Harmonics had used to construct their cities and the catacombs and much of what went into them was not only virtually indestructible, it cleaned up easily. If humans ever learned how to duplicate the para-resonating process used to create the stuff, Lydia thought, it would probably sell well to home builders and remodelers. It would be perfect for use in bathrooms and kitchens, assuming your interior designer liked green.

She turned slowly on her heel and surveyed the dimly lit gallery.

What had Chester been doing here the night he died? Detective Martinez and everyone else assumed that he had come to steal one of the artifacts. On its good days Shrimpton's House of Ancient Horrors was only a third-rate museum. There was nothing of extraordinary value here, but there were some things, such as the tomb mirrors, that would be of interest to small-time collectors. And Chester had a reputation, after all, of being a *petty* thief.

But if she and Emmett had interpreted Chester's note correctly, he had not come here to steal. He had been attempting to conceal the key to his private code.

It was likely that he had been killed before he accomplished his goal. If that was the case, then his killer had the key and there was no point looking for it.

But what if he had been murdered on his way *out* of the museum? What if he had hidden the key *before* someone slit his throat?

She studied the row of display vaults that lined the gallery. On Shrimpton's orders, the green quartz urns, tomb mirrors, and other objects had been dramatically lit so that they glowed eerily in the shadows.

There were literally hundreds of places in this wing alone in which Chester could have hidden his key. He must have known how difficult if not downright impossible it would be for her to search the entire museum.

"Lydia?"

The sound of Ryan's voice behind her startled her out of her reverie. She turned quickly and saw him walking toward her with an urgent stride.

"Hello, Ryan."

"I left a dozen messages for you," he said without preamble.

"I saw them."

"Why in hell didn't you return my calls?"

"I've been a little busy lately."

"Damn it, I've been trying to get hold of you all day."

"In case you've forgotten, Ryan, I don't work for the department anymore. That means I don't always return phone calls to my former colleagues with my former efficiency. I've got other priorities these days."

"Such as your new so-called client?"

A chill of unease shot through her. "Not so-called," she said evenly. "Mr. London is as real as clients get."

"He answered the phone in your apartment this morning. You're sleeping with him, for God's sake. Do you have any idea who he is?"

"Yes."

He ignored that. "London's a Guild boss from Resonance City. I would have thought that you, of all people, would have a few problems with the idea of having an affair with a guy like that."

"He's an ex-Guild boss."

"You know what they say, once in the Guild, always in the Guild."

"My client is my problem, not yours."

"That's not true." Ryan's voice softened. "We're friends, Lydia. Colleagues. I have a responsibility to warn you about London. He's using you."

"Consider me warned. Look, I haven't got time for this. Let's cut to the chase here. What do you want?"

"Damn it, I'm trying to do you a favor."

"The last time you did me a favor, I lost my job."

"Work with me on this and I might be able to get you back into the department."

She had been right, she thought. Only one thing could explain Ryan's persistence today. He must have heard something about the dreamstone.

"What's going on, Ryan?"

"I need to talk to you." He glanced around, apparently assuring himself that the gallery was still empty. "Something big has come up."

It might be smart to find out just how much he knew about the dreamstone. She folded her arms and propped one hip on the corner of the green sarcophagus. "Tell me about it."

"We can't talk here."

"Why not? The museum closed a few minutes ago. We're alone."

He shoved his fingers through his hair and glanced back over his shoulder again. The tension in him was palpable.

He turned back to her and took a step closer. When he spoke, it was in a whisper. "I've got a private client of my own."

"Congratulations. What does that have to do with me?"

He watched her closely. "Last night he approached me about a rumor concerning a piece of worked dreamstone."

She went cold inside, but she managed a derisive chuckle. "Sounds like your hotshot private client is an escapee from a para-psych ward. Everyone knows there's no such thing as worked dreamstone."

"My client is serious." Ryan continued to focus on her with unwavering intensity. "He's no fool. He thinks the rumor is solid, and he's asked me to help him check it out."

She grinned. "Easy money. You wrack up a bunch of hours looking for a bogus piece of dreamstone, and then you tell him it doesn't exist and send him the bill."

"He thinks you may know something about it, Lydia."

"*Me?*" She deliberately widened her eyes, going for stunned innocence. "Why in the world would he connect me to a wild rumor about dreamstone?"

"Because you're working for London, and he thinks London came to Cadence to find the dreamstone."

"Look, Ryan, your client obviously got badly fried somewhere along the line," Lydia said. "Mr. London is not chasing a fantastic rumor. He came here to look for a family heirloom."

"I don't believe you." Ryan moved in closer. "You're not cooperating with me because you want to keep this to yourself. You think you can find the dreamstone on your own."

"Are you crazy? You think I'd be working here at Shrimpton's today if I was on the trail of a piece of dreamstone? Believe me, I'd have quit to spend full time on a project like that. Locating a chunk of worked dreamstone would put me on the cover of the *Journal of Para-Archaeology*. I'd have my pick of posts at the university. Heck, they'd probably make me head of the P-A department. Just think, Ryan, I could have *your* job."

Ryan blinked, apparently startled by that possibility. Then he recovered, his handsome features twisting into a grim mask. "My client is an experienced collector who knows all about ruin rumors. He's convinced the dreamstone exists."

"What's the name of this experienced collector?"

"I can't tell you that." Ryan's shoulders stiffened. "He prefers to remain anonymous."

"Yeah, I'll just bet he does. If people find out he's searching for dreamstone, someone may call the guys in white coats to have him taken away."

Ryan clamped his teeth together so fiercely that Lydia heard the click. "Damn it, Lydia, it's in your best interests to work with me on this."

"Yeah? Why?"

"My client has not only agreed to pay me a fortune if I turn up the dreamstone, he's agreed to allow the artifact to be studied and written up by the department."

She pursed her lips. "That means that your name would go on all the journal articles."

"Naturally, I'd make sure you got credit."

"Oh, boy. Just like the old days, huh? I write the article and you get to put your name on it as lead author. Be still, my beating heart."

He drew himself up. "All right. I promise you will be listed as lead author."

"I don't believe that for a moment. You've tried that line before, remember?"

"Lydia, this is no time to indulge in petty quarrels. If my client is right about this dreamstone, you and I are standing on the brink of the most important career moment of our lives."

She studied him for a moment. "You really believe your client is right about the dreamstone, don't you?"

"Like I said, he talks like an experienced collector. I think he knows what he's doing. He sounds much too smart and too savvy to be chasing a fantasy."

"I dunno. Collectors are weird. They wouldn't be collectors if they weren't a little strange."

"But if he's right, there's a fortune at stake here. And not just in cash. This could wipe out your past for you. No one would give a damn about what happened to you six months ago if you show up with dreamstone."

"Okay, convince me. What do you know about this so-called dreamstone?"

"I'm not going to tell you a bloody thing until you've agreed to work with me," he said warily.

"Well, in that case"—she straightened away from the sarcophagus—"looks like this conversation is over. See you around, Ryan."

"*Wait.*" He grabbed her arm in a fierce grip as she made to walk past him. "You're a pro. You know as well as I do that if there's any truth to this rumor, it would be the find of the decade. This is too important to allow personal feelings to get in the way."

"*If* there's any truth to it." She looked pointedly down at his hand on her arm. "Kindly take your hand off me."

"It's London, isn't it?" Ryan shouted furiously. "He *is* after the dreamstone, and you figure you'll do better to stick with him instead of teaming up with me."

"Take your hand off me, Ryan."

"He's Guild. That means he's dangerous."

"Let me go, Ryan."

"Shit, haven't you figured out what's going on here? He's using you."

"What are you talking about?"

"You know damn well what I'm talking about. He's got an agenda."

"Everyone's got an agenda. Including you."

"Whatever London is up to, you can bet it's outside the law."

"I wouldn't go around accusing Emmett London of being a criminal if I were you." She recalled Emmett's words in the café. "He might not like it."

Ryan flushed a dull red. "What is this? Just because he's screwing you, you believe every word he says? I thought you were smarter than that, Lydia."

"My private life is none of your concern, Ryan. Not anymore."

"Pay attention here," he snarled. "The fact that London hired you in the first place should tell you he's got plans that probably aren't going to do you any good."

"What do you mean?"

"You know as well as I do that if his consulting job had been legitimate, he'd have gone through the Society to hire a private P-A. Instead, he chose you. Doesn't that tell you something?"

"I think you've said enough, Ryan."

"He picked you, a tangler working in a place like this because she got so badly fried that she lost her job at the university. You tell me why he'd want a P-A who will probably never work on a reputable excavation team again."

"Shut up, Ryan," Lydia said steadily.

"Have you seen your own para-psych files?" he demanded. "At least two of the shrinks who treated you after you came out of the cata-combs recommended that you check into a nice, tranquil para-psych ward for an extended stay."

She clenched her fists. "Those files are supposed to be private."

"Ghost-shit. Everyone in the department knows what's in them. You were diagnosed as suffering from extreme para-dissonance, am-nesia, and general psychic trauma. We both know what that means. As far as the experts are concerned, you're liable to crack under the slightest pressure."

"That won't happen."

"For sure you'll never work underground again, at least not with a legitimate team." He flung out one hand. "Hell, you're lucky to get a job in this two-bit carnival house of horrors."

Rage flooded through her. She felt pain in her palm and realized that her nails were biting into her skin. "If you don't remove your hand, I'm going to yell. Maybe I can get you arrested. How do you think the folks back in the lab would react to that? For that matter, how would your new *client* take it? Something tells me that if he's after dreamstone, he'd prefer a little discretion from his consultant."

Ryan's face mottled with fury. For a few seconds she thought she would have to make good on her threat. But he must have read the determination in her eyes.

With a disgusted oath he dropped his hand. "Listen to me, Lydia. You don't know what you're getting into here. I tell you, London is dangerous. There's something else you should know. He's got ene-mies who are also dangerous."

That gave her pause. "Enemies?"

"My client tells me that not everyone in the Resonance Guild likes the changes he made in the organization there." Ryan lowered his voice. "What's more, a couple of the people who stood in his way wound up dead in a catacomb. A lot of people think London arranged for their unfortunate accidents."

"That's absurd. If your client told you that, he really is deep-fried. You'll have to excuse me, Ryan." She made a show of glancing at her watch. "I'm going home."

"Damn it, haven't you heard a word I've said? You can't trust London. He's using you."

"Maybe I haven't made my position clear," Lydia said evenly. "As things stand now, I trust London more than I trust you."

"You should have told me that all it took to buy your trust was a good fuck. Hell, I'd have screwed you myself."

She would not let the bastard make her lose her self-control, she vowed silently. She was trembling with anger, but she kept her voice cool.

"You did ask, as I recall," she said very evenly. "Maybe you've forgotten that I declined. I think I had to wash my hair that night."

His hand came up. She watched in disbelief, wondering if he intended to strike her. Energy hummed silently in the gallery. *Not her own.* Her amber was still only skin temperature on her wrist. The invisible vibrations weren't coming from Ryan, either. This was a ghost-hunter frequency.

With a visible effort Ryan lowered his hand. He seemed oblivious to the energy in the air, though. He was too tense, too emotionally involved in the argument to notice it.

"You're in a very serious situation, Lydia. I can help you. Call me when you come to your senses. It's not just my future riding on this. Yours is also on the line."

He turned on his heel and strode off down the gallery.

Lydia watched him walk away. Energy continued to vibrate gently, protectively, in the air around her.

She turned slowly and watched Emmett step out of the deep shadows cast by a large green quartz pillar.

"How long were you standing there?" she asked.

"Long enough."

"You heard? About his new client and all the rest?"

"I heard."

"Emmett, this means that someone else really is after the dreamstone. Whoever he is, he thinks that's the reason you're here in Cadence."

"Looks that way." Emmett glanced down the gallery to where Ryan had disappeared. "Thought I was going to have to fry him."

"Fry who? You mean Ryan?" She was briefly distracted by that. "Could you? This far from the Dead City?"

Emmett did not answer. Instead he took her arm. "Let's go. We've got an appointment."

"With whom?"

"Miss Helen Vickers."

"Who's she?"

"The good lady in charge of the day-to-day operations of the Transverse Wave Youth Shelter. I'll give you the rundown on our cover story on the way."

"Hey, I've got an idea. I could be your lawyer and you could be some rich, eccentric guy looking to give away lots of money."

"Too late," Emmett said. "When I called Miss Vickers, I told her that I would be bringing my wife with me. By the way, our last name is Carstairs."

CHAPTER 21

As things stand now, I trust London more than I trust you.

Okay, so it fell a little short of a ringing endorsement, Emmett thought as he followed Lydia into the offices of the Transverse Wave Youth Shelter. She could have been a touch more eloquent and maybe a shade more dramatic. *I would trust London with my life, my fortune, and my sacred honor,* would have done nicely. Or maybe, *I would trust London to the ends of the universe.* But he would take what he could get.

Probably should have gone ahead and fried Ryan while he had the chance, though.

The youth shelter's business office was located next door to the main facility. From where he stood, Emmett could see a handful of young people who looked to be in their late teens loitering on the sidewalk in front of the shelter. One of them was idly dribbling a frequency ball.

This section of the Old Quarter of Cadence, situated adjacent to the east wall of the Dead City, had clearly never felt the brush of gentrification. It was a mix of shabby chic, bohemian charm, and genuine urban blight. From the window of the Transverse Wave office, Emmett could see missions catering to the down-and-out hunkering cheek by jowl with pawnshops and seedy taverns. Boarded-up, dilapidated buildings occupied the spaces in between. Panhandlers and prostitutes brushed shoulders on the narrow sidewalks. It was easy to see why Lydia hadn't wanted Zane hanging out in this neighborhood.

Towering above the low, squat structures built by the first human residents of Cadence was the massive green quartz wall of the Dead City. The building that housed the Transverse Wave and its associated offices was one of the oldest in the quarter. It had been constructed in the very shadow of the wall.

Ambient psi energy leaked freely through small, often invisible cracks in the quartz. Emmett ignored the frissons that flickered through his para-senses. He knew Lydia felt them too. The little currents and eddies of energy were part of the atmosphere in the Old Quarters of the ancient cities. Tourists loved the creepy sensations.

He glanced around the dingy, cramped office as the door closed behind him. Two battered metal desks piled high with papers and folders, a couple of file cabinets, a telephone, and some scarred wooden chairs completed the decor. Just the sort of furnishings one would expect to see in the storefront charity run on a shoestring. A narrow hall led to another office and a closed door that looked like a storage closet.

An earnest, somewhat harried-looking woman who appeared to be in her early forties sat behind the front desk. She wore no makeup. Her graying hair was done in a simple, no-nonsense bun. Emmett did not see any amber accessories.

She glanced up expectantly. "Mr. and Mrs. Carstairs?"

Lydia held out her hand. "You must be Miss Vickers. Emmett and I are delighted to meet you."

Emmett was amused by her rich, plummy tones. Her academic accent, he figured.

"Call me Helen." Helen Vickers indicated two of the chairs. "Please sit down. Can I get you some tea?"

Emmett opened his mouth to say no.

"Thank you," Lydia murmured. "That would be very nice."

Emmett glanced at her and decided to follow her lead. "I'd appreciate that."

"I was delighted to get your phone call this afternoon, Mr. Carstairs." Helen got to her feet to pour tea from a pot that sat on the other desk. "May I ask how you heard about the work that we do here at the Transverse Wave Youth Shelter?"

"A friend of ours mentioned your facility," Emmett said easily. "He knew that we were very interested in giving money to an organization that focused on young people."

"That's wonderful." Helen glowed with enthusiasm as she handed them the cups. "You've come to the right place. We here at Transverse Wave have dedicated ourselves to helping young people who have nowhere else to turn."

Lydia sipped tea. "My husband and I have been advised by our accountant to investigate a number of different charities that work with young people before we make our decision. He warned us that there are a number of less than ethical charitable organizations around."

"Unfortunately that is all too true. But we here at the Wave are very proud of the fact that the vast majority of our donations go straight back into the work of the shelter. Only a tiny amount is used for overhead and fund-raising. Let me give you a brochure and our latest annual report."

She went to a file cabinet, opened a drawer, and plucked out a folder. She handed it to Emmett.

He opened the annual report and flipped to the organizational information at the back He studied the list of donors while he listened to Lydia gently question Helen Vickers.

"Can you tell us a little about the history of the Transverse Wave, Helen?" Lydia asked. "We understand it's been in existence for a number of years."

"Over thirty years," Helen assured her. "It was established by Anderson Ames, a wealthy industrialist who came from an impoverished background. He knew the perils of the street firsthand and wanted to set up a foundation that would help young people avoid them."

"Is Mr. Ames still involved in the work of the shelter?" Lydia asked innocently.

"I'm sorry to say that he died two years ago," Helen said. "He had hoped that the shelter would go on without him, but the lawyers discovered irregularities in the trust's finances. Things looked bleak until—"

The front door opened at that moment. A tall, well-built man dressed in gray sweats and a pair of sports shoes strode into the office. He carried a frequency ball under one arm. A film of perspiration gleamed on his forehead.

Helen Vickers smiled. "This is Bob Matthews. He volunteers as our recreational director. Bob, meet Mr. and Mrs. Carstairs. They're considering a donation to the shelter."

"Hey, that's great!" Bob grabbed Emmett's hand and pumped it enthusiastically. "If there's one thing we need more of around here, it's donors. Always glad to meet one."

Emmett nodded and retrieved his hand. "It looks like you do good work."

Bob chuckled. "We try. Mind if I give you my sales pitch for some new gym equipment?"

"Another time, Bob," Helen said firmly. "Mr. and Mrs. Carstairs are just gathering information today."

"Got it." Bob held up a hand. "Helen knows me too well. I tend to get a little carried away when it comes to getting stuff for my kids."

"How long have you been volunteering at the shelter?" Emmett asked.

"Let's see, what is it now, Helen? Six? Eight months?"

"Eight, I think." Helen smiled. "And I don't know what we'd do without you." She looked at Emmett. "Bob has really rezzed up our athletic program. Physical activity is so important for the kids. It helps work off some of their frustration and anger."

"I understand." Lydia rose, cup in hand, and sauntered toward a large calendar that hung on the wall near the closet.

Emmett knew she was up to something.

"Looks like you have a very active schedule here at the shelter," Lydia said, surveying the little squares around each date of the calendar.

Helen glowed. "Thanks in large part to Bob."

Bob grinned. "Don't you believe it. I do what I can, but Helen is the one who keeps this place running day in and day out. Now, if you'll excuse me, I just stopped to pick up some keys from my office. Sorry to interrupt."

"No problem," Emmett said.

Bob went down the hall to the small office, opened the door, and disappeared inside.

Lydia looked at Emmett. "Did you have any more questions, *dear*?"

"Just one." He closed the annual report and glanced at Helen. "I see the Guild is listed as one of your major donors."

"It is indeed," Helen said. "And I can tell you in all honesty that if it weren't for the Cadence Guild stepping in last year when we were going through a bad patch financially, the shelter would have had to close its doors. We have Mercer Wyatt's new wife to thank for our continued existence. A very gracious and caring lady."

"Really?" Lydia mused.

"Indeed, just as we were staring financial disaster in the face, the new Mrs. Wyatt launched the Cadence Guild Foundation. We were one of the first charities chosen to receive grants. The Guild money was a godsend."

"ALL RIGHT, LET'S HAVE IT," LYDIA SAID TWENTY MINUTES later as she got in on the passenger side of the Slider. "What are you thinking about the Guild's involvement in the Transverse Wave Shelter?"

"I don't know what to think yet," Emmett said. "I'm still gathering data. I called my office in Resonance City this morning. I'm having someone there do what the administrators of the Cadence Guild Foundation did."

"Look into the shelter's background?"

"Right." He eased the Slider away from the curb. "A duplication of effort, but I couldn't ask for the Foundation's report without raising questions that I'm not prepared to answer yet."

"Speaking of the Guild Foundation, doesn't Tamara Wyatt's interest in social responsibility strike you as a little hard to swallow?"

"No. Tamara was always very big on enhancing the Guild's social image."

"I see."

He smiled slightly. "I realize you don't view that as an achievable goal. There are, however, some of us who think the Guilds can take their place in society as respectable businesses."

"Next thing you know, some Guild boss will be running for mayor."

"Maybe we should get back to the subject at hand," Emmett said.

"Maybe we should." She hesitated, wondering how far she could go. She decided to take the plunge. "Level with me, Emmett. All personal issues aside, do you think Tamara is involved in this?"

He kept his attention on the narrow, crowded street. "It's not beyond the realm of possibility. Wyatt told me that he started making plans to retire shortly after he and Tamara got married."

"Must have come as a shock to Tamara."

"I think it would be safe to assume that she was probably not thrilled."

"Possibly even stunned," Lydia said dryly. "Just think about it. First she dumps you because she finds out that you're planning to resign your position as head of the Resonance Guild and she won't get to be Mrs. Guild Boss if she goes through with the marriage. Then she sweeps the Cadence Guild boss off his feet, marries him, and he promptly announces that he intends to retire too. What's a girl gonna do?"

"An interesting question," Emmett said. "But knowing Tamara, I wouldn't be surprised to find out that she came up with an idea or two."

"I still don't see what you saw in her."

"Funny, I still can't figure out what you saw in Kelso," Emmett retaliated. "What were you doing back there at the shelter when you were looking at the calendar on the office wall?"

"I thought I caught a trace of rez energy."

He frowned. "The office is right next to the Old Wall. There's stray rez energy leaking all over the place around here."

"If I'm not mistaken, this was illusion trap energy," she said softly.

That got his attention. "Are you sure?"

"No. It was faint." She looked out the window toward the towering green quartz walls.

He thought about the little snare she had discovered in the dreamstone jar. "See anything suspicious in the office when you looked around?"

"No, nothing. It must have been a stray leak. Could have come up through the foundation and the floorboards, I suppose. Some of the experts, including Ryan, think that we haven't mapped more than twenty percent of the catacombs here in Cadence, let alone cleared them of traps. They extend for miles underground."

"Speaking of the professor," Emmett said, "I think we'd better see if we can identify his client."

"Probably just some private collector who heard rumors about dreamstone. Happens all the time."

"How often do private collectors follow dreamstone rumors that lead to you?"

She winced. "Okay, I see what you mean. Whoever approached

Ryan not only knows that I'm involved in this, he's linked you to it too."

"Which means that he may be a hell of a lot more than just a private collector who heard some rumors."

"I agree. And I have an idea how we can find out about Ryan and his new client."

"How?"

"I worked at the university for quite a while. I know a lot of people on the staff. A few of them owe me. I'll make some calls when we get back to my place."

EMMETT WENT INTO THE KITCHEN AND OPENED THE BOX that contained the pizza he had picked up on the way back to the apartment. He listened to Lydia's end of the phone call as he took two plates out of the cupboard.

"No, I am not spying on Ryan. For God's sake, Sid, you think I'm jealous because he's dating Suzanne? That's ridiculous. This is a professional inquiry."

There was a short pause. Emmett took the lid off the pretzel jar. Fuzz tumbled through the doorway and looked up at him with wide blue eyes.

"Why do I want to know if he's got any after-work appointments this week?" Lydia said. "I'll tell you why. I think Kelso is trying to steal a client out from under me."

Emmett fed a pretzel to Fuzz.

"No, I don't want you to do anything that could cost you your job, Sid. I just want to know if Ryan has anything on his calendar this week that looks like a non-academic meeting."

Emmett picked up the plates of pizza and went to lounge in the kitchen doorway. On the other side of the small room, Lydia was ensconced on the sofa, feet propped on the coffee table.

"Am I calling in a favor? Guess you could say that. You're right, you do owe me. If I hadn't covered for you and Lorraine that afternoon . . . well, I don't think we need to go into that, do we?"

There was another short pause. Then Lydia grinned. She gave Emmett a thumbs-up signal.

"Thanks, Sid," she said. "I appreciate it. I really can't afford to lose this new client. That's okay, take your time. I'll be at this number all evening."

She hung up the phone and looked at Emmett. "Mission accomplished."

"Who's Sid?" Emmett crossed the room and sat down on the sofa. He put both plates on the table. "And why does he owe you?"

"Sid's a lab tech." She reached for a slice of pizza. "A year ago he and Ryan's secretary, Lorraine, had a mad, passionate affair. They got a little carried away one afternoon. I walked into Ryan's office and found them on top of the desk."

"I take it they were not reading the minutes of the last departmental meeting?"

"Nope. I covered for them. Stalled Ryan out in the hall with some dumb questions until they had a chance to get dressed and Lorraine could take her place at her own desk."

"What would Kelso have done if he'd found them screwing on his desk?"

"Probably fired them both."

"Kelso's a real stickler for appropriate behavior in the office?"

She smiled slowly. "Not exactly. Ryan was sleeping with Lorraine himself at the time. Everyone knew it. He'd have been furious if he'd discovered that she was two-timing him with a lowly lab tech."

"And here I thought academics were a dull, staid lot. Talk about your shattered illusions."

"We have our moments."

He munched pizza while he pondered the details of the conversation he had overheard.

"About that story you used with your friend Sid," he said after a while.

She licked up a long thread of melted cheese that dangled from her slice of pizza. "The one about my being worried that Ryan was trying to steal my client away from me?"

"I believe your exact words were that you were afraid Kelso was trying to steal your client out from under you."

"So?"

"I'd just like to clarify one point."

"What point?"

"Assuming you were referring to me, let me assure you that I have no intention of being stolen out from under you. In fact, I can't imagine anyplace I'd rather be than under you. Unless maybe on top of you."

She paused in mid-chew. Her eyes widened. Then she swallowed convulsively. "Uh—"

"Sooner or later we're going to have to talk about it, you know."

"What? Talk about what?" she demanded.

"You. Me. Us."

"There's nothing to talk about. We have a business association. Nothing more."

"I thought it was men who were supposed to have a hard time

with relationship discussions." He shrugged. "It can wait, if that's the way you want to handle it. But you can't avoid the subject forever."

"Wanna bet?" She started to reach for another slice of pizza.

The phone rang. She dropped the pizza and grabbed the receiver. "This is Lydia. Yeah, hi, Sid. What have you got?"

Emmett watched the intense concentration gather on her intelligent face as she listened to her friend. He wondered if she knew how incredibly sexy she was when she became so utterly focused.

She waved her hand wildly. It dawned on him that she was signaling for paper and pen. He saw both on the end table, scooped them up, and handed them to her.

Lydia went very still, pen poised over the paper. Then she frowned. "Is that all you've got, Sid? Yeah, yeah, I know. It's better than nothing. Didn't Lorraine have any idea of who called?"

Whatever Sid had to say was apparently not entirely satisfying. Lydia tossed the pen down. "If that's all you've got, it's all you've got. Do me a favor, don't mention this to anyone around the lab, okay? I still entertain a few vague hopes of getting my old job back one of these days. What's that? Right. We'll have drinks after work sometime soon."

She dropped the phone into its cradle and looked at Emmett with a combination of triumph and frustration.

"What did you get?" he asked.

"Sid says he checked with Lorraine. There's nothing on Ryan's schedule that's not routine. But she told him that late yesterday afternoon she answered a call in the office. The man didn't identify himself to her, just asked to speak with Ryan. When he finished the call, Ryan seemed very excited. He came out into the office and asked her for my new phone number."

"Did she give it to him?"

"Yes. Lorraine, figuring there was some hot-and-heavy gossip going down, listened in on Ryan's next call, which was to me. But I wasn't home. Today Ryan was out of the office most of the day. He called in once or twice asking if I had called. When she told him no, he seemed well and truly pissed."

"Pissed, huh?"

"Yeah. I often have that effect on men."

"I'll keep that in mind."

"At any rate," Lydia continued, "she took another call for Ryan just as she was getting ready to leave the office today. It was the same man who had called yesterday. She recognized the voice. She was just about to tell him that Ryan wasn't there when Ryan stormed back into the office."

"Fresh from having just been to see you at Shrimpton's," Emmett observed.

"No doubt. Made exceedingly curious by this exciting turn of events, Lorraine delayed her departure from the office long enough to listen at Ryan's door while he took the call. She heard him agree to meet the caller later tonight. Apparently Ryan was less than thrilled about the location of the rendezvous, however. Lorraine told Sid that Ryan tried to argue about it, but in the end he agreed to meet there."

Emmett glanced at the blank pad of paper. "I assume Lorraine did not get the name of the meeting place?"

"Unfortunately, no." She picked up the pen and irritably tapped the point against the paper. "But I've got an idea."

Emmett helped himself to another slice of pizza. "You want to stake out Kelso's place and see where he goes tonight."

She looked at him. "How did you guess?"
"It just came to me in a blinding flash of the obvious."
Her brows rose. "You mean you were thinking the same thing."
"Right. A case of great minds resonating together, I guess."

CHAPTER 22

SOMEWHERE AROUND TEN-THIRTY LYDIA TRIED TO stretch in the close confines of the Slider's front seat. "If Ryan doesn't do anything exciting soon, I'm going to have to knock on his front door and ask to use the bathroom."

"I tried to talk you out of coming with me tonight," Emmett said with no sign of sympathy.

"Just because you don't mind using the bushes in the park—" She broke off abruptly as the front door of Ryan's condo opened. "There he is."

She leaned forward, excitement bubbling inside her. She could see Ryan very clearly in the streetlights as he walked to his Coaster, parked at the curb.

"There he goes," she whispered.

There was no need to keep her voice pitched low. The Slider's front seat afforded ample privacy, parked halfway down the block in the shadow of a large tree. There was no way Ryan could see, let alone hear, her. But the sheer drama of following Ryan to his mysterious appointment had gotten to her. She realized that the rush was not unlike what she experienced when she tangled with an illusion trap.

"I see him," Emmett said.

She heard the edge in his voice and knew that she was not the only one who was feeling the adrenaline.

"I wonder if we made poor career choices somewhere along the line," she said. "Maybe we should have become private investigators or something."

He glanced at her with amusement as he rezzed the ignition. "I'm told the work is not usually this interesting. Most private investigators spend their time getting evidence of adultery to be used in Covenent Marriage dissolution cases."

"Depressing. Guess I'll stick with my job at Shrimpton's."

Emmett waited until Ryan pulled away from the curb, then eased the Slider out from the dark shadows beneath the tree. Lydia listened to the soft, hungry whine of the engine and willed Ryan not to look in his rearview mirror.

Kelso drove at a slow, cautious pace, as though he was not particularly eager to get to his destination.

"Probably doesn't want to have to explain to his client that he failed to get me to cooperate," Lydia said. "I hope the guy fires him on the spot tonight. Serve him right."

"I detect a degree of personal animosity, possibly even vengeance, in your tone," Emmett said.

"Yeah."

Ryan cruised sedately along the broad avenues of the university

After Dark

district, past elegantly maintained lawns and harmonically proportioned homes and condominiums.

When he left the neighborhood he turned left and started toward the Old Quarter.

"Well, well, well," Lydia said.

"My sentiments exactly."

A few minutes later Ryan reached the Quarter and drove even more slowly into the maze of narrow streets that bordered the east wall of the Dead City. Some areas of the neighborhood, those that catered to tourists, were reasonably well lit. But the rest of the Quarter existed in a pervasive gloom.

A block away from the main drag, the tiny, twisted lanes and alleys depended on the weak, erratic glow that spilled from the windows of the area's taverns and clubs.

"Be careful," Lydia said. "It would be easy to lose him here. Some of these alleys aren't even on the city maps."

"I won't lose him," Emmett promised softly.

There was a new quality in his voice. The edge was still present, but now there was something else, something almost feral. She studied him covertly. His expression was unreadable in the shadows, but she sensed the predatory anticipation in him.

A small shiver went through her. Energy leaking from the Dead City, she thought. They were very near the wall.

But she knew that what she felt had nothing to do with stray frissons of ambient psi energy in the area. Her senses were rezzed, and they were vibrating in response to the core of power that resonated deep within Emmett, power that was at once very male and very dangerous. It was as though he was readying himself for hand-to-hand combat. But that made no sense, she thought. They were only here to observe Ryan's meeting with his client. Why was Emmett radiating such intense energy?

She opened her mouth to ask him if something was wrong. But at that moment she saw Ryan's car pull over and park at the curb. She peered through the windshield and saw the dim glow of a tavern sign.

"Good grief," she muttered. "I think he's headed for the Green Wall Tavern. No wonder he tried to talk his client out of meeting him here."

"Not an upscale, trendy kind of place, I take it?"

"It's a bottom-of-the-barrel dive. Makes you wonder what kind of lowlife Ryan is working for. He's got a lot of nerve bad-mouthing you for being involved with the Guild when *his* client schedules meetings in a joint like the Green Wall."

"Nice to know I'm a step up," Emmet said humbly.

Lydia was grateful for the dark shadows of the front seat. She knew she had gone very red.

She watched Ryan climb out of the Coaster, lock it carefully, and then glance around uneasily.

"He doesn't like the looks of the neighborhood," Emmett remarked as he angled the Slider into a space at the curb.

"I don't blame him."

Ryan started down the sidewalk toward the Green Wall Tavern. He glanced back at the Coaster several times.

"He's afraid that when he returns, he's going to find his windows smashed and his car stripped," Lydia said. It belatedly occurred to her that the Slider made an even more tempting target for street vandals than Ryan's Coaster. "And the same thing might happen to your car, Emmett. Maybe we should park somewhere else."

"Don't worry about the Slider." He cracked the door and got out. "I don't think we'll have any trouble."

Unconvinced, Lydia scrambled out of her side and looked at him over the top of the vehicle. "This is one of the worst sections of the Old Quarter in Cadence."

"The car will be okay." Emmett came around the front of the Slider and took her arm. "I've got insurance."

"Even so, if we come back here and find the Slider's been stripped we'll be stuck." She peered worriedly back over her shoulder, much as Ryan had done a moment ago.

She caught a glint of green.

She stopped in her tracks and turned fully around to stare at the parked car. There was a very faint but unmistakable acid-green glow hovering around the license plate of the Slider.

Emmett stopped beside her and glanced casually back at the glowing license plate. "I told you, I have insurance."

"Whew! You can say that again. No car prowler with an eighth of a brain would touch the car of a ghost-hunter strong enough to leave a small ghost hanging around. How did you do that?"

"No big deal. There's plenty of stray psi energy around here. More than enough for me to anchor a little of it to the car for a while."

If Emmett could summon even a tiny ghost and leave it attached to his car while he was halfway down the street, she mused, he was much more powerful than she had guessed.

Not that the news should have come as a major surprise, she thought. Weak ghost-hunters probably did not rise to the top in the Guild's hierarchy. All the same . . .

"Sheesh," she muttered.

"Come on." He took her arm again and tugged her away from the glowing license plate. "We don't want to lose Kelso."

There would be time enough later to sweat out the implications of doing business with a hunter who could set a ghost to guard his car in a bad neighborhood, Lydia thought. She forced herself back to the problem of Ryan's anonymous client.

"We can't follow Ryan into the tavern," she said. "He'll see us."

"So what? We just want to identify his client. Once we see who it is he's meeting, it won't matter if he spots us."

His logic made sense, but it did nothing to quiet her growing unease. On the other hand, she reminded herself, she was in no position to argue. Following Ryan had been her idea.

Mute, she allowed Emmett to guide her into the synch-smoke-and-gloom-filled interior of the Green Wall. She saw at once that the place was several rungs lower on the tavern evolutionary scale than the Surreal Lounge. Whereas the Surreal exuded a kind of cheerful seediness, the Green Wall was a rough-and-ready, serious drinking place—the clientele had no doubt been asked to leave the premises of other, more upwardly mobile establishments.

Her fears of being seen by Ryan faded swiftly. In places like this, people tended to avoid eye contact. Besides, Ryan was bound to be more nervous than anyone else here. The last thing he was likely to do was look for someone he might recognize.

Emmett found a small booth on the side, and Lydia slipped into the corner. A waitress appeared to take their orders. Emmett sent her away with a request for two beers.

Lydia leaned forward. "Do you see Ryan?"

"He's at the bar. Alone."

"Any chance that he spotted us when we came in?"

Emmett shook his head. "He's got his head down, nursing a beer. I don't think he wants to be seen here any more than we want him to see us."

"Hmm. Maybe his big-time client stood him up." That possibility amused her. "He won't like that. Ryan's used to people worrying about keeping *him* waiting."

The beers arrived a few minutes later. Lydia peered cautiously toward the bar. She managed to catch a glimpse of Ryan, who looked as if he wished he was invisible. He was definitely not having a good time, she thought.

"Looks like he's been stood up, all right," Emmett said thoughtfully. "Interesting."

There was another small break in the crowd. Lydia saw the bartender move down the bar to where Ryan was hunched over his beer. The man must have said something, because Ryan's head came up swiftly.

"We've got a problem." Emmett was on his feet. "Stay here. Whatever you do, don't go back to the car alone. Got that?"

"I've got absolutely no intention of leaving without you. What's going on? Where are you going?"

"The bartender just handed Kelso a note. I don't think it was a thank-you from the mystery client. I'll be right back."

He turned and started toward the bar. Lydia gave him a minute, during which a sense of impending disaster settled on her. Emmett was walking into trouble. She knew it as surely as she knew her own name.

She put down the beer, grabbed her purse, and slid out of the booth. Plunging through the crowd, she made her way toward the bar, arriving just in time to see Ryan slinking uncomfortably toward the dark hallway marked REST ROOMS. Emmett was hard on his heels, gliding through the throng like a shark through the water.

Both men disappeared into the shadowy passageway. Panic wafted through her. Something was going very wrong here.

Clutching her purse tightly, she pushed her way through the tangle of people gathered around the bar. The synch-smoke was so thick she had to wave her hand in front of her face to clear the air.

She paused in mid-wave when she saw the huge man with hot, bleary eyes looming in front of her. He wore badly stained ghost-hunter khakis and leathers. His hair had even more grease on it than his clothes did. The smell of alcohol on his breath was so strong she was tempted to stop breathing.

"Hey, there, you're a cute little thing." He gave her what was no doubt meant to be a devilishly sexy grin, but it fell short and landed somewhere in the vicinity of a drunken leer. "You all alone, honey?"

"No," she said coldly. "I'm with someone. Please let me pass."

"Who is he?" The man swayed slightly as he surveyed the crowd behind her. "Point him out. I'll bet I can convince him to let you go home with me."

"I doubt it. Get out of my way."

"The name's Durant. I'm a hunter."

"No kidding." She tried to step around him, but he slid back in front of her.

"You ever had yerself a good time with a hunter, cute thing?" He winked broadly. "We're a little extra-special. Know what I mean?"

"Odd you should bring that up. I just happen to be here with a hunter tonight, and he's not going to be real happy if he finds out you're putting the make on me. Now get out of my way."

"Don't you worry, cute thing. I'll invite him out back and fry his brains for him. He won't have much to say for a while after I get finished with him."

"I was under the impression that the Guild frowned on hunter duels," Lydia said icily.

"Nah. It just don't like 'em to get into the papers, that's all." Durant stretched out a massive hand. "Why don't you and me have us a drink? When your ex-boyfriend shows up, I'll take care of him."

"You want a drink, Durant?" She grabbed a glass off a passing tray. "Here, have one on me."

She dashed the contents of the glass straight into his face. The smell of cheap Green Ruin whiskey made her wince. Durant howled and staggered backward, wiping off the dripping liquid.

"Well, *shit*." Durant blinked several times, then smiled with delight. "I always wanted me a high-spirited-type female."

Seizing her chance, Lydia hurried past him and plunged into the rest-room hallway.

"Hey, come back here, cute thing." Durant lumbered into pursuit. "Don't go runnin' off like that. I do believe you're the woman I've been lookin' for since the day I turned thirteen. *I love you, darlin'*."

The evening was deteriorating rapidly. Lydia wrinkled her nose when she caught a whiff of the odors that seeped beneath the rest-room doors. She kept going, searching for the rear exit.

She turned a corner and saw the door to the alley. There was no sign of either Ryan or Emmett, but she caught a glimpse of a faint green glow coming through the opening. Ghost light.

Bad sign, she thought.

"Come back here, cute thing," Durant shouted euphorically. "I wanna marry you. I want you to have my babies, darlin'."

She stepped through the open doorway into the rank alley. Psi energy crackled in the air. She spun around, searching for the source of the ghost light. She froze when she saw the tableau illuminated in the eerie green glow.

Two ghost-hunters were closing in on Ryan, who had flattened himself against the back wall of the tavern. The assailants were each manipulating moderate-sized ghosts. They were using the green energy manifestations to pin Ryan. In the acid light his face was a mask of fear.

Lydia realized the hunters must have been waiting for him. They had trapped him, and now they were manipulating the ghosts closer. The slow, inefficient way in which the energy danced in the darkness told her that the assailants were young and inexperienced in the handling of psi energy.

But their intentions were clear. They were going to fry Ryan.

The glowing balls of dissonance energy had to be at least eighteen inches across. Serious-sized ghosts, considering that the young specter-cats were working outside the Dead City. The youths might be clumsy, but they were strong para rezes.

Neither ghost alone would have been enough to do more than knock Ryan unconscious, maybe give him a few hours of amnesia. But together the pair could kill him or, at the very least, scramble his brains, perhaps permanently.

"Well, shit." Durant floundered to a halt behind Lydia and peered out into the alley. "What the hell's goin' on out here? We got us a little hunter duel?"

Lydia ignored him. She was too busy trying to locate Emmett in the darkness.

She saw the ghost he conjured first. Without warning, green fire burst into a sheet of blazing energy that was larger than the two smaller ghosts combined.

Emmett stepped out of the shadows of the Dead City wall on the other side of the alley. Around him, the night shimmered and danced with resonating energy. The ghost he had summoned floated toward the two hunters who had pinned Ryan.

"Well, shit," Durant said again, this time in a tone of near-reverent awe. "I don't believe the size of that ghost. And we're not even inside the wall. Whoever he is, he's gonna fry the lot of 'em."

The two young hunters who were closing in on Ryan must have sensed the large UDEM floating toward them. They whirled quickly.

"What the hell?" The first hunter stared, stunned at the advancing ghost. "There's the other guy. Get him."

"He's too strong. He's gonna fry us."

"We can take him."

They just might be able to do it, Lydia thought, horrified.

"Stop it!" she shouted. "I'm calling the police. This is illegal!"

No one paid any attention to her. The two ghosts the youths had been manipulating toward Ryan reversed course and veered to intercept the energy field that Emmett had summoned. The three shimmering balls of raw energy collided. Green sparks showered the night. Acid-green light flared high, crackling dangerously in the air.

Lydia closed her eyes to keep from being temporarily blinded by the bright flash. When she opened them a second later, fearing the worst, she saw Emmett's face starkly etched in the trailing edge of the eerie glow. She was certain that some of the backwash must have caught him, but he seemed unaffected. He kept moving forward. So did his ghost.

The two smaller ghosts winked out.

"He got mine." The second of the two assailants sounded terrified now. He whirled and ran.

The other youth did not respond. He was already fleeing into the night.

Emmett's ghost disappeared too. But another one, considerably smaller, snapped into existence just in front of one of the running youths.

"I'll be damned," Durant sounded deeply impressed. "Haven't seen anything that quick in years. Bushwhacked the little sonofobitch."

Lydia held her breath as the fleeing youth blundered straight into the energy field. It blinked out of existence as quickly as it had appeared, but she knew it had caught the young man. He stiffened and then crumpled to the pavement. He did not move.

Emmett went to stand beside the fallen youth.

"Is he . . . ?" Lydia took a step toward the pair and halted. "Emmett, is he okay?"

"He'll be fine. He just caught some of the de-rez backwash. He'll be out for a while."

"Thank goodness." She glanced at Ryan, who was still slumped against the wall, looking dazed. When she turned back she saw that Emmett was swiftly going through the hunter's pockets.

"What are we going to do with him?" Lydia asked.

"Nothing." Emmett fished a wallet out of the youth's back pocket, flipped it open. "I just want to see who he is."

"Well, shit," Durant said.

Emmett looked up from the open wallet. For the first time he seemed to notice the big man standing in the open doorway.

"Who's that?" he asked Lydia.

Lydia looked at Durant, who was staring openmouthed at Emmett. "That's Durant. He says he's in love with me. He wants me to marry him and have his babies."

"Is that so?" Emmett gave Durant a speculative look.

Durant gulped and managed to close his mouth. "No. *No.* Big misunderstanding." He flapped his hands in a warding-off gesture. "Just a passing acquaintance, that's all."

"He mentioned something about dueling you for my hand," Lydia said.

"Yeah?" Emmett watched Durant very steadily.

"She's got it all wrong," Durant yelped. He staggered backward, then turned clumsily and disappeared into the darkness of the tavern hall.

"It's exactly like they tell you in all the women's magazines," Lydia said. "Men these days just can't seem to commit."

CHAPTER 23

RYAN SPRAWLED ON THE SOFA IN HIS LIVING ROOM AND gulped brandy from the large glass he held in a hand that still shook. "Look, I'd tell you if I knew anything useful. But the truth is, we did everything over the phone until tonight."

Kelso was not the only one still feeling the aftereffects of the ghost-storm in the alley, Emmett thought. There was a price to be paid for using the intensive level of psi energy he had needed to deal with the two young ghost-hunters tonight. And just to make things interesting, he'd been clumsy enough to get caught in the backwash. He'd been here before. He knew what to expect.

Right now he was in the restless stage, his senses still rezzed, the adrenaline not yet flushed from his system. Lydia's friend Melanie had been right about one aspect of hunter physiology, he reflected dourly. In spite of the more immediate issues that logic told him had to be dealt with tonight, he was very horny. It wasn't something he couldn't control, and he knew the sense of urgency would fade soon. Nevertheless, he would have given anything to be alone with Lydia right now.

Not any woman, just Lydia.

Oh, brother. He was in big trouble.

He watched her out of the corner of his eye, yearning and need twisting through him. She was not paying any attention. She was too busy zeroing in on the hapless Ryan.

"You mean to tell me that you didn't sign a formal contract with your client, Ryan?" Her voice was laced with supercilious disapproval.

She was gloating, Emmett thought. On the surface she was projecting concern and a perfectly appropriate degree of professional dismay, but underneath she was definitely gloating. Kelso had screwed up badly, and she was not going to let him forget it. Served the bastard right, Emmett thought. But they did have more pressing concerns at the moment.

"The guy sounded legitimate," Ryan said defensively.

"You mean he mentioned worked dreamstone and you got all rezzed-up," Lydia retorted. "Honestly, Ryan, what were you thinking? Dreamstone, of all things."

Ryan slumped deeper into his brandy, momentarily, at least, a beaten man.

Lydia tut-tutted and moved in for the kill. "And everyone assumes that *my* brains got fried."

Serious gloating, Emmett thought. But she did look sexy as hell.

Damn, this was stupid. Even if he did have her alone in a bedroom, she would probably kick him out. She would assume that his erection was caused by the energy burn.

She would be right, but only partially so. He did want her— badly—but what he was feeling tonight was not the usual short-lived generalized sexual desire that resulted from a major burn. This was a lot stronger, more potent, and it was focused only on her. He didn't want just sex tonight, he wanted sex with Lydia.

He wondered if she could grasp the significance of the distinction. He certainly did. It left him reeling.

He took a deep breath and clamped down on his hormones. In an hour or so, when the last of the burn effects wore off, he would forget all about sex with Lydia or anyone else. The only thing on his mind would be sleep. He would need a bed far more than he would need to get laid. Until then he just had to tough it out and concentrate on the problem of Ryan Kelso.

He studied the spines on the volumes on the bookcase as he listened to Ryan ramble on about the evening's events. He'd seen many of the same titles in Lydia's bookcases, both the one in her apartment and the one in her office. They included Caldwell Frost's infamous *Dawn in a Dead City*, Arriola's *Theory and Practice of Para-Archaeology*, and several years' worth of the *Journal of Para-Archaeology*. But whereas the books on Lydia's shelves were arranged in a jumbled clutter that gave you the feeling she actually read them, Kelso's library was painfully neat.

Emmett turned slowly to survey the room. The old-fashioned leather furniture, the carved oak desk, and the dark carpet with its intricate, harmonically proportioned design all said, "I Am An Academic Honcho" in capital letters. The place looked as if it was ready to be photographed for a feature on scholarly rooms for *Harmonic Architecture Review*. What the hell had Lydia ever seen in this jerk?

He made himself concentrate on the problem at hand. Turning away from the bookcase, he looked at Ryan. He was pretty sure that Kelso was telling the truth, or at least as much of it as he knew.

Ryan was washed out—still scared and still in shock. He knew he'd had one hell of a close call.

"Someone may have tried to kill you tonight," Emmett said flatly. "At the very least, those two hunters intended to fry you into a short-term coma. Your so-called client lured you to the Green Wall Tavern. Therefore, we have to assume he's the one who wanted you burned."

Ryan scowled into his brandy. "What are you saying?"

"I'm saying that you must know something."

"But I don't," Ryan whispered. "I swear it. All I know is a man calls me on the phone, claims to be a collector, talks like he knows the field, says he's heard a rumor of worked dreamstone and that you're in town looking for it, London. He says you've hired Lydia to help you find it."

"That's it?" Emmett asked.

"That's it. You don't fry a man because of a rumor of dreamstone. Hell, there've been wild stories about the stuff since it was first discovered. Collectors have chased the tales for years."

Emmett began to pace in an effort to work off the last of the adrenaline. "Tell me exactly what your client said this afternoon when you informed him that Lydia would not cooperate with you."

Ryan shrugged weakly. "He said he wanted to discuss some other angles we could take to locate the dreamstone. He told me to meet him at the Tavern at eleven. When I got there the bartender gave me that note telling me that the client wanted to rendezvous in the alley."

"You didn't find that just a little suspicious?" Lydia asked archly.

Ryan winced. "The guy made it clear from the beginning that he wanted to maintain a very low profile. I thought he was just trying to avoid being seen in the bar."

"A meeting in a back alley in the Old Quarter is low profile, all right," Lydia murmured.

Ryan's jaw tensed. "So call me stupid."

"Only if you insist," Lydia said cheerfully.

Emmett groaned. "Entertaining though it may be, we don't have time for the sniping. We need to get Ryan out of town. The last commuter flight to Resonance City leaves in less than an hour."

"What?" Ryan straightened abruptly, his face working. "I'm not going anywhere."

"You are if you know what's good for you." Emmett glanced at his watch. The yellow-gold disk was clouded from the intense burn. He must remember to replace it with fresh, tuned amber as soon as possible. So many details. "You've got five minutes to throw some clothes into a bag. Then we've got to get you to the airport."

"But—"

"Someone will meet you at the gate in Resonance," Emmett said.

Ryan looked truculent. "Who's going to meet me?"

"A couple of hunters from the Resonance Guild."

"Thanks, but no thanks." Ryan slammed his brandy glass down on the table. "No offense, but I'm not real keen on meeting any more ghost-hunters tonight."

Emmett held his attention. "Whoever tried to fry you tonight will probably try again. Maybe real soon. You need bodyguards. Under normal circumstances, I'd call Mercer Wyatt and arrange for protection here in Cadence, but I don't think that's a good idea right now. The local Guild is having some problems."

Lydia sniffed. "You can say that again."

Emmett ignored her. "If you don't get on that plane, Kelso, you're going to have to look over your shoulder every minute until this thing is finished."

"What about Lydia?" Ryan demanded. "If I'm in danger, so is she."

Emmett glanced at Lydia.

"Don't even think about it," she said crisply.

He looked back at Ryan. "I'll take care of Lydia."

"Yeah? And who's going to take care of you? The next time they may use three hunters instead of two. Everyone has his limits."

"I'm in a slightly more advantageous position than you are," Emmett said quietly. "For one thing, I'm a lot harder to fry. For another, if someone does succeed in burning me, he'll have a lot more to worry about than if he burns you."

"What do you mean?" Ryan's chin came up with arrogant disdain. "I'm a full professor at the university. I'm the head of the Department of Para-archaeology, damn it. If anything happened to me, the cops would be all over the case in a minute."

Emmett smiled humorlessly. "Maybe. But if anything happens to me while I'm in Cadence, it isn't only the cops who will be all over this thing. Mercer Wyatt would have to explain the situation to the head of the Resonance Guild. He wouldn't like that."

Lydia gave him a sharp, searching look, but she said nothing.

Ryan blinked in a befuddled fashion. Then comprehension settled in his eyes. "I see. This is a Guild matter."

"Yes."

"That does complicate things, doesn't it?" Ryan got to his feet with weary resignation. "I'd better pack." Shoulders slumped, he turned and walked out into the hall.

Lydia waited until he had disappeared. Then she switched her gaze back to Emmett. "Are you sure you're all right?"

"I'm fine. Just got to replace some amber, that's all."

"Replace it?" she said, concern echoing in her voice. "You melted amber?"

He shrugged. "Happens sometimes."

"Not to most people," she said brusquely. "My God, Emmett, if you used so much energy that you actually de-rezzed your amber, you must be half dead on your feet."

"I'll be okay. For a while, at any rate. Long enough to get Kelso to the airport." He rubbed the back of his neck. "When we get back to your place, though, I'm going to need some sleep."

"I can imagine," she said, then lowered her voice. "What did you find in that young hunter's wallet? Anything useful?"

"He wasn't carrying any ID."

"Oh, damn. I was hoping we'd be able to trace him."

"He was probably ordered to make certain he didn't carry anything that could be traced," Emmett said. "But he was a young man. Not well trained and probably not accustomed to thinking things through. He made one small mistake."

"What was that?"

"He'd removed his ID from his wallet, all right, but he forget his gym locker key. I left it where it was. With luck he won't realize that someone looked at it."

Lydia's eyes lit up with eagerness. "What gym does he use?"

"The key was stamped 'Transverse Wave Youth Shelter.'"

AN HOUR LATER LYDIA PARKED THE SLIDER IN THE apartment complex lot, de-rezzed the key, and looked at Emmett with growing concern.

He was sprawled in the passenger seat, head against the padded headrest. He kept telling her he was okay, but she no longer believed him.

As soon as they had put Ryan on board the last flight to Resonance

City, Emmett had made a phone call to arrange for someone to meet the plane on the other end. He had talked to the person he reached for a few more minutes and then he had hung up. Standing outside the privacy booth, she was unable to hear the details of the conversation.

By the time he rejoined her, she was too concerned about him to ask any questions. She knew that he was in bad shape. When she took his arm on the way out of the terminal, he did not protest. Halfway back to the car, he started to lean heavily on her. She asked him for the Slider's keys so she could drive them home. He didn't argue.

"Emmett?" She put her hand on his shoulder and shook him gently. "Wake up. We're here."

He stirred but seemed disoriented. "Need some sleep."

She wondered if she ought to call someone for advice on how to handle post-meltdown syndrome. The truth was, she could not think of anyone who might know what to do. Melting amber was a very rare event, primarily because so few people possessed enough psi talent to do it. And those who were capable of it probably did not talk too much about the aftermath, especially if they were macho hunters who didn't like admitting to weakness of any kind.

Melting amber was just an expression. The stuff didn't actually melt under too much psi energy, but it did get "fogged." It lost the fine-tuned quality that made it able to focus accurately.

Lydia reached out, caught Emmett's face between her hands, and forced him to look at her. "Listen to me. Do you need a doctor?"

He shook his head once. She got the impression he was annoyed, maybe even disgusted.

"Need sleep." His voice had thickened.

His hand moved. She realized he was groping for the door handle.

"Hang on." She opened her own door and jumped out of the car. "I'll come around to your side and help you."

By the time she reached him, Emmett had managed to get his door open, but the bleak, barely-hanging-in-there look on his face told her that he did not think he could haul himself out of the front seat.

"I'll just sleep it off here," he said weakly.

"You want to spend the night in your car? In this part of town? Don't be ridiculous. It's not safe."

"Can't make it up the damn stairs."

"Wait here," Lydia said. "I'll get Zane and Olinda. We'll get you up the stairs."

Emmett did not protest. He was evidently beyond making the effort. Lydia hurried to the stairwell and took the steps two at a time to the third floor. She was breathless by the time she reached 3A.

Zane opened the door on the second knock. He was dressed in his pajamas. Behind him, the front room of the apartment was lit by the glow of the rez-screen.

Lydia said the first words that came into her head. "Shouldn't you be in bed?"

"I was in bed. I sleep in the living room, remember?"

This was no time to point out that it was far too late for him to be watching the rez-screen. "I need some help, Zane."

His face scrunched in alarm. "What's wrong? Is it Fuzz? Another ghost?"

"No, it's Emmett. He got into a brawl with some other ghost-hunters tonight. He melted amber and now he's exhausted. I need to get him up the stairs. Is Olinda home?"

"He melted amber?" Zane's eyes widened. "Holy shit!"

Olinda loomed in the hallway. Her robust figure was sheathed in an aging chenille robe. "Must be one hell of a hunter. Where is he?"

"Downstairs in the car." Lydia stepped back. "Can you give me a hand?"

"You bet. Can't wait to see this." Zane dashed through the doorway and pelted wildly toward the stairs.

Olinda followed more sedately. She closed the door behind her and joined Lydia in the hall. "I've heard these guys who can melt amber have to crash for a few hours afterward."

Lydia went swiftly back toward the stairwell. "He keeps saying he needs to sleep."

"Doesn't sound like he'll be much fun for a while." Olinda winked. "Maybe you shoulda picked one who wasn't quite as strong as London. I hear that the after-effects of a normal-range amber burn are kinda interesting in ghost-hunters."

CHAPTER 24

THE HIDDEN CHAMBER GLOWED WITH RESONATING GREEN
light. Strange shadows appeared and disappeared on the walls. She
sensed that some were doorways, but whenever she tried to ap-
proach one of the shifting dark patches, it vanished before she
could walk through it.

Panic tightened her throat. She knew she must not let it over-
whelm her. There had to be a way out of the chamber.

She went cautiously toward what appeared to be another dark-
ened opening in the green quartz wall. She put out a hand, half
expecting that this doorway would dissolve, just as the others had.

But instead of the wall, her fingers touched only air. Hardly
daring to breathe, she went through the doorway into the ante-
chamber.

She sensed illusion energy and halted. She searched the deep shadows and saw nothing. But she knew the trap was here, some-where. She could feel it.

Then she saw the small dreamstone chest in the center of the room. She went slowly toward it, reached down, lifted the lid, and saw the photograph inside. Chester grinned at her from the picture.

Lydia awoke with a start. Fuzz was in her lap, his front paws braced on her chest. All four of his eyes were open.

"What's wrong?" she whispered.

She gazed wildly around the small living room, searching the shad-ows. But things appeared normal, or at least as normal as they could when you had a ghost-hunter sleeping on the sofa.

Emmett was stretched out on the cushions, still sound asleep, his head turned away from her.

Fuzz took his paws off her chest, closed his hunting eyes, and curled up again on her lap. He closed his daylight eyes too. The all-clear sign.

She stroked his fluffy gray fur absently. She had probably alarmed him when she was in the throes of her dream. Perhaps she had moved or muttered something.

After a while she picked Fuzz up and nestled him into the corner of the big chair. He did not open his eyes, merely shifted and made himself comfortable again.

She got to her feet and padded to the sofa. She reached down and pulled the blankets up higher around Emmett's shoulders. He did not stir.

She went to the window, pushed her hands into the deep sleeves of her robe, and looked out at her sliver-thin view of the Dead City. The images of the dream wafted through her head.

After a while she turned and walked toward the hall that led to her bedroom. In the nick of time she remembered the little table and avoided it.

When she reached her room she went to the dresser and looked down at the photo she had left there. The light from the partially open bathroom door angled across it. She could see Chester grinning at her, just as he had in the dream. She glanced at the copy of the *Journal of Para-archaeology* in his hand. He had been so proud to be listed as a consultant.

She went back out into the living room and settled once more into the depths of the big chair. Stretching out her legs, she propped her slippered feet on the footstool and pulled the lapels of her robe more snugly around her.

For a long time she just sat there, thinking and gazing out into the night.

EMMETT AWOKE WITH A VAGUE SENSE OF DISORIENTA-tion. Then the memory of the burn-fest in the alley washed through him. He raised his wrist, opened his eyes, and stared at the face of the watch. Five o'clock in the morning. He calculated that he'd had three hours of solid afterburn sleep. Not exactly a good night's rest, but sufficient time for his body to recover from the heavy expenditure of psi energy.

He sensed another presence in the small room and turned his head. Lydia was curled deep into the wing chair near the window, her head pillowed in the corner and her legs tucked beneath the folds of her robe. From the crook of her arm, blue eyes blinked at him.

He pushed aside the covers and sat up cautiously. Glancing down,

After Dark

he discovered that someone, presumably Lydia, had removed his shirt. The thought that she had undressed him was an intriguing one. Then he realized that he was still wearing his trousers. Either she hadn't been able to get them off or the prospect of doing so had not appealed to her. He consoled himself with the possibility that she might simply have lost her nerve.

The blanket fell aside as he got to his feet. He had no memory of pulling it up over himself. He went down the hall to the ever-lit bathroom.

Inside the small room he turned on the faucet and leaned over the sink to splash cold water on his face. When he caught sight of himself in the mirror, he winced.

He went back out into the living room. Lydia had not moved, but Fuzz was gone from beneath her arm. Emmett glanced into the kitchen and saw the dust-bunny on the counter near the pretzel jar. Fuzz didn't appear to need any help getting at the pretzels.

He went back to the sofa, sat down amid the tumbled blankets, and propped his elbows on his thighs. He linked his fingers loosely together and looked at Lydia. Why the hell had she slept in that chair? Did she think she needed to stand guard over him? Was she afraid he was going to go berserk because of the amber burn? Another little hunter eccentricity? Maybe she was worried that he would tear up the place.

He noticed that she was awake now, watching him from the depths of the chair.

"How do you feel?" she asked. Her voice was soft and husky.

"Almost back to normal."

"You gave me a bit of a scare last night. I've never seen a ghost-hunter in that condition."

He ran one hand over his face, felt the rough stubble of his beard. He needed to shave. Soon.

"Speaking personally," he said, "I try to avoid it."

"I can understand that. You still don't look in great shape. Maybe you should go back to sleep."

"I'm okay, damn it."

"You don't have to bite my head off. It's not my fault you look like you just spent the night getting into a brawl behind a sleazy tavern."

He started to answer that and then thought better of it. "Why did you sleep in that chair?"

"I wanted to keep an eye on you. Zane and Olinda seemed to think you would be okay, but I wasn't so sure."

"Shit. I'm not an invalid, you know. The burn-and-crash syndrome is absolutely normal. At least, it is after you've used as much energy as I did last night."

She yawned. "You're welcome."

This was not going well. He was getting edgy again. It seemed to happen a lot around Lydia. He tried to distract himself.

"Thanks for getting me up here," he mumbled. "You were right. Spending the night downstairs in the parking lot was probably not one of my brighter ideas."

"No problem. Zane and Olinda helped."

"Uh-huh." He had a vague memory of everyone dragging, hauling, and pushing him up five flights of stairs. Talk about looking like an invalid. No wonder she had slept in the chair. Probably thought he needed a night nurse.

"Too bad the elevator is out." Great. Now he was rambling.

"You can say that again. Driffield's gonna pay one of these days." She pulled her robe closer around her throat and started to rise.

"Well, since it doesn't look like either one of us is going to go back to sleep, I may as well take a shower and get dressed."

He stood up at the same time she did and blocked her path to the bedroom. She came to a halt directly in front of him and searched his face.

"Are you sure you're all right?" she asked.

"No. I am not all right." He cupped her face in his hands. "But I'm not going to go crazy and rip up your apartment."

"I never thought you'd do anything of the kind," she said defensively.

"Sure, you did. It was written all over your face. You've been nervous about me right from the start. And every time some little quirk related to hunter physiology comes up, your freak out again. That's what happened last night, isn't it?"

"I don't believe this." She stared at him with gathering outrage. "You're upset because I spent the night here so that I could watch over you?"

"I am not upset," he said through his teeth. "But I am pissed as hell. Damn it, I'm not sick. I'm not going to lose it and wreak havoc in your living room. You didn't have to keep a vigil over me as if I was some unpredictable wild beast."

Temper flared, and then, without warning, her expression softened. "Take it easy. Calm down. You're not quite yourself yet. Why don't you go take your shower first? I'll have a nice hot cup of rez-tea waiting when you come out."

Her soothing tone nearly sent him over the edge. "I don't want any damned tea."

Her gentle concern evaporated. "Why are you so irritable this morning? I was *worried* about you last night. You scared the daylights out of me when you collapsed on my sofa."

"I didn't collapse. I fell asleep. Big difference."

"You collapsed."

"I fell asleep. But guess what?"

"What?"

"I'm wide awake now." He pulled her close and crushed her mouth beneath his.

For an instant he thought she was going to explode with outrage. She sucked in her breath, her fingers curled into his shoulder.

And then she was kissing him back. *Fiercely.* Everything within him leaped into high rez. Urgency swept through him. He felt her respond to it. Her arms tightened around him as she fought him for the embrace.

They were definitely on the same frequency, he decided. He wasn't quite sure how the dissonance of their mutual hostility had metamorphosed so abruptly into near-violent sexual resonance, but he sure as hell was not going to take time to analyze it right now.

He yanked open her robe. She fumbled with the fastening of his trousers, got them unzipped. He felt himself surge forward into her waiting hands and groaned aloud. When her fingers tightened around him he wanted to shout.

He turned slightly, taking her with him, stepped back and half-fell, half-sank deep into the big, overstuffed chair. She tumbled down on top of him, warm and soft and scented with desire. Her robe fluttered over the arms of the chair as she settled astride him and closed her thighs around his.

He reached down and found the hot, wet place between her legs. She gasped when he dampened his fingers in her heat, breathed deeply when he stroked her clitoris. Her head tipped back. Her hair spilled down her back.

He gripped the wonderfully rounded flesh of her buttocks and thrust himself deep into her snug, tight body.

"Emmett."

He felt her fingers digging into his shoulders as he pushed himself to the hilt. She started to move on him, swift, urgent, excited motions. He found the swollen little bud once more, inserted his finger under it, just inside the already tautly stretched passage.

"Yes." Her breath was warm in his ear. *"Yes."*

He stroked into her, oblivious of everything now except the driving sense of need that consumed him. He felt her shudder, felt her convulse along the entire length of him. Her delicate harmonic shivers established a resonance as irresistible as the pull of gravity.

His release burned through him, hotter than melting amber. He pumped himself dry and then collapsed in exhaustion for the second time.

HE SURFACED A LONG WHILE LATER. LYDIA WAS STILL astride him, her face buried in the curve of his neck. Her body was damp, and he could smell his own scent on her. A raw, elemental sense of possessiveness surged through him. He wrapped his fingers around her upper thighs.

"I'd like to reiterate my main point," she mumbled.

"What was that? I think I forgot."

"I did not sleep out here because I thought you might go berserk and tear up my living room."

"You're sure?"

"I'm sure." She paused. "But if that's what you really want to do, be my guest."

"Thanks. Some other time, maybe."

"Whatever." She raised her head and looked down at him. In the pale dawn light her throat and cheeks were flushed. Her mouth and eyes were soft. She smiled.

He felt his body stir again. He tightened his hands on her thighs. "On second thought, maybe I will go berserk and tear up your apartment after all."

HE PUT THE WATER ON FOR THE REZ-TEA WHILE LYDIA sliced glistening oranges into two bowls. It occurred to him that he was already starting to feel much too comfortable in the cramped apartment.

He was going to have to come up with an excuse to hang around after he cleared up this mess involving Quinn. He wasn't sure yet what was happening between Lydia and himself, but whatever it was, he didn't want to walk away from it. Not yet.

"What do we do next?" Lydia asked as she sat down beside him at the counter.

Optimism soared. They were apparently on the same frequency again this morning. Life was good.

"Funny you should mention that," he said. "I've been thinking."

"Me, too." She spooned up a mouthful of orange. "Everything points to the Transverse Wave Youth Shelter, right?"

"Right." So much for being on the same frequency. Emmett squelched his brief flash of optimism and refocused his attention.

"The Cadence Guild started funding the shelter earlier this year." Lydia looked at him as she blotted orange juice from her lips. "And we know that Tamara Wyatt was the driving force behind the Guild's new civic consciousness. Mercer Wyatt believes he's got a traitor close to him. Maybe that traitor is even closer than he thinks."

"I know where you're going here, but it doesn't work."

"Emmett, I understand that you and Tamara have a past. You were in love with her. Maybe you still are—"

"No."

"Denial is no way to deal with these kinds of issues."

"I am not in denial. I'm telling you that I no longer have any strong feelings for Tamara."

"Right. She dumped you for another man. Of course you've got some strong feelings about her."

"Can we stick to the subject?" he asked evenly.

She looked as if she was going to argue. But she must have seen something in his face that changed her mind. She cleared her throat instead.

"Okay, fine," she said briskly. "I believe we were considering the possibility that Tamara is involved in whatever is going on at the shelter."

"Don't think so," Emmett said.

She glared at him. "Why do you keep insisting she's innocent? We've already decided that everything that's happened is connected. Chester's piece of dreamstone, his death, the missing youths, and Greeley's murder."

"I know."

"The common link is the shelter."

"Lydia—"

"There is one other fact that you can't ignore. Everything that's happened has taken place in the past few months. After Tamara's marriage to Wyatt. After she directed the Guild to set up a charitable foundation and start funding the Transverse Wave Youth Shelter. It all points to Tamara. Admit it."

He couldn't deny her logic. He pondered the problem for a few seconds, trying to find words for what until now had been only an instinctive reaction to the facts.

"Whatever is going on at the shelter, I agree that it's probably connected to the dreamstone," he said at last.

"So?"

"Think about it. Dreamstone is potentially extremely valuable both as an archaeological discovery and in the private collectors' market."

"Right. Whoever gets his hands on it can use it to establish an instant, brilliant reputation in the academic world. But in order to do so, he would have to turn it over to a museum."

"If someone who wasn't connected to the university wanted to capitalize on the discovery of dreamstone to become a celebrity, he or she would have to go public. That would mean holding press conferences. Giving interviews."

"Hmm."

"On the other hand, if the discoverer was planning to turn a huge profit on the dreamstone, he would have a good incentive to keep the find secret until he could do deals in the private market. That would be especially true if the excavation work was being carried out illegally."

"It's pretty obvious that someone is trying to keep the discovery quiet and that the excavation work is being done illegally. So what? How does that make Tamara innocent?"

"Everything about this operation points to someone who wants to keep it secret," Emmett said. "If Tamara was involved in this, she would be far more interested in the publicity than the money."

"Hmm," Lydia said again.

"As Mercer Wyatt's wife, she's already got access to all the money she could ever want."

"Some people never have enough money."

"What Tamara craves," he said patiently, "is social status and the power that comes with it. She wants to rub elbows with the right people. She wants to sit on the boards of charitable foundations, give fund-raisers for the arts, get invited to the homes of the movers and shakers. Believe me, if she got her hands on dreamstone, she would go public with it in a big way."

Lydia tapped her spoon on the edge of the bowl that held the oranges. "I guess you know her better than I do."

"Yeah." He shook cereal out of the box into his bowl. "I do."

She gave him a quick, unreadable glance, but she did not pursue the subject of his relationship with Tamara. "Okay, so we rule out Tamara based on your gut feeling that her motives don't fit the secrecy scenario we've uncovered. And it doesn't look like Ryan is directly involved, either."

"Someone tried to use him to find out how much you know about the missing piece of dreamstone, though," Emmett said. "Whoever is behind this knows we're getting close."

Lydia put down her spoon. "Last night I did a lot of thinking. Among other things, it occurred to me that whoever lured Ryan to the Green Wall Tavern may have had something else in mind besides getting rid of him."

He grunted and concentrated on eating cereal.

"Emmett?"

"Yeah?"

"Did you hear me?"

"Of course I heard you."

"Last night you made a big point of telling Ryan that you were safe because of your Guild connections."

"Uh-huh."

"But if you had been killed in that alley, the Cadence Guild authorities could have claimed that it was just the tragic consequences of your going to the aid of a mugging victim. One of those wrong-place-at-the-wrong-time crimes. Everyone's sorry, but its nobody's fault."

"Wyatt would still have to explain to the Resonance Guild why the mugging was carried out by a couple of hunters," Emmett said.

"That's just the point. Those two youths probably aren't members of the Guild. You said yourself they were untrained. If and when they're caught, Mercer Wyatt can deny all responsibility."

He shrugged. "That doesn't mean the Resonance Guild wouldn't raise hell. A couple of young, strong dissonance-energy para-rezes like those two should have been under the control of the Guild."

"So the Resonance Guild makes a fuss. Big deal. Wyatt promises to investigate and find the bad guys. And that's the end of it."

He smiled briefly, without any amusement. "Take it from me, Lydia, Guild politics aren't that simple."

"You're deliberately missing my point here," she said very steadily. "I think someone hoped you would follow Ryan last night."

He picked up his rez-tea. "You're telling me that you think someone tried to set me up last night, aren't you?"

"Yes."

He took a swallow of tea and said nothing. There wasn't anything to say. He was pretty sure she was right. He'd been sure of it since he'd followed Ryan out into the alley.

"Well?" Lydia said aggressively.

"I can take care of myself, Lydia."

"Damn it, it *was* a setup. *I knew it.*"

She came off the stool with so much speed that her elbow hit the rez-teacup and sent it flying. She ignored it to grab him by the lapels. Since he was not wearing a shirt, she got two fistfuls of T-shirt instead.

"Take it easy, honey," he said soothingly.

"I'm right, aren't I? Someone tried to kill you last night."

"It's okay."

"No, it is not okay. In case it has escaped your notice, we are in big trouble here. We've got to go something. Maybe we should contact Detective Martinez."

"And get ourselves arrested on suspicion of murder? That's not going to do a whole hell of a lot of good."

"Well, what do you suggest, Mr. Ex-Guild Boss?"

He was silent for a moment. Then he said softly, "I suggest I go ahead with the plans I've already made."

"What plans? Why don't I know about these plans?"

"I haven't had much of a chance to discuss them with you," he said, deliberately vague.

"You mean you didn't intend to involve me in them, don't you?"

"Lydia—"

"Never mind. Tell me what you're going to do."

He shrugged. "I'm going to take a look around the offices of the Transverse Wave Youth Shelter tonight. See if I can turn up anything that will give us an idea of who is using the facility to recruit young para-talents off the street to excavate a cache of dreamstone."

"I'll come with you."

"No, you will not."

"You're going to need me, Emmett."

"Give me one good reason why I can't handle it alone."

She smiled coolly. "I told you that I thought I sensed illusion trap energy somewhere in the vicinity of the shelter's office, remember?"

He watched her, wary now. "We agreed that it wasn't unusual to pick up traces of energy leaks that close to the Old Wall."

"What if it wasn't just some leaked energy I sensed? What if it was emanating from a trap set to protect a cache of dreamstone or a small hole-in-the-wall gate that someone found and wants to keep secret?"

"Everyone knows you tanglers are inclined to be over-imaginative," he said.

"Everyone knows you stubborn, arrogant ghost-hunters think you can handle anything with a dose of dissonance energy, but it ain't so. I'm coming with you, Emmett. We're in this together."

She was right, he thought. They were in this together.

CHAPTER 25

MELANIE TOFT PUT HER HEAD AROUND THE CORNER OF the office door. "Thought this was your day off. What are you doing here?"

"I just came in to take care of some paperwork." Lydia turned away from the bookcase and smiled. "Don't worry, I'm not going to stay long."

"I should hope not. I've told you over and over again, you mustn't give Shrimp the idea that just because you're a genuine professional para-archaeologist, you should put in unpaid overtime."

"I promise I'll be out of here in less than ten minutes."

"Good." Melanie eyed her more closely. "Is there anything wrong?"

"No, Melanie, nothing's wrong."

"Look, I know you've been under a strain for the past several days, what with Chester's death and all. If you need more than just your regular day off, don't be afraid to say so. Shrimp won't mind."

"Don't worry." She picked up a pen and then threw it down, very hard, onto the desk. "I'm not going to crack up under the strain."

Melanie looked instantly abashed. "I never meant—"

"I know, I know. It's okay." Lydia pulled herself together and forced a smile. "Don't worry about me, Melanie. I'm fine." Sheesh, now she sounded like Emmett last night when he tried to tell her he was okay after nearly getting killed.

"All right." Melanie looked dubious. "But just remember, you don't have to prove anything to me or to Shrimp. If you want some time off, just speak up."

"Thanks."

Lydia waited until the door had closed behind Melanie. Then she turned back to the bookcase. She gazed thoughtfully at her volumes of the *Journal of Para-Archaeology.*

She removed the photograph that Chester had stashed in the duffel bag alongside the dreamstone jar and looked at it again. Chester grinned proudly from the photo, his hand firmly clasped around the issue of the *Journal of Para-Archaeology* that contained the article listing him as a contributing consultant.

Fragments of her dream floated through her mind. Along with it came the question she had been asking herself yesterday when Ryan interrupted her.

What if Chester had been on his way *out* of Shrimpton's the night he was killed?

She took a step forward and trailed her fingertip along the spines of the journal volumes. She paused at the one that contained the article naming Chester as a consulting contributor.

She pulled the volume off the shelf and opened it slowly to the familiar page. The title of the article blazed up at her. "An Assessment of Variations Found in the Para-Resonance Frequencies of Ephemeral-Energy Sources."

A slip of paper fluttered to the floor. She bent down, plucked it up, and stared at it. Chester's handwriting was unmistakable. There was a series of numbers. Beneath each number was a letter.

AN HOUR LATER, LYDIA OPENED THE SHEET OF PAPER containing the coordinates and spread it out on the kitchen counter. She put Chester's key down beside it. Then she unfurled the university's official archaeological site map of the Dead City.

"The code is simple enough," she said. "Chester used our birthdays, phone numbers, and the date of the issue of the *Journal* in which my article appeared. I recognized them immediately. After that it was just a mater of connecting the dots."

Emmett watched as she penciled in the coordinates on the map. Her gathering excitement fairly shimmered in the air around her. She wanted desperately to get back underground, he realized. She wanted to prove to herself that she could still handle the catacombs.

"If Brady's information is solid," he said, "it indicates an unmapped hole-in-the-wall gate into the catacombs beneath the shelter."

She nodded, concentrating intently on her task. "There are dozens of them, of course. The university authorities seal them whenever they find them, but the ruin rats discover new ones all the time."

"Same story in Old Resonance."

She put down the pencil and looked up, her face flushed with anticipation. "Somewhere along the line, someone must have discovered this particular hole-in-the-wall gate. For all we know, it's been found and lost many times over the years. But this time someone discovered the dreamstone down there, somewhere in one of the catacombs."

Emmett thought about it. "At the same time, he must have found the passages clogged with ghosts and illusion traps. Probably realized that he needed to put together a team to help him clear the site so that he could excavate."

"But he couldn't put together a legal excavation team because he would have had to report his finds to the university authorities. They would have claimed the dreamstone."

"But it occurred to him that he was sitting on top of a perfect source of unregistered labor. Street kids come and go from the shelter all the time. Some of them are bound to be untrained dissonance and ephemeral-energy para-rezes. Easy to recruit, especially if you promise them a little free training and a share in the profits."

"And if you don't mind risking their young necks," Lydia added grimly. "Excavation work in the unmapped sections of the catacombs is dangerous, even for expert and experienced tanglers and hunters. When I think of a bunch of young people being sent out to clear the tunnels—"

"Cannon fodder," Emmett said softly.

She glanced at him sharply. "What?"

"It's an old Earth term. I came across it once in a book."

"Oh." She let that pass. "Well, one thing's for certain. If someone is using a hole-in-the-wall gate that is accessed via the youth shelter and if he's recruiting kids out of the shelter, then he almost certainly has to be on the staff at the Transverse Wave. It's the only way he could come and go freely."

"Or the only way she could come and go freely," Emmett said quietly.

"True." Lydia agreed. "Hard to believe that anyone could excavate a catacomb right under Helen Vickers's feet without her suspecting that something out of the ordinary was going on. She's got to be involved in this."

"I told you, I've got my people in Resonance checking out her background. With any luck we may get some info tomorrow."

"We're talking a couple of murders, basic training for some hunters, and some serious illusion trap work. Hard to believe Vickers is handling all that alone."

Emmett thought about the locker key he had found in the pocket of one of the young hunters. "When did Bob Matthews say he started volunteering at the shelter?"

"A few months ago."

He studied the map while he ran through his options. He wished like hell that there was another way, but he knew there wasn't. He needed to get inside the unmarked catacomb passage, and he needed a good illusion tangler to help him. Lydia was one of the best.

He felt her watching him. He had a hunch she knew exactly what he was thinking.

"Like it or not, the job requires a hunter-tangler team, and you know it," she said.

She was right.

"We'll do it tonight," he said.

She glanced at Fuzz, who was munching a pretzel on the counter. "Don't worry, we'll take backup."

"What do you mean?"

"Fuzz." She plucked the dust-bunny off the counter and stroked his scruffy fur. "His night vision and sense of smell are much better than any human's." She hesitated. "I think of him as my good luck charm."

CHAPTER 26

LYDIA STOOD IN THE DARKENED SHELTER OFFICE AND looked out at the silent, night-shrouded street. It was two in the morning. The Transverse Wave had been closed since midnight. The doors and windows were locked. There were no street youths hanging around. No one had come or gone from the shelter in two hours. Either the illegal excavation work was not done at night or it was not scheduled for tonight.

The only indication that the neighborhood was not entirely deserted were the pair of drunks Lydia had seen slumped in a doorway as she and Emmett made their way through an alley. The only light in the vicinity was the sickly glow of a tavern sign half a block away.

"Everything okay?" Emmett asked from the shadows behind a metal desk.

She turned quickly, irritated by the query. "I'm fine," she said brusquely. "Just getting the feel of the place. Trying to pick up the illusion trap vibes I sensed the last time we were here."

"Right." There wasn't enough light filtering through the window to show Emmett's expression. His voice was very even. He turned and went down the hall toward Bob Matthews's office.

Lydia followed, fighting the thread of panic that was unfurling deep inside. Not fear of the dark, she thought. At least not yet. This was another kind of fear. Please don't lose faith in me now, she wanted to say to Emmett. You're the only one besides me who thinks I can still do this. Please believe in me.

But she kept silent. Even to voice the plea would be an admission to herself as well as to Emmett that she was anxious about what lay ahead. Ever since she had recovered from her Lost Weekend, she had been desperate to get back underground. Now the moment was upon her, and all she could think about was how she must not screw up.

But what if Ryan and the shrinks and everyone else were right? What if she really had lost some of her ability to tune into the psi frequencies?

Stop it, she told herself. *You de-rezzed that little illusion trap in the dreamstone jar. That was delicate work. If you could handle that, you're okay.*

She reached up to touch Fuzz, who was perched on her shoulder. He did not rumble in response as he usually did when she petted him. She sensed his heightened state of alertness and knew that all four of his eyes were open.

Emmett did not click on the penlight until they reached Matthews's office. Lydia left him to the task of rummaging through the desk drawers. She opened up all of her own senses, physical and paranormal, searching for the invisible traces of ephemeral energy that indicated an illusion trap.

It was never easy sorting out psi sensations this close to the Dead City wall. The overwhelming psychic weight of so much alien antiquity masked frequencies that would have been clearer in another section of town.

She was vaguely aware of Emmett moving around the office, but she concentrated on her job. Quietly she walked back to the door of the interior office and listened. The amber in her bracelet warmed gently against her skin.

Nothing.

As if aware of her tension, Fuzz stirred restlessly. She started to reach up to soothe him and froze. Her amber was heating up.

"There," she whispered.

Emmett paused to watch her intently. He said nothing

Feathery tendrils of dark psi energy swirled in the invisible currents of the air. Easy to miss amid all the other traces of leaked energy in the vicinity, but she had a fix on the trap now.

"Got it," she said, her self-confidence returning quickly.

Emmett closed the drawer he had been investigating and walked toward her. "A stray leak?"

"Don't think so. A nice, steady frequency. Or at least as steady as ephemeral energy can be." She turned on her heel, orienting herself. "Over there, near that other door."

"The storage closet."

Emmett snapped off the penlight and led the way out of the small office. He walked to the closet door and tried the knob. It did not turn in his hands.

"Guess that would have been a little too easy," Lydia said.

"Guess so." Emmett took out the small metal tool he had used to get them into the front door. His palm closed over the amber in the handle.

"There we go," he said after a moment. "Very sophisticated. Not your ordinary mag-rez lock, even though it looked like one."

Urgency swept through Lydia. "Be careful when you open that door."

In the dim recesses she could not see the arrogant disgust on Emmett's face, but she certainly sensed it. He obviously didn't like having his skills questioned any more than she did.

"Not real likely there's an illusion trap inside the closet," he said coolly. "For one thing, there would be nothing to anchor it."

"Don't forget that jar Chester found. The trap inside was a nasty one. Dreamstone seems to function as an anchor even outside the wall."

"Who would leave a priceless piece of dreamstone in a storage closet?"

Nevertheless, he opened the door with obvious caution. Lydia breathed a little easier when she felt no increase in the intensity of the illusion trap energy.

Emmett opened the door wider and shone the light inside.

Fuzz tensed on Lydia's shoulder; he did not seem to be unduly alarmed, just very alert and watchful. He was in full hunting mode, she thought. So was Emmett.

For that matter, so was she.

Emmett's light revealed several filing cabinets, a couple of cartons of business stationery, and a stack of annual reports.

Lydia moved into the large closet. "Watch out for the shadows. It's easy to conceal a trap in them."

"I've been out of the field for a while, but I'm not a novice at this, Lydia."

"Sorry."

"Forget it. Feel anything?"

She moved slowly, staring intently into the patches of darkness between the filing cabinets. The unique psi-energy waves produced by illusion dark were definitely stronger in here, but whenever Emmett aimed the light beam at a suspicious shadow, it vanished.

She put out a hand and brushed her fingertips along the nearest wall. There was no increase in the resonating frequency. She circled the room, touching each wall in turn. When she came to the east wall, she went still.

Energy pulsed, stronger here. Dark, illusion energy. She stared at the row of file cabinets that lined the wall.

"I think the source is behind one of the cabinets, Emmett."

He did not question her verdict. "All right. Probably one of the lightly loaded ones. No one wants to shove a heavy file cabinet out of the way every time he goes through a door. Open some drawers and see if you can find one that's half empty."

Lydia pulled out the nearest drawer. It was stuffed with files. She grasped the handle of the next one in line and hauled it toward her. The drawer was filled with aging files. Heavy files.

"Here we go," Emmett said softly.

She looked up to see him standing in front of the last file cabinet. He was gazing thoughtfully into what appeared to be an empty drawer.

She hurried toward him. "Illusion shadow?"

He aimed the light inside it. "Doesn't seem so."

She came to a halt and glanced into the darkness of the drawer. "It's okay." She concentrated, felt amber warm on her wrist. "The vibes are coming from the wall behind it."

"Give me a hand."

Fuzz hopped off Lydia's shoulder and perched on the top of the nearest cabinet to supervise.

It came away from the wall with unnerving ease. There was nothing behind it. Just more paneling.

Emmett reached out and traced an almost invisible seam in the cheap wood. Excitement rose again within Lydia, dissolving some of her uneasiness.

"Oh, boy," she said.

"My sentiments exactly," Emmett replied.

He pushed on the section of wall. The door swung inward on well-oiled hinges.

Impenetrable, endless darkness clogged the opening. Emmett played the light across it. The shadows did not disappear. If anything, they seemed to deepen.

"Stand aside," Lydia said softly. "This is where I earn the big bucks."

Emmett stepped back. "Be my guest."

There was no hint of doubt or concern in his voice even though they could both see that the trap was large. She moved forward.

Her natural ability to resonate with the peculiar wavelengths of illusion energy had been honed by academic training and practical experience. All of her senses went into high rez as she readied herself to tackle the task of untangling the trap.

With her paranormal instincts she probed the swirling layers of ephemeral energy that concealed the main resonating frequency of the trap. She looked into it with that part of her that saw beyond the normal spectrum of sensation and viewed colors that had no names, felt harmonic pulses that existed on another plane.

The trap was very ancient. One of the oldest she had ever encountered. It must have been set and de-rezzed any number of times by whoever was using this tunnel entrance, but it did not appear to have lost much of its brute force.

She found the frequency and began to resonate with it, deliberately sending back the vibrations that would dampen the invisible psychic wave motion. This was the most dangerous part. If she made a mistake, the energy pulses would rebound on her, swamping her senses, sucking her into an alien nightmare.

Seconds ticked past, but she lost track of the time. The trap was more complex than she had realized. It resisted her dampening efforts. At the same time it seemed to invite a quick, summary action on her part that would de-rez it instantly. She refused the temptation to rush through the process. More than one trap tangler had been ambushed that way.

Intuition, skill, and a delicate touch were the hallmarks of a good tangler.

She fine-tuned the frequency one more time. And felt the energy of the trap abate.

"Nice work," Emmett said.

The alien darkness was now gone from the tunnel mouth. A flight of glowing green quartz steps descended into the catacombs.

"A hole-in-the-wall gate, all right," Emmett said.

"The wall of the Transverse Wave Youth Shelter must have been built right up against the Dead City wall," Lydia said.

"Some ruin rat probably put up the building years ago to conceal the hidden gate." Emmett started down the stairs. "My guess is that someone else rediscovered it sometime within the past year."

Lydia held out her arm to Fuzz. The dust-bunny scampered up her sleeve to her shoulder, and they followed Emmett down the steps.

When they reached the bottom, Emmett switched off the flashlight. They stood together in silence as their eyes adjusted to the eerie green glow that emanated from the ancient walls. Underground, the green quartz gave off a strange light that had evidently been illuminating the catacombs for millennia.

"Ready?" Emmett drew an amber-rimmed resonating compass out of one pocket.

"Ready."

Euphoria bounced high inside her, a combination of adrenaline and relief. She was back underground. She had her own compass. And she was okay.

The curious ambience of the Harmonic catacombs had not changed. Everything felt normal, from the heaviness of sheer age that seemed to seep from the quartz itself to the dim green glow.

"Screw Ryan and screw the psi-shrinks," she muttered.

"Is that your way of assuring me that you aren't going to crack up?"

"Yep."

"Didn't think you would," he said.

"Thanks."

"Looks like we won't need the compasses," Emmett said after a while.

He was right, Lydia thought. There was enough debris, old and new, in the cleared catacomb tunnel to mark a freeway route. She spotted candy wrappers, empty Curtain Cola bottles, and discarded pizza boxes.

"Very unprofessional," she sniffed.

"They're using kids, remember? Kids eat. A lot."

The passageway was a narrow one, unlike some of the larger branches of the catacombs that Lydia had worked during her career with the university teams. In places there was barely room for her and Emmett to walk side by side. As with all of the mysterious underground tunnels, it was impossible to know why the original builders had designed and built them.

This particular stretch was relatively straightforward in construction. It turned and twisted a couple of times, and there were numerous side branches, but it was easy to stay on the well-beaten, candy-wrapper-strewn path.

"They probably work as many hours of the day as possible," Emmett said. "And they're trying to get the job done as quickly as possible. Every time you reset a trap, you have to have someone untangle it the next time you come through."

"Time-consuming. And dangerous with amateurs involved."

They moved deeper into the glowing green passage.

Their soft-soled boots made no sound on the hard quartz. Occasionally Emmett glanced at Fuzz.

"Don't worry," she said. "He'll give us plenty of warning if he senses anyone coming down the corridor."

"If you say so." Emmett studied another bend in the tunnel. "I've never worked with a dust-bunny before."

"Fuzz is now a permanent part of my team. One of these days I'll tell you how he got me out of the catacombs after my Lost Weekend—" She broke off abruptly as she heard Fuzz rumble in her ear. "Uh-oh."

Emmett halted. "I don't hear anything."

"I think Fuzz does. Maybe he senses a ghost."

"I won't argue with him. Both of you stay behind me."

"Damn it, Emmett—"

"I'm the ghost-hunter here, remember? You did your job, let me do mine."

He had a point. Nevertheless, she reached up for Fuzz and settled him on Emmett's shoulder. "Take him. The two of you have something in common."

"Like what?"

She smiled. "By the time you see the teeth it's too late."

Emmett raised his eyebrows but said nothing. He turned and, with Fuzz straining forward eagerly from his shoulder perch, rounded the bend in the tunnel.

Lydia followed, but not too closely. Let the man do his job, she told herself. He let you do yours.

A moment later Emmett's voice drifted back around the corner. "Well, hell!"

Lydia rushed forward. But when she rounded the bend she encountered no ghost light. Instead she saw Emmett standing in front of a large patch of suspicious shadow.

"Can you get rid of it?" he asked urgently.

"Sure." She was getting downright cocky now, she thought. That was not good. She forced herself back into her most professional mode.

She dealt with the trap quickly. When the shadows vanished, she and Emmett stood looking into a small alcove. A lean young man and a woman with long, filthy hair were stretched out on a dirty mattress, sound asleep. The were both clad in stained, ripped clothing that looked as if it had not been washed in a very long time. Next to them were bottles of Curtain Cola and empty sandwich wrappers. A small dreamstone vase stood at the entrance, visible now that the nightmare trap it had anchored had been de-rezzed.

Emmett started forward.

The young man on the floor stirred and opened his eyes. He sat up slowly and blinked several times in groggy disbelief.

"Uncle Emmett?" His gaze cleared rapidly. Relief transformed his face. "I knew you'd come looking for me."

"You took my cabinet." Emmett reached down to haul the young man to his feet. "What the hell else was I going to do, Quinn?"

CHAPTER 27

LYDIA GAVE EMMETT A WITHERING GLARE. HE GOT THE message. She thought he was being callous.

"For heaven's sake," she snapped, "this is no time to lecture your nephew about that stupid cabinet." She turned to Quinn. "Are you all right?"

Quinn looked slightly baffled by her interference. But he nodded quickly. "Yeah, sure. I'm okay."

"Quinn?" The young woman stirred and sat up slowly. "What's going on? Who are these people?"

"Meet Uncle Emmett, Sylvia. I told you he'd show up sooner or later." Quinn helped her to her feet. "Come on, we're getting out of here."

Lydia glanced around. "Anyone else in here besides you two?"

"No, not at this hour," Quinn exclaimed angrily. "They keep Sylvia and me locked up with traps when they're gone. But the others come and go on a schedule. They're really into the whole thing, y'know? Like to wear little chains with three wavy lines around their necks like scout badges or something. The idiots think they're going to get rich."

"What about guards?" Emmett asked.

"Couple of hunters right now. There was another one when I first got here, but he got fried and wandered off into a tunnel. Never saw him again. They haven't had much luck recruiting anyone else."

"Probably figured they didn't need to leave guards to watch us," Sylvia said, rubbing her arms. "The trap was more than enough to keep us inside that chamber while they were gone." She looked at Lydia. "You must be a very good tangler."

"The best," Emmett said before Lydia could respond. "What about your amber, Quinn?"

"Are you kidding? They take it away from us during rest periods. The main entrance is the only branch of the catacomb that's been pretty well cleared. You can't move ten feet down any of the side passages without amber."

"Where's the dreamstone?" Lydia asked curiously.

"Whenever they dig a piece out, they store it in a chamber located in one of the other passages," Sylvia said. "Except for a couple of places like this one that they use to trap this entrance and the one at the top of the stairs."

Emmett did not like the dangerous professional interest he saw in Lydia's eyes. "Forget the dreamstone. We don't have time to look at it now. We'll come back for it."

"Sure." She looked briefly wistful, but she did not argue.

Emmett turned back to Sylvia and Quinn. "Either of you know of another way out of here besides the stairs that lead up into the shelter office?"

Quinn shook his head. "No. Like I said, the side passages are clogged with traps and ghosts. They haven't bothered to clear any of the other passages, let alone explore them. All they care about is getting the dreamstone out."

Sylvia bit her lip. "They're almost finished. Quinn and I have been working as slowly as possible, but we weren't going to be able to stall much longer."

"Really glad to see you guys." Quinn sounded relieved. "We knew they wouldn't have any more use for us once we finished excavating the site."

Emmett put his hand on Quinn's arm. "You did good, kid. Come on, we're getting you out of here. Lydia, neither of them has amber, so we'll put them between us. I'll take the lead with Fuzz. Got it?"

"Got it." She moved into position behind Sylvia and Quinn. "If Fuzz seems to tense or if he sort of growls, be careful."

"Don't worry, I'll pay attention."

Emmett started back along the corridor, conscious of the weight of the dust-bunny on his shoulder. Ahead of him nothing moved in the dimly glowing quartz hallway. There were no inexplicable shadows or shimmers in the air. Fuzz seemed alert but not alarmed.

Emmett was starting to believe they just might make it out of the catacombs without incident when Fuzz froze. Simultaneously he felt the faint tingle of energy.

"Damn." He slapped his arm out to the side to make sure none of the other three blundered past him. Quinn stumbled, then caught his balance.

"What the . . . ?" Quinn began.

There was no time to respond. Ahead of Emmett the corridor exploded with acid-green energy. The huge ghost flared high and wide, blocking the narrow tunnel.

Sylvia gave a muffled cry. Everyone froze.

Fuzz whined softly. A tremor went through his small body, but all six paws remained firmly planted on Emmett's shirt, facing the pulsing green specter.

"Just what we needed," Lydia said grimly.

"I don't understand," Sylvia whispered. "I thought they'd cleared this corridor. The others come through here all the time."

Emmett figured this wasn't the time to explain that this ghost had been deliberately summoned tonight. The unusual patterns of dissonance told him that it was really two smaller ghosts that had been melded into one.

Two hunters working together at the entrance of the corridor, he thought. But the one he'd singed last night couldn't possibly have recovered this fast. Besides, whoever was controlling this double ghost was no untrained novice. It took experience and talent to force two dissonant energy fields into one for any length of time.

Another hunter, then. Matthews?

The ghost started to drift down the corridor toward Emmett and the others.

"Uncle Emmett?" Quinn sounded uneasy.

"It's okay, Quinn. It's really a two-in-one. Got to handle it a little differently. Right now it's shielding us from the two hunters who are behind it. We can't see them, but they can't see us either. I'm going to try to take control of the ghost and send it back toward the two guys who summoned it. But if that doesn't work, I'll have to de-rez it. Either way, in the end we'll have to deal with the hunters. They may be armed."

"Right." Quinn eased Sylvia out of the way and moved up to stand next to Emmett. "But without my amber I'm not going to be much help."

"Trust me, at the rate they're using up psi energy, they won't be able to summon more than a couple of flickers by the time we get to them. But we'll have to move fast. As soon as the ghost disappears we take them."

Quinn nodded in understanding. "Hand to hand, huh?"

"Probably."

"Emmett?" Lydia spoke urgently from directly behind him.

"Take care of Sylvia," he ordered softly. "I'll handle the rest."

He probably came off sounding like one of those macho jerk Guild guys she was always complaining about, he thought. But he didn't have time to be diplomatic. Fortunately, she did not argue. He saw her fall back with Sylvia in tow.

He concentrated on the conflicting dissolution patterns in the double ghost. The mingled energy was both its strength and its greatest weakness. There was a lot of power in a ghost this size, but it was inherently unstable. That made it vulnerable to a takeover—*if* he could locate the two main frequencies.

The ghost picked up speed as it moved toward them, but it still wasn't moving fast. No green UDEM had ever been known to shift position at a pace that exceeded a man's moderate walking speed. Furthermore, the bigger the energy field, the more cumbersome it was. But if it backed you into a corner, you were fried meat.

Emmett searched for the frequency patterns. He found the weaker one first. As he had expected, whoever was driving it lacked firm control. The hunter wielding the dominant ghost had already interfered with the wave pattern to a great extent in order to complete the meld.

The ghost floated closer, flaring and pulsing with angry green light, herding Emmett and the others back down the passageway.

Emmett felt the fresh amber in his watch grow warm against the back of his wrist. He poured more psi energy through it.

The ghost slowed, struggling to maintain its internal rhythms, but it did not stop. Emmett knew the precise instant when his watch fogged. He switched his focus to the backup amber he wore on a chain around his neck.

The double ghost was in trouble now. It stopped, pulsing wildly. Emmett recognized the signs of imminent collapse.

"Got it," he said softly. "I'm going to try to reverse it, but if it fails, be ready, Quinn."

"Right."

Working with all the subtlety he could command, Emmett took control of the weakening ghost. He prodded it gently until it began to drift back the way it had come.

There was a shout of alarm from the vicinity of the quartz staircase.

"Shit! He's got it."

Quinn grinned. "You do good work, Uncle Emmett."

"Let's go." Emmett started forward. "Whoever put it together will try to de-rez it as soon as he realizes what's happening."

"I'm right behind you."

"So am I," Lydia said firmly. "And Sylvia's here too."

The woman did have a way of picking the worst possible times to disobey orders, Emmett thought. He opened his mouth to issue fresh instructions.

But at that instant the fading ghost pulsed one last time and winked out.

"*Now*, Quinn."

Two figures stood silhouetted in the green glow of the staircase. They were less than ten feet away. As Emmett and Quinn closed on them, they both turned and fled back toward the staircase.

Emmett recognized one of the two young hunters who had attacked Kelso in the alley behind the Green Wall Tavern. The other was Bob Matthews. If either had an illegal mag-rez gun, he was too psi-rezzed to use it.

The two pounded up the staircase, into the gloom of the unlit storage closet.

Emmett dashed through the opening after them. The young hunter had already vanished, fleeing out of the shelter office toward the safety of the street.

But Matthews moved more slowly. Emmett knew that the other man's senses were probably badly jangled from the experience of having had his own ghost turned against him. It *hurt* when that happened. Really hurt.

Emmett caught him, whirled him around, and slammed him up against the nearest file cabinet.

Matthews's face twisted with rage and fear. He made a fist and threw a wild punch. Emmett managed to shift barely enough to avoid taking the blow in the groin. It caught him on his side, however, and sent him reeling backward.

Matthews closed in quickly, carrying both of them to the floor.

"Sonofabitch," Matthews roared, straddling Emmett. He shoved his hand into his jacket. When he pulled it out, a knife gleamed in his fist. "Sonofabitch, we almost had it all, you freaking SOB."

Emmett grabbed Matthews's knife arm at the wrist. Matthews yelled again and dropped the knife, point first, straight toward Emmett's left eye.

Emmett whipped his head to the side, heard the blade clatter to the floor beside his ear.

He jerked hard and forced Matthews off of him. There was a sharp thud. Emmett felt the jolt of the impact and realized that the other man had struck his head against the edge of a cabinet. Matthews slumped and went still.

Two figures dressed in stained rags that reeked of spilled alcohol materialized in the storage closet doorway that connected to the outer office. Emmett gave them a sour glance as he got to his feet.

"Where the hell have you two been?" he asked.

"Sorry we're a little late, boss," Ray Derveni said cheerfully. "We ran into a little trouble outside. The woman set an illusion trap at the front door after you and your lady friend went inside."

"Damnedest thing you ever saw," Harry Adler added. "Didn't think you could set one of those babies above ground."

Emmett frowned. "How'd you get past it?"

"A kid came runnin' out a minute ago. Guess he didn't know about the trap. Ran straight into it. Got nailed. Once it had been sprung we were able to get around it."

"Emmett," Lydia said urgently, "we've got a problem."

"*Sylvia,*" Quinn shouted. "She's got Sylvia."

Emmett swung around. He saw Lydia standing at the top of the staircase next to Quinn. Both were peering through the opening.

"Let her go," Lydia shouted.

Emmett went to where the others were gazing down the green staircase. He saw Helen Vickers at the bottom. She was not alone. She held a mag-rez gun to Sylvia's head. He wondered how she'd gotten her hands on one.

"Where the hell did she come from?" Emmett muttered.

"She was hiding in the shadows of the staircase," Lydia said quietly. "She grabbed Sylvia while you were dealing with Matthews."

"I'll kill her if anyone comes after me," Helen warned hoarsely. "I swear I will."

"No one will follow you," Lydia promised in a soft, coaxing tone. "You have my word."

"You think I believe that for one minute?" Helen's face was contorted with rage. "You've ruined everything, you stupid bitch. I'm the one who found that dreamstone. I de-rezzed the first traps. It's *mine*."

Emmett watched her move back another pace. Her foot brushed against what looked like a small heap of refuse.

"Please," Quinn said desperately, "let Sylvia go."

"Shut up. I should have gotten rid of you the day you walked through the front door. I thought I could use you if the Guild came around, but you've been nothing but trouble. I should have had one of the others fry you and dump you in the catacombs."

"Helen, he reasonable. You'll get lost in those tunnels," Lydia said. "You don't want to die underground, do you?"

"I won't get lost. There are other ways out of this branch. I've spent months down here. I know my way—"

She broke off on a shattering scream as the little heap of refuse she had nearly stepped on moved. Fuzz thinned himself into the sleek predator he was and scampered up the leg of Helen's trousers in the blink of an eye.

Helen shrieked and batted wildly with her free hand. "What is it? Get it off me! *Get it off!*"

Fuzz reached her throat. His small teeth gleamed just above her jugular.

Helen screamed again. With a convulsive movement she released Sylvia and dropped the gun to claw Fuzz away from her throat.

"Fuzz—" Lydia started down the staircase. "*Jump!*"

Fuzz leaped off Helen's neck and landed on all six paws. He raced toward Lydia, who reached down to scoop him up into her arms.

Sylvia grabbed the gun off the green floor and dashed toward the stairs. Quinn reached for her. She tumbled into his arms. Emmett discovered that the staircase doorway was suddenly clogged with people. He could hear footsteps as she fled down the corridor.

"Would everyone kindly get the hell out of the way so I can get her?" he snarled.

Quinn swung around to stare into the tunnel. "She's getting away."

"It's all right," Lydia said softly. "She won't get far."

"What are you talking about?" Quinn demanded. "You heard what she said. She knows her way around down there."

"It won't do her any good." Lydia caught hold of Emmett's arm. "Trust me."

Another scream echoed off the quartz walls, a cry that came from the heart of a nightmare. It reverberated for a long moment and then went deathly silent. Emmett decided he now understood the true meaning of the word "bloodcurdling." He looked at Lydia.

"I reset one of the little dreamstone traps while you were dealing with the ghost," she said quietly. "I left it in the corridor behind us, just in case. I thought it might give us some cover if we had to retreat."

He looked at her for a long moment. Then he smiled slowly. "Always nice to work with a pro."

CHAPTER 28

ALICE MARTINEZ TOSSED A FILE DOWN ONTO HER DESK with a tight, angry movement. "You should have filed a missing persons report."

"My nephew was eighteen, and there was no indication of foul play." Emmett lounged against the wall of Martinez's office. "I didn't think the cops would take the case very seriously."

Alice gave him a disgusted look. "With your Guild connections? Give me a break. We'd have been all over the Transverse Wave Youth Shelter."

"That kind of high-profile investigation could easily have convinced Vickers and Matthews to get rid of Quinn. They would have killed him and dumped his body in an unexplored tunnel. As it was, they only kept him alive to use as a hostage in case anyone from the Resonance Guild came looking before they finished excavating the dreamstone."

Martinez was not happy, but Emmett knew there was very little she could do about it. As far as he was concerned, she had no grounds for serious complaint. He and Lydia had, after all, dumped the whole thing in her lap. Thanks to them, the detective had tied up the loose ends of two murders, made several arrests, and exposed the illegal excavation of legendary dreamstone. Talk about a career-making case, Emmett thought. But some people just couldn't look on the bright side.

It was easy enough to dismiss Martinez's irritation, but Lydia's cool withdrawal had him worried. He watched her as she answered Alice's questions with clipped responses. She sat stiffly in the chair, her face angled so that she did not have to meet his eyes. She had retreated behind a veneer of icy reserve. Something was simmering under the surface, but he did not understand it. She had been like this since they had emerged from the catacombs last night. He was starting to wonder if going back underground had triggered some kind of delayed psychic trauma for her after all.

Alice opened the report on her desk. "According to this, your in-vestigator in Resonance City discovered that Helen Vickers was a strong tangler."

"She was also an opportunist," Emmett said. "She went to work for Anderson Ames two years ago and quickly made herself indis-pensable to him. Read, took advantage of him. He was getting senile, apparently. In any event, she managed to get herself into his will. But when he died—a death, by the way, that probably warrants fur-ther investigation—she suddenly discovered that there was no money after all."

Lydia took up the tale. "She went to the shelter to see if there were any assets she could sell off before she closed the place down.

Quinn overheard her mention that she found the old illusion trap guarding the hole in the wall. She de-rezzed it and started exploring the catacombs. She discovered the first piece of dreamstone sitting in the tunnel next to the skeleton of the last ruin rat who had tried to excavate. She realized there might be more. She decided to keep the shelter open as a cover, but she called an old lover and offered to make him a partner."

Alice arched one brow. "Bob Matthews."

"Right. The two of them had worked together in the past. But there was a problem," Emmett said. "Not only was the site filled with ghosts and traps but the dreamstone pieces were all individually trapped. Apparently they both had a couple of close calls. They needed cheap, expendable labor."

Alice's face hardened. "Young, untrained hunters and tanglers from the shelter."

Emmett nodded. "Quinn's friend Sylvia heard about the jobs here in Cadence. Quinn got worried after she phoned him, and he went after her. I followed Quinn."

"Straight to Chester Brady's shop in the Old Quarter," Lydia said. "Chester bought the cabinet from Quinn. But he must have gotten curious and followed him around while he asked questions about Sylvia. Vickers got nervous and had Quinn kidnapped. At the time, she probably didn't know he had Guild connections. Afterward it was too late."

"We figure Brady must have witnessed the kidnapping," Emmett said, "and followed Quinn and the kidnappers into the catacombs. That's probably when he stole the piece of dreamstone."

Thanks to Matthews, who had talked freely after his arrest, they all knew the rest of the story, Emmett thought. Matthews had been in favor of killing Quinn out of hand. It was Vickers who reasoned that they might need him for insurance. In the meantime they could use him to help with the excavating.

But then they found the claim check in Quinn's pocket and realized he had sold a valuable object to Chester Brady. That left a trail, and they knew it. Matthews and one of the hunters followed Chester. When he went to Shrimpton's, they assumed he had gone there to steal an artifact. It looked like a golden opportunity to get rid of him so, they seized it.

But while they were about the business of killing Chester, Helen Vickers discovered that one of the pieces of dreamstone was missing. She knew enough about Chester's shady dealings and his tangler abilities to realize that he might be the thief. But it was too late to question him. He was dead. She sent Matthews to search Chester's shop and his apartment, but he found nothing.

Vickers and Matthews had no idea that Chester had left a clue to the cache of dreamstone in Lydia's office.

When they learned that Emmett was in town and that Lydia was asking questions about the cabinet, they panicked. They sent one of the hunters to her apartment to try to scare her off. When that didn't work, they decided to get her tangled up in a murder investigation. Hence the search of Lydia's apartment. It had been made to look like a routine burglary, but the hunter had gone there to find something that could be used to tie her to a crime scene. He had grabbed one of her personalized amber bracelets.

Martinez looked at Lydia. "They assumed that you and probably London too would, if not actually arrested for Greeley's murder, at least be kept very busy trying to talk yourselves out of charges."

"At that point they were just trying to buy enough time to get the rest of the dreamstone and get out of Cadence," Emmett said.

"When their plan bombed, they made one more attempt to find out what we knew by dragging a colleague of mine into the situation," Lydia explained. "And then they tried to murder Emmett."

"They only needed a few more days," Emmett said quietly.

AT SIX O'CLOCK THAT EVENING SOMEONE POUNDED forcefully on Lydia's front door. It was not Zane's distinctive knock, so she chose to ignore the summons.

She finished pouring herself a glass of wine and reached for the lid of the pretzel jar.

The knock sounded again. She paid no attention.

"At the rate you're going through these," she said, feeding a pretzel to Fuzz, "I'd better buy stock in the company that makes them."

Fuzz rumbled happily from her shoulder and started to crunch with his usual enthusiasm.

"Help yourself, pal." Lydia reached up to pat him. "You deserve it. Don't know what I'd do without you."

She picked up the wineglass and started toward the balcony. En route she paused to listen. The knocking appeared to have stopped. She told herself she was relieved, but deep inside she knew she was lying.

The evening was warm. She opened the balcony slider and left it that way. She had just settled down onto one of the loungers when she heard someone open the supposedly locked living room door behind her.

Fuzz continued to munch, placidly content. Lydia did not look back over her shoulder. She was pretty sure she knew who had just entered her apartment.

"I don't know what the hell is going on here," Emmett said as he came out onto the balcony. "But if you think I'm going to let you pretend I no longer exist, you can think again."

"Believe me, I know you exist." She took a sip of wine, hoping it would calm her. "You're pretty hard to ignore, London."

"So I've been told." He sat down on the opposite lounger. "You want to tell me what's wrong?"

"Nothing's wrong."

"Was it going back underground? Did it bring back some bad memories? Lydia, if you need to see a shrink, I know a good one in Resonance. A friend of the family."

"A friend of the family." She slammed the glass down so hard that wine splattered on the table. "You mean a shrink with a Guild connection, don't you?"

"Well, yes, he has treated dissonance-energy para-rezes who work for the Resonance Guild, but that doesn't mean he can't handle an ephemeral-energy para-rez. He's very well qualified."

"Oh, I'm sure he is," she said through her teeth. "I'm sure he's first-rate. But as it happens, I don't need a shrink."

"Are you sure? You've been acting very strangely ever since we came out of the catacombs. Maybe going back underground so soon after your bad experience six months ago wasn't good for you."

She leveled a finger at him. "Don't start. If you tell me that you've finally joined the ranks of folks who think I've lost my para-rez pitch, I swear I'll throw you off this balcony."

"I know you haven't lost your pitch," he said calmly. "The way you handled the traps in the tunnels proved that. But there are other things that can go wrong."

"Yes." She picked up her glass. "There certainly are other things that can go wrong."

He was beginning to look wary instead of concerned. "I think I'm missing something here."

"You? Nah." She took another sip of wine. "How could you miss anything? You're a Guild boss—"

"Ex-Guild boss. And I've told you, I prefer the term 'CEO.'"

She sniffed. "Pardon me. You're the *ex-CEO* of the Resonance Guild. How could anything escape your all-knowing gaze?"

"Lydia, I'm here because I'm worried about you. You haven't been acting normal for the past two days."

"There's nothing wrong with me," she said very evenly.

"Is that so? Then why won't you take my calls? Why won't you answer the door when you know I'm standing out there in the damned hall? I'm not leaving until I get an answer."

She looked at him, anger bubbling inside, hot and painful, seeking release. "You want an answer? I'll give you one. The only thing wrong is that I'm mad."

"Mad?" He hesitated. "At me?"

"No. At myself."

He relaxed, but only slightly. "Why?"

"For trusting you."

"What the hell is that supposed to mean? What have I done to make you stop trusting me?"

"Let's start with the way you called in those two guys from the Resonance Guild and posted them as guards outside the shelter."

"Harry and Ray? I know it didn't work out the way I planned because of the trap Vickers left at the door, but it seemed a reasonable move. We didn't know if anyone in the Cadence Guild was involved in the excavation work, so I didn't want to risk using someone local."

"You don't get it, do you? Why didn't you *tell* me that you'd called in two Guild men from out of town?"

He shrugged. "For the same reason I didn't mention it to Detective Martinez. Because I hadn't cleared it with Mercer Wyatt. I didn't want anyone to know I'd imported some extra muscle without getting Wyatt's approval. Guild politics are a little tricky at times."

"Guild politics." She wanted to scream with frustration. "That's what it was all about, wasn't it? Guild politics were more important than keeping your partner informed."

He was suddenly very watchful. "You're pissed just because I didn't mention the fact that I brought in some out-of-town help?"

"I'm pissed because I'm wondering how many other things you didn't bother to tell me because *Guild politics* come first."

"Lydia—"

"We were supposed to be partners, remember? Partners treat each other as equals. Partners keep each other informed."

"I kept you informed, damn it."

"You lied to me right from the start, London. First you tracked me down because you thought I'd stolen your lousy cabinet. Then you hired me to help you find it, but you neglected to mention that you were not only a ghost-hunter but a Guild boss."

"Ex-Guild boss."

"Once a guildman, always a guildman."

Without warning, icy anger enveloped him. "Once a tangler, always a tangler. I wasn't the only one who didn't lay all the cards on the table right at the start."

"What are you talking about?"

"You had two objectives in this affair. You wanted to see Chester Brady's killer caught, and you wanted to prove to yourself and everyone else that you could handle going back into the catacombs. You needed me to help you get the job done. You used me."

She was so outraged, she could hardly catch her breath. "You came to me, remember? You claimed you wanted to hire me, but all along you thought I'd stolen your stupid family heirloom. And then you had the gall to seduce me."

He was on his feet, reaching for her before she realized what was happening. His hands clamped around her arms. He hauled her up off the lounger as though she were weightless. Out of the corner of her eye she glimpsed little bursts of wild ghost energy. Flickers.

Fuzz tumbled discreetly off her shoulder and vanished into the apartment.

"There seems to be a misunderstanding here," Emmett said, his voice dangerously soft. "I could have sworn that you were the one who seduced me."

"How dare you imply that I—"

"That you used sex to manipulate me?"

"That's not true and you know it."

"Yeah? Then why *did* you seduce me?"

"I did *not* seduce you," she stormed.

"What would you call it?"

"We had sex, okay? It happens sometimes between two people who—" She broke off, unable to finish.

"Between two people who are attracted to each other?" he suggested. "Is that what you were trying to say?"

She seized on the only face-saving way out of what had become an extremely hazardous quagmire. "Yes. *Yes*. It was just sex."

"Not a deliberate seduction."

"No." She wondered if there was a difference, but decided that this was not the time to go into the issue. "It just happened."

He lowered his mouth until it was only an inch above hers. "It was pretty good sex, though, wasn't it?"

Her mouth went dry. "That is beside the point."

"I don't think this argument has a point. Not one that's worth pursuing, at any rate. Let's get back to the sex."

"Just like a man, to try to use lust to avoid having to discuss a relationship—I mean, to avoid having to talk about a business association."

"Uh-uh." He did not sound particularly interested. His attention seemed to be focused entirely on her mouth. "To be perfectly honest, I don't want to talk about anything right now."

The telltale flickers had disappeared, but she could still feel energy crackling in the air. She was afraid that some of it was emanating from her. She swallowed.

"Emmett?" He was so close she could feel the heat in him. She tried to ignore it. "Sex is not enough."

"You may not trust me completely, but we made a damn good team down there in the catacombs. That counts for something."

He kissed her before she could summon a response. For a moment she hesitated, trying in vain to marshal further arguments. But it was too late. Much too late.

"You're right," she said against his mouth. "That counts for something."

He scooped her up and carried her indoors. She closed her eyes and did not open them until he lowered her onto the bed.

He jerked at the buttons of his shirt, flinging the garment aside. Then his hands went to his belt buckle. She watched him undress, aware of the shimmering excitement coiling deep inside her.

He was big, sleek and fully aroused. The heat in his eyes was hotter than melted amber. When he came down onto the bed and gathered her into his arms, she knew that she was very likely stepping into an illusion trap, possibly the most dangerous one she had ever encountered.

But this was no alien nightmare. This was a dream of another kind. She had made her decision. She would revel in it as long as possible.

And then his hands were on her and she stopped thinking about anything except the sensations that caressed her entire body. Sensual energy swirled through her as his fingers moved on her. She felt herself become hot and damp. She turned her head into his chest and kissed him, inhaling the scent of him.

And then he was on top of her, his weight crushing her into the depths of the bed. He reached down to draw her knees up alongside his thighs, making a place for himself between her legs.

He forged into her slowly, giving her time to adjust to him but allowing no room for retreat. Not that she wanted to pull back, she thought. She had never craved anything in her life the way she craved Emmett tonight.

She sank her nails into the muscles of his back and tightened her knees around him. He made a husky, unintelligible sound and pushed himself deeper inside, filling her completely.

He kissed her again, his mouth at once demanding and desperate. She understood the strange combination because she was experiencing the same driving need. She had to have him, had to find the release that only he could provide. She clutched at him, drawing him closer.

He moved deliberately within her, withdrawing until he was almost free and then sliding heavily back inside. The pressure became more than she could bear. She knew that his control was close to shattering. His back was slick with perspiration.

"Yes," she whispered, clenching him tightly. "Yes, *now*." She lifted herself against him.

"*Lydia*."

He plunged back into her one more time. Her climax swept through her with shattering intensity. She was vaguely aware of the great, wracking shudders rippling through Emmett. She parted her lips on a small scream, felt his mouth cover hers, and then spun away into a darkness made brilliant with sparkling dreamstone.

HE OPENED HIS EYES A LONG TIME LATER AND LOOKED up at the ceiling. Lydia was curled snugly against him. She felt very good. He was intensely aware of her warmth and softness. She did not speak, but he knew she was awake.

"You were right," he said. "I didn't tell you everything."

"No kidding." But there was no anger left in her voice, only a wry resignation.

"There were reasons," he said slowly. "The Guilds are changing, but it's going to take time. Old habits die hard."

"I know." She groaned and stretched languidly. "I can't blame you for keeping secrets. You had to protect Quinn, and you were right when you said that I had my own agenda in this thing. We used each other."

He felt his jaw tighten. "It was a partnership. Maybe we didn't tell each other everything right up front, but that doesn't mean we weren't partners."

"I vote we don't argue about it anymore, Emmett. I don't think either of us can win. Besides, it's over."

"Not quite," he said.

She went very still. After a moment she raised her head and looked down at him. "What's that supposed to mean?"

He hesitated. This was Guild business, after all. Very serious Guild business. But he knew he had already made the decision. She had a right to be in on the finish.

"There's one other loose end to tie up," he said.

CHAPTER 29

"THIS IS GUILD BUSINESS." TAMARA WYATT TURNED away from the study window. The movement of her head caused her amber earrings to catch the morning sun. They glowed a dark yellow gold. "Whatever it is you have to say to us, Emmett, it should be kept within the Guild. There is no reason to involve Miss Smith."

During the drive to Mercer Wyatt's mansion in the hills, Lydia had promised herself that she would keep her mouth shut and allow Emmett to handle this. It was his show, after all. But listening to Tamara talk about her as if she weren't in the room was too much. She consigned her vow of silence to the garbage.

"I disagree, Mrs. Wyatt," she said briskly. "In the course of this mess, a friend of mine was murdered, as was a business acquaintance named Bartholomew Greeley. A young boy was ruthlessly terrorized by a rogue ghost-hunter. On top of everything else, my apartment was scorched."

Tamata whirled to face her. "The Cadence Guild is not responsible for any of those things."

Emmett looked at her. "Wrong, Tamara. The Cadence Guild was involved."

"Can you prove it?" Mercer Wyatt demanded coldly.

Emmett held up the folder he had brought with him. "I may not have evidence that will stand up in a court of law, but I think I've got enough to convince you. And when it comes to Guild matters, that's all it takes, isn't it?"

"Yes," Mercer said steadily. "Convincing me is all that is required."

Tamara looked at Emmett. "If you actually have proof that some-one in the Cadence Guild was responsible for what was going on at the youth shelter, you should discuss it privately with Mercer. He will deal with it. I still say Miss Smith has no business here."

"Too bad," Lydia said. "Miss Smith *is* here, and she's not leaving until this is over."

A soft, discreet knock on the door interrupted Tamara before she could argue further.

"Come in," Mercer ordered.

The door opened. Lydia turned to see an earnest-looking man walk into the study.

"Miss Smith," Mercer said quietly, "allow me to introduce Denver Galbraith-Thorndyke. Denver is the administrator of the Guild Foun-dation. Denver, this is Lydia Smith."

Denver inclined his head in a polite nod. "Miss Smith." He turned back to Mercer with a quizzical expression. "I got a message that you wanted to see me, sir."

"Emmett, here, has some questions for you concerning our Foun-dation grants." Mercer looked at Emmett.

Denver followed his glance. He pushed his glasses up on his nose and smiled slightly. "Yes, Mr. London?"

Emmett did not move from his position near the bookcase. "You told me you ran a thorough background check on Helen Vickers before you funded the programs at the Transverse Wave Youth Shelter."

"That's right," Denver said. "Why? Is there a problem?"

"Yes." Emmett tossed the file folder down onto the nearest table. "There is a problem. I had my people in Resonance run a check on her, too. They turned up several interesting facts. Ten years ago Helen Vickers was involved in an underground excavation disaster. No charges were brought, but two people died and a valuable artifact went missing. The surviving members of the team blamed Vickers."

"Good Lord." Denver stared at him. "I found no such information on Miss Vickers."

"She was using a different name at the time," Emmett said. "You should have found it. My people did within twenty-four hours."

"I don't understand."

"There's more," Emmett continued. "Two years ago the original founder of the Transverse Wave Youth Shelter, Anderson Ames, died in a mysterious fire. Helen Vickers was his sole heir."

Denver drew himself up. "Are you implying that I failed to do a proper in-depth background investigation on Miss Vickers before I authorized funding for the shelter?"

"No," Emmett said. "I think you did a very good background investigation."

His icy voice sent a shiver through Lydia. This was the shadowy, mysterious Emmett London who had once held the Resonance Guild in an iron grip, the man who had single-handedly transformed it.

Ryan had told her that this Emmett London had made enemies along the way. She could well believe it.

"I think you discovered everything that my people turned up and more," Emmett said to Denver. "You had plenty of time to dig deep, and that's just what you did, isn't it?"

"I don't know what you're implying, but I certainly have no intention of listening to these wild accusations," Denver said tightly.

"Yes," Mercer said, "you do."

Tamara looked at him. "I don't understand. What is this all about?"

"All in due time, my dear," Mercer said. "All in due time."

Emmett contemplated Denver. "You realized that Vickers, whatever else she was, was no model of selfless altruism. So you did a little more investigating, didn't you?"

Denver clenched his hands into fists. He was trembling visibly now. "I don't know what you're talking about."

"You learned that she and the man who calls himself Bob Matthews were old lovers. Somehow you uncovered their hole-in-the-wall dreamstone excavation project. My guess is that, acting anonymously, you blackmailed them into cutting you in for a piece of the action. In return, you promised to keep funding the shelter and to keep the Guild off their backs."

"This is outrageous! How dare you insinuate such things?"

"You took charge of the entire operation—anonymously, of course," Emmett said. "I'm sure Vickers and Matthews are already trying to tell their lawyers about the mysterious blackmailer, but no one will take them seriously. After all, there's no proof. You kept your own hands very clean."

"You're insane," Denver whispered.

Tamara frowned. "Denver, is any of this true?"

"No, no, of course not, Mrs. Wyatt." Denver swung around to face Mercer. "You can't possibly believe this nonsense, sir."

"I didn't want to believe it," Mercer said wearily. "But this morning after Emmett called to tell me that he suspected you were involved in the illegal excavation at the shelter, I had your house searched."

Denver blanched. "You sent people into my home? But that's illegal. You can't do that."

"We found the London family heirloom," Mercer said. "The cabinet of curiosities, I believe it's called. It was hidden in your basement storage closet. You stole it from Chester Brady's shop after he was killed. And later you posed as the new owner in order to set Greeley up."

Tamara touched Mercer's shoulders. "Are you certain of this?"

"Yes, my dear," Mercer said gently. "Quite certain."

Right then and there Denver seemed to crumple. He sank in on himself as if suddenly too exhausted to stand. For a moment there was absolute silence in the study.

"How dare you?" Tamara's patrician face twisted into a mask of anger and disgust. "You've ruined everything. *Everything!* For a year I've been working on the Guild Foundation. It was the first step toward changing the Guild's image here in Cadence. And now this. If word gets out about the Guild's connection to the illegal excavation at the shelter, we'll be back to square one. The media will have a field day."

"Don't worry, my dear," Mercer said soothingly. "Word won't get out about any of this. It's a Guild matter. It will be handled in the usual fashion."

Lydia snorted softly. "Figures."

Tamara glowered. "What about her? She's not Guild. Who's going to keep her quiet?"

There was a short, brittle silence. Everyone, including Lydia, looked at Emmett.

Emmett shrugged. He said nothing.

Lydia gave Tamara a cool smile. "You want to start changing the Guild's image? Stop trying to police yourselves. Turn Denver over to the authorities. Take the hit in the press."

"Impossible," Tamara said instantly. "We can't risk the bad publicity. The media already classify the Cadence Guild as little more than a very powerful mob. Turning Denver over to the police would only feed that negative image."

Denver removed his glasses and began to polish the lenses with a cloth. "You can't touch me, you know. My family will see to that. I don't care how strong the Guild is, the Galbraith-Thorndykes can and will protect me."

Mercer studied Emmett, who was standing at the window now, hands in his pockets.

"What do you say, Emmett?"

"Turn Denver over to the cops," he said quietly. "His family can afford good lawyers. My guess is he won't do any time. There's very little hard evidence against him."

"Then why go through the motions?" Tamara protested. "And the humiliation?"

"Because," Emmett said, "in the end the big story won't be Denver's involvement in the dreamstone scheme. It will be the fact that the Cadence Guild went to the mainstream justice system about the situation. Lydia's right. It's a major step toward shaking the mob image."

Tamara whirled to confront Mercer. "Listen to me! We can't take the chance of destroying what we've been working for all year."

Mercer looked thoughtfully at Lydia for a long moment. She had the feeling that she was being weighed and judged. Another little shiver went through her. She'd seen that same calculating intelligence in Emmett's gaze from time to time. Perhaps power always revealed itself that way.

Mercer turned his head to smile gently at Tamara. "They're right, my dear. If we truly want to begin the task of reshaping the image of the Cadence Guild, it must start here. I will call the police myself."

CHAPTER 30

THE LINE OUT IN FRONT OF SHRIMPTON'S HOUSE OF AN-
cient Horrors was three times as long as it had been the day following
the news that Chester's body had been discovered in the sarcophagus. The number of people waiting to see the first public exhibition
of worked dreamstone was growing by the minute. Lydia had never
seen her boss so happy.

"I got a raise," she confided to Melanie.

"You deserve it." Melanie grinned. "I still can't believe you pulled
this off. How in the world did you manage to convince the university
authorities to allow the dreamstone to be put on display here, of all
places?"

Lydia contemplated the crowd filing past the exhibits. "Let's just
say I pulled a few strings."

Emmett walked out from behind a nearby display vault, where he had been studying a small dreamstone vase. "She means she convinced Mercer Wyatt to call in a few favors at the university."

Melanie grimaced. "I won't ask what kind of favors."

"I didn't ask either," Lydia said cheerfully.

"Well, one thing is for certain," Melanie said. "Shrimp will never forget this day as long as he lives. He's positively glowing with pride. I wouldn't be surprised if he leaves you the whole bloody museum in his will."

Lydia held up a hand. "Please. Don't even suggest it."

Melanie laughed. "Just joking. My guess is you'll soon be so busy doing private consulting work you'll have to quit your job here at the museum."

"We'll see," Lydia said. "It takes a while to build up a clientele."

"Especially if you're choosy," Emmett murmured dryly.

She glared at him.

"Excuse me. I'd better go give Phil a hand at the front gate," Melanie said smoothly. "I'm sure he's exhausted from selling so many tickets."

She waved as she plunged into the crowd.

Emmett stood quietly beside Lydia for a while. Together they watched the line of people wind through the exhibits.

"Melanie was right," Emmett said eventually. "You probably won't have any trouble attracting private clients."

"We'll see," Lydia said again.

"Think you might need a partner on your next case?" Emmett asked conversationally.

"I doubt it. I mean, what are the odds?"

"Maybe you'll require the services of a good ghost-hunter," he suggested.

"Hard to say."

"Well, then, how about a date tonight? Need one of those?"

"Thought you'd never ask."

Bridal Jitters

CHAPTER 1

Harmony: Cadence City,
two hundred years after the closing of the Curtain

♣

"SO, IS IT TRUE WHAT THEY SAY ABOUT GHOST-hunters?" Adeline Delmore leaned close and lowered her voice as she helped herself to another orange-frosted cookie. "Are they really *amazing* in bed after they've zapped a ghost? I've heard the sex is unbelievable right after a burn."

The question caught Virginia Burch just as she took a sip of the sparkling wine punch. She coughed and sputtered. Heat infused her cheeks. Unfortunately, she reflected glumly, bright pink was not her best color, especially on her face. She glanced wildly around to make sure no one else had overheard Adeline's outrageous question.

The offices of Gage & Burch were crowded with friends and colleagues, some of whom she could not recognize because, even though they were here to celebrate her engagement, most wore masks and costumes. It was Halloween week, after all; otherwise known here in Cadence as party-till-you-drop week. She wondered if the fact that her friends had chosen to throw a surprise engagement party with a Halloween theme was a bad omen. Not that she needed any more to warn her that her forthcoming marriage was probably a huge mistake.

Luckily someone had cranked up the volume of the music. The throbbing beat of a rez-rock song created a blanket of white noise that effectively shrouded conversations. As far as she could tell, no one had overheard Adeline's question about the sexual habits of ghost-hunters.

"Uh," Virginia said. To buy herself some time, she groped for a napkin decorated with a cartoon picture of a woman in a pointy black hat and a cape, riding a broomstick. "Uh, well—"

"I've heard the stories," Adeline continued, eyes gleaming. "And if you'll recall, I dated that good-looking hunter for a while. The one with the blue eyes and the curly black hair. I can't remember his name."

"Brett." It was hard to keep up with Adeline's ever-changing list of boyfriends, Virginia thought. But Brett had been memorable mostly because he had been a swaggering braggart. Of course, a lot of ghost-hunters were swaggering braggarts.

But not Sam. Whatever else he was, he was not a typical hunter.

She glanced across the room to where her new combination fiancé/ business partner stood talking with one of the guests. Sam Gage didn't have to do any bragging, she thought wistfully. You knew just by looking at him that he could take care of himself and any ghost that happened along.

She was pretty sure he'd be terrific in bed, too, but she was beginning to think she might never find out the truth of that for herself.

"Oh, yeah, right," Adeline said. "Brett. That was his name. At any rate, he made some very interesting claims and promises. Ghost-hunters are not exactly shy when it comes to telling you about their sexual prowess. But our relationship didn't last long enough for me to run an experiment. Anyhow, I'm curious. I realize it's none of my business—"

"No, it's not."

"But I *am* your very best friend in the entire world," Adeline reminded her. "If you can't tell me, who can you tell?"

Virginia cleared her throat and decided to be honest. "Sorry, I'm not in a position to answer your question."

Adeline looked dumbfounded. "You're not? But you're going to marry Sam Gage. He's a hunter. This is your engagement party."

"Oddly enough, it looks more like a Halloween party to me."

"Okay, okay, so we decided to give it a theme. All the best parties have themes. I read it in last month's issue of *Harmonic Home & Garden.*"

"I can't believe *Harmonic Home & Garden* told you that Halloween is considered an appropriate theme for an engagement party."

"Personally, I thought it was kind of original." Adeline looked across the crowded room to where Sam stood. A speculative light glittered in her deceptively innocent eyes. "Are you telling me that you two haven't done it yet? How weird."

"Adeline, I explained that Sam and I intend to apply for a two-year marriage-of-convenience license, not a covenant license."

"So what? That doesn't mean you aren't going to sleep together, does it?" Adeline broke off abruptly, eyes widening. *"Does it?"*

"This is business." Virginia swallowed. "I told you that."

Adeline looked skeptical. "One hundred percent business?"

"Yes."

"No fooling around at all?"

Virginia fought to quell the panic that had been nibbling at her for the past few days. "Like I said, it's a business arrangement."

Adeline groaned. "I don't believe it. You and Sam are a perfect couple."

Virginia paused, her plastic cup of punch halfway to her mouth. "What ever gave you that idea?"

"Are you kidding? You and Sam were made for each other. You've got so much in common."

"Such as?"

Adeline's brow climbed. "Well, for openers, you're both repressed, obsessive workaholics. Neither one of you seems to know how to have fun."

"Thanks a lot."

Adeline chuckled. "Should have seen the looks on your faces when you walked into the office this evening."

"We weren't expecting a party, Adeline."

"Yeah, I know." Adeline smiled smugly. "It was a surprise party. And it worked, didn't it?"

Virginia thought about the way her stomach had clenched when she had opened the door a short time earlier and been greeted with shrieks of *"Surprise."*

"It worked," she mumbled into her punch. "I was definitely surprised."

Adeline gave her an admonishing frown. "A lot of people went to a lot of effort to pull this off. Do me a favor: Try to look like you're having a good time, okay? Sam is taking it in stride."

Sam could take anything in stride, Virginia thought morosely, even an unanticipated engagement party. She caught a glimpse of him through the forest of black and orange balloons that dangled from the ceiling. He was still talking to the earnest-looking man in glasses.

Even surrounded by bobbing cardboard goblins, plastic jack-o'-lanterns and several yards of black and orange crepe paper, he looked, as he invariably did, completely at ease, totally in control.

He was a powerful dissonance-energy para-resonator—a ghost-hunter—but, thankfully, he did not go in for the long-haired, super-macho, khaki-and-leather look favored by most hunters. Tonight he was dressed in a black T-shirt, black trousers, and a tan jacket that fit well across his broad shoulders. He wore his resonating amber in a simple, gold ring rather than set in a massive belt buckle or a flashy pendant.

There was a relaxed air about him. The graceful languor of a natural-born predator at ease between kills emanated from him in psychic waves. Virginia could feel the disturbing energy all the way across the room. No one else seemed to be particularly aware of that aura—both dangerous and deeply sensual—that enveloped him, but it stirred all the tiny hairs on the nape of her neck.

Another twinge of panic zapped through her, unsettling both her physical and paranormal senses. The combined assault on her aware-ness made her shiver. The anxiety attacks were getting worse, she thought. Every time she contemplated marriage to Sam, she felt the small, high-rez shocks of trepidation.

What had she done?

She had agreed to marry Sam Gage; that was what she had done. Granted, it was only a two-year marriage-of-convenience. Neverthe-less, she was going to be legally tied to him for two full years.

What had she done?

She forced herself to take a couple of deep breaths. When that did not block the tide of uneasiness that was doing such strange things to her insides, she tried another sip of the wine punch.

Just a marriage-of-convenience. They were common enough. It would end in two years unless she and Sam elected to renew it for another two-year period. There would be no reason to do that, she assured herself; no excuse to convert the MC into a more formal and far more binding covenant marriage.

Adeline was right; she had to project a little more good-natured enthusiasm here, Virginia told herself. She had agreed to the MC, after all. It was a terrific business move. And she certainly could not blame her friends for throwing a party. They meant well. And she was genuinely fond of most of them.

She was surrounded with a representative sprinkling of the professional and not-so-professional types involved in the many legitimate and not-so-legitimate businesses that had grown up around the excavation of the Dead City of Old Cadence. There were a number of academics from the university who were in the process of building distinguished careers studying the alien ruins. There were also several contract and freelance para-archaeologists, such as herself, and a few of Sam's ghost-hunter buddies who provided security to the excavation teams. In addition, there was a colorful assortment of gallery owners, hustlers, and ruin rats who worked the fringes of the trade in alien artifacts.

It was a mixed lot, to say the least, but they were all bound by their mutual interest in making their livings from the exploration and excavation of the ruins left by the long-vanished Harmonics.

It should have been a cheerful occasion, but she could feel the panic nibbling at her stomach.

"Sorry, Adeline. I guess I'm not in a party mood tonight."

"Fake it," Adeline said with a stern look.

Virginia gave her a reluctant smile. "Yes, ma'am."

"That's better." Adeline searched her face more closely. "What's the matter? I thought you were excited about this arrangement. Why the cold feet?"

"I'm not getting cold feet."

"Yes, you are. This is your old pal, Adeline, remember? I know you better than anyone else. You've been getting increasingly short-tempered and high-strung for the past two weeks."

Virginia glared at her and picked up the punch ladle. "I've been a little busy lately, okay? I just finished the Henderson job yesterday, and Sam and I signed our first joint client this morning. We start work on the project tomorrow. On top of everything else, my family is hassling me about this MC, even though I've explained a hundred times that it's just a business deal."

"Your family is still convinced that Sam is just taking advantage of you?"

"That's their official position." Virginia ladled more punch into her cup. "But the truth is, they want me to settle down in a covenant marriage with Duncan."

Adeline shrugged. "Can't blame them. Duncan is a great catch. Good family, good connections. Nice guy."

"Duncan and I are friends, but it will never amount to more than that." Virginia dropped the ladle back into the bowl and took a hefty swallow of the punch. "Duncan and I both know it, even if our families don't."

"You mean you don't love him, and he doesn't love you."

"Yes. That's exactly what I mean."

Adeline raised her brows. "So, instead of a nice, safe marriage to good ol' Duncan, you're going to take a flyer on a two-year MC with a man you hardly know and who is a ghost-hunter to boot. Gee, can't imagine why the family is upset about that decision. Nope. Can't think of a single reason why your relatives would have a problem with your plans."

Virginia gave her a speaking glance. "It's business."

Adeline assumed an infuriating all-knowing expression. "Know what I think?"

"What?"

"I think you've got a radical case of nerves. Bridal jitters, as my aunt Sally would say."

"That's ridiculous. Why would I be nervous?"

"Excellent question."

"This is just a business deal." Virginia suspected that she was beginning to sound desperate. She tried to temper her tone. She wanted to sound calm and cool. As calm and cool as Sam had sounded when he had presented her with the proposition three weeks ago.

"This section of the Old Quarter is slated for gentrification within the next couple of years," he had explained. "Investors and developers are already starting to nose around. This house is going to be worth a fortune soon. But in the meantime, I've got to find a way to hang on to it."

She gazed at her new landlord in genuine alarm. She had rented her office and her upstairs apartment from him less than two months ago. She had found the old house at the end of a long, fruitless day spent tracking down the addresses of virtually every affordable rental in the Old Quarter of Cadence City. It had not been an advertised rental, but she had decided to make inquiries after noting the small sign on the door, which read Dead City Security, Sam Gage, Prop.

Her intent had been to ask the unknown Mr. Gage, who was clearly a small businessperson like herself, if he was aware of any suitable space in the neighborhood. The choicest rentals, she had learned, were frequently obtained by word of mouth rather than through the want ads.

Her initial impression of Sam Gage, the owner and sole employee of Dead City Security, was that he was not what one expected in a ghost-hunter who had set up shop as a security consultant. She had found him in his office, ankles propped on his desk, deep into the current issue of the *Journal of Para-Archaeology*. Heavy reading for a ghost-hunter, she thought. Most of the ones she knew preferred *Sex-Starved Psychic Playmates* and *Naked Amazon Maidens of the Alien Catacombs*.

Before the end of the conversation, Gage had offered her an office on the first floor and an apartment on the second. She had fallen in love with both spaces the moment she had seen them. She was beginning to think that she had fallen in love with her new landlord at approximately the same time, but that was another issue altogether, one she did not want to confront.

"Hang on to it?" she repeated warily. "Is there a problem?"

"Just the usual. Taxes, upkeep, repairs." He spread the fingers of his amber-ringed hand in a gesture that encompassed all the trials and tribulations of home ownership. "This house was built right after the Era of Discord. That makes it over a hundred and fifty years old. It was built to last, so it's sound, but it needs a lot of work."

"I see." She looked around at the elegant molding, gleaming wooden floors, and uniquely framed windows.

The place was perfect for her one-person consulting business. The location, only two short blocks from the great, green quartz wall that surrounded the Dead City, was ideal. Her work required frequent trips both above ground and deep into the catacombs of the ancient alien ruins. From here, she could walk to her job site, which meant she would not have the expense of a car.

She cleared her throat uneasily. "Are you thinking of raising the rent already? Because, if so, I'd like to remind you that I do have a one-year lease."

He braced his hands on the top of her desk and leaned slightly forward. His amber-colored eyes were steady and intent. "No, I'm not going to raise your rent. I've got a proposition for you. If things work out the way I think they will, we'll both make a killing."

His idea had been a straightforward business arrangement. A marriage-of-convenience and a merger of her consulting business with his Dead City Security. He'd painted a dazzling picture. Operating as a single entity, Gage & Burch Consulting, they would double their resources overnight. Together, they would be able to compete for larger, more lucrative clients. The increased revenue would go into maintenance. The MC would ensure that they paid lower taxes. When the house was sold to developers in two years, they would share equally in the profits. A win-win situation.

All she had to do was find a way to be as cold-blooded about the arrangement as Sam. Unfortunately, the closer they drew to the date of the wedding, the less certain she was that such a thing was possible.

"I told you," Virginia said to Adeline. "Sam wants to hang on to this house until some developer is willing to pay big bucks for it. He offered to cut me in on the profits. It's a terrific business opportunity for me." Who was she trying to convince? She wondered.

Adeline reached for a piece of neon-orange candy. "Maybe the fact that it's just a business deal is part of the problem. Maybe that's not what you want."

No, Virginia thought. It most definitely was not what she wanted. Late this afternoon, after a long walk and a cup of coffee in the lonely little park at the end of the street, she had finally forced herself to face that fact. She was in love with Sam, but all he wanted from her was her signature on a contract. Marriage, especially a marriage-of-convenience, would be hell. The frustration factor alone would probably drive her to the nearest para-psych ward within a month. She was almost sure now that she could not go through with the arrangement.

But she had not yet figured out how to tell Sam.

She had planned to get things out in the open tonight. Then she had opened the door of the office and walked straight into the engagement party.

She could hardly bring up the subject now in the midst of a party. She would wait until morning. Tomorrow would be soon enough to tell him that she was having second thoughts.

She felt a guilty sense of relief at having made the decision to put off the inevitable for another few hours.

SHE WAS GETTING COLD FEET. HE COULD FEEL THE CHILL clear across the room. Every time he caught her eye, she averted her gaze or started up an earnest conversation with whoever happened to be standing nearby.

The last of the guests finally departed shortly after midnight. Sam closed the door behind the laggard and turned to see Virginia sinking down into the chair behind her desk. His bride-to-be looked both relieved and exhausted. She also looked cross. But then, lately she frequently looked tense and irritable. Bridal jitters. The odd thing was that the more anxious she got, the calmer and more certain he became.

She leaned back in the chair and closed her eyes. "Thought they'd never go."

"They meant well," he said.

"I know." She rested her head against the back of her chair. "But they don't understand."

"Sure they do. We're getting married. People like to celebrate marriages. Even MCs."

"I don't see why."

"Because there is a streak of the romantic buried somewhere inside most people," he explained patiently. "Deep down, everyone hopes that marriages-of-convenience will morph into the real thing."

"That's a highly unrealistic expectation. Statistically speaking, most MCs end on the first or second renewal date unless someone makes a mistake and gets pregnant." She paused meaningfully. "And there is absolutely no excuse for that kind of mistake."

"Right. No excuse."

Few mistakes of that sort were made because the First Generation colonists who had settled Harmony had crafted very strict legislation covering marriage and family. The more liberal social policies of Earth had been abandoned when the energy Curtain that had served as a gate between worlds had unexpectedly closed, stranding the settlers. The founders, desperate to provide a social structure that would ensure the survival of the colony, had opted for stern laws. But in their wisdom, the First Generation planners had also understood that harsh rules that did not take human weaknesses into account would ultimately fail. Failure of the social structure of the tiny band of desperate settlers would mean catastrophe.

In an effort to deal with basic human foibles, the founders had provided the socially and legally sanctioned marriages-of-convenience to cover many of the traditional and less-than-romantic reasons that drove people into wedlock: family pressure, business, or simple passion. Couples who elected to have children were expected to file for the more formal covenant marriage.

The muted warble and twang of a high-rez rock guitar sounded from the street. Sam crossed the office to the window, made a space between the blinds, and studied the night-shrouded sidewalk.

The Old Quarter teemed with revelers tonight. The heavy river fog that had cloaked Cadence nightly for the past several days had deterred no one. People dressed as witches, goblins, and ghosts—the fairytale sort, not the very real remnants of dangerous alien energy known as *unstable dissonance energy manifestations*—drifted in and out of the mists. Orange lights came and went eerily in the shadows. As Sam watched, a grinning jack-o'-lantern appeared out the gloom. Someone shrieked in pretended fright. Raucous laughter echoed in the night.

This was Halloween eve, and the noise level was already high. Tomorrow night, Halloween night, would be bedlam. Half of Cadence would flock to the Old Quarter to party. There was no place in town quite as atmospheric at Halloween as the seedy districts adjacent to the ancient walls of the Dead City.

In this part of town, ambient psi energy leaked continuously through tiny, often invisible cracks in the emerald-colored stones. It seeped up from the endless miles of green quartz tunnels and corridors beneath the pavement. The little currents and eddies of energy were part of the lure of the Old Quarters of all the cities on Harmony that had been built near the sites of ancient ruins. Tourists and locals alike loved the creepy sensations, especially at this time of year.

Maybe there was something to the theory that the flickers of psychic and para energy were stronger at this time of year, Sam thought. Ever since he had been a kid running loose on the streets, it had always seemed to him that he was more aware of the traces of ancient alien psi energy at Halloween. Tonight was no exception. The not-quite-human trickles of power that leaked out of the Dead City felt very strong. The stuff whispered through his mind, making him deeply aware of the unseen paranormal world that hovered just beyond the range of the physical senses. The surge in power levels that he detected were probably nothing more than the result of his overactive imagination, he thought. The same imagination that had conjured up the brilliant idea of talking Virginia into a marriage-of-convenience.

In hindsight, all he could say was that it had seemed like a good idea at the time.

Behind him, Virginia yawned. "We'd better get some sleep. Mac Ewert will be expecting us early tomorrow morning. He's anxious to get his excavation site cleared so that he can get his team back on the job. He made a big point of reminding me of how much money he's losing with every day of lost work."

"You're right. We need some sleep. Don't want to doze off in front of Gage & Burch's first client." Sam turned away from the window. "I'll see you to your door."

For a few seconds, the tension in her eyes retreated. She gave him a familiar, laughing smile, the kind of smile she had bestowed on him frequently until he had asked her to merge her business with his and file for an MC. At the sight of the glowing look, he felt his whole body tighten. The desire he had worked so hard to conceal for the past two months heated his blood. With every passing hour it was getting harder to quash the rush of sexual anticipation that stirred him whenever he was near Virginia.

By the time his nonwedding night arrived, he would be a basket case.

What the *hell* had he been thinking? A marriage-of-convenience in which he slept on the third floor while Virginia slept on the second floor was going to make him certifiably crazy.

She rose from the chair and stretched. "I thought it was my turn to see you to your door."

"Want to flip a coin?"

"Okay, but this time let's try one of my mine. I don't trust that one that you like to use. It always comes up heads." She dug a quarter out of her pocket. "Call it."

"Heads." He moved toward her.

She flipped the coin into the air. He caught it before it struck the polished surface of her desk.

"Heads," he said without bothering to look at it.

She wrinkled her nose. "You're in luck. I'm too tired to argue."

At the door of the office, she paused to switch off the lights. He followed her out into the front hall and locked up. Together, they climbed the elaborately carved central staircase to the second floor and went down the corridor to the small suite of rooms she used as an apartment.

She opened her door, stepped inside, and swung around to face him through the narrow opening. Her green-and-gold eyes were big and deep in the shadows. He could feel the tingle of awareness in his paranormal senses and knew that he was responding to her on the psychic plane as well as on the physical level. Sensual psi energy shimmered disturbingly in the small space that separated them. Couldn't she sense it? He wondered. Was she really oblivious to the attraction between them?

The wariness in her eyes made him uneasy. With each passing day, she appeared to be growing more restless. His fears of being driven crazy by sexual frustration were submerged beneath a new concern: What if she changed her mind? What if she canceled the MC?

Stay focused, he told himself. *This will work.* It had to work.

"Good night," he said as casually as he could manage. He forced himself to take a step back. What he really wanted to do was pick her up and carry her through the small living room, straight into her bedroom. "I'll see you in the morning."

She hesitated. "Sam?"

"Yeah?" He realized that he had stopped breathing.

She sighed. "Never mind. It's not important. Good night."

Very gently, she closed the door in his face.

He reminded himself to breathe.

CHAPTER 2

HE DID NOT SLEEP WELL THAT NIGHT. IT WAS NOT THE noise from the crowds in the street or the whispers of Dead City psi energy that kept him awake. It was the realization that Virginia was getting ready to tell him that she did not want to go through with the marriage. He knew it as surely as he knew that when she called off the engagement, his world was going to become as bleak and gray as the tide of fog that had boiled up out of the river.

He rolled out of bed at dawn, shaved, showered, and dressed for the meeting with Ewert. He was still mulling over various means of convincing Virginia that the MC was a terrific idea when he went downstairs to collect the morning edition of the *Cadence Star*. He opened the front door and was greeted by a wall of gray mist. The fog was so thick that it had blotted out the early-morning sun, creating an artificial twilight that looked as if it would last all day.

Perfect Halloween weather.

He shrugged off the fog. It would not affect today's job. He and Virginia would be working underground in the catacombs. Down below in the endless miles of glowing green corridors, there was no day or night.

He saw the small package on the step just as he started to reach for the newspaper. A faint hiss of all-too-familiar psi energy whispered through his para senses in silent warning.

"Damn." Hell of a way to start the day.

He crouched on his heels to get a closer look at the square object wrapped in brown paper. It was addressed to Gage & Burch Consulting. There was no return address. He did not pick it up.

"Something wrong, Sam?" Virginia called out from halfway down the stairs.

"An unscheduled delivery." He did not take his eyes off the package.

"What is it?"

"I think you'd better take a look at this. If I'm right, it falls into your area of expertise, not mine."

She descended the rest of the stairs quickly and hurried across the wide front hall to the door. She came to a halt beside him and looked at the package.

She pursed her lips thoughtfully. "Uh-oh."

"I hate it when you use that professional jargon." He glanced at her. "What do you think?"

"The same thing you're thinking, I imagine. It's an illusion trap. I can feel the energy pattern. Someone left us a nasty little trick. I'll bet it was some idiot who had one too many bottles of Green Ruin to drink last night. Probably thought it would be a great Halloween prank."

"I think he'll change his mind when I find him," Sam said softly.

Virginia glanced at him, frowning slightly. "Don't worry, it's just a small trap."

"Can you de-rez it?"

"Does amber resonate? Of course I can de-rez it. But I'm not going to do it out here on the front step. Let's take it into the kitchen."

She reached down and scooped up the box with a nonchalance that made Sam wince. He followed her into the big kitchen at the back of the house and watched her set the box down on the scarred counter.

"You might want to stand back a little," she said as she clipped the string. "Just in case."

"We're partners, remember?" He moved closer to the counter.

She smiled as she began to unwrap the package. "Yes, but you've never seen me work. I wouldn't blame you for being a tad cautious. Even small, simple illusion traps can be very unpleasant if they aren't untangled properly."

"I've spent a lot of time underground and I've worked with some clumsy tanglers. I've caught the flashback from an accidentally sprung trap more than once."

"Well, there won't be any flashback this time. You have my personal guarantee."

Her cool, professional arrogance amused him. He watched her peel away the brown paper. A small cardboard box was revealed. With a good deal more caution than she had exercised a moment ago, she raised the lid and gazed inside.

"Well, well, well," she murmured. She sounded as cheerful as if she had just received a bouquet of flowers.

Personally, he could think of a number of other things he would rather find on his doorstep first thing in the morning besides an illusion trap. But if the challenge of de-rezzing it lifted Virginia's spirits and gave her something else to think about besides calling off their marriage, he might be willing to overlook the prank.

"What is it?" he asked.

"A very nice piece." She angled the box to allow him a closer look at the object inside. "A little unguent jar. Museum quality. Not spectacular, but quite excellent. It would bring a good price in a gallery. I can't imagine anyone in his right mind wasting it just to play a vicious Halloween trick."

Sam eyed the small green quartz jar. It was elegantly rounded in a shape that was not quite comfortable for a human hand. The top was carved in an airy, fanciful design similar to many he had seen in the course of his career. The art and sculpture left behind by the long-vanished Harmonics always reminded him of the Old Earth poet Goethe's description of architecture: *frozen music*.

"You're right," he said. "It's not unique, but it's definitely valuable. Whoever our prankster is, he must be a wealthy collector if he could afford to use an artifact worth a couple of grand just to pull off a Halloween stunt."

An illusion trap had to be anchored to an artifact or to old green quartz from the ruins.

"Probably too drunk to realize what he was doing." Virginia carefully lifted the top of the jar and peered into the dark interior. "Okay, here we go. It's a simple pattern. This won't take long."

"Easy for you to say." He looked down into the shadows inside the little unguent jar. The darkness there was not normal. There was a dense quality to it, the only visible warning of the tiny trap. In the eerie glow of the green catacombs of the Dead City it was all too easy for a member of an excavation team to mistake illusion dark for ordinary shadow, but here in the brightly lit kitchen, the difference was obvious to the trained eye.

Obvious, but no less dangerous.

He had seen other tanglers work, but this was the first time he had watched Virginia in action. She'd only had a handful of clients during the time she had been renting office space from him, and she had dealt with them on her own.

He felt psi energy spark and shiver in the air. Very high-rez. He was impressed. She was as powerful as her academic credentials claimed.

Technically speaking, she was an ephemeral-energy para-resonator; a tangler in common parlance. With the aid of the specially tuned amber that she wore in her earrings, she could focus her particular type of paranormal energy in a way that allowed her to neutralize the vicious and sometimes deadly illusion traps. The wicked snares were one of the hazards of para-archaeological work in the alien ruins. The vast majority of tanglers became para-archaeologists. It was one of two natural career paths, the second being the illegal antiquities market.

An illusion trap was tricky. Once tripped, it released a web of ephemeral psi energy in an alien nightmare that enveloped the mind of the unlucky person who had triggered it. No two traps produced the same harrowing visions. Some were simple to de-rez, especially the really old ones. But in later Harmonic traps, the energy had been woven into complex patterns that defied all but the most skilled tanglers.

No one who had ever survived the experience of being caught in an illusion trap's web could ever fully describe the nightmares. Sam had sensed enough on the occasions when he had been zapped with some of the flashback energy from a poorly sprung trap to know that the visions were composed of unimaginable colors and a vertigo-inspiring darkness. The experts claimed that the nightmares lasted only a few minutes before the human brain sought refuge in uncon-sciousness. The resulting coma, however, could last for hours or days. When the victim eventually awakened, he or she invariably suffered an amnesia that cloaked most memories of the event. Some never recovered completely. They tended to end up in the para-psych wards of mental institutions. Others were so traumatized they could never work underground again.

No one knew why the Harmonics had booby trapped their under-ground catacombs. Whoever their enemies had been, they were as long gone as those who had set snares for them.

"Got it," Virginia said with soft satisfaction. She took a breath and looked up from the jar. "Didn't even heat up my amber. It's clean."

"Nice job." He picked up the jar and turned it in his hands, ex-amining it from every angle. The fizz of malign energy that had warned him of the trap had ceased. The trap could be reset by a skilled tangler, but unless that was done, the unguent jar was safe to handle.

He looked down into the interior. The unnatural, viscous shadow was gone. In its place was the ordinary darkness one expected to find in the interior of any small vessel. There was also something else inside the little jar. He pulled out a square of folded paper.

Virginia frowned. "It looks like a note."

"Yes, it does, doesn't it? Maybe our prankster wants to brag. Thoughtful of him to provide a clue." He unfolded the paper and read aloud the single sentence typed on it. " 'Happy Halloween. The ghosts and goblins are real in the catacombs this week. Stay out. This will be your only warning.' "

"What in the world?"

"Not real original," Sam remarked.

Virginia snatched the paper from his hand. "Let me see that." Her brows drew together in a stern line as she read it silently. Then she looked at him. "What do you think this is all about?"

"I think," Sam said, "that one of Mac Ewert's competitors doesn't want us to go to work for him. Wouldn't be the first time a rival has tried to scare off another team's consultants."

"Huh." She dropped the note into the trash. "Obviously whoever sent this doesn't realize who they're dealing with. The firm of Gage & Burch doesn't get scared off *that* easily."

Sam saw the gutsy determination in her eyes and smiled. For some reason he suddenly felt a lot more optimistic about his marriage prospects than he had when he had come downstairs earlier.

"DAMNDEST THING I'VE EVER SEEN." MAC EWERT RAN A blunt-fingered hand through his thinning gray hair. "I've heard of waterfalls, but I've been mapping catacombs for twenty years, and this is the first one I've ever run into."

"They're rare," Sam agreed. "But I think we can handle it for you."

Virginia felt her jaw drop. She barely managed to conceal her shock. She was amazed by Sam's casual response to Ewert's announcement. They were going to have to de-rez a *waterfall?* She almost groaned aloud. Of all the bad luck. This was just what they did not need for their first time out as the new firm of Gage & Burch; a nearly impossible assignment. She was the one who had taken the call yesterday morning from Mac. He had certainly not mentioned anything about a waterfall.

She reminded herself that waterfalls fell into Sam's area of expertise. She had to admire him for projecting an image of professional confidence, but she seriously doubted that he'd had any experience with waterfalls. Few people had.

She had read about them, of course. They were described in the textbooks as unique cascades of unstable dissonance-energy manifestations—ghosts—that could block entire corridors. Unlike most UDEMs, they did not drift aimlessly through the underground tunnels of the Dead City. Instead, they were anchored in one place, forming impenetrable walls of seething psi energy that could fry anyone dumb enough to get too close. Little was known about them because so few had been discovered. Those that had been found had been de-rezzed by teams of very expensive, highly specialized experts, not by small-time security consultants. Sam would be on his own with this one. Her name was now on the newly repainted door of the office, but that didn't mean she could help him with the waterfall. This was a job for a ghost-hunter. A really, really good ghost-hunter. All she could do was cheer him on.

Ewert gave Sam a look of mingled desperation and aggressive demand. "Think you can handle it, Gage? This project is already running behind schedule. I've had one delay after another in the tunnels during the past month. I can't afford any more."

"I'll take a look," Sam said. "I can give you a firm answer as soon as I examine it."

Ewert planted his hands on his desk and glanced at the khaki-and-leather clad man who lounged against the wall. "Leon, here, doesn't think any single hunter can deactivate it. He tells me I'm going to have to contract with the guild for a team of specialists. Trouble is, my budget won't stretch that far."

"It's big," Leon drawled. "More ghost energy than I've ever seen in one place and I've been working underground for damn near fifteen years."

Virginia glanced at him. Leon Drummond was the Ewert team's ghost-hunter. He was working on a standard guild contract. He had made it clear that he resented having a private consultant brought in to handle the waterfall problem.

Leon was everything that gave ghost-hunters a bad name, as far as Virginia was concerned. He was arrogant, macho, ill-mannered, and he had poor taste in clothes. His oversized belt buckle was studded with so much amber that if he ever fell into the river, she was pretty sure that he would sink like a stone.

"Like I said, I can give you an answer after I've had a look at the waterfall," Sam said calmly.

"Suit yourself," Leon muttered.

Ewert leaned wearily back in his chair. "Leon will take you to the site. I can't allow anyone else into that corridor until the waterfall is cleared. Too dangerous. For God's sake, don't do anything stupid. If you and Miss Burch can't handle it, just say so. My insurance won't cover any lawsuits."

Sam nodded as he got to his feet. "We'll keep that in mind. Ready, Virginia?"

If nothing else, this was going to be interesting, she thought. Not many people got an opportunity to see a real ghost-energy waterfall. In spite of her misgivings, anticipation rose within her.

"Ready," she said.

With a shrug, Leon managed to straighten himself away from the office wall. He turned and sauntered out through the door without a word. Sam and Virginia followed him outside to where the utility vehicle waited.

THE EERIE GREEN GLOW GIVEN OFF BY THE EMERALD-hued quartz that lined the alien catacombs always had the same effect on Virginia: It sent a tiny chill of dread and wonder down her spine. The sensation was not a thrill of fear exactly; more a deep, elemental response to that which was not human. She had grown up in the very shadow of the ancient ruins, and she had been aware of her own psychic response to the peculiar energy that resonated within its walls since childhood. But she did not think that she would ever be entirely comfortable in the mysterious tunnels. Some part of her would always feel like an intruder here.

No one knew what the ancient Harmonics had looked like. No pictures or records of physical descriptions had ever been found. None of the art that had survived depicted the vanished beings who had created it. No one could even guess why Harmony's original inhabitants had built these endless miles of catacombs, most of which had never been charted. But one thing was certain: The business of exploring, mapping, and excavating relics from the ruins was big. And the competition could be fierce.

Virginia sat next to Sam on the second bench of the small, open-sided utility truck. Leon Drummond took the wheel, piloting the vehicle through the maze of intersecting corridors with the aid of an amber-rez locator. He had remained sullenly silent since leaving Ewert's office.

Sam had not had much to say, either. Virginia studied him out of the corner of her eye. He was playing it cool, she thought. But, then, Sam always played it cool. If he had any doubts about confronting a dangerous waterfall of unstable dissonant energy, he did not allow them to show.

Virginia wanted to ask him why he had not mentioned the illusion trap they had found on their doorstep that morning to Mac Ewert, but she was not about to bring up the subject in front of Leon Drummond.

There was another, more personal matter that she had not yet gotten around to this morning, either, she reminded herself: marriage. She had promised herself that she would tell Sam about her growing doubts, but then had come the business of the illusion trap, and after that they'd had to hurry in order to make the meeting with Ewert.

What with one thing and another, she had found excuses not to deal with the issue of their marriage.

She glanced at the glowing green maw of an intersecting corridor as Leon drove past. There was a warning sign posted at the entrance. Keep Out. Unmapped Zone. Sort of like her engagement, she thought. Another little chill went through her, but this time it had nothing to do with the alien catacombs. She would talk to Sam this evening, she promised herself. Right after they had finished this consulting project.

She could not put it off another day. Her nerves couldn't take the stress.

She studied the quartz walls as the utility truck traveled along the corridor. The endless green stone passages were interrupted here and there by small, slightly less than human-sized openings that, she knew from experience, led to chambers. Most of the rooms and anterooms discovered in the underground regions of the ancient city were small, but some vast, exotic spaces had been found. Explorers had untrapped chambers so large and elegantly proportioned that many para-archaeologists assumed they had been used for ceremonial functions or royal tombs. But they could just as easily have been employed as underground aircraft hangers for all anyone knew.

Twenty minutes later, Leon slowed the cab and turned into the entrance of a branching tunnel. Virginia caught a glimpse of another warning sign. Keep Out: UDEM Ahead.

Leon brought the cab to a halt and finally deigned to speak. "The waterfall is down that corridor on the right."

The announcement was unnecessary. The pulsing, acid-green light of the unnaturally large concentration of ghost energy was already visible. It throbbed at the entrance of the corridor. Virginia gazed at it, amazed. She had never seen that much ghost light in one place in her entire career. She could only guess at the size of the UDEM itself. It was still out of sight around the corner.

Beside her, Sam moved. He got out of the cab and walked toward the entrance of the branching corridor. His hard face was etched in lines of concentration and keen anticipation. He was looking forward to this, Virginia thought. Well, what else had she expected? He was a ghost-hunter, after all, and this was undoubtedly the most dangerous, most challenging energy specter he had ever been called upon to de-rez. She would probably be feeling the same excitement if they were confronting a particularly complex illusion trap.

Sam paused at the entrance of the tunnel. He glanced back at her over his shoulder "Wait here. I'm going to take a closer look."

Leon draped his arms on the steering wheel and watched Sam disappear around the corner into the pulsing green light. "This won't take long. Once he sees the size of that thing, he'll be back. He'd have to be a fool to try to tackle that sucker on his own."

Virginia did not like his tone. The last thing she wanted to do was wait here with Leon.

"I'm going with him." She hopped lightly down from the truck.

Leon scowled. "Are you a hunter, too?"

"No, I'm a tangler."

"This ain't no job for a tangler," Leon said. "That's a ghost in there, not some wimpy little illusion trap."

Virginia ignored him. She went quickly toward the tunnel entrance. When she rounded the corner, she was nearly blinded by the fierce, oddly cold glare. She narrowed her eyes against the intense glow and saw Sam. He was silhouetted in front of a cascading wall of pure green energy: the waterfall.

It was an astonishing sight. Light tumbled, swirled, and flowed in oceanlike waves that poured in an endlessly circulating fountain from ceiling to floor and back again. The wall of churning energy blocked the entire corridor, which was narrower than most. The interior dimensions were much smaller than those of the outer tunnel where Leon Drummond waited in the truck.

For some reason, the silence of the waterfall struck Virginia as strange, even though she had seen enough ghosts in her time to know that there was rarely much noise associated with them. A few pops and crackles and the occasional hiss of the ice-cold energy constituted the usual range of the sound effects.

"It really does look like a waterfall," she exclaimed as she went forward to join Sam. "You'd almost expect to see a river or a pool of psi energy forming at the bottom."

Sam frowned at her. "I thought I told you to wait in the truck."

"Not a chance." She gazed at the tumbling green waves. "We're a team, remember?"

"This isn't illusion energy."

"Right. You're the expert on this stuff. I'll just supervise."

He hesitated. "I've always worked alone."

"Not anymore." She turned toward him. "It was your idea to merge our businesses, remember?"

He gave her an odd look. "Yeah. I remember."

She turned back to the cascades of green fire. "Well? What's your professional opinion, Mr. Ghost-Hunter? Can you handle it?"

Sam did not answer immediately, but his eyes gleamed in the reflected glow. His mouth curved slightly.

"Does amber resonate?" he asked with just a hint of old-fashioned ghost-hunter arrogance. "Yeah, I can handle it. But I'll have to de-rezz it one section at a time."

"Why?"

"Because it's not really one large ghost. It's composed of a number of smaller UDEMs that have been linked to create the waterfall effect."

"Aha. That makes sense. Whoever did this also figured out how to anchor it in place, too, like an illusion trap. I've never heard of a ghost that didn't just drift aimlessly."

Sam moved a little closer to the waterfall. "It's old. Very, very old. Probably been here for eons."

"I can believe it." Virginia shivered. "I'm sure the ancients knew a lot of Halloween tricks that we humans will uncover the hard way."

"Might as well get to work." Sam walked slowly across the width of the tunnel, as though measuring the breadth of the waterfall. He came to a halt at one side.

Virginia felt the invisible rush of human psi energy. A lot of it. She had seen Sam work before but never on a project that demanded so much para-talent. She took a respectful step back, not wanting to get in his way or disturb his concentration. De-rezzing this monster ghost was going to take a great deal of focused psi power.

Silence hummed for a few minutes.

Waterfall light flared, glinting off Sam's strong cheekbones. The green glare transformed the hard planes and angles of his face into an eerie, menacing mask. He gazed, seemingly riveted by the water-fall.

It was probably because he was concentrating so intently on the job at hand that she was the one who heard the high-pitched whine of the utility truck's engine first. She glanced back over her shoulder, surprised to see that Leon had braved the corridor, after all.

The small truck barreled toward where she stood with Sam in front of the waterfall. It was moving quickly; too quickly. She put up a hand to warn Leon to halt.

Then she realized that Leon was not at the wheel. No one was in the open sided truck. Someone had rezzed the engine, slammed it into gear, and sent it hurtling down the narrow corridor toward Sam and her. It was a tight fit. Assuming the vehicle continued to travel in a straight line, there would be only a foot of clearance on either side. With a sickening sensation in the pit of her stomach, she realized that even if they could flatten themselves into that small space, it would do them no good. When the truck slammed into the energy waterfall, there would be an explosion. The flashback of ghost energy would crash over them. If they survived the experience, the tide of raw alien energy would fry their brains. She and Sam would not be able to do much more than sit in front of a rez-screen watching sitcoms twenty-four hours a day for the rest of their lives.

If they survived. And that was a very big if.

"*Sam.*"

He swung around, taking in the situation in a single glance.

"Sonofabitch." He scooped her up in his arms. "Hang on. Tight."

She wanted to argue, but there didn't seem to be much point. There was no place to run. She wrapped her arms around his neck and buried her face against his chest, filling her senses with the scent of him one last time. If they were going to go, she couldn't think of anyone she would rather go with than Sam.

"I love you," she whispered into his shirt.

But she knew that he had not heard her. For one thing, the utility truck was almost upon them now. The fully rezzed engine was screaming too loudly to make even normal levels of conversation possible.

The second thing that made a dramatic farewell impossible was that Sam was projecting an enormous amount of psi energy. She could feel it enveloping her as he held her tightly against his chest. So much power required the use of all of his internal resources, both physical and paranormal. The last thing he could do at that moment was pay attention to what she had muttered into his shirt. It was a wonder he had the strength to hold her in his arms.

She heard the whine of the swiftly advancing truck, felt Sam tighten his arms fiercely around her, and then, impossibly, she was suddenly aware of being surrounded by a rushing sea of alien energy. Ghost energy.

She realized that Sam had chosen to escape the utility truck by leaping through the waterfall with her in his arms.

The acid-green waterfall washed over her in a giant wave. She braced herself for the searing mind burn but, incredibly, the energy did not touch her. She could feel the weight of it pressing on her from all sides, sensed the raw power that seethed in the cascade, *but it did not touch her.* It was as if she was protected by an invisible envelope.

The world whirled on its axis. She felt a jarring thud that took her breath. She heard Sam grunt and then she felt the cool green quartz beneath her. She realized that they had both landed on the floor of the corridor—on the other side of the waterfall.

Sam rolled with her in his arms, carrying her to the edge of the tunnel. They came up hard against the quartz wall.

Sam released her and got to his feet. He swung around to face the cascade of green energy. Dazed, Virginia sat up slowly, pushing hair out of her eyes. She stared at the waterfall. Sam had carried her through that mass of alien energy. Without a scratch.

Unless, of course, this was how you felt after your brain got fried.

Maybe her mind hadn't yet assimilated the fact of its own destruction. Perhaps a lifetime of sitcoms still awaited her. Heaven help her, maybe she would actually enjoy them.

Before she could mention that awful possibility to Sam, she heard the explosion on the other side of the UDEM waterfall. She knew what had happened because she had seen similar events, albeit on a far smaller scale. The utility truck had slammed into the energy wall and been bounced back like a rubber ball. The inevitable blast that accompanied the meeting of an immovable object and an unstoppable vehicle had taken place at the point of impact on the other side of the waterfall.

Here on the back side of the energy cascade, it was business as usual. There was no backwash of energy.

A stunning silence descended. Nothing broke it except the occasional hiss and crackle produced by the tumbling fountain of ghost energy.

"You did it." Virginia tore her gaze off the waterfall and looked at Sam. "You got us through it in one piece. How in the name of Old Earth did you manage it?"

"I didn't try to de-rez the whole damn waterfall. Just neutralized a section big enough to allow us to pass through for about thirty seconds." He spoke absently, as if his thoughts were on something else that was far more important. "Couldn't hold it any longer than that. At least not while I—" He broke off.

"You mean, you couldn't de-rez it for more than a few seconds and carry me through it at the same time," she said. "You don't have to spell it out. I know how much psi power that little leap through the waterfall must have cost you. I must have felt as heavy as that damn truck in your arms."

His brows rose. "A gentleman never calls attention to a lady's weight."

"I appreciate that." She frowned. "You must have melted your amber."

He glanced at his ring. "Yeah, it's fused. I've got a backup chunk, but I won't be able to use it for a while."

She looked around warily. The section of corridor in which they stood looked very much like the section on the other side of the waterfall. The same pale, luminous green glow infused the impermeable quartz. Here and there she caught the telltale trace of illusion shadow that marked the concealed door to a hidden room or antechamber. The dizzying maze of intersecting tunnels stretched out ahead as far as she could see.

The difference between this section of the catacombs and those on the other side of the waterfall, of course, was that this sector had not yet been officially mapped. The safest way out would be to go back through the waterfall, but that would not be possible until Sam had recovered from the aftereffects of melting amber. Besides, Leon Drummond might be waiting on the other side.

She checked her earrings. "My amber is still good. At least we won't lose our sense of direction."

Underground, the only thing that kept you oriented was tuned amber. Without it, the endless miles of eerie quartz tunnels became a hopelessly impenetrable labyrinth, even with a locator.

"Drummond tried to kill us," Sam said without inflection. "My guess is he's our Halloween trickster."

"The one who left that trap on our doorstep last night?"

"Yeah. Someone must be paying him very well to sabotage Ewert's map team. The guild frowns on that sort of thing. Bad public relations."

"Especially now when the guild is trying so hard to build a good public image." Virginia scrambled awkwardly to her feet. She glanced down, half-expecting to find scorch marks on her trousers. She saw nothing but a few new wrinkles. She looked up again. "Sam, you must be exhausted."

"Not yet. The afterburn is still kicking in. The buzz will last for about an hour. Then I'm going to have to crash for at least two or three hours. No way to beat it."

She nodded. The syndrome was well-known. Ghost-hunters who expended large amounts of psi energy needed time to recover.

Sam studied the corridors that branched off in different directions behind her. "We need to find a place where we can hole up for a while. In an hour I'm going to be asleep, like it or not."

She glanced around. "Why can't we just stay here? No one else is going to come through that waterfall."

"Probably not," Sam agreed. "But that's not what's got me worried."

"Well? What is worrying you? Aside from the fact that Drummond just tried to nail us?"

"It occurs to me that whoever hired Leon Drummond to keep Mac Ewert from making any progress in this corridor may be working illegally on *this* side of the waterfall."

Virginia widened her eyes as understanding hit her. "Yes, of course. An illegal excavation project on this side would explain a lot. But if you're right, we could run into Drummond's pals any minute."

"I'd say that's a definite risk." He started toward her. "Come on, we've got to find a place to hide until I can sleep off the afterburn."

"There are bound to be some chambers or rooms we can duck into for a few hours," she said. "All we have to do is pick one that doesn't look like it's been charted yet. Odds are no one will find us during the next few hours. Heck, I doubt if anyone will even come looking for us. Drummond must think we're dead. He'll no doubt report that we got reckless, got ourselves fried by that waterfall, and that the firm of Gage & Burch is out of business."

"True. He can't have any way of knowing that we survived. All the same, I don't want to take any more chances than necessary." Sam looked at her. "We haven't got a lot of time."

The prowling urgency in him worried her. She opened her mouth to say something reassuring, but the words got caught in her throat. He was only a short distance away now. For the first time since they had come through the waterfall, she got a close look at his eyes. What she saw there stilled her breath for a few seconds.

Hot, intense, brilliant; sexual desire, elemental and dangerously compelling, blazed in his eyes. His gaze literally glittered with what, in any other circumstances, she might have mistaken for the first evidence that he felt a degree of genuine passion for her.

Adeline's question came back to her in an uncomfortable rush. *"So, is it true what they say about ghost-hunters? Are they really amazing in bed after they've zapped a ghost? I've heard the sex is unbelievable right after a burn."*

What she saw in Sam now, she realized, was no more than the aftereffects of a massive expenditure of ghost-hunter psi talent. Chemically speaking, it was the result of a combination of testosterone, adrenaline, and the potent biological cocktail his paranormal powers had dumped into his bloodstream.

Nothing personal, she reminded herself. He wasn't attracted to her, per se. It just happened that he was rezzed for sex, and she was the only female in sight. Anything in skirts would probably do just fine for him at that moment.

"Uh, Sam? Are you okay?"

"No." He went past her, heading for the first branching corridor. "Let's get moving."

CHAPTER 3

HE WAS FREAKING HER OUT. HE KNEW IT, BUT THERE wasn't much he could do about it. Hanging on to his self-control required every shred of what little willpower he could muster. Getting them both safely through the waterfall had required more power than he'd ever used in his life; more than he'd known he possessed. He did not intend to tell Virginia the truth: that it had been damned close. They had made it, but in the process he'd poured so much psychic wattage through his amber that he'd destroyed the resonating properties of the precision-tuned stone. Melting amber meant you'd pushed the envelope. There was always a price to pay.

He'd experienced the sexual buzz that often occurred after a major burn before. In the past, he'd always felt fully in control of the predictable arousal. But this time things were different. It wasn't just that the burn had been bigger; the real problem was that this time, he was alone with Virginia, the woman he'd been lusting after for nearly two months.

He was in the grip of a feverish desire that was all the worse because he had worked so hard to suppress and conceal it.

All right, so he had a major hard-on. Just a few rampaging hormones. So what? He wasn't a kid. He could control himself. He *had* to control himself. If he lost it now, he would probably terrify her and turn her against him forever. Any chance he had with her would go up in smoke.

He tried to concentrate on moving ahead down the corridor, searching the walls for the barest hint of illusion energy that would indicate a hidden chamber they could use. All of the rooms that had ever been discovered in the corridors had been found sealed with illusion traps. If they could find a sealed room that looked as if no one else had ever de-rezzed the trap that guarded it, Virginia could unseal it, and they could hide inside for a few hours.

Simple. All he had to do was concentrate and not think about the fact that she was only a few inches away.

"Sam, you're shivering." Virginia touched his forehead with gentle, questing fingers. "Good heavens, you're burning up. You must be running a temperature. Is this normal?"

"Damn it, *don't touch me*." He closed his eyes briefly and drew a deep breath. Great. Now he was snapping at her. "We'll both be sorry if you do."

She frowned; not with fear or trepidation but with a concern that horrified him. If she started in with the sweet, nurturing stuff, he was doomed.

"This can't be normal," she insisted. "I think that burn must have made you ill."

"Trust me, it's normal," he said through set teeth. "A little intense, but normal."

He could not screw up and lose control. Not now. It was crucial that he did not scare her to death. Because maybe, just maybe, he really had heard her say "I love you" in those few seconds before he carried her through the waterfall.

"Slow down, Sam, I can't keep up with you."

He realized that he was loping down the corridor as he raked the walls for telltale signs of illusion dark. "Sorry." He forced himself to slow somewhat.

"It's okay. Let me worry about finding a trapped chamber. We're back into my field of expertise now." She moved out ahead of him. "I think I see something up ahead. Yes, I can feel it."

He tried but he did not pick up the psychic tang of illusion dark. "I don't feel a damn thing."

"Probably because your para-senses are temporarily over-rezzed. But I'm sure there's something up there." She broke into a quick trot. "Positive. And it's big. A big trap usually indicates a large chamber. Maybe we'll luck out and find a palace. They always have lots of little antechambers around them. Plenty of places to hide."

He hoped she was right. Beneath the clawing surge of sexual need and the rush of the burn buzz, he thought he could detect the first warnings of the crash that would soon follow. He could not afford to collapse here in the open corridor. Not when there was a possibility that Leon Drummond's cohorts might be in the neighborhood. He had to stay on his feet long enough to make sure Virginia was safe.

He followed her around a bend and saw that she had come to a halt in front of what, at first glance, appeared to be a section of green quartz wall. But there was something not quite right about the center portion. He peered more closely, blinking to clear his jumpy vision. The wall wavered slightly before it came back into focus. Illusion dark.

"Big," he muttered.

"Yes. Very unusual. Also very, very old."

The thoughtful, decidedly academic tone of her voice worried him. The last thing they could afford to do was waste time while she analyzed the trap from a professional point of view.

"You can write it up for an article in the *Journal of Para-Archaeology* when this is over," he said roughly. "Right now, we need to get into the space behind it."

She gave him a disgruntled look. "I know. Give me a minute here, though. There's something different about this trap."

A new wave of concern washed through him, rezzing up the already fizzing effects of the afterburn just as it had started to fade. "Can you handle it? Because if not, we've got to find another—"

"I can handle it," she assured him. "It's just . . . different, that's all. I can't explain—" She broke off. "Never mind."

She went to work untangling the trap that barred the door. Restlessly, he watched the corridor in both directions while she de-rezzed the entrance.

"Got it," Virginia whispered softly.

There was a disturbing note in her voice, but he did not have time to question her about it. He swung around and saw that there was now an opening in the green wall. Virginia had already moved through it.

He followed her quickly, surprised that he had to give his eyes a moment to adjust to the shadowy interior of the chamber. His first impression was of a vast space filled with green-drenched shadows.

His surroundings glowed, just as the tunnel did, but the light emitted by the quartz was much weaker and much dimmer in here. The effect was an emerald twilight.

The only thing he could tell for certain was that this chamber was large, much bigger than any of the others he had ever seen. In the gloom he could not make out the far walls or the ceiling. The space was filled with a number of structures of various sizes, all fashioned of the familiar green quartz. They were packed closely together and piled on top of each other, forming what looked like miniature city blocks crammed with a number of small apartments. The blocks were separated by narrow, twisting lanes.

He started toward the nearest of the apartments, assessing it as a potential hideout. He saw a narrow opening. It looked large enough to provide access to the interior of the building but small enough to be protected by a single man armed with a mag-rez gun.

Perfect.

"Hang on while I reset the trap," Virginia said behind him.

He paced restlessly while she worked. In a matter of seconds, illusion shadow once more obscured the entrance of the chamber.

"It won't deceive a trained tangler," she said as she turned back to face him, "but it might go unnoticed by a hunter or an excavation team worker, especially if he or she is in a hurry."

"With luck, there's no one out there looking for us."

"But you don't want to depend on luck, do you?"

"No." He scanned the dim chamber. "What the hell is this place?"

"Who knows?" She walked slowly toward him, searching the narrow canyons between the apartment-like structures. "I've never seen anything quite like it. Maybe it was a zoo. All those little cubicles and small rooms might have once been cages for animals."

"Maybe. Could just as easily have been a storage locker facility or an office park or a prison."

"We'll probably never know."

He came to a halt in front of the nearest apartment structure. It appeared to be several stories high. He could see many rows of neatly marked openings on the side.

"There must be a hundred little rooms in there," he said. "We can use one of them."

"Sam?" Virginia sounded uneasy again. "Are you thinking of hiding inside that particular building?"

"Uh-huh. Is it trapped?"

She went closer to examine the nearest entrance.

"Yes," she said.

He frowned. "Well? Can you untangle it?"

"Yes," she said again very evenly.

He waited for a few seconds, but he did not sense any psi energy. She was staring at the trapped entrance, but she wasn't working.

"What the hell's wrong?" he asked. "It's not like we've got all day here."

She turned slowly to face him. In the green twilight her eyes were more shadowed than the interior of the cubicle.

"Not this one," she said. "Let's try another one."

He started to argue and then reminded himself that when it came to traps, she was the pro. "All right, pick another one, but hurry."

She was already moving down the narrow lane between two looming structures. He paced behind her, controlling his temper when she passed up three more trapped entrances. Silently he willed her to make her choice so that he could get on with the task of rigging up some sort of defense that would protect her while he slept off the afterburn.

She turned at an intersection and went down another lane. Just when he was ready to take charge and make the choice for her, she came to a halt.

"Here," she said. She sounded relieved. "This one is okay. We can go inside."

"About time," he growled. "Do what you have to do."

She glanced at him. "No problem. There's no trap at this entrance."

"Damn." He took a closer look. The doorway she had chosen looked more elaborate than the others. It was wider, more ornately carved. It was taller, too. He shook his head. If push came to shove, it would not be as easy to defend. He turned away, scanning the ranks of darkly glowing openings in the green walls.

"No good," he said brusquely. "Pick one with a trap that you can reset after we're inside. It will give us an extra level of protection."

"This is the only one I've seen that feels okay."

He scowled. "What the hell do you mean, it feels okay?"

"Just what I said. This one is okay." Stubborn determination gleamed in her eyes. "This is my area of expertise, and I'm telling you that this will be a safer place to hide than any of the other possibilities that I've seen so far."

"But it's not even trapped."

"There's something wrong about those traps on the other entrances," she said. "I could untangle them, but I don't think that I should."

"You don't think you *should?*" He wanted to shake her. Didn't she realize he was trying to protect her? "What kind of a reason is that? If we get cornered in this chamber by a couple of hunters trying to protect an illegal excavation site, we're going to need all the help we can get. I want a doorway that's well-trapped."

She wrapped her arms around herself and looked at him with

unshakable conviction. "We can't go into any of those other rooms. Trust me on this, Sam. This is the only chamber I've seen yet that feels safe."

He hesitated. "Safe?"

"Yes." She unhugged herself and touched his cheek. She dropped her hand immediately when he flinched. "Sam, we've got to get you inside. You're in bad shape. You're scaring me."

"Just don't touch me," he warned. "Not until I've slept this off."

"Don't be ridiculous. How can it hurt if I touch you? Sam, you're not yourself. If you've got an ounce of sense, you'll admit that you're in no condition to be in charge of the firm of Gage & Burch at the moment."

She was right, but he did not want to admit it. Another wave of shivering swept over him. "Find a trapped room."

"We don't have time to keep looking. You need sleep."

"In a while. Not just yet."

"I'm officially declaring myself the boss of this partnership, at least for now. And I say you need sleep. Come with me."

She reached out without warning. Her hand closed around his arm, sending a tide of sensation screaming through his senses. This time he knew he was lost. The raging hunger roared past the last of his defenses. A great shudder of need wracked him. He no longer possessed the will to resist.

When she tugged him gently toward the doorway, he lurched once and then stumbled after her. At that moment he would have followed her anywhere; straight into hell, if that was where she wished to lead him.

She seemed oblivious to the storm that had him in its grip. She drew him through the untrapped doorway into a wide, softly lit room.

He was vaguely aware of a tall piece of statuary in the center of the space. It soared toward the ceiling, delicately carved in the familiar airy, abstract designs the Harmonics had favored. There was a shallow pool beneath it. Emerald streams of sparkling energy poured gently from the top of the ornately designed quartz. The gentle waves bounced and splashed in the pool.

"A fountain," Virginia breathed in wonder. "I've never seen anything like it. Never even *heard* of anything like it. Maybe this place was some sort of park, or maybe it was a garden in some wealthy Harmonic home. But why all the little tiny rooms in that warren outside?"

"Maybe the neighborhood went bad. Turned into a slum." Sam shook his head, unable to concentrate on the fountain or any of the other questions she had brought up. All of his over-rezzed senses were riveted on her.

"This way," she said.

He did not reply. He knew that he was so far gone now, that if he tried to speak, nothing coherent would come from his throat. He stared longingly at the back of her head as she urged him through an interior doorway. She had a beautifully shaped head, he decided. And the color of her hair, a warm reddish brown, was perfect. The urge to pull her down onto the hard quartz floor and cover her body with his own was nearly overwhelming. He prayed that he would crash into deep sleep before he succumbed to the torrent of desire that was pulsing through him.

Inside the smaller antechamber, Virginia paused. "This will do, I think. You can sleep it off here."

He caught a glimpse of some large chests arranged around the room, saw a green staircase in the corner, but all he could think of was Virginia. He closed his eyes to shut out the sight of her. The attempt to banish her vision from his senses did not work. The scent of her hit him like a narcotic.

Crash, he thought. *Just crash, and this will all be over.* Then he remembered something else; something he had to do first. He reached into his boot and removed the slender little mag-rez gun. He held it out to her.

"Take this. If anyone comes through the door of this chamber before I wake up, use it."

She looked at the gun and then raised startled eyes to his. "Since when did you start carrying a mag-rez?"

"Since I ran into my first ruin rat on my very first consulting assignment," he said brusquely. "I nearly got myself killed. After that, I started carrying one. I also carry a flashlight, even though no one's ever found a darkened tunnel, and extra tuned amber. Call me superstitious. Do you know how to use this?"

"No, of course not," she said primly. "Instruction in the use of mag-rez weapons is not included in the curriculum of the department of archaeology at the university. Probably because it's illegal to carry one underground."

He gritted his teeth and pointed at the weapon. "This is the safety. Disengage it before you use it. When you want to fire, just point it in the general direction of that doorway and squeeze the trigger. Don't worry about aiming. This thing will stun a man regardless of where you hit him."

She looked dubious. "Do you really think I'll need it?"

"I can't think clearly at all right now," he said flatly. "So just take it and promise me you'll use it if necessary."

"Okay." Gingerly she took it from his hand.

He looked around for a place to lie down. But he was still humming with afterburn sizzle and the sexual energy continued to wash through him. It would be a few more minutes before he could take refuge in sleep. He closed his eyes, fighting back raw need. When he raised his lashes, he saw that Virginia was watching him with intense concern.

"Sam?"

"I want you."

She blinked but she did not draw back.

"Sorry," he muttered. He wiped his damp forehead with the back of his sleeve. "Can't help it."

"I know." There was no fear in her eyes, but there was something else; something that could have been sad resignation. "It's all right. I understand about the effects of the afterburn."

"The hell with the afterburn." Unable to keep his hands off her any longer, he gripped her shoulders. "I've wanted you since the day you walked through my front door."

She stared at him with what could only have been amazement. "You have?"

He groaned, pulled her hard against his chest, and tilted her chin. "More than I've ever wanted anything or anyone else in my life."

He kissed her before she could respond. He had to kiss her. Just one kiss, he promised himself. Drain off a little of the sexual charge. By the time it was over, surely the crash would have overtaken him. It had to hit soon. Any second now. Then he would escape into the merciful oblivion of sleep before he did anything else real stupid.

As a plan, it seemed simple and straightforward. Then again, he might have been hallucinating by now, he thought.

But however brilliant the scheme seemed, he knew as soon as he took her mouth that something was going horribly, wonderfully, terrifyingly wrong. Virginia put her arms around his neck and kissed him back.

"Oh, *Sam*."

"Oh, *shit*."

Her response was the last straw. He cradled her face in his hands and drank hungrily from her lips as if he could consume the essence of her vibrant spirit. She moaned softly and tightened her grip on his neck. He could feel the swell of her breasts beneath the sturdy twill of her shirt. The inside of her mouth was warm and welcoming, just as he had imagined.

For the first time he feared that the crash would overcome him before he could finish what he had started. A whole new sense of urgency slammed through him.

Not daring to raise his mouth from hers for fear that he might somehow lose her, he started to undress her. It was not an easy task. His hands were shaking so badly that he could barely manage the buttons.

He felt her fingers slide beneath the waistband of his trousers, gliding up beneath the hem of his shirt. Her palms flattened against his chest, and he thought he would go through the roof. He realized that she was shivering now, too.

"Sam, are you sure you're not ill?"

"I'm okay." He struggled with her shirt.

"I was so afraid that you—"

"Nothing to be afraid of." He managed to wrench his mouth from hers long enough to kiss her throat. "I swear it. You don't have to be afraid of me. I won't hurt you. I could never hurt you."

"I know. That wasn't what I meant."

He finished fumbling with the last of the buttons that closed her shirt. He peeled the garment off her shoulders and hurled it aside. Then he heard himself utter a thick, husky groan. He could feel her firm little nipples pressing against the sleek fabric of her bra.

She was working on his belt now. The sweet torture was almost beyond endurance. Every time her fingers brushed against his skin he thought he would explode.

He dragged the straps of her bra down her arms, freeing her breasts. He leaned his hot forehead against her cool brow and looked at the taut, peaked curves.

"You are so beautiful," he muttered, awed.

She gave him a smile laced with infinite mystery. "No, but you're making me feel beautiful."

He lacked the patience to argue. She was beautiful; the most beautiful, most desirable woman he had ever seen in his life. He knew that, even if she did not.

He scooped her up in his arms, intending to lower her to the floor. Out of the corner of his eye, he saw a wide chest carved of quartz. It would not be any softer than the floor, but at least it looked vaguely like a bed.

He carried Virginia to the hard couch and put her down on it. She lay back on the emerald stone, her hair spilling around her head, her eyes glowing with desire, and watched him with great expectation as he unbuckled his belt.

Her expression nearly finished him.

He yanked impatiently at his clothing. The cocktail in his bloodstream made him clumsy and awkward. But when he finally lowered himself onto the chest and pulled Virginia into his arms, he had never felt better in his life.

Nothing had ever been this good.

He slid one leg between hers and dampened his fingers in her liquid heat.

She gasped, trembled, and closed her eyes. She slid her palm down his chest, across his belly, and lower. He felt her fingers close around him and thought his heart might stop.

"*Sam.*"

Another wave of need thundered through him. "No, don't touch me like that. I won't be able—"

"It's all right."

"Stop saying that." He came down on top of her. Her green-gold eyes were luminous with desire. "Virginia, this isn't the way I wanted to do this, but I can't wait. Not this time."

"It's all right," she said. She opened her legs for him, drew up her knees, and wrapped her arms around him. "Really."

"Hold me." It was half plea, half demand. "Promise me you won't let go."

"Never."

He squeezed his eyes shut against the riptide of need that was threatening to sweep him out into a dark sea. She shifted a little beneath him, and the glide of her silken skin against him nearly ended the matter right then and there.

He plunged deep; sinking recklessly, exultantly into the snug, tight channel of her body. He felt the initial resistance and then she closed around him. She cried out and clung to him, fighting him for the embrace.

He rocked violently against her, driving himself to the hilt with every thrust, needing to forge a bond that would hold long after this encounter.

The climax hit him. Simultaneously he thought he felt Virginia convulse beneath him, but he could not be certain. He barely had time to register a sensation so intense that it could not truly be described as pleasure. But it was not pain, either. Something else, he thought vaguely, something infinitely more important.

There was no time to analyze the incredible feeling. Hard on its heels came the crash. He could only marvel that it had not struck sooner.

He collapsed on top of her, aware that he was trapping her against the quartz chest with his weight. But there was nothing he could do about it. The deep, dreamless sleep took him.

CHAPTER 4

IT FELT AS IF ONE OF THE ANCIENT STONE CORRIDORS had caved in on top of her. Sam was no lightweight to begin with and, as she quickly discovered, he seemed to be built mostly of muscle and bone. There was no softness in him and there was none beneath her.

Talk about being between a rock and a hard place, Virginia thought.

She took a deep breath, braced her hands on Sam's chest, and heaved upward with all of her strength. She managed to gain some wiggle room and, with another strong shove, she was finally able to slide out from underneath his inert body.

She sat up and got cautiously to her feet. There was something wrong with her knees. They were not quite steady. A tremor went through her. She had to grab hold of the edge of the chest to get her balance. *For the record, Adeline, everything you've ever heard about sex with a ghost-hunter in the midst of an afterburn is true.*

Or maybe this was just the result of sex with Sam, she thought cheerfully. She didn't have an extensive amount of experience to call upon when it came to this kind of thing, but it didn't take a lot of experimentation to know what she'd just shared with Sam had been very special. At least she no longer entertained any doubts as to whether or not there were fires of passion burning somewhere inside Sam.

They were there, all right. Enough to set a whole forest ablaze.

Of course, his response to her could have been ignited simply by the legendary ghost-hunter buzz, she reminded herself. Her euphoric spirits sank as suddenly as they had risen. Anything in skirts might have had the same impact on him at that particular moment.

Reality returned with a jarring thud. With a sigh, she steadied herself and glanced around the gloom-filled room. The carved stone chest on which Sam slept was one of several in the chamber. There were also a variety of vases and urns set in softly glowing alcoves. The drenching shadows created a solemn but surprisingly tranquil effect. Perhaps this had once been a meditation room in a Harmonic home. Assuming the Harmonics had meditated.

Questions, questions.

She dressed quickly and picked up the little mag-rez gun. She checked the safety as Sam had demonstrated and then shoved it into her belt.

She glanced uncertainly at Sam. He certainly looked magnificent stretched out stark naked on the stone chest, and she knew he was not cold because the temperature in the catacombs was always the same, comfortable and dry, day and night, year in, year out. But the sight of him was more than a little distracting. The muscled, well-defined contours of his chest and shoulders sent a pleasant little shiver through her.

Their lovemaking had been fast and furious. There had been no time for her to indulge herself in an exploration of his body. She had been intensely aware of the thick, heavy size and weight of his erection, but she had not really *seen* him. Now, she could not stop gazing at him. He fascinated her, she thought. She had wanted to stroke him and touch him for weeks, but this was the first opportunity she'd had to satisfy her longing.

She examined the fierce planes of his face, relishing the determined angle of his jaw and the pleasing, masculine shape of his ears. His dark hair was seductively ruffled where she had run her fingers through it earlier. With his eyes closed he was all hard edges and tough, sleek male. But when his eyes were open you saw the intelligence and the self-control that defined his nature.

When Sam loved, she thought, his emotions would be as steady and as enduring as the glow of Harmonic quartz.

Unable to resist the temptation, she reached out very carefully and slowly closed her hand around the top of his muscled thigh. He was hard and warm beneath her fingers. She drew her palm slowly down to his knee, savoring the feel of him.

Sam shuddered and mumbled something in his sleep. Startled, she snatched her hand away and stepped back. But when he did not awaken, she reached out once more.

This time she traced a path upward toward his chest, curling her fingers in the crisp hair there. He shifted slightly, but she knew from the steadiness of his breathing that he was still sound asleep. A part of him was stirring, she noticed. She stared at his penis, fascinated to see that it appeared to be swelling in length and width once more. Apparently, the deep sleep of afterburn did not shut down all systems.

There was probably a law against looking at him like this, she thought. If there wasn't, there should have been. It was entirely too much fun.

On the other hand, she was going to marry him soon. Surely that gave her some rights.

"Enough with the voyeuristic fun and games," she muttered. "You're supposed to be standing guard."

She picked up Sam's discarded clothing and covered his torso with his shirt. Then she folded his trousers and placed them neatly beneath his head to serve as a pillow. She was already starting to feel quite wifely, she thought, amused.

With a last glance at him, she turned and walked out into the fountain room. The green energy continued to flow and splash in the small pool. It had no doubt been doing so for several thousand years.

She braced one hand on the thick edge of the doorway and looked around with professional interest. This room had the same somber, curiously reflective feel as the smaller antechamber in which Sam slept. She could not explain, even to herself, why these spaces felt safe while the countless little cubicles outside did not.

She took her hand off the wall and made her way across the fountain room to the outer door. She gazed into the narrow aisle that separated this block of cells from the one across the way and listened intently with both her physical and para senses.

Nothing. No indication that the unusual trap that guarded the main entrance to this weird complex had been breached. No voices or footsteps echoed on the paths that intersected the ranks of cubicle-laced buildings. She detected nothing that indicated that anyone who might be looking for them had discovered the zoo chamber.

She waited quietly in the fountain room for a while longer, uncomfortably aware of the weight of the mag-rez gun on her hip. Gradually, boredom set in. Professional curiosity followed closely on its heels. Whatever this place was, it constituted a spectacular new find. She had a degree in para-archaeology, and she was diligent about keeping up with the research on the subject. She was quite certain that nothing remotely resembling this nest of tiny, illusion-trapped cubicles had ever been written up in the academic literature.

She stepped cautiously out into the shadowy lane, visions of an article in the *Journal of Para-Archaeology* with her name on it as author dancing in her head. That kind of publicity would do wonders for the reputation of the new firm of Gage & Burch.

She walked slowly along the gloom-filled path and paused in front of the first of the small cells that lined the little alley. She examined the dense shadow that glinted just at the edge of her vision. The human eye could detect the stuff that the Harmonics had used to weave their dangerous snares, but it could not focus directly on the nearly invisible psi energy.

She crouched down, concentrating with her para senses, and probed the pattern. As she had concluded earlier, there was nothing particularly complex about the design. She could undo it easily enough. But the sense of wrongness was deeply disturbing. Everything within her resisted the notion of untangling the trap.

With a shock, it occurred to her that perhaps it was not the trap itself that was dangerous. Maybe the true threat existed—or had once existed—*inside* the little room. Perhaps the trap was just a warning.

Maybe this place had once been a Harmonic hotel and all of these little traps were nothing more than ordinary Do Not Disturb signs hung on doorknobs to keep the maid from entering unexpectedly.

She contemplated that possibility for a moment and then returned to her zoo theory. She liked it much better. The traps might have functioned as fences to keep dangerous creatures locked inside or to keep curious visitors from getting too close to the beasts inside the cages.

She straightened and walked a few more feet to examine some of the other illusion-darkened entrances. Every single one of them gave off the same clear psychic warnings.

After a while, she returned to the fountain room. A quick check on Sam showed that he was still totally out of it.

She sat down on a glowing quartz bench facing the untrapped doorway and took the mag-rez gun out of her belt.

She wondered how long Sam would sleep.

SAM CAME AWAKE WITH A SENSE OF URGENCY, AS IF someone had just yelled *fire*. He sat up quickly, memory returning in a heated rush. But there was nothing to indicate that the situation had changed while he had slept off the worst effects of the afterburn. If any of Leon Drummond's pals had burst through the doorway, he would have awakened with his hands and feet bound in duct tape, if he had awakened at all.

Relief swept through him. Something soft slid off his chest and fell to the floor. He looked down and saw his shirt. Virginia must have covered him with it after he had nodded off, which had been right after he had taken her with all the finesse of a specter-cat in full rut.

Virginia. He briefly closed his eyes as the images cascaded through him, burning more intensely than ghost fire. For a few seconds he savored them. Then reality closed in. He knew that his recollection of her passionate response might be nothing more than an illusion concocted by his singed senses; some sort of weird para-psych rationalization for what he had done to her.

Yet he could still feel the softness of the skin on the insides of her thighs and the damp, clinging clasp of her body. Just remembering made his insides tighten all over again.

He had wanted her more than he had ever thought it possible to want any woman. But no more so because of the buzz from the afterburn. The truth was, he had been wanting her just as badly for weeks. The only difference was that two hours ago he had lost control.

The flash of relief he had experienced after waking evaporated. In its place was a bottomless pool of dread. He had to face the grim truth: After weeks of being so cautious, so careful, there was a damn good chance that he had destroyed the glowing future he had worked so hard to build.

He had no one to blame but himself.

Virginia had had a bad case of bridal jitters before they embarked on this venture. After what he had done to her here in this room, she no doubt despised him. It would be a miracle if he hadn't scared the living daylights out of her. She was probably making plans this very minute not only to call off their marriage but their business partnership as well.

He picked up his shirt and got to his feet. Anger washed through him. He was furious with himself. The loss of control had been inexcusable. He could only pray that he had not hurt her.

How long had he been out? He glanced at his watch. Two hours. Long enough to restore some but not all of his depleted psi energy. He needed more sleep to function at full capacity but he could manage with what he had regained during the nap.

He grabbed his trousers and pulled them on. The only thing he could do to make amends to Virginia was to get her safely back to the surface.

A shadow moved in the doorway that separated the antechamber from the fountain room. Not illusion-shadow, but it might as well have been, given the hopelessness of his situation.

"Sam." Virginia hovered anxiously in the doorway. "You're awake. Everything okay?"

"Good enough." He realized with a jolt that he did not want to meet her eyes. He did not want to see the accusation and the wariness that he knew he would find there. "Nothing new outside?"

"We're still alone in this place. I'm beginning to think I was right when I suggested it might have once been a zoo. Something about the nature of the traps makes me think they were set to keep visitors away from whatever used to live in all these little apartments or cages."

"Whoever or whatever once lived in the cells is long gone." He reached for his boots. He did not remember removing them. His jaw tightened. "Got the mag-rez?"

"Right here." She took a few steps into the room to hand it to him. "Sam, are you really okay?"

"Don't worry, I'll be able to get us out of here." He took the narrow little gun from her and shoved it back into his belt. "There's probably another exit around here somewhere, but I think our best bet is to go back out the way we came."

She halted. "Back through the waterfall?"

"Yeah. It's the last thing Drummond would expect. Especially after all this time has passed. By now he'll have reported us officially missing, probably killed by an explosion of dissonance energy. I doubt if we'll find him hanging around on the other side waiting for us. But just in case, I'll have the mag-rez in my hand when we go through the waterfall."

"All right. Whatever you think best. You're the expert on ghost-energy."

He glanced down and realized that he was dressed. He could find no more excuses for avoiding her eyes. Time to act like a man. He turned slowly around to face her. "Virginia—"

"Sam—"

They both broke off, staring at each other. In the gloom it was impossible for him to read the expression in her eyes. If she was frightened of him, she was hiding it well, he thought.

He braced himself and tried again. "I'm sorry for what happened," he said evenly. "I don't know what else to say. I could promise you that it won't ever happen again, but I don't know if I can keep that promise."

She did not pretend to misunderstand. "I see."

He drew a deep breath. "I realize that you're probably having second thoughts about our business arrangement as well as our marriage. I don't blame you. I've been doing some thinking about it, too."

"You have?"

He glanced around the tranquil little room. "This is not the time or place to talk about how we're going to terminate our business futures."

"No, it's not." There was an unsettling, flat note in her voice.

"Yeah, well, let's save that conversation for later." He started toward the door, aware that even in the depths of the disaster, he was still trying to buy himself some time. The odds were strongly against him coming up with a way to talk her into going through with the marriage after what had happened, but he could not give up without a fight.

She looked at him as he went past her. "Sam, do you really regret what happened?"

"Hell, yes, I regret it." He planted one hand against the green stone doorway and turned to face her. "Making love to you was the last thing I wanted to do."

She stiffened. "I realize that you were rezzed up because of the afterburn."

"That was no excuse."

"Just tell me one thing. Would anything in skirts have worked for you two hours ago?"

He frowned at her trousers. "You aren't wearing skirts."

She narrowed her eyes. "That was a figure of speech."

"It's never smart to use figures of speech when you're talking to a hunter who's still recovering from an afterburn. We tend to be literal, even on our good days."

"For heaven's sake, this is no time for wisecracks. We're talking about our future."

"I thought we just got through deciding to talk about it later." He took his hand off the wall and stalked into the fountain room.

"Damn it," she called out behind him, "don't you dare walk out on me when I'm talking to you. Come back here, Sam Gage."

"What the hell do you want from me?" He felt his temper ignite. "I said I'm sorry. I don't usually lose control, not even during an afterburn. But things got out of hand this time."

She swept out her palm to indicate the quartz chest on which they had made love. "Didn't what happened in here mean *anything* to you?"

"Of course it did. It meant I screwed up everything. But what's done is done."

She raised her chin, eyes glittering with anger. "Would you undo it if you could?"

"Didn't I just get through saying that I—" He broke off abruptly. There was no point lying about it. The damage was done. He set his back teeth. "I wish it had happened under other circumstances. I wish I had done things differently. I wish I hadn't scared the hell out of you."

"But you aren't really, truly sorry that you made love to me?"

He hesitated. "Well—"

"Just say it."

He felt cornered. Despair, anger, and frustration boiled together, a dangerous stew spiced with emotions he knew he did not handle well. "You want the truth? The truth is what I said to you just before I tossed you down onto that damned stone chest. The truth is that I've been wanting to make love to you since the first day I saw you."

A short, intense silence gripped the chamber.

Virginia's brows bristled in a ferocious scowl. "Good. Because that's pretty much how I've felt from the first moment I saw you, too."

He felt as if he'd just been struck by lightning. For a few seconds he was too stunned to do anything more than stare at her. "It is?"

"Yes." She glared at him. "But you seemed so distant and cool. So businesslike. You kept talking about how many new clients we would attract working as a team. You went on and on about how much money we'd both make once we sold the house to developers."

He finally managed to unfreeze himself. He took a step toward her. "I never wanted to sell the house in the first place. I came up with the idea because I thought it would be a good way to talk you into a marriage-of-convenience. I figured if I—" He stopped. "Hell, I don't know what I was thinking."

She cleared her throat. "We're both adults. We're single. There's no reason we can't simply admit that we're attracted to each other. Marriages-of-convenience are designed for just this sort of situation."

"A legal, socially acceptable, two-year affair."

"Exactly." She shrugged. "If it's just passion, it will probably burn itself out in that length of time."

"Yeah. Sure." Never in a million years. How could he possibly let go of her in two years? Better not to go there in the first place if he knew that he would eventually lose her. But how could he not take what she offered, given the lonely alternative. "Virginia—"

"That's what you wanted, wasn't it? That was the deal. A two-year MC." She smiled a little too brightly. "And I agreed."

She was acting weird, and it made him more uneasy than ever. What the hell was the matter with him? He had gotten exactly what he'd asked for, what he'd wished for when he'd concocted the plan in the first place.

"You know, you were right when you said that this was not the time or place to discuss this sort of thing," Virginia said briskly. "We'd better get going."

He moved toward her. "Is sex all you want out of this?"

"Isn't that what you want out of it?"

"Sex is good. Great." Anger pulsed in him. "I can work with sex."

Her face tightened in renewed concern. "You know, you really don't look normal yet, Sam. You could still be suffering from afterburn. Maybe you'd better get some more sleep before we attempt to go back through that waterfall."

"You're right about one thing. I'm not feeling real normal."

Her eyes widened as he closed the distance between them. "Now hold on just one damn minute. If you think we're going to have sex every time you claim to be in the throes of an afterburn buzz, you can think again. I'll admit it's interesting, but—"

She stopped talking abruptly when he caught her wrists and pinned her to the wall.

"You just got through telling me that you were in this deal for the sex," he reminded her.

"I've got nothing against sex." Her voice was tight with anger. "But the next time we do it, I want to make sure it's for real. Not just the result of a bad burn buzz. Don't you get it?"

"No." He leaned in closer. "Explain it to me in short words."

"I want to be sure it's me you want. I want to be absolutely certain that not just any female would do."

"Trust me, no one else will do."

There was a short, tense silence. Then she cleared her throat and wriggled her fingers in his grasp. "In that case, stop acting like some macho jerk hunter."

He kept her wrists anchored against the wall. "But I am a macho jerk hunter."

"No, you are not," she muttered, seriously disgruntled now. "Stop talking like that."

"You've as good as said I behaved like a macho jerk hunter a couple of hours ago when I made love to you just before I crashed. What happens the next time we get into this kind of situation? Am I going to have to listen to a lot of accusations about how anything in skirts would do? When it's over, will I have to explain that I knew it was you I was having sex with?"

"Just because I wanted to be sure you knew it was me—"

"Believe me. I knew it was you. Just like I know it's you now."

He kissed her, hard and deliberately, letting her feel the frustration and temper she had aroused in him, letting her know that this time he knew full well that she was the woman he had pinned against the glowing quartz wall.

She went rigid. Despair knifed through him.

"Virginia." He released her wrists and caught her head between his hands. "Damn it, Virginia. I want you so much."

She gave a muffled cry and threw her arms around his neck, kissing him feverishly. "I didn't mean to call you a stupid, macho jerk hunter."

"Don't worry about it." Relief surged through him. "Sometimes I am a macho jerk hunter."

"No." She clenched her fingers in his hair. "Never. I knew from the first day that you weren't a macho jerk hunter."

"Yeah?" He took her tender earlobe between his teeth and nibbled hungrily. "What was your first clue?"

"You were reading the *Journal of Para-Archaeology* instead of the latest issue of *Sex-Starved Psychic Playmates*."

"Lucky for me my subscription ran out three months ago," he said very fervently against her throat. "I never got around to renewing it."

She laughed softly. Her head tipped back against his arm. "Oh, Sam, do you really think this will work?"

"We'll make it work." Two years. He had two full years to make it work. He touched the edge of his tongue to the soft skin beneath the collar of her shirt.

She stiffened.

"Sam?"

"It's okay. Even without the skirts, I'm positive I'm dealing with the right lady here."

"No, wait." She planted her palms against his shoulders and pushed him away from her.

He stilled, aware that something was wrong. "What is it?"

"Psi energy. I can feel it. Someone is trying to take down the big trap at the entrance to this zoo."

"Drummond's friends. So they did come looking, after all." The charge of sexual anticipation that had been arcing through him instantly transmuted itself into another kind of high-rez buzz.

"Wait here." He turned and went swiftly across the fountain room. He halted in the outer doorway and listened intently. Sound carried underground. So did the feel of psi energy.

He heard voices reverberating in the distance. They came from the vicinity of the entrance to the vast zoo chamber.

". . . waste of time. Don't care what Drummond says. No way the S.O.B. coulda made it through that waterfall with the little lady tangler. No small-time security guy could be that good. Even if he was that good and even if he did make it through with her, he'd have one hell of an afterburn. He'll be wasted for at least another hour or two."

"We're working for Fairbanks, not Drummond. He said not to take any chances, and he's the one paying us. The orders were to check out every possibility in this damned corridor, so that's what we're gonna do. Now, shut up and untangle this trap."

"Okay, okay. Give me a minute. It's a big sucker."

Sam left the doorway and went to where Virginia stood waiting.

"Let's go." He took her arm.

"Where?"

"Up." He took her arm and started toward the emerald staircase. "It's easier to hunt when you've got the high ground."

"Whatever you say."

She followed him up the narrow, twisting steps to the next level. He saw the gloom-shrouded entrance to another chamber similar to the one below. An energy fountain cascaded silently in the center. Several more ornately carved chests were arranged in an artful manner around the room.

But the thing that interested him the most was the narrow window. He hesitated before he crossed the threshold and glanced at Virginia.

"Trapped?"

She shook her head, frowning intently. "No. This room is clear. Maybe this was the zoo's souvenir shop."

"Or the visitors' room in the prison." He went to the window, braced one hand on the wide ledge, and looked down into the lane. "This will work. If they bother to search this far, I'll have a clear shot."

". . . Got it. We're in."

"Shit. What the hell is this place? Look at all those little rooms. Some kinda cheap hotel, d'ya think?"

Virginia stirred hesitantly in the doorway. Then she walked slowly into the room, careful to keep a respectful distance from the energy fountain. "I don't like this."

"Don't worry. I've got a hunch that once they get a good look at all these little cubicles and realize how long it will take to search this place, they'll figure out something else to do. If they do get this far, I can handle them."

"I know that." She folded her arms very tightly beneath her breasts. "Sam, I'm afraid that tangler will try to de-rez some of the traps."

He sank deeper into the gloom and watched the lane. "So?"

"I told you, I don't think they should be touched. If he starts fooling around with some of them, looking for us—"

She broke off.

He gazed at her. "You're really worried about the nature of the those illusion traps, aren't you?"

"Yes." Her mouth tightened. "I told you, there's something very, very strange about them. One way or another, they all seem to spell out Do Not Disturb in great big capital letters.

"Whatever didn't want to be disturbed is long gone, Virginia."

"I know, but it just doesn't *feel* right."

He shrugged. "Maybe that tangler down there will come to the same conclusion, and he and his hunter pal will leave us in peace."

". . . Gonna take a couple of hours to go through this place room by room. Must be hundreds of little cubicles in here. And they're all trapped, I'm telling you."

"If they got this far, neither one of 'em would be in great shape. Gage will have crashed, and the tangler will be scared out of her wits. I'll bet they would have picked one of these little cubbyholes near the entrance. Start working, man. I'd rather find the bastard before he recovers from the crash. Easier to handle that way."

"Uh, Drake, I don't like the looks of these traps."

"I don't give a damn how they look to you. Start takin' 'em apart."

"There's something real weird—"

"Shut up and get to work, Chaz. Unless you wanna explain things to Fairbanks."

"Sure. Okay. I'm workin' on it."

"Oh, damn," Virginia whispered. "He's going to do it."

Sam took his eyes off the lane long enough to look at her. The stark alarm in her voice worried him. She was scared, he thought. Genuinely, thoroughly, deep-down scared.

"What is it with you and these traps?" he started to ask.

"Sam." Her eyes widened in sudden alarm. "Get down. Now."

"Take it easy, honey, I've got to keep watch—"

"He's got it. He's undone the first trap. I can feel it."

"It's okay—"

"No, it's not okay." She flew toward him across the room and seized his arm. "Get away from the window."

Automatically, he started to resist the tug of her fingers. But the urgency in her was not to be ignored. He reminded himself that traps fell into her area of expertise. They were partners. He had to respect her instincts.

He allowed himself to be drawn away from the window. She pulled him deeper into the room.

"Down," she whispered, dragging him down behind a large quartz chest. "Hurry."

He crouched beside her, the mag-rez gun in hand. "I hope you know what the hell you're doing."

Before she could respond, an inhuman shriek of mingled rage and despair rent the gloom of the alien zoo. It echoed endlessly off the walls. Sam froze, his hand tightening convulsively around the gun. Beside him, Virginia shuddered.

"What in the name of Old Earth . . . ?" Sam whispered.

A very human shout went up, a high, keening cry of terror.

"There's something in there."

Chaz, the tangler, Sam thought.

". . . Get outa here . . ."

Another alien scream rose, joining the crescendoing wail of the first. And then a torrent of screeches, shrieks, howls, and dreadful cries arose. There was a hellishly mournful quality to the unnatural sounds, as though whatever had once inhabited the small cells had been aroused from their centuries-deep sleep to protest the disturbance. The cacophony of otherworldly cries drowned out the screams of Chaz and Drake.

The vast zoo room began to darken. The green gloom seemed to thicken and grow dense. Sam followed Virginia's gaze. They both looked out the narrow window. It was like looking into the depths of an alien sea.

"Dear heaven." Virginia said in amazement.

He knew what was going through her mind. There was no such thing as night and day in the ruins. The glow of the quartz was always steady. True, there had been more than the usual number of shadows in the zoo chamber, but there had been light, and it had remained at a constant level.

Until now.

Only the chamber in which they crouched remained luminous.

Jagged shards of green lightning flashed outside the narrow opening, shattering the heavy darkness that enveloped the zoo. The alien shrieks grew louder.

More lightning sizzled. As Sam watched, an acid-hued bolt of energy illuminated some thing that floated in midair outside the window. He caught a glimpse of a green phantom so gossamer thin and transparent that he could see straight through it to the opposite wall. As he watched, another specter joined the first.

"UDEMs," Virginia whispered. "When Chaz untangled the trap he must have disturbed some."

"Whatever the hell those two things are, they aren't standard-issue energy ghosts." Sam probed cautiously, feeling for the telltale trace of psi energy emitted by normal unstable dissonance energy manifestations. What he picked up with his para senses felt wrong. He cut off the probe immediately. He did not want to draw the attention of the strange specters.

"If they're not UDEMs, what are they?" she asked very softly.

"They're energy ghosts of some kind but not like any I've ever dealt with. Look at the way they move."

"As if—" Virginia hesitated. "As if they're headed somewhere."

"Yeah. Right toward Chaz and Drake."

"But that's impossible."

"Uh-huh."

She was right, of course. UDEMs were not sentient beings. They certainly weren't the ghosts of long-dead aliens, although more than one or two hucksters and con men had tried to convince the gullible of that over the years.

Technically speaking, UDEMs were nothing more than balls of residual psi energy left behind by whatever had once powered Harmonic technology. The only reason they were called ghosts was because they tended to drift through the ancient corridors like ghosts.

Green lightning zigzagged through the misty darkness outside the window. More ghosts drifted past the opening, streaming toward the entrance of the zoo chamber.

"Damn," Sam said. "What the devil is going on out there?"

"I don't know, but I can tell you that this is Chaz's fault," Virginia said grimly. "He set them off. I knew there was something strange about those traps."

The hideous wails continued to rise and fall in the unnatural night.

"Sounds like a reunion of lost souls," Virginia whispered. "I can't even hear Chaz and Drake now. Wonder what's happened to them?"

"Maybe we don't want to know."

"Maybe you're right."

Virginia huddled close, but Sam noticed that she was careful not to impede his gun hand. Not that the mag-rez would be effective against whatever was out there, he thought. If one of the things changed course and drifted through the window, their only hope would be his psi-talent.

More lightning sparked violently. Again and again it shattered the night. But there was no accompanying roll of thunder, Sam noticed. For some reason that only made the energy flashes seem all the more bizarre.

"It's like there's a storm going on out there," Virginia muttered.

"Maybe that's exactly what it is," Sam said, thinking about it. "An energy storm triggered by the untangling of the first trap."

"But to what purpose?"

"Who knows? We're talking about the Harmonics here. No one has a clue about why they did anything. If the place was a zoo or a prison, it's possible those in charge installed some unusual security measures. Maybe we're witnessing some kind of system meant to round up the escapees."

"*Sam.*" Virginia touched his arm, her eyes fixed on the window. "Look."

"I see it."

One of the phantoms had halted in front of the opening. Sam told himself that it was just a mindless UDEM, but it was all too easy to imagine that it was peering into this room as if it sensed prey.

He readied himself, not wanting to use psi energy unless there was no alternative, because he could not be sure that his talent would work against this stuff.

The ghost hovered. The brightest portion of it was at least three feet in length, but its aura flared out in a much wider band of acid green.

It drifted through the window.

"Damn."

Beside him, Virginia sucked in a deep breath, but she said nothing.

Decision time, Sam thought. He could either try to prod it back out the window or he could attempt to clobber it. He opted for the gentle nudge.

He sent out a pulse of psi-talent, gently summoning energy from the quartz walls, ceiling, and floor. A small ball of glowing green fire took shape in the center of the room. He propelled it gently toward the intruder.

The strange UDEM that had drifted through the window paused as though confused. Then, to Sam's enormous relief, it retreated from the smaller ghost.

It wafted back out through the window and disappeared in the wake of the school of phantoms roaming through the streets of the zoo.

Virginia exhaled on a long, soft sigh. "Nice. Very nice."

He could almost taste his own relief. For the first time, he realized that his shirt was stuck to his back. "Don't ever say I don't know how to show a lady a fun time on Halloween."

"A lot of hunters would have tried to blast it to smithereens," she said very seriously. "For some reason, I don't think that tactic would have worked."

"No," he said, "I don't think it would have."

The storm crackled and blazed. An endless parade of desolate-sounding specters and phantoms flitted past the window.

The tempest seemed to rage for hours, but when at last it began to abate, Sam looked at his watch. He was startled to see that only twenty-three minutes had passed.

"I think it's ending," Virginia said.

Gradually, the unholy wails receded. The flashes of lightning grew pale, then ceased altogether. As if some invisible hand had flipped a switch, the familiar green glow seeped back into the atmosphere. The strange darkness retreated into the pooling shadows from which it had come.

"Must have seemed like an eternity to Chaz and Drake," Virginia whispered.

"It may have turned out to be just that."

"Are you saying you don't think they survived it?"

"I don't know what was going on out there, but whatever it was, they were caught out in the open." Sam smiled slightly. "Thanks to you, we were safe in this room."

He got cautiously to his feet and went to the window. When he looked out he saw that everything looked very much as it had just before the tempest had been triggered.

Virginia stood slowly behind the chest. "Now what?"

"Now we get the heck out of here before someone else sets off another storm." He moved swiftly back toward her. "Ready?"

"If you're waiting for me, you're backing up."

They found Chaz and Drake lying on the floor near the main gate into the zoo. It was obvious that the two desperate men had tried to flee back through it, but something had caused the illusion trap there to reset itself. The energy storm had caught up with the pair before Chaz could untangle the trap a second time.

Virginia hesitated and then went down beside one of the men and checked for a pulse. She looked up in surprise. "He's unconscious, but alive."

"Same here." Sam rifled through the pockets of the man dressed in leather and khaki until he found a guild license and an amber-powered grid locator. "This is all we need. The locator shows three exits in this sector. We won't have to go back through the waterfall, after all."

"What are you going to do with that man's guild license?"

"I'll give it to Mercer Wyatt. He can take it from there." Sam got to his feet. "The guild polices its own."

Virginia gave him an odd look. "You're, uh, friends with the head of Hunter's Guild?"

"Let's just say that Wyatt and I have a nodding acquaintance. He owes me a couple of favors." Sam studied the illusion trap that guarded the exit. "Go ahead and de-rez it. I'll drag these two out of here. We'll leave them in the corridor. Wyatt can send one of his staff to clean up this mess."

CHAPTER 5

"WE WERE WORRIED SICK." ADELINE HELPED HERSELF TO a leftover black-and-orange cupcake from the plate on Virginia's desk. "First we hear that you and Sam have gone missing in the corridors; a report which, I hasten to add, none of your buddies believed for one tiny minute, because we all know how good you and Sam are; and then we learn that the two of you got zapped by some sort of massive ghost called a waterfall."

"The waterfall part was for real." Virginia rocked back in her chair and took a sip of hot, spiced cider. "But, as you can see, neither of us got zapped."

She peered at her watch, wondering what was keeping Sam. After talking to the police, he had gone to meet with Mercer Wyatt. She had not liked that. It was no secret in Cadence City that Wyatt ran the guild as though it was his own, private fiefdom. A lot of folks, including an editorial writer on the *Cadence Star* considered him no more than one or two steps removed from being a gangster. But she could not argue with the fact that if you were a ghost-hunter, you had to form some sort of business relationship with the guild. She had not asked Sam just what kind of terms he had worked out with Wyatt. She was not sure she wanted to know.

"So what, exactly, was going on down there in the tunnels?" Adeline asked around a mouthful of cupcake.

"A band of ruin rats headed by a recently fired employee of the University Museum named Fairbanks uncovered a hole-in-the-wall just beneath the museum's basement. They were using it to siphon off some of the museum's holdings. Stuff that had been in storage for years, which might not have been missed for years. If Mac Ewert hadn't accidentally stumbled onto that waterfall and asked us to help him de-rez it, the rats probably would never have been caught."

Holes-in-the-wall were not uncommon. They usually took the form of tiny cracks and fissures through which little more than ambient psi energy could squeeze. But some of the openings in the thick quartz walls and underground corridors were large enough for a man to crawl through. A few were even bigger: eons-old stairwells and empty shafts that no longer ascended anywhere. It was one of those that Fairbanks, a powerful tangler, had discovered while laboring in the basement of the huge museum.

Adeline gazed at her with the look of a professional inquisitor. "What now?"

Virginia shrugged. "The cops take it from here. Last I heard, they'd picked up everyone involved except Leon Drummond. But I doubt if he'll escape. Not with the guild looking for him as well as the police."

"I wasn't talking about your big case. I know the firm of Gage & Burch has closed it. Probably be all over the evening news." Adeline selected a black-and-orange petit four. "I meant what happens now with you and Sam?"

Virginia took another sip of hot cider and contemplated the heavy mist that drifted in the street outside the office window. She thought about the passion that had exploded between them in the little fountain chamber.

"Good question," she said quietly.

THE NARROW STREETS AND TWISTED LANES OF THE OLD Quarter were thick with fog, but that did not deter the throngs of hobgoblins, ghosts, witches, and assorted monsters who had come to the district to celebrate Halloween.

Virginia walked out of the little corner restaurant with Sam at her side shortly after ten. She could feel the stray pulses of psi energy that leaked from the ruins. They seemed stronger than usual tonight. Maybe it was true that the Dead City was more alive at Halloween than at other times. She was aware of constant little frissons across her para senses. Some just tickled; some were more disturbing. But she could not be sure that all of them were caused by ambient Harmonic energy. She knew that some of the ripples were attributable to Sam, who seemed blithely oblivious to the new level of awareness that pulsed between them.

When he had suggested dinner together earlier, she had been sure that he wanted to talk about their future. But the only thing that had been discussed over a bottle of wine and a leisurely meal of tapenade-tossed cheese ravioli and good bread had been their case.

She did not want to hear another word about their case. She was heartily sick and tired of discussing their case.

Sam paused on the restaurant step and eyed the tide of costumed celebrants that flooded the street.

"I don't know about you, but I've had enough of ghosts and goblins for a while," he said. "What do you say we take a shortcut home and drink a private toast to the successful finale of Gage & Burch's first case?"

Home. To talk some more about their stupid case. Virginia steeled herself. "Sam, we need to talk about us."

"I know," he said.

She was so surprised by his casual agreement that she was momentarily speechless. His mouth curved slightly as he took her arm and steered her along a side street, away from the crowds of revelers.

She shoved her gloved hands into the pockets of her coat and slanted him a sidelong glance. His expression was as enigmatic as ever, but she sensed something going on beneath the surface.

She had come to know him better than she had realized during these past few weeks. And much of what she now knew for certain verified her initial impression. Her instincts had been right that first day. The cool, self-contained veneer was a cover for the deep passions, the unyielding determination, and the rock-solid strength that was at the core of this man. If Sam Gage gave you his word of honor, you could take it to the bank.

If Sam Gage ever said he loved you, you could depend on that love forever.

Commitments like that were dangerous things. Sam probably knew that better than anyone else, she thought. Maybe that was why he was so cautious about making them in the first place.

She decided to take the plunge.

"Sam, about our marriage—"

"I don't want an MC," he said bluntly.

That brought her to an abrupt halt in the middle of the sidewalk.

She stopped and swung around to face him. "You've changed your mind?"

"Yes." He watched her with unreadable eyes. "It won't work. I can't handle it."

Despair jolted through her. "You can't handle it? But you're the one who suggested it in the first place."

"It was a mistake. I think I knew it all along, but after what happened in the ruins, I'm sure of it."

"I see." She did not know what to say. This was not how she had anticipated the conversation would end. "I thought that after what had happened, you might feel differently, but I didn't realize—"

"A marriage-of-convenience will drive me crazy," he interrupted. "I don't want—"

He broke off suddenly as a goblin-masked figure in a long black coat stepped out of the shadows. Light gleamed wickedly on a mag-rez gun.

"I'd say trick or treat," Leon Drummond growled behind the hideous mask. "But you haven't got a choice. You're going to get the trick, whether you want it or not."

Virginia caught her breath. Drummond ignored her. She could see the baleful glitter of his eyes through the holes in the mask. His attention was focused on Sam.

"I'm surprised you're still hanging around, Drummond," Sam said. "Wyatt's got men out looking for you."

"You sonofabitch, you screwed up everything," Leon hissed. "We were nearly finished. Two more days and we would have shut down the operation with no one the wiser. The museum wouldn't have missed the pieces we took until the next full audit. But Ewert had to call you in, and you ruined the whole damned project."

"What can I say?" Sam smiled coldly. "It's what I do."

"Well, it's gonna be the last damned thing you do." Drummond raised the mag-rez gun. "Nobody messes with Leon Drummond and gets away with it. Especially not some two-bit private detective."

Leon was concentrating so fiercely that he never even noticed the ball of green energy that was forming rapidly behind him. Virginia was impressed. Not every hunter could summon a ghost outside the Dead City, let alone control it.

The energy ghost flared and pulsed, gathering strength as Leon continued with his tirade.

"Wyatt's security people are watching my house, thanks to you. I can't even get to my car. They're covering the airport, too. I'll have to use the tunnels to get out of Cadence."

"Risky," Sam said, sounding mildly interested. "Not many people get far in the tunnels once they get beyond the mapped sectors. Unpleasant way to go, all alone in a maze filled with traps and ghosts and who knows what else. They say that even if someone survives the experience, he isn't real sane afterward."

"I'll make it." Leon's hand tightened on the mag-rez. "But I'm gonna make sure you pay for what you did first."

The ball of ghost fire was quite large now. The energy aura pulsed outward abruptly, enveloping Leon Drummond. He jerked wildly when the fringes of the green field touched him. His hair stood on end. His mouth parted on a silent scream. The mag-rez fell from his hand and clattered on the pavement.

A few seconds later, Drummond collapsed, unconscious, beside his weapon.

Virginia exhaled slowly. "You really are good, partner."

Sam gave Drummond a dismissive nod and turned back to her. "Where were we?" he asked.

She swallowed and managed to drag her eyes away from the still and silent Drummond. "I, uh, think we were discussing the fact that you no longer want to get married."

He frowned. "I didn't say that. I said I didn't want a marriage-of-convenience."

"Oh." Her heart was suddenly weightless. "You did say that you were kind of literal on your good days."

"I thought an MC would give you time to get used to the idea of a real marriage," he said with an air of dogged determination. "But I don't think I could take it, knowing that you were just trying me on for size."

"Size? But there's nothing wrong with your size. I already know that you fit. Perfectly."

"I want a commitment. I want kids. I want to know you'll be there ten, twenty, forty years from now. I don't want to play house with you. I want a home."

"Oh, Sam, that's what I want, too." She threw herself against him so hard that it was a wonder he did not go down. "Why didn't you say something sooner?"

He caught her close and wrapped his arms around her. "I was afraid I'd scare you off," he said into her hair. "I came up with the deal on the house and the MC plan as a way to make sure I could hold on to you until I could convince you to fall in love with me."

"I fell in love with you the day I rented the office and the apartment."

"Why the hell didn't you say so? Look at all the time we've wasted."

She raised her head and smiled. "How was I to know that you had fallen in love with me? You never said anything. You were always so cool, so controlled. I was beginning to wonder if you ever got excited about anything."

His eyes gleamed. "You want excitement? Let's go home. I guarantee I'll come up with something exciting."

She hesitated, pointing down at Drummond. "What about him?"

Sam groaned. "I guess I'd better make sure Mercer Wyatt sends someone out to collect him. If I leave him here, he's liable to wake up later and make a nuisance of himself."

"Call Wyatt," Virginia smiled, aware of the happiness blossoming deep inside. "I can wait."

CHAPTER 6

THE RECEPTION FOLLOWING THE LENGTHY, FORMAL COV-enant wedding service was held in the downstairs offices of Gage & Burch. Virginia's beaming father and brothers toasted the bride and groom so many times that her mother had to call a cab to take them home. Adeline performed brilliantly as a bridal attendant. Mercer Wyatt created a small stir when he showed up with a gift for the newlyweds—a fine, museum-quality Harmonic vase that had to be worth several thousand dollars. Virginia made a mental note to ask Sam the precise nature of the favors he had done for the head of the guild.

When it was all over, Sam insisted on carrying Virginia up the stairs and through the doorway of the darkened bedroom. The long sweep of her white satin skirts cascaded over his arm. Her veil was a gossamer cloud that clung to his sleeve.

He put her down on the wide bed in a tumble of satin and silk and went to the dresser. She curled up against the bedpost and watched him remove his cuff links. He took off his white shirt and then he removed the bottle of champagne from the ice bucket that sat on a stand.

The cork made the appropriately cheerful sound when it came out of the bottle. Sam poured two glasses full of bubbling champagne and carried them both back across the room to the bed. He handed one to Virginia.

"To us," he said softly.

"To us." She smiled.

They did not take their eyes off each other as they drank the toast to their future. When Virginia had drained her glass, Sam took it from her and put it down beside his on the night-stand.

She saw the steady glow of love and happiness in his eyes when he turned back to her. She knew that he saw the same expression mirrored in her own gaze.

She slid off the bed and got to her feet. He reached out to lift the veil from her hair. She turned her back to him. He kissed the nape of her neck and went to work on the tiny buttons that secured her gown.

A thrill of pleasure went through her when the bodice of the dress fell to her waist. Sam put his arms around her from behind and cupped her breasts. His thumbs grazed across her nipples. He bent his head and kissed the side of her throat.

"I love you," he said.

She leaned back against him, savoring the warm, sleek feel of his bare chest. "I love you."

A moment later, the frothy gown cascaded into a pool at her feet. He unbuckled his belt. When she turned around, she found him ready for her, his hard body fiercely aroused. He picked her up again and settled her against the pillows. She reached for him with a kind of hunger she had never known.

He crushed her into the soft bedding, his mouth hot and deeply sensual on her skin. All of her senses opened at his touch, the paranormal ones as well as the physical. Effervescent, invisible psi energy hummed in the air that surrounded them. She knew it came from both of them, sparked by their passion and fueled by their pleasure.

Sam took his time with the lovemaking, crafting a slow, sensual dance. She felt his mouth on her breasts, his teeth light and tantalizing on her taut nipples. She kissed his shoulder, using her own teeth in ways that made him murmur husky, sexy threats.

When, eventually, he did retaliate, she wanted to scream with delight. But she made no sound because he had stolen her very breath.

He parted her legs, settled himself between them, and forged slowly, deeply into her. She sank her nails into the hard contours of his muscled back and gloried in the full, heavy heat of his erection.

He eased himself partway out of her channel and then pressed forward again. The intense, impossibly stretched sensation was almost too much. She lifted herself against him, silently demanding that he move more quickly.

But he only laughed softly in the darkness and whispered wicked things that exacerbated the sensual torment.

Finally she could not stand it any longer. She pushed against his chest. His eyes gleamed as he allowed himself to be rolled onto his back.

She came down on top of him, fitting herself to him, kissing his chest and his throat, riding him with a wild abandon that carried them both into the heart of pure ecstasy.

A LONG TIME LATER, SHE CAME AWAKE, AWARE THAT Sam was not asleep. She stirred and stretched and drew her toes up along his leg.

"Something wrong?" she asked.

"No." His arm tightened around her. "I was just thinking about that place where we hid out while I recovered from the burn."

"The zoo?"

"The more I think about it, the more I think that maybe it wasn't a zoo."

She shrugged. "A down-market apartment complex or a cheap hotel. Maybe a prison, as you suggested. I doubt if anyone will ever know for certain, even when the experts get through untangling all the traps."

"True, but there is one explanation for the chamber that we overlooked. It fits with everything we experienced while we were in it, and it explains a lot."

She propped herself on her elbow and looked down at him. "What's that?"

"Maybe what we stumbled into was a Harmonic graveyard."

For a moment she could not believe she had heard him correctly. And then the implications hit her. Her mouth went dry.

"You think it was a *cemetery?*"

"That would account for all the small chambers," he said seriously.

"Graves and crypts." She shuddered. "Good grief. Now that you mention it—"

"It would also account for the weird feeling you got from the traps that guarded the cubicles. Maybe they were set as warnings against disturbing the dead."

"But that fountain room and the little antechamber off of it," she interrupted quickly. "Why wasn't it trapped?"

"Probably because it wasn't an actual grave site. It may have been a meditation chamber or a viewing room. Or it could have been the place where the caskets were displayed for sale, for all we know."

"Aaargh." She flopped back on the pillow. "Do you think we really spent Halloween in an alien graveyard?"

"I think there's a good chance that we did, yes."

She stared at the ceiling. "Kind of boggles the mind." Abruptly she sat up amid the sheets. "But what about that strange energy storm that Chaz triggered when he untangled one of the traps? And those things that we saw drifting past the window. You don't suppose they were—" She broke off, unable to put the thought into words.

Sam smiled slightly. "Real ghosts?"

"No." She shook her head violently. "I absolutely refuse to believe that. The only ghosts are unstable dissonance energy manifestations. UDEMs. Composed of ambient psi energy. There is no such thing as real ghosts."

"Whatever you say." He threaded his fingers through her hair. "Who am I to argue with an expert such as yourself?"

"Definitely not real ghosts," she reiterated very forcefully. Then she frowned. "But about that antechamber off the fountain room."

"What about it?"

"If it was a funeral room or some sort of viewing chamber, then that big chest where we . . . where we—"

"Where we made love for the first time?"

"It must have been a—"

Sam grinned. "Yeah, I think it might have been a casket or a sarcophagus."

She swallowed. "We did it on top of a casket? Our first time to-gether took place in an alien funeral parlor? On top of a *coffin*?"

"I'm pretty sure it was empty," Sam said. "There was no trap, re-member?"

"That's not the point. What am I supposed to tell our grandchil-dren when they ask us about our first real romantic date? That you took me to an alien cemetery and made wild, passionate love to me on top of a *sarcophagus*?"

Sam roared with laughter and eased her onto her back. He lowered himself until he covered her body with his own. Then he braced his arms on either side of her head and looked down at her with eyes that gleamed with sensual amusement.

"Maybe we ought to make it our own, private Halloween tradition," he suggested. "We could hunt up a new alien graveyard every year."

"Don't even *think* about it."

He smiled slowly. "Then what do you say we get busy on creating some children so that one day we'll have those grandchildren you mentioned a minute ago."

"At last, a truly brilliant idea." She wrapped her arms around his neck and urged his mouth down to hers.

He kissed her until she stopped thinking about Halloween and graveyards and alien sarcophagi; until she could think of nothing else except their love and the future that they would build together.